As it was no goo[...] lacked the skill to crea[...] *ilo*, and instead adapted [...] it found to hand. The first living organism it encountered was a crab of the type which is known to the Hindrix-Prodorgotz system of taxonomy as Thorbakrodomon Rantharchardaliz. Therefore the Hermit Crab adapted the biology of this animal for its own purposes, and dwelt thus thereafter on the shores of Jod.

Thousands of years passed.

During those millennia, the Hermit Crab slowly changed and adapted the form it had learnt. In nature, Thorbakrodomon Rantharchardaliz grows to no great size. A typical specimen will have a carapace which is scarcely a finger-length across at maturity. However, the Hermit Crab found it inconvenient to remain at this size, since it was often attacked by seagulls. These it obliterated, thanks to those powers to modulate probability which it still retained from its earlier mode of existence. However, seagulls remained a danger, since even the Hermit Crab had to (and has to) sleep sometimes.

Hence the Hermit Crab increased in size until the depredations of seagulls were no longer a danger. However, increased size brought it to the attention of humans, who proved even more of a nuisance than the seagulls had been.

Many tragedies ensued . . .

Also by Hugh Cook

THE WIZARDS AND THE WARRIORS
THE WORDSMITHS AND THE WARGUILD
THE WOMEN AND THE WARLORDS
THE WALRUS AND THE WARWOLF
THE WICKED AND THE WITLESS

and published by Corgi Books

THE WISHSTONE
AND THE
WONDERWORKERS

Hugh Cook

CORGI BOOKS

THE WISHSTONE AND THE WONDERWORKERS

A CORGI BOOK   0 552 13536 4

Originally published in Great Britain by Colin Smythe Limited

PRINTING HISTORY
Colin Smythe edition published 1990
Corgi edition published 1990

This book is set in 10/11pt Baskerville by Kestrel Data, Exeter

Corgi Books are published by Transworld Publishers Ltd.,
61-63 Uxbridge Road, Ealing, London W5 5SA, in Australia by
Transworld Publishers (Australia) Pty. Ltd., 15-23 Helles Avenue,
Moorebank, NSW 2170, and in New Zealand by Transworld
Publishers (N.Z.) Ltd., Cnr. Moselle and Waipareira Avenues,
Henderson, Auckland.

Made and printed in Great Britain by
Cox & Wyman Ltd, Reading, Berks.

FOREWORD

Mighty are the labours of the redactors of Odrum, and merciless is their diligence. As it endured redaction in the dungeons of Odrum, the Text which follows became encumbered by a full two million words of explication and interpolation. In the interests of convenience, readability and sanity, most of this overgrowth has been cut away.

The enormity of the labours expended by Odrum upon this Text boggles the imagination. Upon the foundation of this historical account there was erected a terrifying redactatorial monument complete with an elaborate apparatus of footnotes, screeds of etymological speculation and hundreds of thousands of words of textual analysis.

Only a few (a very few) of the comments by some of the more prominent redactors have been left to give a faint indication of the flavour of the Text in its redacted form. The rest of Odrum's additions have been soundlessly elided. Which is only fair, since Odrum's scholars were equally ruthless in their abbreviation of the Originator's writings.

Common sense tells us that the reader needs no editorial help to understand a straightforward history such as this. Even so, a few words to explicate the Hermit Crab are in order. Drax Lira, Redactor Major of Odrum, plainly misunderstood and grossly underestimated this entity. The Originator of the Text knew better, yet never learnt of the Crab's origins. In fact, the Originator knew not even the Hermit Crab's name.

As it happens, the Hermit Crab originated in the fires of the local star. It belonged to a race of creatures which are not formed from flesh as we understand it, but instead exist as dynamic, highly localised modulations of probability. As a result of a theological dispute, the Hermit Crab was forced to flee from its fellows. Since to stay was to die, it abstracted itself from the inferno which had served it as a home for the better part of seventy million years, and fled into the unutterably cold wastelands of outer space.

At length, it reached a planetary surface. It was sick and injured by the time it made landfall on the shores of Jod, and therefore had no time for the fifty thousand years of careful thought and diligent analysis which would have been advisable under the circumstances. Instead, it had an urgent need to embody what was left of its life processes in corporeal form, lest those processes be altogether extinguished.

You must understand that the Hermit Crab was and is entirely lacking in divinity. Like us, it was and is mortal. In its original form, it was fit only for life in the seas of a sun. Therefore it found the shores of Jod entirely inimical, and was forced to evolve with extreme rapidity in order to survive.

As it was no god, devil or demon, the Hermit Crab lacked the skill to create organic form and process *ex nihilo*, and instead adapted what it found to hand. The first living organism it encountered was a crab of the type which is known to the Hindrix-Prodorgotz system of taxonomy as Thorbakrodomon Rantharchardaliz. Therefore the Hermit Crab adapted the biology of this animal for its own purposes, and dwelt thus thereafter on the shores of Jod.

Thousands of years passed.

During those millennia, the Hermit Crab slowly changed and adapted the form it had learnt. In nature, Thorbakrodomon Rantharchardaliz grows to no great size. A typical specimen will have a carapace which is scarcely a fingerlength across at maturity. However, the Hermit Crab found it inconvenient to remain at this size, since it was often attacked by seagulls. These it obliterated, thanks to those powers to modulate probability which it still retained from its earlier mode of existence. However, seagulls remained a danger, since even the Hermit Crab had to (and has to) sleep sometimes.

The soft-bodied castle crabs which live in discarded seashells can never risk growing beyond the size of the available armour. However, the Hermit Crab suffered no such limitation, since it was a true crab with its own exoskeleton which it could shed at will whenever it wished to enlarge itself. Hence it was able to increase its size until the depredations of seagulls were no longer a danger. However, increased size brought it to the attention of humans, who proved even more of a nuisance than the seagulls had been.

Many tragedies ensued in the long years before the Hermit Crab managed to learn the local languages, and to modify its anatomy so that it could vocalize its simple and understandable demands (for peace and quiet and an adequate source of nutrition). After that, life went more smoothly. And the Hermit Crab had the leisure in which to contemplate further changes to its organic structure.

Any form would have been a burden to the Hermit Crab, for, in its previous mode of existence it had enjoyed freedoms which we can scarcely comprehend. Imagine yourself re-incarnated as a paving stone, and enduring several millennia of such entrapment. This will give you a measure of what the Hermit Crab had to suffer.

However, while any form would inevitably have been hard to endure, the Hermit Crab realized its frustrations would at least be diminished if it could assume human shape. It would gain freedoms of action and intercourse which were totally impossible while it remained trapped within a crab's carapace.

Unfortunately, attempts by the Hermit Crab to modify its structure further always failed. First forms are like first languages: once learnt, they are near impossible to unlearn. In the end, the Hermit Crab realized it could not learn a second form without freeing itself of the first. It would have to step away from its flesh and (briefly, at least) exist once more as a disembodied modulation of probability in an environment totally unsuited to such a mode of existence. In theory, this was possible; if it decided to abandon

7

crab-flesh for human, it had at least a 3 per cent chance of success. And a 97 per cent chance of dying a swift and painful death.

Such odds did not appeal to the near-immortal Hermit Crab, which therefore retained its first-found form. And suffered. Hence its somewhat grumpish disposition, its unambitious philosophical outlook and its eremitic mode of existence.

That is all the reader really needs to know about the Hermit Crab. Its name is (strictly speaking) irrelevant. However, for the record, let us note that the wizard Paklish once sojourned on Untunchilamon and was long in discourse with the Hermit Crab. (We mean of course Hablos Paklish the philosopher, not the brilliant but ill-fated Alkibiades Paklish, would-be domesticator of dragons.) It was the philosopher Paklish who bestowed upon the Hermit Crab its name, Codlugarthia, which in the Janjuladoola of Yestron South means 'Son of Thunder'.

However, as you will see from the Text which follows, this name had quite fallen out of use by the year Alliance 4312.

AN OPENING EDITORIAL NOTE

This Text purports to be a true and correct account of certain events on Untunchilamon. However, as complete Verification has proved impossible, scholars are advised to treat it with caution. To accept it as the whole truth (or as nothing but the truth) would be rash, to say the least.

I myself have been to Untunchilamon and to Injilta-prajura in days gone by, during the rule of the late Wazir Sin. I then met some of those who feature in this Text, notably Justina Thrug (later to be the Empress Justina), Aquitaine Varazchavardan (then chief adviser to Wazir Sin), and Nixorjapretzel Rat (then an eager young scholar who earned himself some coppers by serving as my interpreter-guide).

I also saw the magical fountains of dikle and shlug which spring from the island of Jod, where I was shown the Analytical Engine by Ivan Pokrov. His explanations of the Engine were most unsatisfactory; I remain convinced that this conglomeration of titanium cogs is incapable of cognition, and that Pokrov is a fraud. The Hermit Crab I also saw, but all it said was 'Go away.' As I possess a parrot with a vocabulary far more extensive, I remain unimpressed.

But I swear by my fingernails that I never heard any mention of this maze of sewer-works said to exist Downstairs, or of this dorgi and this Shabble, or of this mythical 'Golden Gulag' which the Originator of this Text has conjured with. Such surely belong to the realm of fantasy. In this Translation, we have not endeavoured to dignify the Fantastic by scholarship, which could in any case say only that the cryptic is cryptic; hence references to such semantic entities as 'zulzers', 'ionising radiation', 'transponder', 'vocal identities' and 'spectral analysis' remain unglossed.

It is for the Originator to say what True Meaning these semantic entities have (if any). However, for reasons which need no elaboration (we are hardly dealing with ancient history, are we?!) the Originator is not likely to be available for Interrogation. Ever.

It is with every confidence that I repeat the original conclusions of the Report I made to the Battle Council on my return from my Survey of Untunchilamon: there is nothing and nobody on this sunburnt little island capable of materially assisting us in the Conquest.

Given under my hand on this the morning of the twelfth day of the fifth month of the 15,436,794th year of Din Civil.

    Drax Lira.
    Redactor Major

CHAPTER ONE

Untunchilamon is an equatorial island girded by reefs of red coral, an island of magic and mystery which lies mid-ocean between the continents of Argan and Yestron.

Since that is our setting, what then is our story? You will have heard much of Untunchilamon in saga, song, chronicle or legend, and will doubtless expect this tale to deal with the fate of the famous bard of that island. But it does not. The precious bard of Untunchilamon was stolen some years before our story opens when a ruthless band of waterthieves ventured to Injiltaprajura and looted the treasury. Thereafter the bard was fated elsewhere. To the west, in fact. To Argan.

But this history does not touch upon Argan.

This account deals instead with the wishstone, the fabulous bauble ornamenting the sceptre of the Empress Justina, who came to power in Injiltaprajura after Lonstantine Thrug went mad (another good man destroyed by syphilis!) and was incarcerated in the Dromdanjerie.

Our history opens in the year Justina 5. To be precise, it opens in the season of Fistavlir, time of the Long Dry, when the doldrums have settled over Untunchilamon. Then the wind is nil or chancy, and precipitation is zero. Not that this worries the good folk of Injiltaprajura, for the fountains sourced Downstairs supply them with all the water one could wish for, and then some.

Justina 5.

Which year is that?

By the Cosmos Clock of Din Civil, it is the year 15,436,789. By the Holy Calendar of the Golden Sepulchre it is Jintharth 424. The Wind Worshippers, on the other hand, denominate it as the Year of the Tinted Quail, whereas the Disciples of the Golden Monkey know it as Fen 4 of Asio 5699.

Those versed in the history of Yestron should note that Justina 5 is the seventh year of the Talonsklavara, the disastrous civil war instigated by Aldarch the Third. In Argan, far west of Untunchilamon, historians reckon Justina 5 to be the year Alliance 4312, whereas in the northern continent of Tameran it is Khmar 5, that is to say the fifth year of the rule of the Red Emperor.

As for the Ngati Moana, the people of the Great Ocean – why, by their reckoning it is the Year of the Flying Fish in the 376th Generation Cycle.

The time, then, is Justina 5. The place is Untunchilamon. With that settled, let us now have . . . action.

Let us survey the city by night.

The city?

Injiltaprajura, of course. There is no other city on Untunchilamon. Study then this city, Injiltaprajura, pearl of the Laitemata Harbour – not to be confused with that monolithic chunk of bone which is itself known as Pearl. Injiltaprajura, lit bright by candles, star lanterns and the blue-green glimmer of walls adorned with moon paint.

Injiltaprajura is a metropolis of some 30,000 souls. The city is governed from the palace which stands on the heights at the inland end of Lak Street, and this imposing edifice of pink marble is currently the home of the Empress Justina. The pink palace sits atop Pokra Ridge, that half-circle of rock which separates Injiltaprajura's urbanised portside from the northern desert side where one finds barracks, quarries, cemeteries, and the many market gardens which flourish thanks to a limitless supply of water sourced Downstairs.

Let us ignore Injiltaprajura's desert side for the moment, since the portside has a virtual monopoly on life and action. Let us start at the steps of the pink palace, then follow Lak Street as it winds its way downhill past the houses of the great and the grand, past the mysterious ship-sized chunk of bone which is known locally as Pearl, and then past the

Cabal House of the wonderworkers of Untunchilamon.

If we wished, we could make a diversion at this point. We could leave Lak Street and risk the precipitous slopes of Skindik Way. Do we so wish? Of course we do not! For if we were thus to dare our way into the slums we would inevitably encounter the lunatic asylum, then the enormous rotting doss house known as Ganthorgruk, and then the city's slaughterhouse.

And beyond?

Things still worse! The clutter of hovels and scramble-walks known as Lubos, which is without doubt the worst quarter of the city. There we would find such dubious people as the corpse master Uckermark, asleep amidst the stench of decomposing meat.

Let us not, therefore, turn down Skindik Way. Instead, let us continue to make our way down Lak Street. Past the Cabal House. From which there issues sound and light – a pluff, then a cascade of red sparks.

What lies within?

A dragon, mayhap?

No, only the wonderworkers themselves, busy with the exercise of magic. This cascade of sparks is, one hopes, but a harmless epiphenomenon of their endeavours.

Exactly what, you ask, are those endeavours? What precisely are they doing in the Cabal House? Why, nothing original. The wonderworkers of Injiltaprajura – that is to say, the city's resident sorcerers – are engaged in the attempt to turn lead into gold, which is a feat theoretically within their capabilities but in practice near impossible.

So far, tonight's experiments have seen the wonder-workers turn lead into spaghetti, chaff, peacock feathers, black marble, musk, the jawbone of a jackal, the mummified flesh of an archer a thousand years dead, pumice, salt water, wax and a great big heap of carpet fluff. Yesterday they succeeded in converting the same substance into cheese, pyridine, basalt and sawdust. And tomorrow – who knows?

The truth is, the powers of the sorcerers of Yestron are

third-rate when compared with those of the wizards of Argan. Yestron's wonderworkers are capable of spectacular effects, but lack the fine nuances of control of which wizards are capable. Furthermore, sorcerers (unlike wizards) cannot create objects which in themselves possess powers magical or attributes uncanny.

Therefore, while a sorcerer might (might!) be a match for a wizard in combat, sorcerers could never make the magic rings, enchanted gates, bewitched bottles, philtres, potions, slaughter-swords, flying sticks and flame-trenches that the wizards of Argan's Confederation create.

Ignore then the Cabal House of the wonderworkers, and observe instead Lak Street. Something is moving on that thoroughfare. What is it? Precisely what is it that has caught our attention? It is not the virgular serpent sliding from a sewer-hole. Nor is it the tiny jade button which lies by that sewer-hole, a button which was attached to Troldot Turbothot's dress uniform until it became detached during a brief scuffle with a would-be pickpocket. Nor has our attention been drawn by the dead dog (as yet unconsumed by carrion eaters) which has attracted the scavenger snake into the open air.

No, the subject of our interest is the Princess Sabitha. Out on the night, out on the town, out on the prowl. Hoping (expecting!) to be seduced, seized and subjected to – well, let us leave the business of subjection to the imagination. At least for the moment. And while the imagination does its work, let us watch the Princess Sabitha, who steps out lively even though the night is hot enough for mosquitoes to be drowning in their own sweat.

[I personally went to the trouble of obtaining fifty mosquitoes which I then placed within a sealed retort. Subjecting these vampiric reptiles to increasing degrees of heat in an effort to elicit an outflow of sweat secured at length their utter dehydration and their death yet failed to bring about any visible production of moisture. The necessary conclusion is therefore that the autodestruction of mosquitoes through the mechanism suggested by the Text is impossible, which implies that the Originator is here in error, or else is perpetrating a deliberate Untruth. *Oris Baumgage, Fact Checker Minor.*]

What do we know of the Princess Sabitha, this gay young aristocrat?

This we know: she was not born on the island of Untunchilamon. No, she was born far to the east in Yestron. To be precise, she was born in Ang. With more precision still, we can place her nativity in the city of Obooloo, in the very heart of the Izdimir Empire. Her full name was Sabitha Winolathon Taskinjathura. She was a descendant of the famous Ousompton Ling Ordway whose lineage has been dealt with at such length in Lady Jade's Book of the Higher Aristocracy, and thus she could trace her ancestry back for at least some three thousand years.

In due course, the dictates of fortune brought Sabitha to Untunchilamon. There, as befitted her royal station, she was domiciled in the palace of the Empress Justina. Unfortunately, thanks to the slapdash way the palace was organised, nobody has made the appropriate arrangements to supervise her amusements. In fact, far more care is taken of Justina's grossly over-indulged albinotic ape Vazzy.

In all the time the princess has been resident in the pink palace, nobody has seen fit to remedy this situation. Hence she is free to come and go as she pleases, without so much as a chaperone. Thus, on the night on which our history opens, here she is out on her own on the streets of Injiltaprajura.

By daylight she looks every bit the young royal, preening herself for her admirers, delicately supping upon fresh fish or zabaglione, accepting (as of right) those compliments and courtesies which come her way. But now it is night, and she is out for action. She is hot, hot, there's no doubting it. She walks with a strumpet's roll, her xanthic eyes alight with a leam of lust as she quits Lak Street and ventures down Skindik Way. Swiftly she reaches the depraved depths of Lubos. There she does not vacillate, but recklessly plunges into the stews.

One does not expect such things from the aristocracy. But there it is. The truth must be told, and the uneffaceable truth is that she is pursuing carnal satisfaction with no sense of aidos whatsoever, shamelessly strutting her stuff in the streets, ready (more than ready!) for the first male with the energy to take her.

She has not gone far through the wagmoire of the waterfront slumlands when she encounters a virile young mariner. He is a sailor fresh off a ship, a mangy street-fighter who has but one ear. Hunk is his name, and he has sailed the waters of the Great Ocean from Yam to Manamalargo. He has seen the cruel cliffs of Odrum, the jungles of Quilth, the storm-torn shores of Wen Endex and the limpid waters of Parengarenga Harbour.

He has tasted the exotic pleasures of a thousand ports, yet still is ready for more. Furthermore, the glamour of his pintle is alone sufficient to persuade the Princess Sabitha that he is the one. For when appetite goads the flesh sufficiently, questions of class, decency and caution go right out of the window.

Thus Hunk meets Sabitha, and, in the manner of all idiothermous animals lusting in heat, they decide without preparation or preamble to engage in that interesting activity which the scholarly Arwin has dealt with in such exhaustive length in his five-volume magnus opus, *On The Generation Of Species.*

But before genetic data (or organic secretions and their concomitant diseases) can be transmitted from one to the other, the would-be lovers are interrupted by the advent of an apparition in appearance formidable indeed.

It is a Thing which hangs in nightdark heights near the gable of the nearest speakeasy. A globular Thing the size of a fist. It crackles with electric auras of gangrene blue and corpse-love yellow. Then it speaks unto them in a voice of brass and cymbals, saying:

'I am the demon-god Lorzunduk. Behold! And know your doom!'

Whereupon the Princess Sabitha flees, yowling.

Hunk stands his ground. His back arches, his hair stands on end, and he hisses and spits ferociously as the apparition descends. Then his nerve breaks, and he too flees.

Which is just as well.

For if the lovers had not been thus separated before the consummation of their passion then this chronicle would have had to touch in some way upon that aforesaid consummation. Which would have been unfortunate. For this work is meant for the literate, and the literate are by definition more interested in the life of the intellect than the life of the organism, the life of the aforesaid organism being – is it not? – essentially repetitive and thus tedious.

So let us be glad that we are not forced to waste our time by contemplation of an unoriginal act at which frogs, newly-weds and blowflies are equally competent. Let us be glad that we need here insert no account (doubtless to be skimmed or impatiently skipped by those in search of deeper revelation) of the shimmering scream of pleasure with which the Princess Sabitha accepted the hard-driving Hunk into her body, about the thrust of his drive questing deep in the humid velvet of her tight yet tender—

Well, you know the rest.

Anyway, to return to our chronicle. Both cats have fled in terror. Yet the glowing ball still hangs there in the air.

Sniggering.

Those of you who have been to Untunchilamon yourselves or who know the place by reputation will likely have guessed already that the glowing ball is nothing more than Shabble.

Shabble?

Yes, Shabble.

'Shabble! Shabble!' the children are wont to cry as they go chasing through the streets. 'Shabble, come play with us! Shabble, Shabbiful, Jabiful, Shabajabalantiful.' And sometimes Shabble will. Or, if not in a cat-chasing mood, then Shabble may condescend to amuse Shabbleself with a kitten to the kitten's delight.

(Shabbleself? Itself. Himself. Herself. Theirselves. Choose

any one at will or at random – and you will know at least as much about Shabble's psychology as the so-called experts.)

Shabble, then.

In appearance, a miniature sun, though coloration tends to be changeable and idiosyncratic. In voice eccentric, speaking at will in any of the accents heard ever on Untunchilamon, even those unplaceable foreign accents otherwise voiced only by the conjurer Odolo. In behaviour feckless, for Shabble has scant regard for consequences.

That is Shabble.

While Shabble is still hanging there in the air, an untoward incident occurs. There is a massive energy drain which affects all of Injiltaprajura. Lights darken. Fires go out. Candles die. Then, to Shabble's horror, Shabble feels Something trying to seize Shabble's own energy. Shabble squeaks in fright and flees down the nearest drainpipe. The drainpipe (naturally) leads Downstairs.

Downstairs!

There is horror down there, and Shabble fears it greatly. Yet the alternative is death.

Thus Shabble flees.

We in our mortal flesh, living never more than a skin away from pain, are like to think of Shabble as a careless immortal. But, while it is certain that Shabble lives longer and safer than any of us – for Shabble's body is a full-size sun set in its own separate universe, interfaced with the local cosmos only by means of a cunning transponder which outwardly looks like a sun in miniature – yet even Shabble can be hurt, and has been. It is difficult to hurt Shabble, but the therapists of the Golden Gulag knew how. Oh yes! They knew how, and on occasion put theory into practice.

The therapists?

The Golden Gulag?

These will have to await their own chroniclers. For this is but a modest tale, dealing only with a few days in the life of Untunchilamon, with a struggle for the wishstone and the fate of some of the wonderworkers (and others) who became involved in that struggle.

This is not, then, the Omnium conceived of by the literary theoretician Sinja Larthelme, he whom those who would have themselves thought of as wise must pretend to hold in such high regard. In this account, many things are touched upon which 'thou must pursue in scholarship thyself if thou wouldst know more of them,' as Eric the Wise said to the over-valorous Uri of legend on the occasion of their famous debate outside the notorious Stench Caves of Logthok Norgos (into which the bright-smiling Uri ultimately ventured alone, and may be venturing still for all we know).

[The Golden Gulag mentioned by the Originator appears to be his personal invention. Despite the claim made above, the Originator does later elaborate this invention at length, claiming in the course of such elaboration to reveal the Truth which lies hidden behind the veils of the Days of Wrath. Yet an exhaustive search of the Archives for collaboration of these tales of the Gulag uncovers no mention of it whatsoever. In truth, scholarship knows virtually nothing of humanity's mode of existence before the wars of the Days of Wrath. *This Insertion by Order of Indorjed, Archivist Superior.*]

[The naive should note that the unrelenting labours of the world's best scholars have failed to produce even so much as a definitive date for the Days of Wrath. They are generally supposed to have taken place between 9,000 and 20,000 years Before Present; it is generally agreed that no closer dating can be arrived at. The airy exactitude of the Originator should be seen against this background. *This Insertion by Order of Than, Chronologer Superior.*]

[Here seventeen spurious Insertions by various hands have been deleted. One suspects that Insertions by some are valued for their own sake. That some see careers in terms of the creation of quantity rather than quality. The over-ambitious younger generation must learn that, in scholarship as in other things, continence is a virtue. *By Order, Jonquiri O, Disiciplinarian Superior.*]

Well, then.

You have seen the start of our history.

A malign Power of some description – most probably a hideous demon in the process of breaking through into our innocent and unsuspecting world from the World Beyond – has subjected Injiltaprajura to a massive energy drain. Shabble, the bright-voiced imitator of suns, has been forced to flee Downstairs lest this energy drain end Shabble's life entirely.

What now?

Why, the tale of the wishstone and the wonderworkers begins, and proceeds to its conclusion.

You know the setting and the scope of the action. If then you deem our history to be worthy of your attention, read on. If not, then may the mephitic stench of a million dead scorpions enfold you, may cesspool fevers rack your bones for the next five thousand years, may worms the colour of mastic ooze from your ears, and may your flesh decay until it becomes soft as a mango lost for a month in a dungheap.

And may you dwell in the house of your mother-in-law forever.

CHAPTER TWO

Chegory Guy was a knifefighter. Perhaps that is not entirely accurate. If truth be told, he had never been in a knife fight in his life. Yet it is still far from misleading to describe him as a knifefighter since he owned a number of blades and had been trained to kill with them. Furthermore, he trained with his weapons on a daily basis, practising feinting, shifting, slashing and slicing, stabbing and hacking.

Once you know this, you will not be surprised to hear that he was an Ebrell Islander. These people are, of course, notorious for their violence. Such generalisations are, or so we are told by the Ashdan liberals, odious, untrue and misleading; nevertheless, it would be hard to make sense of the world without them, and in the case of Chegory Guy they make a great deal of sense.

This dangerous young man dwelt in the fair city of Injiltaprajura (or, shall we say, the bloodstone-complexioned city of Injiltaprajura?). To be precise, he was domiciled in the Dromdanjerie.

The Dromdanjerie.

What and where?

What is easy. The Dromdanjerie is the lunatic asylum of Injiltaprajura. It is a huge building fabricated from the native bloodstone of Untunchilamon. It has 2 kitchens, 27 showers, 44 stench holes, 6 high-security cells and 19 dormitories. One of the many fountains sourced Downstairs has been linked directly to the plumbing. This provides unlimited fresh (potable!) water for the showers with their floors of glistening green tiles, for the sluice rooms, for the kitchens gay with sun-faced representations of flowers, and for swabbing out those filthy dormitories so drearily painted in institutional brown and grey.

The Dromdanjerie, then.

What of it?

Does my acquaintance with the place seem too intimate? If so, know this: the Brin think me normal enough. Though what is 'normal' if one metabolises silicon, as do the Brin? Never mind. Enough of that. Let us not return to it again. Let us return to Chegory Guy. And to the action:

As Shabble was sliding down a drainpipe to escape the massive energy drain which threatened Shabbleself's very existence, the Dromdanjerie was waking. All the lights had gone out, waking those many who could not sleep in the dark. They screamed as if they had swallowed acid. They raved as if fresh-returned from hell. This set off most of the others. The dogs in the Dog Worshipper's Temple at the back of the Dromdanjerie began barking and howling. So, with uproar rising to heights unendurable, the staff of the Dromdanjerie was waking.

Chegory Guy was not on the staff – he was in fact a rock gardener who worked on the island of Jod – but as he boarded in the Dromdanjerie's staff quarters he too was wakened by the racket.

He kindled fire, then helped light (or, as the case may be, relight) lanterns by the dozen. Jon Qasaba took the first dozen, and, carrying them on a bablobrokmadorni stick, strode away into the depths of the bedlam. Guy loaded a second bablobrokmadorni stick for Qasaba's daughter.

Olivia.

Olivia Qasaba. She of the uncertain moods, at one moment a playful gamine, then on an instant a sophisticated ice lady, as remote and as distant as the stars. A female creature who was suffering that confusion of the blood which besets a girl who is in the process of becoming a woman. There are several symptoms of this confusion, the most notable being a propensity for slamming doors and a tendency to burst into tears upon provocation which should by rights produce (at the very most) no more than the briefest of scowls.

Chegory Guy was at least in part responsible for her

erratic emotional weather. What did he do? He was there! That was enough. Sometimes Olivia wished to romp with him like a boy at play with a peer, giving expression to simple high spirits and the natural ebullience of youth. At other times, she imagined him as an ardent suitor into whose arms she could swoon in a waking dream of passion.

Either way, Chegory disappointed her, for he daily grew more remote. Why? Because he had a nice regard for his own safety. He sensed her confusion. (He sensed it: but to most of the other people in the Qasaba household that confusion needed no sensing whatsoever, as it was clearly written in the girl's every action.) He feared that if he let her within his guard, she would one day go further than she was ready to, and would then scream rape. Or, alternatively, that she would go hardly any distance at all, and that he would then yield to temptation and rape her in truth.

Why did the young man take this business of rape so seriously? He was not one of those earnest young philosophers who pass through a phase of diligent asceticism at the age of eighteen. No: it was a survivor's caution which governed his flesh.

Chegory Guy was, as we have said already, an Ebrell Islander. By breeding at least, though not by birth. Yes, though Chegory Guy had been born on Untunchilamon, his parents had both been of Ebrell Island stock. Now the Ebrell Islanders are a race of drunkards, knifefighters and fornicators cursed by a genetic tendency to wanton dissipation. You doubt this? Are you then one of these Ashdan liberals who hold that hereditary traits are but illusory, and who believe (or at least claim to believe) that all things are possible for all people? Read on! And you will be enlightened.

The Ebrell Islanders had long been a troublesome minority on Untunchilamon. They had always been for the most part unemployed. Gambling, drug abuse, violence and venereal disease were rife amongst them. They were customarily involved in smuggling, theft, prostitution, extortion and organised crime. They were a cancerous blotch upon civilisation.

Therefore, when Chegory Guy was but nine years of age, the wise and magnanimous Wazir Sin had organised a pogrom against the Ebbies. The slaughter had been efficient in the extreme, and only a few of the underpeople had escaped into the wilderness. Among those few were the nine-year-old Chegory Guy, his father, his uncle Dunash Labrat and his cousin Ham.

Strangely, the slaughter of the Ebrell Islanders failed to end unemployment, crime and prostitution in Injiltaprajura. Wazir Sin was vexed. He decided he had not gone far enough. So he drew up a Program of Purification. First he would hunt down any and all Ebbies who had fled into the Wastelands. Then he would slaughter the few survivors of the Dagrin – the aboriginal race of Untunchilamon. Then he would kill the crippled, the insane, the mutant, and anyone over the age of seventy. Then he would—

But it is pointless to detail further this Noble Experiment, for it was not to be. Before the saintly Wazir Sin could enact his visionary program, the horrors of Talonsklavara threw the Izdimir Empire into disarray. The Yudonic Knight Lonstantine Thrug took advantage of the confusion, overthrew the innocent Sin, then murdered that upright imperial servant. Two years later, Thrug was imprisoned in the Dromdanjerie when his mounting insanity had reached the point where it had become undeniable. His daughter Justina installed herself in the belfried palace at the top of Lak Street and proclaimed an amnesty so general that its provisions extended even to the few remaining Ebrell Islanders.

Some of the Ebrell Islanders who still survived in the wilderness returned to Injiltaprajura. Dunash Labrat came home to reclaim his properties, which had been managed in his absence by his wife. Though Chegory Guy's father stayed in the heartland of the Scorpion Desert, Chegory himself came back to Injiltaprajura with his uncle (the aforesaid Dunash Labrat), and began an apprenticeship as an apiarist. This was aborted when young Chegory proved to be allergic to bee stings. Thereafter he took various forms of irregular employment until at last he landed himself a steady job on the island of Jod.

On Jod, Chegory came into contact with Ivan Pokrov, and thus met Pokrov's friend Jon Qasaba. An Ashdan. An Ashdan liberal, in fact. Jon Qasaba and his sister-in-law Artemis Ingalawa found the civilisation of Chegory Guy to be a project which appealed to their hopelessly optimistic liberal tastes. They collaborated with Ivan Pokrov on this civilisation experiment, arranging for Chegory's working day to end at midday so he could study throughout the afternoon while still drawing his pay from Jod's Analytical Institute. Soon enough, Chegory was boarding with Jon Qasaba in the Dromdanjerie's staff quarters, and was thus thrown into daily contact with the nubile Olivia.

Is there any need to further elaborate the reasons for Chegory's caution? He was a member of a despised minority which had recently been almost hunted to extinction on Untunchilamon. By reason of his race, people would expect him to rape, kill, cheat, steal and lie, and also to indulge in the worst forms of drug abuse. Therefore he acted always with the greatest of caution, avoided compromising situations, and showed his thorns to Olivia.

This delicious young damsel, seeking friendship at least (and sometimes thinking she might be seeking more), found his remoteness hard to endure.

By now you may be asking: how are such things known? How have the dynamics of Chegory's relationship with Olivia been discovered? How can we be sure that this is how it was?

Why, because there is such a thing as gossip, of course. You must realise that institutions (prisons, armies and asylums) are great places for gossip, because there is intimacy, the cheek by the jowl, the free speaking of the loquacious in front of those so familiar they have become invisible, and because there is time. Time to study hints, to theorise on fragments.

And if most of the witnesses to these events were mad, what of it? The intellectual powers of the insane are no weaker than those of people fool enough to accept the status quo. You may doubt this. But reflect! Suppose one has done something heinous. Suppose one has raped one's brother, burnt down a temple, embezzled half a million dragons or finally settled accounts with one's mother-in-law. What is smarter? To throw oneself on the mercy of the court, and get oneself executed? Or to discover that one is in truth insane and really indulged in delinquency because one was, for example, frightened by a goldfish in early youth.

Believe me, unless one is truly demented it takes a lot of calculated intellectual discipline to maintain one's madness in the face of the implacable investigations of that most scholarly of all therapists, Jon Qasaba.

Suppose one has yet again been hailed to the Dromdanjerie's interview room, there to face the tenth interview in as many days with the formidable Qasaba. The ever-resourceful Ashdan thinks he has at last found a clue which will explicate one's behaviour. He enters. He seats himself. He shuffles through a great heap of notes, observations and laborious speculations. Then he looks one in the eyes (he is still ignorant of the fact that my people consider such eye-to-eye contact extremely rude) and he says:

'Why did you use an axe to kill your mother-in-law?'

'Because I wanted her dead.'

'Yes, yes, I know that. But why an axe? Why that particular implement and not another?'

In the teeth of such a question, what is one to do? One's natural reaction will be to laugh. Or voice one of the quips which come so easily to the tongue:

'What was I supposed to use? A toothpick?'

But one cannot safely do either of these things. The mad are supposed to be serious and devoid of wit. So: will the truth serve? No. For the truth is too simple. It was pleasure, pure pleasure, to see the bitch smashed apart, to see her skull burst like a rotten cantaloup, to see great globs of blood—

[Here a lengthy descriptive passage has been excised. *By Order, Drax Lira, Redactor Major.*]

Anyone can understand this. Or should be able to. However, Jon Qasaba is so obsessed by his pursuit of arcane knowledge that he has lost touch entirely with the blatantly obvious. So one thinks long and carefully, then answers:

'Weight.'

'Weight?'

'Yes, it ... the axe, it ... I mean, it was heavy. Oppressive. It was ... there was a memory. I mean, what I'm trying to say is that there's all these ... these ...'

'Go on.'

'It goes back to ... to when I was little, that's when the weight, the weight, the pressure, it first ... or maybe it was before then.'

One observes Jon Qasaba writing. One deciphers his eager notation: Birth Trauma?!

When Qasaba looks back, one is staring at nothing. Slowly, one says:

'Blood, too. That comes into it. Somehow, it's ... there's blood mixed up in this. The memories, I mean.'

You get the picture? This is the kind of intellectual endeavour it takes to remain suitably mad while one resides in the Dromdanjerie. So don't write off the insane. While they are not necessarily totally accurate in their observations, who is? Would you trust Qasaba to author this history? Qasaba, who truly believes that Rye Phobos did what he did because his mother subjected him to the Second Indignity when he was aged but three? No, Qasaba—

[Here the Originator libels Qasaba at length, then argues that the status quo itself is not necessarily sane. Hence (he says) that majority which dwells outside the lunatic asylum is possibly the group which is truly mad. Surely (I say) such argument is absurd. In terms of logic and the law, lunatics are by definition those incarcerated in lunatic asylums. What more need be said? *Drax Lira, Redactor Major.*]

Thus, to return to the question of the provenance of our facts.

Believe me, all this is known. Or most of it. Very, very little is surmise, and the logic of such surmise is inescapable. Truly, Olivia Qasaba was at the age of change, of ripeness, of hot juice and urgent dreams, that age when nine thoughts in ten are unspeakable because of their impropriety. In her days of youth and vigour she was domiciled in close quarters with Chegory Guy, and had no other appropriate target of sexual opportunity in sight.

Ergo, she was infatuated with him. Or, at a minimum, she was continually considering (perhaps continually rejecting, but definitely considering!) young Chegory as a potential sexual partner. For such is the nature of the blood. Such is the nature of the organism. And who can deny that the organism has, shall we say, at times a certain priority? When the flesh is gorged and the urge is upon them, even the wise must—

[Here by Order of the Redactor Major a gratuitous crudity of considerable obscenity has been excised. Also an unpardonable elaboration of that crudity, complete with the baseless attribution of regrettable personal practices to several of History's more dignified Perpetrators.]

Let us have an equation, then, in the manner of the famous literary theorist Sinja Larthelme. Boy plus girl equals the necessity for diligent onlookers to be ever considering the probable consequences of propinquity.

Does that satisfy?

The followers of Sinja Larthelme will doubtless answer: no. The equation is too simple. Too true. Too close to life as it is lived. Too close to commonsense. They want different equations, elaborate expressions of curves and intersections, velocities and accelerations, subsets and matrices. They pretend to be in possession of a generalised mathematics of existence which (this is their conceit) treats with human disorder (chaos, coincidence, collision) in terms of a mode of discourse possessed of a logic as rigorous as that used to clarify the dance of the stars.

Which is a nonsense.

Because—

[To spare scribes, readers and overburdened library shelves alike, some seventy thousand words of impassioned exegesis have here been excised by Order of the Redactor Major.]

Well, where were we?

We were at the point where Chegory Guy was loading lanterns on to a bablobrokmadorni stick for Olivia. Once the stick was loaded, she followed her father into the depths of the Dromdanjerie to help calm the inmates. She walked with a firm, confident step. She knew the mad by name, and was used to dealing with their moods and panics. Nevertheless, it is worth noting that she had a lead-weighted cosh in her back pocket.

The daughter of an Ashdan liberal, yet she carried a cosh?

Well, yes.

Life in the Dromdanjerie does tend to inject a certain degree of realism into one's actual behaviour whatever one's ideological outlook.

Chegory Guy did not follow. Not because he was scared, but because Jon Qasaba had often explicitly forbidden him to venture into the dormitories. Instead, he lit more lanterns, then sat silent. Waiting. As he waited, he heard all the dogs of Injiltaprajura begin to bark and howl.

What did he think of as he sat there thus? We can only guess. Perhaps he thought of Olivia, of her heat, her nipples, the marginal hairs, the faint-breathing odour easing from her secret. He was young, was he not? So what else would he think about? And Olivia was worth thinking of, oh yes, she was worth it, very much worth it indeed.

But I never touched her, I swear it.

CHAPTER THREE

While Shabble was exploring Downstairs and Chegory Guy was lighting lanterns, other events were taking place elsewhere in Injiltaprajura. To the treasury housed deep below the pink palace there came a band of robbers. These brigands were the Malud marauders Al-ran Lars, Arnaut and Tolon.

How did they get in?

How did they get past the guards, bars, doors and walls?

Why, by using a secret passage.

Al-ran Lars, you see, had helped loot that treasury before. He had been to Injiltaprajura years before in an ill-famed ship known as the Kraken and captained then by the notorious Log Jaris. On that raid, Al-ran Lars and his companions had snaffled the bard of Untunchilamon. Now Al-ran Lars was back for a second helping.

Some will call his intentions immoral, but surely this is unjust. What benefit has the world from treasure which does naught but sit in the dark for year on year, unchanging? Treasure thus restrained is dull stuff, not process but form. Once it is released into the world, it joins that endlessly fascinating interplay of energy which we know as the economy.

This is what it is all about.

It?

Life, strife, existence!

So Da Thee, a Korugatu philosopher near unique in his sobriety, says simply that life is energy.

Remember that while the treasure of Injiltaprajura lay untouched in doom-dark silence, its existence was (in practice) purely theoretical. In practice, it made no difference whether the treasury was filled with gold or with shadows. Therefore let us not libel the Malud marauders by calling them witless criminals. Let us see them by the light of philosophy, and know them as life-makers, releasers of energy, creators of new potential for the world's existence.

'Where is it?' said Arnaut, youngest of them all and hence the most excitable.

He spoke, of course, in Malud, since that is the language of the people of the island of Asral. Not only is it their name for their tongue – it is also their name for themselves. Although, as far as the eye is concerned, they are outwardly identical to the Ashdans.

'Hush,' said Al-ran Lars as he raised his lantern.

Light spangled from eye-bright diamonds, from coins in cascades, from gold-woven tapestries and other wealth beyond ennumeration. Pearls the size of pears. Almandine glowing as red as roses. Carbuncles lit by their own inner fire. The glamour of ultramarines. Globes of amber. The sombre ochre light of a solitary firestone, work of the wizards of Arl, masters of both the merely luminous and the incandescent.

'There,' said Tolon, the big one, the muscle-man.

He pointed.

'That's it,' said Al-ran Lars, and slipped his hands into a pair of mailed gauntlets.

With his hands thus armoured, he picked up the sceptre of the Empress Justina. This ornament terminated in a glittering bauble, a fierce-blazing flare of rainbows, a soft-humming triakisoctahedron. Al-ran Lars raised it to his lips. Kissed it.

'No snakes,' said Arnaut.

'I noticed,' said Al-ran Lars dryly.

When he had first come here years before, the greatest wonders of the treasury had been guarded by snakes and by worse. But security had grown slack in the intervening years. Which is not surprising, since it takes a fair amount of hard work and enterprise (not to mention raw courage) to maintain a sizeable colony of poisonous reptiles in good health in an underground treasury.

Al-ran Lars passed the sceptre to Tolon, who hefted its

weight easily. Tolon bent back the copper clasps which bound the triakisoctahedron to the sceptre, freed that fabulous bauble, then let the denuded sceptre fall. It clanged against the flagstones.

'Let me see,' said Arnaut, eagerly claiming the wishstone from Tolon.

The triakisoctahedron was warm to the touch. It vibrated constantly, as if it was not a jewel which he held but a huge insect, its wings ever seeking to urge its mass to flight. Arnaut raised the wishstone in both hands and said:

'I wish I may I wish I might have a – a loaf of bread tonight.'

Nothing happened. Al-ran Lars laughed.

'I told you,' said he.

'It was worth trying,' said Arnaut, crestfallen.

'Come,' said Al-ran Lars. 'Let's be gone.'

Then he led the way to the door through which they had entered. It closed with a heavy thlunk-clunk, and the treasury was once more in darkness. Before venturing back through the tunnels Downstairs, Al-ran Lars searched first Tolon and then his nephew. But neither had taken any trinkets which might betray them.

'Good,' said Al-ran Lars, pleased with their discipline.

But this discipline was only to be expected. This raid had been planned and rehearsed for two years. It was slick, professional and cunning. Oh, how cunning!

When the loss of the wishstone was discovered, Injilta-prajura would be turned upside down by thief-seeking soldiers. Any foreigners who had just arrived in town would naturally be under suspicion. This was why Al-ran Lars had brought the Taniwha to Untunchilamon shortly before the beginning of the Long Dry. For long dull days of windless weather the brig had floated at anchor while Al-ran Lars bought and sold in the markets of Injilta-prajura. Now his ship was so familiar to all the city that it was but part of the scenery.

When the season of Fistavlir ended and the trade winds blew once more, the Taniwha would sail from Injiltaprajura with the wishstone aboard. Even her crew would be ignorant of this special cargo, knowledge of which would be restricted to Al-ran Lars, to his nephew Arnaut, and to his blood-brother Tolon.

Al-ran Lars was sure the wealth the wishstone would win would be worth all the effort and the danger which went with it. The two years of planning. The long, dangerous journey east from Asral. The days of trial and tension which yet lay ahead. Wealth would compensate for all. So he thought. Little did he know what horrors awaited them! What dangers fearful! What doom near-inescapable. But he was to learn. Oh yes, he was to learn soon enough.

The Malud marauders hustled along through the underways Downstairs till they came to a flight of stairs. Up they went. Al-ran Lars extinguished his lantern then opened the sally port at the top of the stairs. He and his companions then sallied out of it. They were in the open air again. To be precise, they were in Thlutter, the steep, jungle-growth gully just east of Pearl.

Injiltaprajura's portside slopes steeply from Pokra Ridge to the waterfront. Gullies steeper yet gash the slope. For the most part, roads and houses avoid these gullies, which are choked with vegetation in which there dwell indestructible black pigs, snakes, spiders, scorpions, centipedes half as long as your arm, bush dogs, numerous cats and mosquitoes in their millions.

Many of these mosquitoes began to bite the three pirates (for such the Malud marauders were, surely, though they guised themselves as honest merchants) as soon as they emerged into the night air. Muggy night air, air alive with the splitter-splatter of a dozen fountains, with the smells of dank earth, coconut rot, over-ripe bananas, decayed mangos and frangipani.

'Dogs!' said Tolon.

'I'm not deaf,' said Al-ran Lars.

Dogs in their hundreds were barking. To north, south, east and west. It sounded as if every dog in Injiltaprajura had been roused to wakefulness.

33

'Come on,' said Arnaut. 'Let's get out of here.'

'Wait!' said Al-ran Lars.

Next moment, the bells of the pink palace rang out. These were the midnight bells, marking the end of undokondra (that quarter of the day which lasts from dusk to midnight) and the start of bardardornootha. The bells had scarcely died away when rainbows flourished through the heavens. The peacock-plumage blaze of colour lit up Thlutter. Lit up the broad-leaved banana trees, the trailing scorpion vines and the faces of the Malud marauders. Faces which clearly revealed their dismay. Then the rainbow light snapped out. Vanished! Gone!

The three Malud blinked blind at the darkness.

'The wishstone!' said Arnaut. 'The wishstone, the stone, that's what's doing it!'

'Nonsense,' said Al-ran Lars, closing his eyes in an effort to recover his nightsight.

'Maybe it's the wonderworkers,' said Tolon. 'Warning us. Hunting us.'

'Rubbish!' said Al-ran Lars. 'They can't know anything. Not yet.'

But he was worried. The rainbows in the sky had echoed the inner life of the wishstone. The relationship between sky and stone might be spurious, accidental, coincidental. Nevertheless, the sky-brightening had surely been a symptom of a fearful exercise of magic.

Al-ran Lars came to a swift decision.

'We're going back,' he said. 'Back Downstairs.'

'You really wish to run?' said Tolon.

'Rather that than fight my way through Injiltaprajura street by street.'

'It's not far,' argued Tolon. 'We could be back aboard soon enough.'

'With these dogs on the rouse?' said Al-ran Lars. 'With the sky amok with colour? The whole city will be awake by now.'

Arnaut said: 'I think—'

'Think later!' said Al-ran Lars. 'Thinking we can do when we're safely underground.'

So saying, he led his comrades back Downstairs. Down there, of course, Shabble was still on the loose.

What precisely did cause those dogs to rouse, those rainbows to flourish through the sky? With the benefit of perfect hindsight we can say, without a doubt, that those phenomena were associated with the arrival of a demon in Injiltaprajura. Yes, a hideous Thing had broken through from the World Beyond, and would in due course do appalling damage to the dignity of some of the city's leading citizens.

But this was not known at the time, hence the shock, alarm and bewilderment felt by the Malud marauders was shared by others in the city. Priests roused themselves from bed and went to pray to their gods and to make whatever sacrifices their religions demanded. Sentries standing watch woke their superior officers and were cursed for their pains. Fishermen in canoes which were working the Laitemata and the lagoon by night extinguished their lamps, stowed their gear and began rowing for shore, fearing the sea itself might be next to manifest an unexpected disturbance – perhaps one which would doom their frail craft.

We see, then, that many of the worthy citizens of Injiltaprajura were disturbed by these manifestations which were, at that time, so inexplicable. One of those who suffered a certain degree of angst as a result of the phenomena-of-unknown-origin was Justina's Master of Law, Aquitaine Varazchavardan.

The name rings a bell?

I wouldn't be surprised.

Varazchavardan is a formidable figure who has doubtless found his way into many histories by now, so there is every possibility that you will have encountered him already in your reading. Nevertheless, let us tell him in detail even so.

Aquitaine Varazchavardan, who had fingernails as long as the fingers themselves, dwelt in a villa on Hojo Street. Varazchavardan, who was sorcerer and civil servant both, liked his sleep. Yet he was wide awake, even though bardardornootha had begun. There is no mystery about this. His mind was occupied by an urgent question: *What the hell is going on?*

Earlier in the evening, the lean albino had been woken by the massive energy drain which had extinguished every light in the city. He had known at once that it was nothing to do with the wonderworkers dabbling with the transmutation of metals in the fastness of the Cabal House. No. Someone or Something was tampering with the Fundamentals. Who? Or What? Could it be that the Hermit Crab had been roused to action?

Gods forbid!

Shortly after the energy drain, something had set every dog in Injiltaprajura to barking. Varazchavardan had immediately suspected earthquake. Yet the earth had stayed stable. It was the sky which had next shown signs of disturbance. Rainbows had briefly lit up the entire dome of the heavens from one horizon to the next.

And what next?

Varazchavardan grimaced, watched and waited.

He was standing on the balcony of his villa's uppermost storey. He looked up and down Hojo Street, and saw lanterns on the move as nervous worshippers began to flock to their temples.

Hojo Street is the most desirable piece of real estate in Injiltaprajura, and consequently attracts land taxes quite astronomical. So astronomical, in fact, that most buildings on Hojo Street are owned by institutions which can live tax free – most notably religions.

Aquitaine Varazchavardan flexed his talons and looked across the Laitemata Harbour to the island of Jod where dwelt the Hermit Crab.

Is it the Hermit Crab?

He remembered his first (and last) interview with that sinister sage. He had dared a trifling piece of magic to test the island's eremite, and had nearly been turned inside out. That brief encounter had been sufficient to convince him the Crab could do whatever it wanted.

36

But why would it eat energy, wake dogs, conjure with rainbows? There's no sense to it.

The night's manifestations were more in the nature of an experiment. Who but the wonderworkers indulged in experiments? Ivan Pokrov, of course! The man was always playing with mysterious objects recovered from Downstairs or dredged up from the seabed in fishermen's nets.

Demon's claw! What's Pokrov up to now?

So thought Aquitaine Varazchavardan. After thinking such, he vowed to visit Pokrov soon to see precisely what was afoot on Jod.

If it's Pokrov, we can bring him to heel.

And if not?

Varazchavardan, of all people, should have been able to deduce from the evidence that Untunchilamon was probably feeling the will of Something from Beyond. A Power of some kind. A demon. A minor god. Or (greater gods forbid!) a major god. He had the requisite knowledge, experience and intelligence. But all he thought was:

Time will tell.

The truth is, though Varazchavardan was alarmed by the sudden manifestations, he had a lot of other things on his mind which worried him far more. Political things.

Abandoning his fruitless scrutiny of the night sky, Varazchavardan opened the mosquito screens and went back inside. He poured some sherbet into a glass, opened an amphora and clawed out a chunk of ice which he dropped into his drink. Ice, sourced Downstairs, was dirt cheap in Injiltaprajura. Otherwise Varazchavardan would scarcely have found life in the tropics bearable. He hated the heat.

This was his fifteenth year on Untunchilamon. Much of that time had been tolerably enjoyable – the eight years he had spent as chief adviser to Wazir Sin. At the start of Talonsklavara he had considered going to Yestron to join the struggle for control of the Izdimir Empire, but had abandoned the notion since the probable outcome of the continental civil war had at that time been unclear. Shortly afterwards, Varazchavardan's old friend Sin had been murdered by Lonstantine Thrug.

Then life had become difficult.

Still, by adroit political manoeuvring, Varazchavardan had managed to stay close to the heart of power. He had been helped by the fact that he was head of the wonder-worker's Cabal House. Lonstantine Thrug had not wished to pick a quarrel with Injiltaprajura's sorcerers, and his daughter Justina had been similarly cautious, allowing Varazchavardan to retain his position as Master of Law.

All in all, life had been good. Particularly as Varazchavardan had certain extracurricular interests which had brought him wealth sufficient to pay for both the villa on Hojo Street and the taxes on the same.

But the good times were over. Talonsklavara was almost at an end, and it seemed Aldarch the Third, the dreaded Mutilator of Yestron, was sure to be victorious in the struggle for control of the Izdimir Empire. Once Aldarch III had made himself master of Yestron, he would surely take steps to reintegrate Untunchilamon into his realm. Then Varazchavardan would have to flee – or else make his peace with the Mutilator.

How?

Varazchavardan could scarcely hope to conceal the fact that he had served Injiltaprajura's illegal regime for the last seven years, working first for the murderer of the rightful governor, the eminent Wazir Sin, then for the murderer's daughter. Aldarch the Third was unlikely to look favourably on such activities.

If Varazchavardan were to seize power on Untunchilamon in the name of Aldarch III, he might win the confidence of that formidable conqueror. But if he were to act, he would have to act quickly indeed. For all he knew, Talonsklavara might have ended already. No news of Yestron's civil war could reach Untunchilamon in the season of Fistavlir when the doldrums made intercourse with distant shores near impossible.

Of course, the canoes of the Ngati Moana still sailed the seas. But in this season they came only from the west, using the Coral Current to supplement the breezes which the weather rationed out a single breath at a time.

These were the political questions which were occupying Varazchavardan's mind and distracting him from an analysis of unexpected paranormal phenomena. That night, as he sat in his grand house in Hojo Street, quietly sipping his sherbet, he at last came to a decision.

He would mount a coup. He would overthrow the Empress Justina and burn her to death. He would drag her mad father from the sanctuary of the Dromdanjerie then butcher him. Then he would raise a memorial to the memory of Wazir Sin and strive to complete the great work which Sin had begun. He would slaughter the surviving Ebbies. Then begin on the aboriginals, the deranged, the mutant and the senile. Such resolute action would surely commend him to Aldarch III.

'I'll do it!'

Thus said Varazchavardan, and drained the last of his sherbet.

'Do what?' said Nixorjapretzel Rat, who had entered the room without Varazchavardan being aware of him.

'What are you doing here?' said Varazchavardan, startled from reverie.

'I came to wake you up,' said Rat, the young sorcerer who had till recently been Varazchavardan's apprentice. 'There's strange things afoot in the city.'

'What kind of things?' said Varazchavardan. 'Crocodiles? Trolls? Walking rocks?'

'None of those,' said Rat. 'Something invisible which eats lamplight and swallows the flames of candles by the thousand. Something invisible also which rouses dogs by the hundreds. Something which lights the sky with rainbows.'

'You think I don't know about that already?' said Varazchavardan. 'Do you think I haven't got eyes? Or ears? Stop wasting my time! Get out of here!'

Then he fished a lump of ice from his glass and flung it at the fast-retreating Rat.

So.

We have discussed Varazchavardan and his thoughts, motives and intentions in some detail.

What is our authority for such discussion?

If you have personal knowledge of Aquitaine Varazchavardan, you will doubtless know that the eminent Master of Law lived without friend, lover or confidante. Yet without the testimony of such, who could ever guess at the thoughts behind that inscrutable maggot-white face? Nobody. You will have noted that the young Rat was not admitted into Varazchavardan's confidence, but fled without having any discourse of consequence with his master. So who betrayed Varazchavardan to this chronicle?

The answer is simple.

Varazchavardan betrayed himself.

Know then that there later came a time when Aquitaine Varazchavardan shared a pallet with an intellectual of scholarly disposition in the dungeons of Obooloo. Both at the time were under sentence of death, and the stress of such sentence can change much. Certainly it changed Varazchavardan, and he sang to his scholarly companion as if to a lover. Hence knowledge personal and private passed to another, and in due course to this history.

You wish to know more of this? More could be told. But it is a cruel story, a tale as grim as an executioner's axe, a history dark with blood, an account of pain and hate, of gloating oppression and deaths obscene, of fear amidst the shadows. It is painful even to begin to remember those days of horror. If you have an appetite for such, then you must satisfy that appetite elsewhere.

For the moment, let us be content to watch Aquitaine Varazchavardan as he salvages another piece of ice from his well-stocked amphora. It melts in his hand. Drops of water slide to the coconut matting which covers the floor. He slips the ice between his teeth. He crunches. Cool, so cool! He closes his eyes and thinks of: Obooloo in winter.

Of ice and snow.

Now the moment is over. Let us flee through time and space, for our history bids us elsewhere.

CHAPTER FOUR

Very close in time and space, Shabble was still hiding out Downstairs. Shabble hated it down there, for far too many things from the Golden Gulag still survived down there. Evil evil evil! Evil was the Gulag, and accursed is its name.

There is no need to delve too deeply into the details. There is enough death, fear and horror in the world without us dredging up the sorrows of days bygone. Furthermore, it is surely wrong to gratify that all-too-common appetite which feeds on pain for its own sake, death for its own sake, fear for its own sake.

Therefore we will say nothing of the sewer pits, in which political dissidents were kept for days on end in cages waist-deep in the effluent of a metropolis. We will not mention the commercial wards, where those too sick to long survive were maimed and blinded by researchers questing for safer cosmetics. We will keep silent about the Proving Grounds, where weapons of all descriptions were tested on human subjects. We will pass over the subject of the carnivals staged to gratify the jaded tastes of debauched hedonists.

We will simply note that the Gulag was a commercial empire devoted to therapy (treatment of recidivists a speciality), and Shabble, who was once on the receiving end of some of that therapy, still had nightmares about it.

(Shabble sleeps? Even sharks sleep, my darling.)

Thus Downstairs most definitely aroused in Shabble memories most painful which (for the reasons given above) we will not detail.

The Malud marauders who were skulking in the depths Downstairs knew nothing of the Golden Gulag, but Al-ran Lars did think he knew all he needed to know about the dangers of those depths. He had briefed Arnaut and Tolon about the same, assuring them that Injiltaprajura's under-parts were basically safe. Therefore the Malud were most surprised to be challenged without warning by a voice from the shadows.

'HALT!' cried that doom-dark voice. 'HALT! THROW DOWN YOUR WEAPONS AND SURRENDER!'

Being who they were and where they were, the Malud marauders instead drew their weapons and charged, their voices raised in battle-bright onslaught. There was a flare of white-hot energy. Their weapons twisted and melted in their hands. Metal splashed molten to the floor where it puddled and cooled. A bright, bright sun-bright sun-globe hung in the air.

Burning, burning, burning.

Then it said:

'I am the demon-god Lorzunduk. And you have offended me.'

If the Malud marauders had been natives of Untun-chilamon then they would have answered:

'Shabble! Don't be silly! This is no time for games! Look what you've done to our beautiful swords! You should be ashamed of yourself!'

But instead the alien pirates fell grovelling to the ground, all courage gone now that they had been so spectacularly disarmed. Soon, very soon, they were pleading, praising and Confessing All.

Thus we leave the Malud marauders Al-ran Lars, Arnaut and Tolon as prisoners of the irresponsible Shabble as we shift in space (though not in time), leaving Injiltaprajura's underworld in favour of the corridors of Ganthorgruk, that creaking doss-house which broods above Lubos in Skindik Way. Ah. As yet, nothing of interest is happening here. So let us shift in time after all, moving forward to the heart of bardardornootha. At this intersection of time and space we find the conjurer Odolo, enduring bad dreams.

It is hot in his room.

A gecko clings to the wall. A mosquito circles by his ear. A kamikaze bug bumbles noisily from wall to wall. But

Odolo dreams not of the gecko, the mosquito or the kamikaze bug. No. Even when the mosquito settled on his cheek and thrust for his blood he dreamt not of it but of . . .

Strange things.

He dreamt of a loathsome yale, a *lusus naturae* which hunted him through a forest of thorns. He dreamt of ants made of honey, of candles quick-burning and rainbows bright. But never in his darkest, deepest, most murderous nightmares did he dream that the wishstone had been stolen.

If he had known of its theft, then he would have had nightmares indeed, whether he was sleeping or awake. For in the last few years the Empress Justina had smiled upon Odolo, and had granted him a few lightly paid sinecures. Among other things, he was Official Keeper of the Imperial Sceptre, which meant that the wishstone which adorned that sceptre was his responsibility.

For him, the day ahead offered every chance of disaster.

Let us shift again.

Not in place, but in time.

To dawn.

The sun has touched the glitter dome of the imperial palace. The dawn bells ring out from the pink palace, announcing the end of bardardornootha and the start of bright-favoured istarlat. Already the air is alive with the smells of curry and cassava, of saffron-flavoured rice, of braised flying fish and fried banana. Breakfast is cooking!

Ah! Dawn on Untunchilamon! Memories, memories! The rising sun shines hot on the monolithic mass of Pearl and ignites colour in the bloodstone of Injiltaprajura. The sea burns incandescent. A distant surf shatters on the Outer Reef. Within the lagoon, waves minor lap tamely at beaches incarnadine, the sands of which are made of red coral and bloodstone mixed.

Even at dawn it is still warm. Hot, even. For Injiltaprajura cools but little in the night. The sun glorious rouses flies and butterflies alike. The colours and choruses of a million million insects stir amidst Injiltaprajura's gulleys. There many flowers, heavily perfumed, flaunt themselves amidst the jungle, which flourishes thick thanks to the urging sun and the water fresh-flowing from the eversprings sourced Downstairs. There parrots squawk and screech, there monkeys squabble and wild dogs with wilder cats contend.

This, then, is dawn on Untunchilamon.

This is what Odolo woke to.

Or, rather (to abandon nostalgic imaginings for historical truth) he woke to a hot, muggy, heavily shuttered room with a sagging roof. He reached for the jug by his bed, poured some water into a coconut-shell bowl, then drank.

A liquid thicker than water slid down his throat. He gagged and spat. Blood splattered across the floor. In horror, he clutched his throat, retched, gagged again, then spat some more. He had visions of a huge bleeding sore in his mouth, of ruptured arteries in his throat, a burst blood vessel in his lungs, a lethal ulcer in his stomach.

He lent over the side of the bed, the better to clear the blood from his gullet. Upset the jug. And saw a brief torrent of blood spurt from its neck and slither across the floor in all directions.

'Falamantatha!' he said, in high amazement.

Then amazement gave way to anger. Who had staged this obscene and vicious joke? He immediately suspected his feckless gossoon. But his bedroom door was still barred from the inside. The boy could not have entered while Odolo slept. Nobody could have got in during the night.

'Some work of the wonderworkers!' said Odolo. 'That's what it is!'

But which of Untunchilamon's sorcerers would have done such a thing? And why? Was it a threat? A message? A warning? Had he offended one of the island's mages by his agile conjuring and his lighthearted jokes about magic and its practitioners? If so, then who precisely had he offended? And how could he make amends?

'Varazchavardan,' said Odolo slowly. 'Maybe that's who it is.'

Odolo was cursed with incurable levity, which had got him into trouble many times in the past. Maybe his wit had once again landed him 'upside down in boiling dung' as the local expression so nicely put it. Maybe he had finally told one albino joke too many.

'Well,' said Odolo, 'Varazchavardan forgets. The Empress Justina likes me very well.'

The thought gave him confidence, but the confidence was misplaced. For the blood was but a token of horrors greater yet to come, and the Empress was to prove powerless to protect him from those horrors.

A little later, Odolo descended to Ganthorgruk's dining room. He slapped a damn on to the chef's counter and breakfast was served to him. It was a mess of something grey and brown with bits of wiggly stuff poking out of it.

'Gods!' said Odolo, swilling it round in his bowl. 'Is there a doctor in the house?'

'Enough of your cheap cracks,' said Jarry the chef, who had a hangover. 'If you don't like it, don't buy it.'

'Cheap?' said Odolo. 'No joke is cheap if loss of life be its inspiration. Unless the life in question was yours, dear Jarry. A joke would be a bargain if that were its price.'

Jarry hawked and spat, missing Odolo by a fingerlength. The conjurer retreated, bearing his breakfast away to a table out of spitting range. Then he began to eat.

Usually, part of Odolo's daily routine was to play animal–vegetable–mineral with his breakfast, to the general amusement of all in earshot. But this morning he slopped down the food without comment, scarcely tasting it. He was still thinking about the jug of blood.

He finished his breakfast, pushed the bowl away from him, and paid out another damn to buy himself a cup of cinnamon-flavoured coffee, which he took to his favourite window. From here, one could look over the roofs of Lubos to the waters of the Laitemata, to the island of Jod, to the island of Scimitar which lay yet further south, to the lagoon beyond Scimitar, to the Outer Reef and then to the scintillating immensity of the open sea.

Odolo loved that view.

As he sipped his coffee, he thought of all the things he had to do that day. By rights he should go to the Vidal mansion to make a formal apology for the joke he had made at the funeral of Old Redlegs. He had to placate his bank manager, and try to convince the old monster that the overdraft was not nearly as large as it seemed. Since there was to be a Petitions Session on the morrow, he should drop by at the treasury to clean the Imperial Sceptre. It would only take a few moments. Then he had some tricks to rehearse for his performance at the banquet which would follow the Petitions Session.

Okay. And what else? The room, of course! Have to get someone to clean that bloody room.

As Odolo was so thinking, the clearing maid screamed. Moments later, he knew why. Miniature rainbows were dancing above the breakfast bowl which he had so lately emptied, and the bowl itself was boiling with frenzied blue scorpions.

CHAPTER FIVE

The island of Jod.

What and where?

'What' is easy enough. It was the home of the Hermit Crab and also of the marvellous building of imported white marble which housed the Analytical Institute. 'Where' is equally easy. The island of Jod lay – and lies still, one presumes – in the middle of the Laitemata Harbour. To the north, the mainland of Untunchilamon and the city of Injiltaprajura. To the south, the minor island of Scimitar, then the Outer Lagoon, the last reef rocks and the limitless blue sea beyond.

What and where are accounted for. So what about why? The hell with why! This is a history book, not a treatise on philosophy. If the island of Jod had, in any sense, a 'why', it is not for us to enquire into it.

Who, then.

A question more worth asking.

There were many people on Jod. There was, for example, Ivan Pokrov, head of the Analytical Institute. Then there were algorithmists, mechanics, kitchen hands and others. But let us start at the bottom. Let us start with the lowest of the low, which must mean, of course, that we find ourselves starting with an Ebrell Islander.

With, to be precise, young Chegory Guy.

When do we start with him?

In the morning. Not the early morning, where we left the conjurer Odolo staring aghast at a bowl full of scorpions. Not the mid-morning, either, for we have passed over that in silence. No, we start with Chegory Guy in the late morning, at the tail end of istarlat.

It was late morning on the island of Jod, and, as per

47

usual, Chegory Guy at work on the rock gardens. He was proud of his job, and of his reputation as a good, reliable worker who needed no supervision. Stupid Ebby! His pride was grossly misplaced. Despite all his endeavours, no rock under his care ever enlarged itself by so much as a fingerlength. His rocks were sterile, and did not multiply. Barren were his labours, and bitter were the fruits thereof.

[It is doubtful that this criticism is seriously intended. While the Originator doubtless hates and despises Ebbies (and who can blame him?) he here appears to be making an ill-advised attempt to indulge in humour. Unlike market gardeners, rock gardeners are neither required nor expected to fecundate the earth. Habble Skim argues that crystal flowers are known to grow in deep desert, and that the rocks of Untunchilamon may possess a similar potential for enlargement. They do not. Here I speak from personal knowledge. An alternative theory has been advanced by Gin Anvil, who claims that insanity is here in evidence. But is it? While that is a possibility, it is hard to locate another passage where the Originator deviates even slightly from accepted dogma regarding the nature and potential of the physical universe. Therefore, while I do not claim to understand the attraction of 'humour' (and would regard any insinuation that I am a 'humorist' as being libellous) I nevertheless believe that all evidence and research supports my contention that we are here in the presence of a joke. *Drax Lira, Redactor Major*.]

Nevertheless, Chegory was happy in his work, even though his pride in his labours was fatuous. However, he was scarcely going to get rich through such employment, since his job paid him but five damns a day.

Untunchilamon still used the official currency of the Izdimir Empire, in which there are forty damns to a single dalmoon and ten dalmoons to a dragon, with each dragon containing one standard pearlweight of basilisk-grade gold. Note that the dalmoon herementioned is not to be confused with the coin of identical name which is used in Dalar ken

Halvar solely for the ritual purchase of aborted foetuses. Note also that in the Malud of Asral, 'dalmoon' denotes a gaff-rigged boat rather than an item of coinage.

Things are unlikely to have changed since my departure from Injiltaprajura, so a traveller planning a visit to Untunchilamon should be able to rely on the imperial coinage. However, if one is starting out from Obooloo, please note that the turquoise strings so often used as a medium of exchange in the markets of Ang find scant acceptance on Untunchilamon, where money-changers will give you naught but ten per cent of their customary value. The money-changers are also highly suspicious of the spings, flothens, ems and zeals issued by Obooloo's Bondsman's Guild. On the other hand, saladin rings are treated as cash, just as they are in the imperial heartland, and have a similar purchasing power.

With that noted, let us return to Chegory Guy, still rock gardening on Jod, and still earning no more than five damns a day. In Injiltaprajura, a damn buys no more than it buys in Obooloo, and five damns will scarcely purchase a kiss, far less one of the greater pleasures. Thus we see that Chegory was without a doubt impoverished. However, his needs were few. He got his lunch for free, and paid but fifty damns a month to board at the Dromdanjerie. Hence he managed.

Chegory was still working some time later when the noon bells rang out. Their brazen voices carried clearly across the sun-hammered waters of the Laitemata. Young Chegory quit work and took lunch to the Hermit Crab. He emptied lunch (two pails of broken meat) into the trough in front of the Crab's cave. Then he lingered, wondering if he dare ask the Hermit Crab what had happened the night before.

What had made the lights go out, the dogs of the city wake, and rainbows burst across the sky? The Crab should know, for the Crab was (at least by reputation) omniscient. Chegory was curious; he wanted to know for the sake of knowing. Furthermore, if he won a reply from Jod's most notable resident, it would give him the confidence to ask for help with graver matters.

What Chegory really wanted to do was to change his race. His skin marked him for what he was. Thanks to his genetic inheritance, he could never escape the relentless categorising of a society which regarded him with (at the least) disdain. Consequently, Chegory had developed two elaborate lines of daydream, one pessimistic, the other optimistic, but both offering certain attractions unavailable in reality.

At times, he imagined himself transformed into a rock. A solid, inert object disregarded entirely by the public which trampled it underfoot. To some people, this would be the stuff of nightmare, but Chegory drew pleasure from such inauspicious reverie because as a rock he was safe from scorn, immune to pain, a world removed from injury. In his more optimistic daydreams, he changed not into a rock but into – into something else. It mattered not what, as long as that something was not an Ebby. He longed to clothe his soul in the flesh of an Ashdan, or to garb his spirit in the smoke-grey of the Janjuladoola people of the imperial heartland. Even the pallor of the people of Wen Endex appealed, though aesthetes everywhere despise it.

Since Chegory worked in such close proximity to the Hermit Crab, and daily served lunch to that entity, he was ever aware that the stuff of fancy could be made the stuff of flesh, or (to put it another way) that his red-skinned flesh could be made into something more to the world's fancy. But he had never yet been able to nerve himself up to ask the Crab for assistance.

'What,' said the Hermit Crab, 'are you waiting for?'

Chegory did not dare speak his mind. He did not ask for miracles. Instead, he meekly asked: 'Is there anything else I can do for you?'

To which the Hermit Crab answered: 'Stand out of my sunlight.'

Chegory took the lunch pails back to the lunch pail stand, where they would remain until the butcher's boy who brought the Crab's daily meal to Jod refilled them on the morrow. Then Chegory washed his hands in a free-flowing fountain. Then he dressed for lunch.

To work in the blazing sun Chegory wore a loincloth and boots. An odd combination but one appropriate to his job, since he was often putting his toes in danger by sledgehammering rocks. For lunch, he put a light knee-length robe over his loincloth. Later in the day, when it was time to leave Jod, he would change into his evening wear, which was long lightweight linen trousers and a lightweight longsleeved shirt, both worn primarily as a defence against night's mosquitoes.

This history has concerns weightier than fashions to deal with but those who have an interest in such things will note that this was fairly standard wear for males of the lower classes on Untunchilamon, except that most would go barefoot or wear sandals rather than encumbering themselves with boots. Lower-class females, however, would wear trousers and shirt exclusively, regardless of the time of day. People of a higher station, such as Ivan Pokrov or Artemis Ingalawa, would tend to wear ankle-length robes at all times, while sorcerers would never be seen dead or alive in anything other than long, flowing silken robes most richly embroidered.

Thus clothing.

When Chegory had washed his hands and had dressed for lunch he entered the white marble building which housed the Analytical Institute. There the windchimes sang:

Tangle tongle schtingle schtong . . .

It was the season of Fistavlir, the Long Dry. Yet even so, there was just enough wind to idle the chimes into music.

Meanwhile, back on the mainland – but you have guessed already. Of course. The conjurer Odolo, Official Keeper of the Imperial Sceptre, was in the treasury. And had found the imperial sceptre lying on the floor where the hand of a thief had discarded it. And Odolo's heart was hammering, for the wishstone, priceless ornament of that sceptre, was gone!

51

By the time Chegory Guy was ready to sit down to his own lunch on the island of Jod, Odolo had already raised the alarm, and troops were already beginning the search for the guilty – or for scapegoats. But Chegory knew nothing of that, therefore his appetite for his lunch was entirely unspoiled. He was feeling hungry, relaxed and tolerably happy as he strode into the formal dining room.

The usual company was there, politely waiting for Chegory to enter before they seated themselves. There was the olive-skinned Ivan Pokrov, head of the Analytical Institute and master of the Analytical Engine. The Ashdan mathematician Artemis Ingalawa, who had been labouring as usual to develop algorithms for the use of the aforesaid engine. Olivia Qasaba, who had worked all morning in the Dromdanjerie before making her way to Jod. Last but not least, Chegory's coeval Ox No Zan, the foreign student who had come all the way from Babrika to study under Ivan Pokrov. Today young No was looking decidedly miserable because he had an appointment that afternoon with Doctor Death the dentist.

As Chegory entered the room there was a scraping of chairs as these habitual dinner companions seated themselves. All but Ingalawa, who had one thing she had to do before she relaxed.

'What's for lunch?' said Chegory.

'Sea slugs,' said Olivia.

'Oh, good,' said Chegory, with predictable enthusiasm.

'And flying fish,' said Olivia.

'Better still!' said Chegory, pulling out a chair as if to sit.

'Hands!' said Ingalawa.

This hand-check was the one duty restraining her from relaxation. She took it very seriously indeed.

Reluctantly Chegory extended his paws.

'I did wash them,' he said. 'Right after I fed the Hermit Crab. I gave them a good wash.'

'They're filthy!' said Ingalawa. 'Look! Black gunge under the nails!'

Chegory blushed so fiercely that the flush was visible even though he was redskinned to start with.

'Well, what do you expect,' he said. 'That's rock gardening for you.'

'You've got rakes, shovels and god knows what. Why do you need to go grubbing about with your hands?'

'Because,' said Chegory. 'It's technical.'

'What's technical about rocks?' said Ingalawa.

'If you must know,' said Chegory. 'I was cleaning out the grease trap, you know, where all the kitchen water—'

'What on earth were you doing that for?'

Chegory began to get worked up. Angry, even.

'Well, it was rocks, okay, my rocks had got into there, I mean I didn't put them there, it was probably those kids, you know, that Marthandorthan bunch, they come over the harbour bridge in the evenings, they just run riot. Okay, so it's all rocks in there and a whole lot of filth and muck and stuff. So what am I supposed to do, make some big thing out of it? I mean, who does it if I don't?'

'You still could have—'

'Oh, leave the boy alone,' said Pokrov. 'Let's eat.'

'Before he's washed his hands?' said Ingalawa.

'He's not going to suck the stuff from under his nails, is he? Sit down the pair of you. Eat, eat!'

With some reluctance Ingalawa abandoned the civilisation of Chegory Guy for the moment and seated herself. Chegory, smarting still from Ingalawa's reprimand, took his own place. Olivia grinned at him from across the table. She already had a flying fish on her plate and was teasing its wings open and shut with her fingers as if pretending it was still flying. Her grin was inciting Chegory to do the same. He was sorely tempted – but a glance at Ingalawa showed him the scholarly Ashdan female was still dragonising him.

A moment later, she saw what Olivia was doing.

'Olivia!'

This said to the accompaniment of a hand slammed down on the table.

53

'It's Chegory's fault,' said Olivia, dropping the wings of her flying fish. 'He dared me to.'

Chegory kicked her under the table. Olivia kicked him back, hard. He caught her ankle. Drove his thumb into a pressure point between the heel's tendon and the associated bone. Olivia wrenched her leg back. Such was the violence of her reaction that her knee slammed into the underside of the table with a resounding thump which upset the curry powder and spilt the flying fish sauce.

'That's enough!' shouted Ingalawa.

Olivia looked at Chegory.

Chegory looked back.

He winked.

Olivia clutched her hands to her face as if vomiting. Actually, she was trying to stifle a fit of giggling. She was not entirely successful.

'I'm serious,' said Ingalawa, in her now-you-are-adults-not-children-and-I-expect-you-to-behave-accordingly voice. 'Any more nonsense out of either of you and you can get down from the table and go and eat in the kitchen.'

'Oh, can we?' said Olivia eagerly.

'No!' said Ingalawa.

'Would anyone care for some iced water?' said Ox No Zan.

He was sorely distressed by the display of bad manners which had disrupted the meal. In his home city of Babrika such conflict would be unthinkable. Any young person rude enough so to misbehave in front of an elder would be . . . well, skinning alive would be the least of it.

'Thank you,' said Ingalawa, seeing No's discomfort and thus, out of courtesy, allowing his attempted diplomatic intervention to succeed and bring the scene to an end.

Some time later, when the meal was well underway, Artemis Ingalawa broke the news to Ivan Pokrov. He had been invited to dine at the Qasaba household that evening. He said he would think about it.

Why such hesitation?

Because Jon Qasaba was in the habit of probing Pokrov.

54

Who preferred to conceal his true age, provenance and past. Ivan Pokrov was a some-time citizen of the Golden Gulag, and, even though the Gulag had collapsed in war twenty thousand years ago, old habits die hard.

Pokrov was reticent about his true identity because he was a criminal on the run. He had offended against Injunction AA709/4383200/1408 of version 7c of the Authorised Penal Code of the Golden Gulag. A heinous crime indeed! What's more, a crime unpunished to date, for so far Ivan Pokrov had escaped the extended algetic tutoring he so richly deserved.

'You must come,' insisted Ingalawa. 'Jon keeps saying we haven't enjoyed your company for . . . why, he says it feels like a passage of millennia.'

Ivan Pokrov, who was already sweating because of the heat of the day, began to sweat all the more. Was Ingalawa hinting that all was known already?

Before Pokrov could worry about it further, a servant entered to say that a visitor was demanding an audience with him.

'We're in the middle of lunch,' said Pokrov.

'The visitor,' said the servant, 'is the Master of Law. Aquitaine Varazchavardan.'

'Oh,' said Pokrov. 'That puts a different complexion on things! Show him in immediately.'

Very shortly, Aquitaine Varazchavardan was shown to the dinner table. Chegory Guy was most embarrassed to find himself in the presence of a member of the Imperial Court. In obedience to the dictates of courtesy he rose to his feet and made reverence in the Janjuladoola manner: palms of the hands pressed together, knees bending slightly to lower height as head makes a short bow toward the fingertips. Varazchavardan did not bother to acknowledge this homage. He seemed unaware that Chegory existed as he rounded on Pokrov, saying:

'Pokrov! Have you anything to say to me?'

Varazchavardan oft used this open-ended question on his victims in an effort to intimidate them and startle them into incontinent confession. But it had no such effect on the master of the Analytical Institute, who said:

'Why, yes. Welcome, welcome! Won't you sit down? Please. We've sea slugs today. Look. Green, succulent. Did you ever see anything more beautiful?'

Pokrov knew his man. Varazchavardan was not a glutton, nor was he an epicure, but he did have a notorious weakness for sea slugs. He accepted the invitation. Nevertheless, he did not allow himself to feed for long before he got down to business.

'Pokrov,' said he, 'did your Analytical Engine by chance have anything to do with the events of last night?'

'No,' said Ivan Pokrov. 'What happened last night suggests someone was tampering with probability itself. My Engine lacks the power to do such, for it is but pieces of metal in conglomeration.'

'Nevertheless,' said Varazchavardan, 'it thinks.'

'It does not think,' said Pokrov. 'It merely manipulates. As the prestidigitation of a conjurer is to the magic of a true sorcerer, so the manipulation in which the Engine indulges at my pleasure is to the freedoms of my thoughts and of yours.'

Despite Pokrov's denials, Varazchavardan insisted that he would inspect the Analytical Engine after lunch.

By this time Chegory had realised Olivia was casting little avid glances in the direction of the wonderworker. He found himself possessed of a ferocious jealousy. What did old man Varazchavardan have that Chegory Guy didn't? Answers numerous could be postulated, for, after all, Varazchavardan was a member of the Imperial Court whereas young Chegory was but a dragonless rock gardener. But let the truth be known. The sweet Ashdan lass had not conceived a lust for the wonderworker himself but for his robes, silken ceremonial robes most marvellously embroidered with serpentine dragons ablaze with goldwork and argentry, with emerald and vermilion, with incarnadine and ultramarine.

Chegory, who did not know this, was relieved when lunch drew to a close.

When lunch did end, Ox No Zan absented himself so he could keep his appointment with Doctor Death. Artemis Ingalawa went back to her algorithmic labours. Pokrov told Chegory and Olivia to busy themselves with the mathematical studies which were (as always) to occupy their afternoon, then he led Varazchavardan into the Counting House where the Analytical Engine was at work.

Pokrov gave his standard explanation of the Engine's function, and concluded by saying:

'Thus what we see here is no more than the mechanical manipulation of patterns. The person who devises the protocols by which those patterns will be manipulated is exercising intelligence. So too is the person who designs the actual mechanisms which enable data to be processed by such algorithms. There is however no demon in the machine itself. It knows nothing, lacks all sense of self, and is ruled by the same mechanical necessities which rule a stone rolling helplessly downhill. In other words, it cannot think, does not think and never will think.'

But despite Pokrov's explanation, the Master of Law found the Analytical Engine no more scrutable than before. The collosal construction (otherwise known as the mills of Jod) still defied his understanding. It was still no more than a maze of brass and steel, of intermeshed cogs made of titanium (the sole source of which is fire vanes taken from the corpses of dragons), of levers and wires and ratcheting mechanisms.

'What is it doing now?' said the Master of Law.

'A statistical analysis of the recent census,' said Ivan Pokrov. 'The inland revenue wants to know how best they can screw more money out of the populace. We'll give them the answer. In time! The mills of Jod grind slowly, but they grind exceedingly small.'

The albinotic sorcerer could take a hint. He knew what Pokrov was telling him. That the Analytical Institute had friends in high places. It worked for the inland revenue, no less. Very well then! Even Varazchavardan was reluctant to go up against the inland revenue department, at least for the moment. Nevertheless, when he seized power on Jod he would make a point of smashing the Engine and burning Pokrov alive.

On principle.

What principle?

A very simple principle: namely, that anything occult is dangerous. Varazchavardan's main objection to the existence of the Analytical Engine was that he could not for the life of him understand it. Oh, he could see the hard-muscled engine operators sweating at the treadmills. He could see how the transmission system worked, feeding the energy of manpowered cylinders to whirling metal.

He saw copper cards with their inscrutable arrays of punched holes. He saw other operators feeding these cards into the interstices of the Engine. He saw needles descend upon the cards – and, in his imagination, he substituted Ivan Pokrov's flesh for the insensate cards thus tortured.

All this he saw.

But – how did any of this senseless insectile activity allow the Engine to think? And it did think, it did, it must, it had to! Else how could it outperform even the hard-headed analysts of the inland revenue? Pokrov was lying. Had to be lying. This conglomeration of metal was a farcical front. There was true magic hidden here. Somewhere. There was Power. And Varazchavardan vowed to win its secrets from Pokrov's seared and bleeding corpus before he made that corpus a corpse.

With his inspection completed, Varazchavardan took his leave of Ivan Pokrov at the door of the Analytical Institute and began to walk down to the shore. He had almost got there when fluids began to well up from the wealth fountains which studded the slopes below the Counting House.

'Oh no!' said Pokrov.

Oh yes! It was happening! Nothing could stop it!

As Pokrov watched helplessly, familiar pungent odours filled the air as chemicals flooded out of the wealth fountains. The flood swelled around the ankles of Aquitaine

Varazchavardan then rose higher yet with prodigious speed. The albinotic sorcerer was suddenly waist-deep in a veritable torrent of bile-green dikle and filthy grey shlug. He lost his footing and was swept away into the sea.

'I hope he drowns,' muttered Pokrov.

Don't get the wrong idea. Pokrov was a very nice man. But he knew the Analytical Institute and everyone associated with it would be ten thousand times safer if Varazchavardan came to a nasty end.

However, Aquitaine Varazchavardan swam with remarkable facility to the harbour bridge and hauled himself aboard. Then he stood up. The Master of Law was not given to histrionics, and therefore did not turn and shake his fist. Nevertheless, as he set off for the shores of Injiltaprajura, something about his purposeful stride made his mood perfectly clear.

CHAPTER SIX

One would like to think that all this time Chegory Guy and Olivia Qasaba were hard at work on their mathematical studies. But they were not. Olivia had a considerable aptitude for figures yet disliked them. Her redskinned companion lacked both aptitude and liking entirely.

It must be admitted that, in spite of lacking such, young Chegory had nevertheless made considerable progress in the study of numbers both real and unreal, positive and negative, whole and fractional, prime and partial, imaginary and obscene, and by now the construction of basic algorithms was second nature to him. He was familiar also with the mathematics of potentials and unpotentials, of points and infinities, of singularities and of blanks.

Furthermore, while Chegory lacked Olivia's intellectual finesse, he had nevertheless absorbed basic games theory, and understood the sociopolitical implications of the same. He had attained a degree of competence in the slippery contextual arithmetic of hyperspace, in the calculus of probability curves in n-dimensional true space and in the calculation of the structure of fundamental topographical harmonics in polydimensional non-space.

However, he had been defeated entirely by Thaldonian Mathematics, which is essential to a correct understanding of everything from the nature of reality to the construction of trans-cosmic junctions, for it is that branch of theory developed to assist with the description of that event-class associated with the manifestation of klayta, or, as Habada Kolebhavn has so elegantly termed them, 'dynamic objects of intermittent existence and indefinite probability'. To put it more crudely, it is the mathematics of the stresses which exist between the probable and the improbable, without which an understanding of true Advanced Theory is impossible.

I can understand Chegory's problems, since I myself studied under Ivan Pokrov for thirty years yet remained equally defeated by Thaldonian Mathematics. Nevertheless, Chegory's failure to persist in his studies in the absence of his tutor shows the Ebrell Islander in him manifesting itself beyond a doubt.

[One's opinion of the Originator is much diminished by finding the Originator equating his own talents with those of an Ebrell Islander, albeit in a very minor field of endeavour. One also feels that the Originator has here indulged in language which is unnecessarily pretentious, with the consequence that much is here mentioned which is difficult to explicate. 'Games theory', for example, presumably refers to score-keeping in so-called amusements such as the ritualised conflict known in the Ebrell Islands as ruck, but you would not know it from the Text. One regrets the lack of any footnote to identify the briefly cited Habada Kolebhavn, unknown to our own researchers. (There is a minor poet of Obooloo called Handana Kodendarden, but this is most unlikely to be the person referred to.) The term 'klayta' is unknown to our lexicographers. Context suggests that it refers to dreams, or, possibly, to memories, to shadows or to lies. But how could one have a mathematics of dreams? Or of shadows? Here it is worth repeating that a diligent search of all the authorities has confirmed that only four mathematical operations are possible, these being addition, subtraction, multiplication and division. Some of our Readers have suggested that the Text above implies otherwise. If so, then the Text is wrong. A brief application of common sense will soon show why this is so. *This Commentary inserted by Order of Jan Borgentasko Ronkowski, Fact Checker Superior.*]

Usually Chegory was at pains to hide his idleness, but on this occasion he was caught out, for when Ivan Pokrov returned to the study room he found Olivia and Chegory playing paper–stone–scissors.

'Why aren't you working?' said Pokrov.

'With that stink?' said Olivia. 'How can we possibly work when we can't hardly breathe?'

It must be admitted that the stench of so much dikle and shlug was hard to endure. Nevertheless, Pokrov refused to admit to sympathy.

'We will work,' he said. 'We will begin with a review of basic solid-shape topology. With a *viva voce* examination, in fact.' So saying, he opened a dusty cupboard untouched for many months, took out a box of shapes and began. 'What is this?' he said, holding up a solid wooden model resembling an octahedron with a three-faced pyramid on each face.

'That,' said Chegory Guy, 'is a triakisoctahedron.'

Pokrov was dismayed by this languid response. He had hoped to stir up some passion in his pupils, which was why he had deliberately insulted them by turning their attention to such kindergarten stuff. But obviously the Ebrell Islander at least was incapable of intellectual arousal, or at any rate not today.

In truth, Chegory couldn't care less whether they studied the most basic of basics or the Higher Arcana. He disliked the study of the inhumanities entirely. Even the presence of Olivia Qasaba failed to add enjoyment to the study session. He almost wished he was with Ox Zan, enduring the tender mercies of Doctor Death.

On and on went the lessons, until at last they took a break for afternoon tea, for which Artemis Ingalawa joined them. Afternoon tea! Ah yes! One of the greatest achievements of the Izdimir Empire is to have universalised this custom. How pleasant it is to sit outdoors drinking green tea and making educated guesses as to the provenance of the same while watching the clouds form and reform.

Only on Jod in the season of Fistavlir there were no clouds. There was only the aching blue sky. And the stench of dikle and shlug outpouring from the wealth fountains. And there was no mystery in the provenance of the tea. It came of course from Chay, that harbourless highrise island which lies southeast of Untunchilamon, mid-ocean between Injiltaprajura and the shores of Yestron.

Chay, of course, is the leading source of tea, coffee and spices of all descriptions for the area—

[Here an extensive geography lesson has been excised. *By Order, Eder Digest, Redactor Minor.* There is nothing more tedious than the Originator of this Text when said Originator yields to the didactic impulse.]

There thus they sat, drinking tea, looking for all the world as if they were aristocrats in Ang. While they were thus amusing themselves, a small sun-bright sphere came bouncing through the air.

'Shabble!' said Ivan Pokrov sharply. 'You're too bright.'

The impersonator of Powers turned the light down to a dull glow. Then, in high excitement, began to tell a wild story of adventures Downstairs, of dangers encountered and prisoners captured. Chegory, Olivia, Ingalawa and Ivan Pokrov listened till Shabble was done.

'So you captured some pirates,' said Pokrov, only half-believing this story. 'What have you done with them, then? Have you eaten them?'

'I went to sleep,' said Shabble simply. 'When I woke up, they were gone.' Then, in very hurt tones: 'But they said they wouldn't! They promised! I made them! They said they'd be as good as gold, they wouldn't go anywhere, they wouldn't run away. But they did, they did, they did! Alone, I was all alone, all alone Downstairs, I woke up and they were gone, gone, they left me, oh, oh, oh!'

'There now!' said Pokrov, in his most soothing tones. 'You're not alone now. You're with us.'

'Yes, so I am!' said Shabble, brightening both literally and metaphorically. 'Let's go hunt them, shall we? I don't like Downstairs, but it's all right if you go with me. We could catch them. We'd be famous. They've got the wishstone, we'd be heroes if we found them.'

'The wishstone?' said Pokrov. 'You didn't tell us about that!'

'Oh, they stole it from the treasury,' said Shabble.

Pokrov thought this most likely untrue, for the treasury of Injiltaprajura was heavily guarded. If pirates had fought their way into it overnight the whole city would have heard about it by now.

'I think you're fibbing,' said Pokrov.

'I'm not!' said Shabble, justifiably hurt.

'Well, it doesn't matter either way,' said Pokrov. 'I'm not going Downstairs. We might meet a dorgi.'

Immediately Pokrov wished he had kept silent. He had spoken about dorgis! In front of Ingalawa! Unless he was careful he'd find himself next confessing knowledge of the Golden Gulag.

'All the dorgis are dead,' said Shabble. 'They died a hundred thousand years ago.'

'What,' said Chegory, 'is a dorgi?'

'A type of dog,' said Pokrov, inventing furiously to cover his blunder.

His intent was to lie, but it happens that he accidentally told the truth. For there is a breed of dogs known as dorgis. They are ferocious killers bred in Dalar ken Halvar by cross-breeding Lashund hunting hounds with the heavy-weight canines known as thogs.

'A type of dog?' said Ingalawa. 'I've never heard of dogs Downstairs.'

'They're not dogs!' said Shabble in high excitement. 'They're killers, killers, that's what they are. The Golden Gulag had thousands of them.'

'Gulag?' said Olivia. 'What's a gulag?'

'Something from Shabble's imagination,' said Pokrov.

'It is not neither,' said Shabble. 'It's an empire, that's what it is. A huge empire with seven planets and fifty thousand million people, oh, and the sunships, they were the best, I got a ride to the sun once, that was the very best of all. I'm a sun myself, really, but I can't see myself. But I saw the sun we went to. And there was music, music, all over the Gulag there was music, you don't have music like that now.'

'Very nice,' said Artemis Ingalawa in her adult-to-child

voice. 'Now tell us, friend Shabble. Have you any idea what made the lights turn strange in the night?'

Shabble pleaded ignorance. But had uncomfortable memories of the Days of Wrath when weapons such as the psionic torque were in common use. Weapons for disrupting probability. That war was a terrible thing because Shabble got hurt, and badly hurt, and almost died. Worse – most of Shabble's friends did die. Shabble refused to answer any more questions.

'You know!' said Ingalawa. 'You must tell us!'

In response, Shabble began to sing in a monotonous tang-tong imitative of a bell.

'Stop that!' said Ingalawa.

Shabble did, and imitated instead cantor and choir exalting in the manner of the Temple of the Higher Waters. When Shabble was in such a mood, one could curse or landdamne the lonely one all day to no effect. Ingalawa, losing patience, stuffed Shabble into a teapot and stalked off to renew her algorithmic labours.

'Come on,' said Pokrov to Chegory and Olivia, 'let's get back to our studies.'

On through the afternoon they studied, with the two students growing ever more languescent despite valiant efforts on Pokrov's part. While they studied, ever did the dikle and shlug pour forth from the wealth fountains and pollute the waters of the Laitemata.

Dikle and shlug. What precisely are they, these strange substances? They are of course two of the most important exports of Untunchilamon, and at the time with which this chronicle deals they were also the main source of income for the Analytical Institute.

Shlug is everywhere sought by the best metalworkers, for it is the ideal grease for preserving metalwork of any description against corrosion, particularly during long-term storage. This is precisely what shlug was used for in the days of the Golden Gulag. It is thick, stable, vile-smelling and boring, except when it combines its dull grey with the bile-green of dikle to form a thin, rainbow-hinting fluid.

Dikle, on the other hand, is intrinsically far more interesting, for it is a thixotropic substance which will abruptly convert from solid to liquid when suitably excited by heat or vibration. When it converts from a slightly yielding solid to a free-flowing liquid it forms a fluid which has the texture and constituency of olive oil. Peasants lubricate the axles of their carts with it. It is said that swordsmiths use it to judge temperature, for it is at welding heat that dikle changes from fluid to liquid. It is also known that the whores of the Flesh Temple of—

[Excised! *By Order, Drax Lira, Redactor Major.*]

—and thereby excite their customers to heights of pleasure unheard of and undreamt of elsewhere. But in the days of the Golden Gulag, dikle was used exclusively as a high-temperature lubricant in the sunships of the Systems Patrol.

So now you know.

All the time that Cheogry and Olivia were studying, servants of the Analytical Institute were busy on the foreshore, filling amphorae with these precious substances. Meantime the musically obsessed Shabble, still floating in a teapot, sang on and on and on.

Shabble had of course been telling the truth about capturing some pirates (the Malud marauders Al-ran Lars, Arnaut and Tolon) in the depths of Downstairs. Furthermore, Shabble had indeed been lied to by these ruthless cutthroats, who had broken their most solemn promises and had slipped away when the innocent one at last went to sleep. The reckless one had also been telling the truth about the wishstone. It really had been stolen.

Even now, events of some note were taking place on the mainland. Undesirable elements (such as Ebrell Islanders) were being rounded up to be interrogated about the missing wishstone. Many were being beaten up as they were rounded up. Furthermore, it was most unlikely that the trouble would be over by the time Chegory Guy was due to return to the mainland.

CHAPTER SEVEN

Late in the afternoon, Ivan Pokrov was summoned to the Counting House. That was the official name for the room in the Analytical Institute which housed the Analytical Engine itself. A transmission shaft had snapped, bringing the operations of the Engine to a grinding halt, and he was needed to supervise the repairs. He left Chegory and Olivia with plenty of work to do, and at first they worked diligently, or at least pretended so to work.

But the day was hot, and Chegory soon abandoned scholarship for dreams. Wild dreams! Fantasies in which a benevolent Hermit Crab granted him thighs, nipples, breasts, buttocks and watermelons by the thousands. Then Olivia seized her Ebrell Island friend and shook him into wakefulness.

'Pokrov's coming!' she said.

Thanks to this warning, Chegory Guy was the very picture of diligent scholarship when Ivan Pokrov returned in the company of Ingalawa.

'How far have you got?' said Pokrov.

'Not far,' admitted Chegory.

'There's always tomorrow,' said Pokrov. 'It's time to go home. I'll be coming with you. I've decided to accept the dear doctor's invitation. I will dine at the Qasaba household this evening.'

As the westering sun sank in the west they packed up. Chegory changed into his evening wear – trousers and shirt – leaving his loincloth on the island for the morrow.

They were ready to make the trip back to the mainland. There were of course four of them – Chegory, Olivia, Ingalawa and Pokrov – but unfortunately there were only two pairs of stilts left in the rack at the main entrance to the Analytical Institute. The flow of dikle and shlug from the wealth fountains had eased but it was still more than ankle-deep.

'Let Olivia and Artemis have the stilts,' said Pokrov. 'We men can wade.'

'No need,' said Chegory. 'There's more in the workshop. They were getting repaired yesterday. The glue should be dry by now. I'll go and get them.'

With that said, off he trotted.

Ah, how pleasant it is to have servants! An obedient Ebrell Islander willing to run for the stilts without even being asked! However . . . appearances are deceptive. These animals cannot really be domesticated. As you will see.

While Chegory was off on his errand, the others did not sit, nor did they retreat into the shadows. Pokrov was lost in thought (a common occurence for him) and thus paid no heed to heat or discomfort. As for the two women, why, they were not going to be the first to admit to the weakness of the flesh. They were both Ashdans, the pride of which race has not been exaggerated by the many commentators who have remarked on it.

'Look,' said Olivia, pointing to the south-west. 'A canoe.'

Indeed, a double-hulled canoe was being paddled through the Rajavakoram Channel between Scimitar Island and the mainland. They knew it at once to be one of the seagoing canoes of the Ngati Moana for it was far larger than the frail outriggers which fished in the local lagoon.

'They'll have news,' said Olivia.

'Only of the west,' said Ivan Pokrov.

In the season of Fistavlir the only canoes to reach Untunchilamon were those which came from the west. In such vessels the Ngati Moana dared the shallows of the Green Sea, helped by the Coral Current. A canoe adrift in that flux of water will be carried at least thirty leagues to the east between one sunrise and the next.

This canoe would in all probability have come from the island of Yam, which lies due south of Asral and Ashmolea.

Its crew would have aided their eastward drift by salvaging whatever scraps of wind came their way, or by paddling, maintaining their strength by feeding on sharks and turtles caught fresh from the sea.

'We could get away on one of those,' said Pokrov softly.

Artemis Ingalawa laid a hand on his shoulder and said: 'It's too early to think of that.'

She was in no hurry to flee Untunchilamon. Life here was good. Anyone could have told that just by looking at what she was wearing: not the plain robe which would have been appropriate to one of her rank but a trouser suit of yellow silk and a silken alizarine cloak fringed with gold and cinnebar. She had known poverty in the past and liked her present financial status much better. What's more, on Untunchilamon she was free to indulge her mathematical passions to the full, yet was far removed from the competitive pressures which sometimes made life in her homeland very difficult indeed.

Artemis Ingalawa had found her utopia and was determined to enjoy it till the end.

Besides, there was still a chance that Aldarch III might lose the war for control of Yestron. But, certainly, if he did win, and then stretched out his claws toward Untunchilamon, there would be many good citizens of Injiltaprajura who would be prepared to pay heavily for a place on one of the canoes of the Ngati Moana. Usually, the Star Navigators take no passengers, for the journeys they make in their open canoes are long and hard, even to those habituated to such a life.

What motivates these people to dare where no others will? Trade, obviously. These matchless navigators traffic in pearls, ivory, dragon teeth, sponges and spices. But above all else it is the lust for pounamu which drives them. This brittle green stone they love as much as do the aesthetes of Ang, and so to acquire it they will sail the length and breadth of the Great Ocean, touching on shores so distant that one is scarcely more than a legend to the other.

While Pokrov and the Ashdans were still watching the

canoe, Chegory returned with the extra stilts. But with him as well was Shabble. Chegory had liberated the irresponsible one from the teapot. The living jewel was bobbing now at his shoulder, still humming softly. You see? You would not really want an Ebrell Islander as a servant. Off it goes on the simplest of errands: to get some stilts. Yet back it comes with the most feckless delinquent on all of Untunchilamon.

'Chegory,' said Ingalawa, chiding him. 'I thought we could have done without Shabble's company tonight.'

'But Shabble loves dinner parties,' said Chegory.

'Shabble loves them all too much!' said Ingalawa.

Shabble was to formal dining in the Dromdanjerie what the Empress Justina's albinotic ape Vazzy was to banqueting in the pink palace. Need more be said?

'Don't worry about Shabble,' said Ivan Pokrov. 'I'll keep our spherical friend in order.'

'I'll hold you to that,' said Ingalawa. 'You know what happened last time.'

'Yes,' said Pokrov with a sigh. 'I remember.'

Shabble loves to gossip. Shabble loves to sing. Shabble loves to imitate voices with malicious intent, and is the most adroit ventriloquist imaginable. Shabble is (socially, at least) a menace.

But Shabble did naught but hum softly as the four humans went stilt-striding through the chemical outpour to the harbour bridge. There they dismounted, put their leg-lengtheners in the stilt-rack, then began to walk toward the mainland. They went slowly, slowly, for the heat was unendurable, the humidity suffocating.

Day was almost at an end, and, in its death-throes, the bloody sun set the oily waters of the Laitemata ablaze with baleful fire. Fish in their thousands floated belly-up in those poisoned waters. Lifeless their silver, swift-fading their orange and green. An octopus groped for survival one last time then slackened and died.

If the flow from the wealth fountains did not abate there would be nothing left alive in the Laitemata by the morrow.

Then the dikle and shlug would spread out into the lagoon. A few days' outflood would suffice to double the price of fish in Injiltaprajura. Still, who could complain? Production of such poisons was one of the mainstays of Untunchilamon's economy, and there was no stopping that production even if people had wanted to.

Chegory stopped to watch another sick octopus struggling in the water. The dying beast was kin to the gigantic krakens which dwelt in the Deep far to the north. Such monsters shun the shallows and will never dare water low enough to be plumbed by human divers. Hence Injiltaprajura was safe from their depredations, for the Laitemata Harbour could only be approached through lagoon passages scarcely deep enough to float a ship.

'Come on, Chegory!' said Olivia, and he hurried to catch up with the others.

The harbour bridge rocked beneath the feet of the trampling humans, for it lacked all foundation and was afloat upon pontoons. Its boards of unpainted coconut wood creaked underfoot as creak the bones of an animated skeleton as it wrestles the lid from its coffin.

As Chegory drew level with Olivia she dropped back. He halted immediately, knowing she meant to tap his ankle and send him tumbling. He paused, as if admiring the view. The clutter of stalls and shops scattered along the waterfront all the way from the harbour bridge to the far end of Marthandorthan. The crowded slumclutter of Lubos directly ahead. Further uphill, the hulk of Ganthorgruk, with the Dromdanjerie – home – directly above it. Higher yet, the inscrutable mass of Pearl. Then, riding the heights of Pokra Ridge, the pink palace itself and the temples and mansions of Hojo Street.

'Come on, Chegory,' said Olivia, skipping past him. 'Come on, or you'll be late for dinner.'

He followed.

They were only halfway to the shore when the sun-bloody sky flashed into rainbow. Its gaudy colours writhed like the feathers of a million peacocks afloat upon an ocean of boiling red oil. Then the waters of the Laitemata buckled, then flailed, then reared toward the sky as a monstrous shape erupted from the sunfire sea. Up from the waters it came. Huge, bulking, loathsome, vast. A kraken! Its gorged tentacles of purple-brown shed water in flurries as they thrashed.

It was close, close, close enough to seize them. Its eyes were bloody as the sun, swollen with rage, engorged with lusts anthropophagous. Knowing that it was themselves that the eyes perceived, the humans tried to flee. The kraken groped for the harbour bridge. Shook the bridge. The shockwaves skittled the scampering humans.

Olivia screamed in fear. She scrambled to her feet then tripped and fell. Chegory grabbed one of the rope handrails and hauled himself upward. Pokrov stayed down, clutching a knee in agony. Ingalawa got up. The kraken shook the bridge again. But this time Ingalawa kept her footing. She slid into the whirlwind stance with a combat shout so shattering it could be heard for half a league away. All praise for her courage! Yet what use was such defiance? The kraken was already hauling its vast, slovenly bulk toward its prey. Could Ingalawa outfight it? To that question, what fool requires an answer?

Even Shabble seemed unprepared to contend with the loathsome thing from the depths, for the imitator of suns was sliding upward into the sky, singing, sweetly singing, soft-lilting in an ecstasy of music.

Shabble's brightness caught the eye of the kraken. Which lazily uncoiled a spare tentacle and sent its fearsome strength questing for Injiltaprajura's oldest juvenile delinquent. The tentacle caught the ever-rising Shabble and snapped tight around the surface of the shining one.

There was a brilliant flash of light.

A burst of searing heat.

A convulsion as the kraken writhed in pain, the remnants of its Shabble-ensnaring tentacle racked by spasms of uncontrollable agony. Bright burnt Shabble, though this brightness was somewhat obscured by the fumes of incinerated tentacle which hung around the shining one.

'Shabble!' yelled Chegory. 'Kill it kill it kill it!'

The kraken recovered itself. Groped toward the humans.

'As you love us, kill it!' screamed Chegory.

One tentacle of swollen purple-brown coiled round Olivia's ankle. Chegory fell upon it in fury. In a berserker rage he wrestled with the monster. But he wrestled uselessly, for the remorseless strength of the monster began to drag the Ashdan lass toward its waiting maw. In panic Chegory tore at the tentacle with his teeth. But the rubbery substance refuted the onslaught of his incisors.

Olivia screamed incoherently as she was torn away from the harbour bridge. Chegory grabbed her hand. Her eyes bulged with panic as she clutched him. The tentacle upreared. Chegory, still clutching, was yanked off his feet.

Then Shabble—

Shabble spat fire.

The kraken convulsed in agony.

It outflung Olivia. She fell. Landing heavily on Chegory Guy.

The kraken screamed.

High and shrill it screamed.

Shabble let rip with a blast of fire which tore the monster clean in half. Huge clouds of steam ascended from the sea, tainted with the stench of burnt monster and by fumes released by superheated dikle and shlug.

The monster was dead. Dead, dead, dead and destroyed, while they were still clutching to life.

Olivia was sobbing, sobbing, sobbing, clutched close by Chegory and clutching close. Artemis Ingalawa eased out of her fighting stance. Ivan Pokrov, the pain in his knee abating, picked himself up. He was eager to observe the monster's corpse at close hand before it subsided beneath the waters of the Laitemata. He could be heard to mutter:

'How interesting. How very interesting.'

Shabble, still softly singing all the while, floated down from the heavens like a feather.

'Chegory dearest,' said Shabble, 'there's more than one.'

73

The Ebrell Islander untangled himself from Olivia and looked round. Shabble was right! There were at least half a dozen monsters in clear sight, thrashing madly in the harbour waters. The nearest was only a league distant.

'Kill them!' he said curtly.

'Oh, I don't really want to kill anything else, Chegory dearest,' said Shabble.

'Don't worry about the other monsters,' said Pokrov. 'They'll die from a surfeit of dikle and shlug before they can do any harm. Come and look at this, Chegory. Isn't it fascinating?'

'It's gross, it's horrible,' sobbed Olivia. 'I hate it, I hate it, I want to get out of here, I want to go home.'

'Come along then, darling,' said Chegory.

Then, soothing her as best he could, he led her shorewards along the harbour bridge.

In the heat of the moment he did not realise that he had called her his darling. As for Olivia, if she noticed his presumption, she did not choose to comment on it.

*   *   *

The conjurer Odolo, Official Keeper of the Imperial Sceptre, had endured all manner of terror that day. He had been arrested as soon as the loss of the wishstone was discovered. He had been beaten, interrogated and threatened with torture. Only the personal intervention of the Empress Justina had spared him from the loss of toenails and fingernails both.

Late in the afternoon, Justina had set Odolo at liberty. But that gesture of imperial liberality meant little on its own. Doubtless he was still under suspicion. He had declined the meal she offered him (his interrogators had starved him on principle) and had fled.

Odolo had been physically and mentally exhausted by the time he got to Ganthorgruk. It had been too late for lunch and too early for the evening meal, but he had persuaded the chef to rustle up some soup. Then he had taken himself to his bed where he had collapsed. To dream grim dreams of monsters various.

Last and most vivid of his dreams was one in which krakens upheaved themselves from the waters of the Laitemata. This dream lacked the slapdash incoherence of image and narrative which characterises most of our sleeping delusions. Worse, it stayed bright and sharp in memory when Odolo awoke.

Why should that worry him?

Because he remembered the morning, and the scorpions which had swarmed to life in his breakfast bowl. Scorpions real enough, mind you! In the end, it had been necessary to pulp them with a rolling pin.

Odolo hurried to the nearest window which had a view of the Laitemata. What he saw therefrom increased his worries a thousandfold.

CHAPTER EIGHT

Olivia was still shaking and shuddering when they reached the shore, where the harbour bridge ended at the bank of crushed red coral and broken bloodstone which ran the length of the entire waterfront of Injiltaprajura. They had scarcely stepped off the bridge when Ox No Zan hailed them.

'I've been waiting for you!' he said.

'That much we could have guessed for ourselves,' said Pokrov. 'Did you see the show?'

'Oh yes, oh yes!' said Ox Zan. 'Shabble was marvellous!'

Shabble did three rapid pirouettes and squeaked with undiluted pleasure. Injiltaprajura's master of irresponsibility has never been averse to accepting compliments.

'It's Chegory we've got to thank,' said Ingalawa. 'He's the one who brought Shabble along.'

This is the worst thing about these Ashdan liberals. They're always so ready to think the best of people! Doubtless the kraken would have snacked on Ingalawa and her companions unless Shabble had been on hand. But did Chegory Guy have that in mind when he fetched Shabble from the teapot? Hardly!

'Yes, Chegory!' said Ox Zan. 'That's why I'm here! You have to go back, now, now, right back to Jod.'

'Why?' said Chegory.

'Because, because,' said Ox Zan in high excitement, 'because the wishstone's missing.'

'So Shabble was telling the truth!' said Chegory. 'The wishstone was stolen!'

'If Shabble knows about it,' said Ox Zan, who had yet to hear Shabble's story of encountering pirates Downstairs, 'then maybe Shabble can help get it back. Meanwhile, you'd better run, Chegory. Soldiers are hunting the streets for – what's the word? – undesirable elements, that's it! Everyone they catch is getting smashed up to make them tell about the wishstone.'

'Chegory,' said Artemis Ingalawa severely, 'is not an undesirable element.'

'Well, you know that and so do I,' said Ox Zan, 'but the soldiers—'

'Oh, we all know about the soldiers,' said Chegory. 'I'm off.'

He turned as if to retreat to Jod. But Pokrov caught him by the sleeve.

'Wait about,' said Pokrov.

'You don't understand,' said Chegory, already in a panic. 'They'll kill me!'

This was the stuff of nightmare. Soldiers on the street. Hunting. Hunting him!

'Nonsense!' said Ingalawa. 'You're innocent.'

'What's that got to do with it?' said Chegory. 'I'm an Ebrell Islander, aren't I? Pogrom! Doesn't that mean anything to you?'

'Stop being melodramatic,' said Ingalawa. 'The pogroms went out with Wazir Sin. You're a free citizen. You should act accordingly.'

'What?' said Chegory, scarcely able to believe his ears. 'Get myself beaten up?'

'You won't get beaten up,' said Ingalawa in her lecturing voice. 'Untunchilamon is under the rule of law. People don't get assaulted in the streets for no reason.'

'Oh, you might not,' said Chegory. 'But I'm—'

'You're with us,' said Ingalawa firmly. 'You're under our protection.'

'Thanks but no thanks,' said Chegory. 'I'm going back to Jod.'

'Oh Chegory!' said Ingalawa. 'You can't just run away like this. You're a disappointment to me. Haven't we always done our best for you? Can't you see? If you always act like a doormat you'll always get stepped on. You have to stand up for your rights.'

Chegory knew she was talking nonsense, yet knew he would sorely wound her pride if he told her as much. Pride is the dominant vice of the Ashdans, and Ingalawa had more than her fair share of it. Moreover, he did not want to disappoint her if he could possibly help it.

'You're coming with us,' said Ivan Pokrov. 'If we run into any soldiers we'll vouch for you.'

'Yes, Chegory,' said Shabble. 'And if they hurt you I'll burn them up.'

'Shabble!' said Pokrov sharply. 'You are not to burn anyone up! Do you hear me?' In reply there came a soft swelling of orchestral music. 'I mean it!' said Pokrov. 'If you incinerate even one soldier, there will be consequences! I'm talking about therapy!'

The music cut off abruptly.

'Really?' said Shabble.

'Indubitably,' said Pokrov.

'Oh,' said Shabble, in a most crestfallen voice. Then, rebelliously: 'But why shouldn't I? Boom! I could burn them up just like that. All gone. What fun!'

'If you go round doing things like that,' said Pokrov, 'then nobody will play with you, not ever again. They'll all be too afraid. They'll run away. I mean it! Everyone! You'll be left all alone. Now and forever.'

'Really and truly?' said Shabble.

'He's not kidding,' said Chegory. 'But if you do want friends, how about finding the wishstone? You could do it!'

'I know where it is already,' said his orchestrally inclined companion.

'Where is it then?' said Chegory.

'East of sun and west of moon,' sang Shabble. 'Supping on soup with the scorpion's grandam.'

'Shabble would tell if Shabble knew,' said Ivan Pokrov, 'because Shabble is a prattlemouth and can't help Shabble-self. If we could win back the wishstone, why – well, with Shabble's help, maybe we will. Then we'll see.'

On this optimistic note Pokrov led the way forward. Ox No Zan mumbling something about having to fill a prescription – then headed off in the opposite direction. Despite Ingalawa's denials, No knew that in a situation like this the presence of an Ebrell Islander meant trouble, and trouble was the last thing No wanted. Pokrov's party continued on its way without any further desertions, though Chegory was still fearfully worried.

Elsewhere, in the dining room of Ganthorgruk, another fearfully worried man was sipping at a fresh cup of coffee. It was the conjurer Odolo, who was standing by an open window overlooking the Laitemata Harbour, now darkening to squid's ink in the evening. All the krakens which had upreared from the water were already dead, poisoned by dikle and shlug. The Ngati Moana in the freshly arrived canoe had halted by one of the bloated corpses. Elsewhere, a few rowing boats were setting out to investigate the others.

Suddenly, Odolo's attention was attracted by something in his coffee cup. He looked closely. A whirlpool was forming in the coffee. Something was shaping in the whirlpool, was—

Abruptly, Odolo flung his coffee out of the window.

Miniature rainbows flashed momentarily from his fingertips.

He heard a hooting scream from the neighbouring Dromdanjerie, and, wondering if he would shortly join the lunatics there housed, he shuddered. Surely he was going mad. Or was he? Could it be that he was suffering something worse still? Persecution by a sorcerer of surpassing skill, perhaps.

Or—

Or what?

He had no idea.

Comparing the predicament of these two people, we see immediately that the conjurer Odolo had problems which threatened to be far more serious in the long term. He was going mad; or else he had discovered within himself vast, uncontrollable sorcerous strengths which were activated by his dreams; or else a wonderworker was attacking his sanity

79

by exercise of magic; or else, most fearsome prospect of all, he was in the process of being possessed by a Power of some description.

Nevertheless, one suspects that Chegory Guy would readily have swapped places with the conjurer had the opportunity arisen. For Odolo was (probably) in no serious immediate danger, whereas things might go very badly for Chegory at any moment. All it would take would be for him to run into a few soldiers who didn't like the look of his face.

At first, however, all went well. With Pokrov still leading, they trod the creaking boardwalks of the slumlands of Lubos then gained the precipitous slopes of Skindik Way, where the bloody light of the setting sun was echoed by the bloodstone paving slabs of the road itself. Past the slaughterhouse they went, then past the looming hulk of Ganthorgruk.

They were at the Dromdanjerie!

'Home safe,' said Olivia Qasaba.

But the Ashdan lass had spoken too soon. For a moment later a door was flung open and soldiers came boiling out of the Dromdanjerie itself.

'An Ebby!' cried one.

They grabbed Chegory, threw him against the nearest wall and began to search him for weapons. They found them, too. A business blade in a boot sheath, no toy but heavyweight steel sharpened to murder. A skewer-shiv holstered alongside the other boot. A knuckle-lance tucked in a back pocket.

'You got a licence for these?' snarled a soldier.

'Yes, yes,' said Chegory. 'In the Dromdanjerie, my room, in there, all paid for, all legal.'

Weapon licences were ten damns each, a heavy price in terms of Chegory's wages, but he had such a fear of getting into trouble that he had bought them regardless. The other alternative, going without any weapons at all, was not tenable for someone who had to walk through Lubos every day on his way to and from work.

'He's legal!' said Ingalawa. 'You see? All legal. You can't arrest him. Let him go! And me!'

'Shall I burn them?' said Shabble eagerly.

'You stay out of this,' said Pokrov. 'We'll sort it out.'

Ingalawa was already doing (or trying to do) just that.

'Stop that!' she shouted, grabbing at one of the soldiers who was holding Chegory Guy.

'Shove off,' said the soldier, pushing her away.

'That's Chegory Guy you've got there!' said Ingalawa. 'A free citizen of Injiltaprajura who enjoys the full protection of the law.'

Chegory inwardly groaned. Only an Ashdan liberal would make speeches like that at a time like this. Worse, she had named him! They were mad, these Ashdan liberals. Completely detached from reality. As he had expected, Ingalawa's intervention was useless. Nevertheless, she persisted.

'We can vouch for him,' said she. 'So can Qasaba, Jon Qasaba, Qasaba. He's just in here, in the Dromdanjerie.'

'Oho!' cried a soldier. 'So this is a madman we've caught! An escaped lunatic!'

'Don't be ridiculous,' snapped Pokrov. 'This is an honest rock gardener you've caught.'

'Who are you then?' said one of the soldiers.

'I am Ivan Pokrov, master of the Analytical Engine,' said Pokrov with great dignity. 'Who's in charge here?'

'I am,' said a stalwart warrior. 'Coleslaw Styx at your service.'

'What's your rank, Styx?' said Pokrov, in tones which owed more to anger than to etiquette.

'I'm a guard marshal in the service of her imperial majesty Justina,' said Styx.

'Right!' said Pokrov. 'Sort out this mess, Marshal Styx!'

'Oh, that's easily done,' said Styx. 'You're all under arrest!'

Whereupon soldiers manhandled Chegory and his friends up Skindik Way to Lak Street, across Lak Street and down Goldhammer Rise. Shabble bobbed along after them in a state of high anxiety, and it was Shabble's light which illuminated the party as the quick-falling gloom of the equatorial night overtook them.

'Where are you taking us?' said Ingalawa.

'To the Temple of Torture,' said Styx, thus precipitating disaster.

All Injiltaprajura knew the Temple of Torture had ceased functioning as such when its patron, Wazir Sin, had come to a sticky end. Ingalawa presumed (rightly) that Justina's soldiers had taken over the empty building on Goldhammer Rise to use it as a detention centre.

But Shabble made no such sensible presumption. Instead, the lord of gossip panicked. His friends were going to be hurt, maimed, tortured, killed! They were being dragged to the hideous Temple of Torture! There to endure the unspeakable, the unmentionable, the unthinkable! Shabble acted without further thought. Moments later a dozen burnt and temporarily half-blinded soldiers were staggering around the street.

'Kill them!' roared Styx. 'Catch them and kill them!'

So Chegory, Ingalawa et al. fled for their lives. They ran blind through the night, chancing life and limb as they pelted down Goldhammer Rise. They only halted when they reached Marthandorthan, the dockland area. There Shabble joined them and cast a cone of light around them.

'Shabble Shabble Shabble!' said Ivan Pokrov in something like despair. 'What have you done?'

'Nothing,' said Shabble defensively.

'You crazy gloop!' said Chegory, beside himself with anger. 'You burnt a dozen soldiers half to death!'

'I did not,' said Shabble heatedly. 'I only singed them a little, that's all.'

Shabble was telling the truth. None of the soldiers under the command of Coleslaw Styx had been seriously injured. But it made no difference. Chegory and his companions were suddenly wanted criminals on the run. He said as much.

'But Shabble's to blame!' said Olivia.

'Chegory's right,' said Pokrov. 'The law is the law. Anyone with Shabble when Shabble runs amok gets punished.'

That was indeed the law, or part of it. A good law it was, too. Shabble was potentially a master of arson, espionage and public disorder, so it was best to have the strongest possible sanctions to stop people exploiting Shabble's weakness of character.

'What – what will they do with us?' said Olivia. 'When they catch us, I mean.'

'There now,' said Ingalawa, holding her niece close and tight. 'There there.'

This refusal to provide specifics told Olivia that things were very bad indeed. She started weeping.

'We, um, off the streets,' said Chegory, conscious of their urgent need to take immediate evasive action. 'Under cover, we have to get under cover, as soon as possible.'

'You told me once of your cousin, Firfat Labrat,' said Ingalawa.

'No!' said Chegory in alarm. 'Not him! We can't go to him!'

'But we'd be safe there,' persisted Ingalawa. 'Wouldn't we?'

'All we need is a haven for this evening alone,' said Ivan Pokrov. 'Come morning, we can get a good lawyer and sort this thing out.'

Chegory was not at all keen on the idea. But what else could he do? If he had been on his own, he would have found one of the entrances to the depths Downstairs, and would have taken his chances in those realms of danger. But he durst not lead Olivia into such places. Reluctantly, he agreed. He would lead them to the lair of Firfat Labrat.

But where was that?

Though Chegory was well acquainted with all quarters of Injiltaprajura, he was so upset by the turn events had taken that at first he was lost. Shabble brightened to reveal their surroundings entirely, but young Chegory found that the streets of Marthandorthan were as strange to him as those of an alien city. Then he got a grip on himself, got his bearings, and began to lead the way to safety.

CHAPTER NINE

Firfat Labrat was a drug dealer. The drug in question was the dreaded alcohol, a fearful carcinogen which shrinks the breasts of women and enlarges the breasts of men, which gnaws the liver and addles the brain. It rots the unborn while they lie within the womb. It blights the marriages of young and old alike and turns good workers into filthy, unkempt layabouts.

Such is the demonic allure of this drug that the helpless junkies who become addicted to it will persist in their course of self-destruction despite vomiting, impotence, gastric reflux and uncontrollable outbursts of unpredictable violence or shameless confession. In the final stages of their degradation they cannot live without this hellish brew to which their bodies have become hopelessly addicted. Their limbs shake constantly with fever; the walls around them crawl with nightmarish delusion; all that awaits them is a remorseless descent into insanity and death.

What kind of depraved person would traffic in such filthy stuff? What foul, leprous ghoul would seek to profit from such? Why, an Ebrell Islander of course! Such was Firfat Labrat. And in the slumlands of Injiltaprajura, where the vice of poverty is at its worst, he found plenty of people ready to work for him. Yes: it is truly remarkable what people will do to avoid starvation.

Wazir Sin would have put an end to all this, of course, for he was preparing to wipe out the poor entirely when Lonstantine Thrug overthrew him. Since then, men like Labrat had flourished. In fact, in the absence of any strong-minded utopian like Sin, it looked like the poor would be with Injiltaprajura always, and their vices likewise.

When Chegory brought his friends to Labrat's lair – a rotting warehouse in a most insalubrious part of Marthandorthan – they experienced some difficulty gaining admission because the search for the wishstone had heightened the sense of paranoia which attended the activities of the loathsome Labrat.

However, Chegory was not entirely unknown to Labrat's men, for on occasion he had earnt himself a little mango money by helping shift mysterious cargoes in the depths of bardardornootha. You see? He was an Ebrell Islander through and through. Tainted already by his willing association with the traffic in disease, insanity and death.

Thus in due course Chegory's negotiations at the door to Labrat's lair met with success, and he was admitted together with his companions. So there they were in a drug dealer's den with soldiers doubtless scouring the streets for them.

'Wait here,' said a minion. 'I'll get friend Dunash.'

Off went the minion. Chegory and his companions settled themselves on barrels and prepared to wait.

Olivia stared around with the widest of eyes. She had never before been in a place like this. Shabble supplemented the efforts of a few feeble oil lanterns, illuminating a large hall studded with doors opening on to offices and strongrooms, the air heavy with the scent of joss sticks being burnt to conceal the taint of the drug which was stored in this house of evil.

'How are we going to get out of this mess?' said Chegory. 'Shabble? You got us into it. Got any bright ideas?'

'Burning, burning, burning,' chanted Shabble in a lilting, high-singing voice. 'Injiltaprajura entire, I could burn it, Chegory. The whole lot! Nothing left! All gone! No more problem then! Right now, that's what I'll do, I'll burn it right now.'

'You will do no such thing!' said Pokrov.

'Why not?' said Shabble.

'Because I,' said Pokrov, 'would be most annoyed. I might even send you to the therapist!'

Shabble squeaked with fear and ascended to the ceiling.

'Could Shabble really incinerate Injiltaprajura?' said Chegory, with a kind of horror.

'No, of course not!' said Pokrov briskly. 'Or not at a single blow, in any case. It would probably take our bubbly little friend several days to barbecue the entire city.'

'You know a lot about Shabble,' said Ingalawa.

'Yes, yes,' said Pokrov, affecting impatience. 'We chat, you know. Shabble tells me things. Why, it was Shabble who helped my grandfather design the Analytical Engine.'

Pokrov was lying. It was not Pokrov's grandfather whom Shabble had helped. It was Pokrov himself.

'I've seen a portrait of your grandfather,' said Ingalawa. 'He looks remarkably like you.'

'What's remarkable about family resemblance?' said Pokrov. Then, without waiting for an answer, he continued: 'Look, enough of this idle chit-chat. We have to think seriously. Shabble's got us in a mess. What are we going to do?'

'Justina,' said Olivia. 'The Empress.'

'We know who the Empress is, child,' said Pokrov.

'Yes,' said Olivia, 'but, I mean, we could petition her, you know. People do it all the time. Up at the pink palace, I mean.'

'Oh, we know all about the petitions process,' said Pokrov.

'She does have a point,' said Ingalawa. 'It might be the swiftest way out of our difficulties.'

'Well I don't want to get mixed up in any petition,' said Chegory.

'Why on earth not?' said Ingalawa. 'The Empress is very nice. She's kind, sensible and merciful. Very few petitions fail, you know. If they're at all reasonable she'll grant them. She'll understand about Shabble getting out of hand.'

'I still don't want to go petitioning,' said Chegory. 'Not Justina, not anyone.'

'What's the problem?' said Ingalawa. 'It's a perfectly logical thing to do.'

Chegory was silent. This woman didn't understand anything! A petition to the Empress was the most public matter imaginable. What if his uncle was to learn of it? If Dunash Labrat learnt that Chegory had fallen foul of the law, Chegory would be ashamed to ever again show his face at the worthy beekeeper's smallholding.

Ingalawa, Qasaba and Pokrov began to bully Chegory. He must stop running; he must stand up for himself; he must act like a citizen, not like a furtive criminal. Meantime, the miscreant arch-illuminator of Injiltaprajura descended from the heights to join in the debate.

'Yes, yes,' said Shabble. 'Do it, Chegory! Do it!'

The Ebrell Islander's will began to crumble in the face of this combined onslaught. But he was still terrified of publicity, exposure, notoriety. He thought it safer by far to run, to hide, to vanish, to disappear from the face of the earth. At last, unable to defend himself directly any more, he begged leave to think things through overnight.

'Don't prevaricate like that,' said Ingalawa. 'Show some decisiveness for once. Make a decision!'

Fortunately, Chegory was rescued by the arrival of Firfat Labrat and his henchman Hooch Neesberry. Labrat himself was incongruously garbed in a green singlet, a white dhoti and pink slippers. He was a big man built in Ebrell Island red, his flesh largely smothered by luxurious red hair which grew from his cheeks, his chin, shoulders and the back of his hands; indeed, he was so furry that in a certain light he looked more like a rare kind of ape than a man.

This, then, was Firfat Labrat, son of Chegory Guy's mother's brother Vermont and hence Chegory's cousin, and a cousin also of Dunash Labrat's son Ham. He greeted Chegory warmly, and laughed when Chegory explained the troubles which had brought them to Marthandorthan.

'That Shabble!' said Firfat, shaking his head. 'Always up to some mischief!'

'Yes,' said Chegory, 'but it's my fault really. I should have stayed on Jod. But these – these people persuaded me otherwise. I'm sorry we're here, it puts you in danger.'

'Danger's my business,' said Firfat, slapping him on the shoulder. 'More, it's my life.' Then he laughed again. Then, growing serious, turned to one of Chegory's companions. 'You're Ivan Pokrov, aren't you? The man from the Analytical Institute, right?'

'The same,' acknowledged Pokrov.

'Then maybe you can help me,' said Firfat. 'There's this little thing I have to sort out with the inland revenue.'

'If there's accounting work to do,' said Pokrov, 'then Shabble can help us. We can get it done in no time.'

Shabble immediately began to drift away. Shabble was the best accountant on Untunchilamon and knew the intricacies of the tax system inside out, but nevertheless hated figurework of any description.

'Come here,' said Pokrov. 'Or do I have to send you to a therapist to get any work out of you?'

'It's my holiday,' said Shabble rebelliously. 'I haven't had a holiday for five thousand years. I'm taking one now. So!'

But Pokrov was insistent, and at last Shabble, with the greatest of reluctance, followed him into Labrat's office.

These Shabbles! Lazy, idle, mischievous, wilful, wanton, irresponsible! Surely the collapse of the Golden Gulag is no longer a mystery once we realise that the Gulag relied heavily upon Shabbles for expertise of all descriptions. As it has often been remarked in Injiltaprajura, for practical purposes Shabble is scarcely worth a damn, since this creature must be supervised constantly and badgered incessantly if any work is to be got out of it.

Nevertheless, the invention of Shabbles remains the crowning achievement of the Gulag. The best brains of the Gulag laboured mightily for fifty thousand years to produce intelligent life which would surpass human genius ꓶ and, in the Shabbles, they succeeded.

'Taxes!' said Neesberry, once Labrat had vanished into his office with Pokrov and Shabble. 'Things were simpler in Zolabrik, eh?' And he slapped Chegory on the back. 'You remember?'

'Yes,' said Chegory sourly. 'Though I was young.'

'Of course you were! Then but a boy, but now a man. Come, man-thing, let's drink with the men. You Ashdans coming?'

'We don't drink,' said Ingalawa severely.

'But you're coming regardless,' said Neesberry.

Ingalawa protested. Neesberry insisted. Ingalawa capitulated, and she and Olivia accompanied the two men into Firfat Labrat's private saloon. There they were introduced to the few favoured guests who were enjoying Labrat's hospitality. These guests included the harbourmaster, two bankers, three priests, a couple of tax collectors and a judge.

'Give our friends a little Number One,' said Hooch Neesberry.

The barman complied, serving up small tots of Number One in white porcelain cups. Chegory Guy regarded the fluid with disfavour. It was hard liquor. He knew, all too well, the consequences of indulgence in such. Intoxication. Addiction. Then the slow descent into degradation and madness in which the addict sweats through waking nightmares, hands and body shaking as imaginary spiders swarm in the fireplace and dead flesh walks by daylight.

'Drink up!' said Neesberry.

'We are his guests,' said Ingalawa, gently reminding Chegory of the demands of etiquette.

So Chegory gritted his teeth and took a swallow of the Number One. The vicious fluid seared his throat. Tears started from his eyes. His head spun and his knees buckled. He staggered, but kept his balance. He could feel the gut-rot liquor burning, burning, burning as it gulleted down to his stomach.

He took a deep, slow breath. Then another. Calming himself. Steadying himself. How did he feel? Well . . . actually, not too bad. In fact, he felt fine. He felt good. He realised the initial shock had been due more to his own fear than the liquor's chemistry. He reminded himself that he was, after all, an Ebrell Islander. For generations, anyone born on the Ebrells had perished in youth if they lacked the capability to handle hard liquor. Centuries of selective breeding had given Chegory a distinct genetic advantage when it came to handling strong drink.

I won't die tonight. Not if I'm careful.

Thus thought Chegory Guy.

But, nevertheless, he warned himself to be very, very careful. He nursed his drink, and was nursing it still when a trio of soldiers entered the saloon.

'Peace,' said Hooch Neesberry, seeing Chegory's alarm. 'These are regular customers of ours.'

Then – doubtless out of devilment – he introduced Chegory to the newcomers.

'So!' said one, 'so you're the infamous Chegory Guy! Shabble's companion in crime, are you? Oho, are you in trouble! There's men burnt bad who've sworn to burn you alive.'

'I'm innocent!' protested Chegory.

'You're an Ebby, aren't you?' said the other soldier. 'So how can you be innocent?'

This witticism set both soldiers to laughing.

Chegory's fingers were already fists. A sullen anger hardened his face. He was but a joke away from brawling.

'Come, friends,' said Neesberry, seeing that brawling was imminent. 'Finish your drinks and come with me. I've something to show you.'

Then he led Chegory and his two Ashdan companions from the saloon and into some quiet back rooms where there were a few pallets on the floor.

'Here we sleep at times like this when it's best to lie low,' said Neesberry. 'Likely you're tired. Feel free to get your heads down and get some rest.'

Chegory said he would be more than happy to do so. Indeed, he was tired. It had been a long, long day. His sleep the night before had been disrupted by disturbances at the Dromdanjerie; he had worked hard physically all morning and mentally all afternoon; he had been shaken up by an encounter with a kraken then further traumatised by his sudden arrest and Shabble's foolhardy assault on the arresting soldiers.

He was exhausted.

'You sleep, then,' said Ingalawa. 'I'm going to have a word with Ivan and friend Firfat.'

Go she did, with Neesberry departing with her. But Olivia elected to stay. Strangely, Chegory found fatigue miraculously dispelled once he found himself thus alone with the young Ashdan lass in a room well-equipped with shadows, beds and privacy.

How long must we speculate before we divine the thoughts which must necessarily have presented themselves to his mind?

'Precious is the day and precious is the flesh which enables the day.' So says the Creed, which also tells us that 'Great is the Gift of Life and sacred is the preservation of the same.' Yet in our day-to-day life habit dulls our appreciation of existence, our awareness of what life has to offer and our knowledge of our own mortality.

Since Chegory Guy had long sought safety in habit, routine and the renunciation of ambition, he had long been more dull than most. In childhood he had endured the terrors of the pogrom which had claimed the lives of his mother, brother and sister. Thereafter, his greatest ambition had been to be a rock, something utterly insignificant and inoffensive, something the world would never think worth the effort of destruction. Chegory had lived by rote for a long, long time. (Here we are of course dealing with time as youth measures that mystery, for old age would think young Chegory had scarcely been born.)

By rote he had lived till this day, when events both major and minor had disrupted the even tenor of his cherished routines. His brush with death and with the law had awakened him to a terrifying appreciation of his own mortality. He also found himself alive to the world of the flesh.

To the world of beauty.

Olivia Qasaba!

Long had he denied the lust which urged him to possess

her. Yet in the here and now it was hard to deny his desire. Soft were her curves and bright was the sheen of her skin. A light was alive in her eyes, and he allowed himself to imagine that she was remembering the valour with which he had contended against the kraken on the harbour bridge.

The caution which had governed his relations with Olivia in the Dromdanjerie was at low ebb. He was possessed by something akin to the recklessness which stirs the blood in time of war and sets the appetites seething. He imagined Olivia indulging him with a kiss. He was conscious of the gloss of her hair and of a certain fragrance which hung about her. He imagined—

But we all know exactly what he imagined. There is no need to elaborate further. Suffice to say that he studied the young woman intently while pretending to scrutinise his fingertips.

Olivia of the moods uncertain! What was she thinking of? What thinking? What? Only one way to find out. Ask!

'Olivia,' said Chegory.

He meant to make her name itself a poem. But he was truly tired despite his enthusiasm for the life of the moment. His tongue slurred her name, thickened it, made her middle-aged and dowdy, insulted her beyond redemption. Or so thought Chegory. Yet Olivia answered him:

'Yes?'

Yes. She said yes. But to what? To nothing, for the moment. But one day, surely, she would say yes to all. To him, to his strength, to his need, to his urgency.

Chegory found himself trembling.

Then an outbreak of uproar abruptly ended this delightful dalliance. The two young people got to their feet in alarm as the building echoed with shouts, screams, the thumping of trampling boots and the resounding crash of sledgehammers smashing down doors.

'Gods!' said Olivia. 'What is it?'

'We're being raided,' said Chegory. 'Come on! Let's get out of here!'

But attempts to escape were futile. Chegory and Olivia

93

had scarcely got out of the bedroom when shadows jumped them. Chegory was seized. Slammed up against a wall. Mobbed by a good half dozen soldiers.

'Help!' screamed a nearby panic.

His own throat shouted:

'Olivia!'

Then he was slammed again, hit, struck, pounded. All voice knocked out of him by twenty knuckles, thirty. An elbow hard against his face then sharp, sharp, a swordpoint sharp-needling into his throat.

'Don't move, Ebby!' said a snarl. 'Or you're dead!'

'You're under arrest,' said an authority.

Chegory felt his legs buckling.

'Don't move, I said!'

But down he went regardless, helpless to save himself, the world crashing around him as he fell.

He was kicked to his feet.

'You're under arrest,' said a triumph.

'I told him that already,' said an authority first heard but moments before.

Then another voice:

'The charge is drug pushing.'

'Wha—'

Thus his throat, mouthing a single syllable void of meaning. His legs void of strength. Curt efficiency dragging him away already. His feet kicking behind him. Screaming. Someone screaming. Olivia, Olivia!

But Chegory was helpless to save her. All fight, all sense, all thought had been knocked out of him. Like a carcase he was carried, dragged, handled, thrust. He had lost track of where he was, where they were taking him, how far they had come.

Then a bright and blinding light lit his surroundings. He was in the main hall of the warehouse. Artemis Ingalawa was struggling, fighting four soldiers who had hold of a limb apiece. Firfat Labrat and Ivan Pokrov were being hustled out of an office at swordpoint, protesting loudly. Above—

Light light light!

Shabble, surely.

'Chegory!' cried Shabble. 'Chegory, dearest!'

Then, in extremis, Chegory Guy found his voice.

'Don't do anything!' yelled Chegory.

If Shabble let rip and fried a few soldiers, then Chegory Guy would most certainly get the blame. Then the army might of its own initiative launch a pogrom against all Injiltaprajura's surviving Ebrell Islanders, no matter what the Empress said.

'Burning,' chanted Shabble. 'Burning burning burning.'

Then Pokrov's voice rose above the uproar in a shout large-volumed by his desperation.

'Shabble! Come here! Right now! Or I will send you to a therapist immediately!'

To Chegory's great relief, the lord of misrule obeyed, and no further threats of incineration were issued from that source as Chegory and his fellow captives were hustled outside into the night.

CHAPTER TEN

Shortly after the raid on Firfat Labrat's premises in the dockside quarter of Marthandorthan, some prisoners were brought to the gates of the Temple of Torture in Goldhammer Rise. Firfat himself was not one of those prisoners. At that very moment he was back at his warehouse remunerating the soldiers who had just done him a favour by demonstrating to him the manifest inadequacy of his security arrangements.

Chegory, however, was in no position to buy himself out of trouble. For a start, he had no money. Also, unlike Firfat he did not have friends prepared to help him with negotiations. Firfat, on the other hand, had a judge, three priests, a couple of bankers and Injiltaprajura's harbourmaster all on his side.

Could Firfat have saved young Chegory Guy? Perhaps. If he had really exerted himself. But then again, perhaps not. After all, the soldiers did have a quota to fill, and thus were glad to be able to deliver Chegory Guy, Olivia Qasaba, Artemis Ingalawa and Ivan Pokrov to the detention centre.

Shabble was not technically under arrest but bobbed along with them anyway, soaring out of the way whenever an irritated soldier tried to swat the beacon-bright summoner of all night-flying insects.

At the temple gates the prisoners were signed for, as if they were a consignment of cassava or so many sacks of coconuts. Then they were taken into the temple precincts, which were crowded with detainees of all ages, races and sexes, many slumped in sleep already despite certain obstacles to peaceful repose in the form of squalling babies and squabbling in-laws.

'Oh well,' said Chegory, 'it doesn't look too bad. Let's find a quiet corner and get settled.'

To Chegory's horror, Ingalawa and Pokrov had no intention at all of quietly settling down. Instead, they began to protest long and loud, demanding lawyers, bail, release, apologies. Chegory feared they would all get beaten up. He was already stiff and sore from the thumping he had taken in Firfat's warehouse, and had no wish whatsoever to add to his injuries. To his relief, Ingalawa's protests diminished after a fellow captive explained that they could not get access to lawyers because a State of Emergency had been declared.

'Oh,' she said. 'That explains it. Okay then, we'll make the best of it. But I do wish we had mosquito nets.'

These Ashdan liberals! Weird is too weak a word for it! Ingalawa typifies some of the attitudes of the breed. She had protested vehemently solely on the grounds that she was being deprived of her legal rights. On a point of principle, in other words. For that she had risked a beating. Then, once she knew their detention was lawful, all her objections had ceased. It was not being locked up that worried her – no, for she was tough, she was with freinds, she could hack it. No trouble!

Chegory, far more concerned with mere survival than with his rights, found Ingalawa's attitudes alien, to say the least. He was not nearly so sanguine. If truth be told, he was near frantic with worry. He was under arrest on a drugs charge. What worse could happen?

'Shabble!' said Pokrov. 'Turn down your light! You're pulling in every bug in creation!'

But Shabble made no reply. Instead, the imitator of suns sang sweet madrigals, quite lost in a musical fugue. So the humans ignored the lord of chaos, tried (less successfully) to ignore the swarms of insects lured by the light of the singing one, and endeavoured to compose themselves for sleep.

Olivia produced an ivory comb and began to stroke it through her long, silky black hair. Chegory watched her out of the corner of his eye. Shortly he had to carefully compose his limbs so no evidence of his uprising passion would be visible. He was not at all embarrassed at this; it was such a common occurrence that he indulged in the necessary manoeuvres without thinking.

'Shall we tell our dreams?' said Ingalawa.

The telling of dreams is an Ashdan custom followed in Ashmolea South and Ashmolea North alike. One does not tell the dreams one has endured already; instead, one tells the dreams one wishes to have.

'You first,' said Olivia.

'I wish to dream myself . . . living in the usual,' said Ingalawa. 'No alarums in the streets, no prison walls, no soldiers. Instead, the Dromdanjerie as always. My own room, my own bed, the peace within my own mosquito net.'

Ingalawa was a skilled dreamer with years of training and experience behind her. Since that was her chosen dream that was surely what would grace her sleep that night.

'I wish,' said Olivia, still soothing the comb through the free-flowing fantasy of her hair, 'I wish . . . I wish the same.'

But the way in which she said it hinting of things unspoken, of visions altogether different, of dreams intended yet unvoiced.

'You now,' she said, glancing at Chegory.

Then glancing away. Too quickly, too casually. His dream? He saw Pokrov watching him, saw the smile on Pokrov's lips. Knew Pokrov knew. But he denied all, and said stolidly:

'I wish to be a rock. That's all. That's what I'll be tonight. A rock, nothing else.'

'Oh, Chegory!' said Ingalawa. 'What will happen to you if you can't dream more than that?'

'It's only dreams,' said Chegory.

'But dreams shape life,' answered Ingalawa.

Reason was with her. The shaping of aspirations is never

a matter to be taken lightly. In part, the Ashdan discipline of dream-telling is such a shaping. It is also a sharing, and, indeed, a profoundly effective method of socialisation. By declaring that he would be a rock, Chegory was rejecting the aspirations which Ingalawa wished to foist upon him; he was shutting himself off from the elite intellectual society which she wanted him to enter; he was declaring his life hopeless even though he was her pet project. He was being, in a word, offensive.

'They do shape life, you know,' persisted Ingalawa. 'Chegory, Chegory, what will become of you if you don't try?'

'Well, I don't know,' said Chegory, in scarcely more than a mumble. He was too tired for this. Debate, rhetoric, ideology – Ingalawa had an endless appetite for such. But Chegory was exhausted, and longed for sleep. To avoid further argument he said: 'I have to excuse myself for a moment.'

Then he stumped off to find the toilet, which he located at the rear of the temple. It was nothing fancy. Just a shaft bored straight down into the ground until it debouched into one of the tunnels Downstairs. In this case, the tunnel in question was lit with unearthly green light, some of which filtered up the bog-hole. By that light Chegory saw a heavyweight metal grille halfway down, a focus for filth which prevented anyone escaping down this makeshift sewer, and also stopped any occult horror creeping up into the temple from Downstairs.

By the toilet was the customary bowl of water, but smell alone told Chegory it was foul with the filth of dozens of people. He was disgusted, and found himself immediately constipated. Nevertheless, he took a piss, then mooched back to his companions, hoping to find them seriously attempting to sleep. But instead he found them arguing with soldiers. By the time Chegory realised his danger, he had been spotted.

'Zounds!' cried one. 'It's him!'

He turned to run, but they were too quick for him.

Scorched uniforms, singed hair, angry sunburn and patches of blisters told him who they were. These were the soldiers Shabble had burnt. They were exceedingly sore, very angry and definitely in a mood for murder.

'Ebby!' said one, punching him.

'Stop that!' shouted Ingalawa, grabbing the bully.

'You stay out of this,' said the soldier, shaking her off.

Then the soldiers began to shove Chegory around, pushing him so he went reeling from one to the other.

'What next?' yelled one.

'Skin him alive,' growled one dragon-bitten veteran.

'Eat him alive,' shouted another.

'No, no. Stake him out in Lak Street for the rats to eat.'

'Oh, too easy, too easy. The lagoon, boys. Tomorrow. Blood in the water. Sharks.'

All the while Chegory stumbled helplessly from one shove to the next, knowing he would be pulped if he fought back. Swiftly, a consensus formed. The soldiers would prove their own virility and the inferiority of members of lesser races by castrating the Ebrell Islander.

'You can't!' screamed Olivia.

'Ebby lover!' said a soldier, administering a slap along with the insult.

There followed loud noises from Qasaba, Ingalawa and Pokrov with reference to lawyers and lawsuits. All the while Shabble bobbed about in the air, making music that got steadily louder and louder. This the soldiers ignored until the torturer of harmonies began to imitate a skavamareen.

[*Skavamareen:* despite hints made below by the Originator to the effect that this is a species of mechanical device, it is actually a type of demon rumoured to scourge the lands west of the Great Ocean. In those benighted lands, a fearful populace propitiates these demons with human sacrifices to obtain their silence, for to endure the wail of a skavamareen is agony undiluted. *Ritha, Annotator Minor.*]

[Ritha's note on the skavamareen is in error. The great lexicographer Zero Twink has proved beyond a shadow of a doubt that the word 'skavamareen' denotes a rabid wildcat. *Sot Dawbler, School of Commentary.*]

To the skavamareen the demented Shabble then added ghoul-drums, a two-tone gong, a set of babble-tongs, the sound of a dragon with a bad case of flatulence, the cry of a cockerel and the bray of an ass.

The guards took exception to Shabble's musical taste, particularly when the genius loci of Injiltaprajura added a second skavamareen to this makeshift orchestra. By now you will be asking the obvious question. What, you ask, is a skavamareen? Ask away! The device will not be described here, lest some reckless spirit be tempted to build one from description. Ignorance is bliss!

Let it merely be recorded that the soldiers were truly justified in attacking Shabble with shovels. This they did, battering at the imitator of suns in a truly terrible fashion. But it is almost (not entirely – the therapists of the Golden Gulag knew how!) impossible to hurt or kill Shabble, just as it is impossible to damage a rainbow.

Such was the fury of these men at arms that they quite abandoned Chegory Guy as they onslaughted Shabble. Chegory promptly collapsed. Sick, dizzy and disorientated. Olivia and Ingalawa comforted him as best they could while Ivan Pokrov made notes by Shabblelight for the trial (of certain members of Justina's brutal and licentious soldiery) which would surely result from this night of outrage.

The noise grew even louder as Shabble competed in volume with swearing soldiers, the incessant screaming of sundry babies and the groans, moans and assorted abuse of disinterested parties who merely wished to sleep.

These proceedings were interrupted by the advent of a senior officer whose stentorian voice nearly shattered eardrums as he roared:

'What the hell is going on here?'

This officer was the commander of the detention centre, a lean Ashdan whose every word and gesture bespoke the habit of command. Nevertheless, neither his impressive appearance nor his thunderblast query won him reply. His men were in too much of a fighting frenzy to be distracted by anything less than a bucket of cold water.

The commander promptly found such a bucket and tossed it over Shabble's assailants who sobered up with amazing alacrity.

'Shut that thing in the shit pot!' said the commander.

Men scurried to obey.

Shabble of the many musics was too intoxicated by melodic raptures to resist this indignity. Thus the potential incinerator of soldiers was bundled into the shit pot. The lid was put on, muting the cacophony emanating from within. Some twine was produced and used to tie tight the lid.

'Throw it into the well!' said the officer.

Again he was obeyed.

The shit pot tumbled away into the darkness and hit the water below with a muted splash. For the time being the troublesome one was lost to eye and ear alike and something close to silence reigned. Naturally Shabble would burn Shabbleself free once the musical fit was over, but for the moment the innovative one had no thoughts for anything but creative ecstasy.

The officer then ordered one of his subordinates to march away all idle soldiers and put them to work.

'Wait a moment,' said Ivan Pokrov. 'I want the names of these people. I want them brought to justice.'

'Take them away,' said the commander.

His subordinate marched the soldiers away. Some cast dour glances at Chegory Guy as they filed past his recumbent body, and one or two muttered unveiled threats against his person. Once they were gone, Ingalawa abandoned Chegory to Olivia's exclusive care, and got to her feet to confront the commander.

'Who are you?' said Ingalawa.

'That should have been my question,' said the commander with something of a sneer. 'But I know enough about you without a name.'

Why was this said with a sneer?

Because he was addressing a woman who was also a child of the effete culture of Ashmolea South. The commander was from the north, where they breed ferocious fighters who value physical supremacy above all else. Ingalawa did not like his attitude at all. He was dismissing her as if she were of no account, which was intolerable. Ingalawa was a scion of one of the few fighting clans of Ashmolea's south, and when her temper was roused the liberal Ashdan intellectual soon gave way to the homicidal berserker.

So she said:

'Have you a name?'

In Ashmolea, this is fighting call, and always compels a response. For to be silent is to accept dishonour to oneself and to one's family.

'A name? Shanvil Angarus May! Is that name enough for you? May of Rest Acular! Is that genesis sufficient?'

'That's all we need to sue you,' said Ivan Pokrov. 'We'll have a summons drawn up as soon as we get out of here.'

'You're crazy,' said Shanvil May, speaking to Pokrov with a contempt equal to that which he had displayed when addressing Ingalawa.

'I doubt it,' said Pokrov. 'Our good friend Chegory Guy has been beaten nearly to death by your soldiers. I hold you responsible. Doubtless the courts will take a similar view of your culpability. Either you ordered it or else through gross negligence you failed to prevent it.'

'You're the one who's in trouble, not me,' said Shanvil May, totally unimpressed by this fancy little speech. 'You're being held on charges of the utmost gravity.'

'Trumped-up charges!' protested Pokrov.

'That's as may be,' said May, 'but the law is the law and the law will be obeyed because it is the law. You will stay in detention until you have answered the charges.'

'What are we charged with?' said Ingalawa.

'Consorting with drug dealers to start with,' said Shanvil May. 'Do you deny it?'

'I'll answer that question in court,' said Ingalawa.

So she said, though her plan was still to resolve her difficulties by petitioning the Empress Justina. If she had to fight the matter out in court she must necessarily lose, since she was as guilty as hell, because she had indeed been consorting with drug dealers. She had even drunk of the dreaded alcohol, and the taint of the same drug was still on her breath.

'I,' said Shanvil May, 'will enjoy watching you try to wriggle out of this one in a court of law.'

With that said, he turned to leave.

'You can't just walk off like that!' said Ingalawa. 'We need protection. Your soldiers have already tried to murder us. I'll hold you responsible if one of us gets murdered. Look – this Ebrell boy is so badly beaten he can't even stand.'

'Not a problem,' said Shanvil May briskly. 'I'll send your Ebby friend to the palace to be Tested.'

'Tested?' said Olivia. 'By what?'

'By the squealer in the treasury, of course,' said May. 'What else?'

Upon which Chegory, who was not nearly as badly hurt as Ingalawa had made out, thought:

Thanks, Ingalawa! You've really done it this time!

He did not want to go to the palace. He wanted nothing to do with any Test. Also he did not want to be removed from Olivia who was so sweetly treasuring his bruises.

'How will taking him away to the palace help?' said Olivia. 'He'll still get beaten up.'

'No, no,' said Shanvil May, in a voice which was two parts of soothing balm to nine parts of lordly condescension. 'The Test of the squealer will take all night. By the time your boyfriend gets back here those soldiers sharking after him will have gone off shift. It'll be a new day.'

'You're wrong,' said Pokrov decisively. 'I know all about that thing you call a squealer. It gives judgement in less than a heartbeat. How can that take all night?'

'There'll be a queue,' said May.

Then set about organising Chegory's journey.

So it came to pass that Chegory Guy was very shortly

marched out of the Temple of Torture, up Goldhammer Rise and then up Lak Street. Through the night went Chegory and his escorting soldiers, sweating as they laboured through the coffin-close heat of the tropical night. Past the ship-sized chunk of bone known as Pearl they went. So cool it looked, but nevertheless the night was stifling. Past the grand houses glimmering with the blue-green light of moon paint. Cool these looked also, but heat was still breathing out from the sun-tormented slabs of bloodstone over which Chegory and his escorts walked. Then at last there bulked ahead the pink palace of the Empress Justina, jewel of Injiltaprajura.

[Here an ambiguity. Was the palace that jewel, or the Empress? Whichever way this ambiguity is resolved one must find the Originator guilty of bad taste, for the Empress was a pandornabriloothoprata, as they so neatly put it in Janjuladoola, whereas the palace itself was a monument to kitsch of the worst possible kind. *Oris Baumgage, Fact Checker Minor.*]

Chegory was marched up the steps to the portico. Between the huge carven pillars he was led. Into the foyer he was taken. There he was handed over to the palace guards.

'Another one for the squealer,' said a soldier. 'To go back to the detention centre when finished with.'

Chegory was paperworked then taken into the deep-delved interstices of the palace underlevels, there to await the Test. Shanvil May was correct in thinking the Test would not take place in a hurry. In the corridor leading to the treasury there was a long, long queue of Ebrell Islanders and similar undesirables waiting to be tested by the squealer.

Suspects were taken into the treasury one by one. The squealer (an antique device of uncertain origin) would wail long and loud if anyone presented to it had been in its presence in the last ten years.

Chegory was content inasmuch as he knew himself to be innocent. At least here in the palace no disaster could befall him. There was nobody here who wanted to kill him; Ingalawa was far away and hence unable to bully him further; he need not worry for the moment about petitions, publicity and the dire punishments which would surely fall upon him as an inevitable consequence of the crime of being an Ebrell Islander.

The queue moved but slowly.

The suspects emerging from the treasury after clearance by the squealer had bloody noses and worse, suggesting that the guards within were amusing themselves at the expense of the captives. Chegory scarcely reacted to this. He had sunk into a fatalistic mood. A beating? What mattered a beating in the face of the absolute disaster which had befallen him?

He started worst-casing his predicament.

What worried him most was the prospect of the agonising embarrassment of public exposure, the shame he would suffer when he had to face his straightbacked uncle Dunash Labrat, and the prospect of exile.

Apart from that, he did not think anything too terrible would happen, as long as he could evade the murderous vigilantism of the soldiers whom Shabble had burnt. The standard punishments of the Izdimir Empire had largely fallen into disuse after Wazir Sin had been overthrown. Such crimes as treason still attracted heavy penalties, but minor malefactors were no longer thrown to pits full of vampire rats. Nor were they—

[Here a loving account of the seven hundred Standard Punishments of the Izdimir Empire has been deleted in the interests of concision. Those interested in the details will find them admirably explicated in an encyclopaedic work by Boz Reebok entitled *The Compleat Manual of Mercy*. *Drax Lira, Redactor Major*.]

Thus Chegory could count on keeping possession of his limbs, senses and sanity. Nevertheless, exile was a definite possibility. Injiltaprajura would think itself well rid of an Ebrell Islander who brawled in the streets, consorted with drug dealers and indulged in the dreaded alcohol.

Exile to Zazazolzodanzarzakazolabrik!

To many, such a prospect would have been nightmarish, for those wastelands to the north of Injiltaprajura were fearsome indeed. A desert of rotten rock undermined by sea-flooded tunnels where dwelt huge sea scorpions and sea centipedes. Ancient ruins haunted by evil metal which hunted and killed. The encampments of the aboriginal people of Untunchilamon, a hunted race feared and despised by those who dwelt in the city.

In Zazazolzodanzarzakazolabrik it was easy to die, hard to live. Or so it was said in Injiltaprajura. In Chegory's case, things were somewhat different. Wazir Sin had launched his pogrom againt Ebrell Islanders when Chegory was but a child, resulting in the young redskin's spending years in the wasteland. He knew how to survive there unaided. Moreover, his father dwelt there yet as stillmaster for the warlord Jal Japone, hence a welcome awaited Chegory if he had to flee Injiltaprajura.

Chegory did not like the idea of exile.

Life in Zazazolzodanzarzakazolabrik was hard, tough and monotonous. Jal Japone was a ruthless taskmaster who drove his men hard. Those men were dangerous killers, trained knife-fighters all. In such company in such a place death could be all too casual. In contrast, Injiltaprajura was a place of luxury. Sweet water unlimited! Green coconut cheap. Cassava, mangos, breadfruit and sugarcane sold fresh from the city's market gardens all year round. Wealth undreamed of in the wastelands.

But . . .

He would survive.

In Japone's court there would be men who would recognise him, who would remember him from his childhood and would be pleased to meet him again as a man.

One might expect Chegory to slip off to sleep once he had assured himself his survival was certain. But he did not. It was not the comfortless stone which kept him awake. He was tired enough to have slept on a bed of nails. But he was beginning to worry about the alcohol he had drunk at Firfat's warehouse.

He shouldn't have.

He shouldn't have let Ingalawa force him to drink it.

What would happen to him? Would he become an addict? Would he find himself crawling through the streets on the morrow craving for drink?

Chegory shared Injiltaprajura's full knowledge of the evils of alcohol. Furthermore, he had been heartily impressed at a tender age by the attitudes of Jal Japone. The warlord made his living by brewing rotgut booze in the wastelands, but he had placed an absolute interdict on the stuff as far as his own men were concerned. Chegory's father had oft reinforced Japone's ban by telling his son of the terrible damage alcohol had wrought on the Ebrells themselves.

Tales of men who had lost ships when they were incapably drunk. Of families which had fallen to fighting because of demon rum. Of the depraved horrors of drunken ceremonies in the temple of the evil Orgy God of the Ebrells. Of—

[Here another of the catalogues with which the Originator of this Text was incurably beglamoured. Deleted by Order. *Drax Lira, Redactor Major.*]

Thus Chegory was for long kept awake, but at last he fell asleep. Nobody bothered to wake him up when the queue moved on. There were already fifty people lined up behind him, none unhappy to leapfrog past the sleeping one, since all were innocent (at least of theft from the treasury) and most were impatient to be scrutinised by the squealer and to be gone. The guards never bothered to rouse the sleeper since it made no difference to them who was first and who last. They had in any case settled to dicing and playing at cards by the light of star lanterns.

Chegory dreamt of Zazazolzodanzarzakazolabrik, that region of desolation known also as the Wastes, the Scorpion Desert, the Scraglands, and as Zolabrik for short. He dreamt of red rock in a red sunset. Of his father, grizzled and gnomish, muttering under his breath as he pottered around in his distillery.

Then Chegory woke.

Then he *Woke Up!*

Because all hell was breaking loose.

The guards were down, riot was loose, uproar ruled, and the prisoners were mobbing into the treasury. Chegory was swept along with them. Helpless to resist. He knew already that this insurrection was madness. They would never get out of here. Palace guards would seal all exits then starve them into submission. Then there would be trials indeed and punishments of unabated horror.

He screamed in frustrated rage, then screamed no more for he needed all his strength to fight for footing in the tussling mob. In through the entrance he was swept, into the treasury. There wealth was heaped upon wealth, and there lanterns and other lights illuminated a scene of outright anarchy.

Prisoners in their dozens were scrabbling for treasure of all description then bearing it away through a hole in the wall which led into yawning darkness. Chegory knew at a glance that this breach must issue into the undermines Downstairs.

Man after man dared the dark, bearing away armloads of gold and silver, of opal, japonica, celestine and carnelian, of amber and pounamu. Two were flailing at each other, fighting over a trifle which had caught the fancy of both – a green globe of stone, no larger than a fist, in which the souls of fireflies glowed like frozen pinpoints of essence of rainbow. While the fighters contended, another man seized it and was off.

'You crazy bastards!' screamed Chegory.

Nobody paid him any attention at all.

Then there were cries of panic from the corridor in which the prisoners had so lately queued while awaiting audience with the squealer. In moments, alarm-shouts warned everyone that reinforcements from the palace guard were fighting their way towards the treasury.

A panic flight ensued. An irresistible floodtide of bodies swept young Chegory Guy through the hole in the wall of the treasury and into the yawning darkness beyond.

Down tunnels they went, blundering through confusions of darkness where elbow argued with chin and boot with instep. They jostled down echoing stoneways, sludged through mephitic passages ankle-deep in sewage, climbed stairs going up then found those same steps descending, and ever they sought for light, light, light, a glimmer of light to free them from the terrors of the darkness which yet oppressed them though their numbers were many.

Intersections were many and each thinned the mob. As intersective decisions lessened the density of the crowd so its pace and urgency lessened also. It became not a mindless flux of squalling flesh but small, disparate groups of in-dividuals who began to think, talk and argue.

Chatter broke out.

'Go north.'

'North, he says! Where's north?'

'You doubt my sense of direction?'

'I doubt your sense, man. There's no way out of here!'

'Of course there is. Must be.'

'Nay. Bones wander here for years. Become dust. No hope for them, no hope, we're lost, lost.'

'We're dead. We're dead, and this is hell.'

'If you weren't with us I'd disbelieve it.'

'Oh! Is that you, Thagomovich?'

'None other. Just my luck to end up with you. Now – what's this? Name yourself!'

'Datkinson Rowen. Tailor by trade. Born Wen Endex. What else you want to know?'

'The way out of here, fool! And you – what have we here?'

So saying, a voice grabbed Chegory by the elbow. He broke away, for he did not care to identify himself. Two steps he took, and that was all. Then he stood still, very still, in the darkness.

'A guard, by chance?' said the voice. 'Perhaps it is. Get it, boys!'

But nobody showed any enthusiasm for games of chase and thuggery in the overbearing dark. Instead, on went the arguing voices. Thirty paces further they went, then halted at an intersection.

'Stinks!' said one.

'Dikle,' said another.

'Can't go down there,' said Datkinson Rowen, the tailor from Wen Endex. 'Stuff's poison. Gets into your skin. Does for you.'

'But it's solid.'

Sound of someone stamping. Thrice. Thonk thonk sploosh!

'There! Turns to liquid, see. Goes solid when it's cool enough but liquid when it's walked on.'

'Thixotropic,' said a scholar.

'Thixotropic! Is that what you call it? Bloody perverse, that's what I call it. Stinks, anyway, as the man said.'

'But there's light at the end.'

'Aagh, there's light for an ending to every tunnel. Come on. Any direction will bring us to light in the end.'

'Oh no. Not so. It's ghosts down here. Ghosts and jaws. Sharks which float in the thinness of air.'

'Oh yes! That I'll believe when pigs shit silver, when sun burns blue, when my mother-in-law turns sweet . . .'

With that, the voices were on their way, choosing ways other than that which led down a tunnel awash with dikle. Chegory footpadded through the dark to that passage. There was indeed light at the far end, some four or five hundred paces distant if he was any judge. A cool blue light which glimmered on the dikle.

Chegory had no fear of dikle, which he knew to be no poison. Furthermore, if he was to go on alone then the sooner he found some light the better. Vampire rats shun the light, whereas he would be easy prey for such monsters if he continued to wander the dark on his own. He hesitated. Run after the others? Or strive to the light?

The others were part of the mob which had fought for treasure in the depths of the pink palace. Such criminal actions had already multiplied Chegory's troubles beyond measure. Previously he had faced charges of brawling, of consorting with drug smugglers and (possibly) of inciting Shabble to violence. Now he was on the run, a hunted man implicated in riot, looting and civil disorder, guilty (though it was not his fault!) of escaping from lawful custody and (a crime equally as serious) of consorting with escaped prisoners.

Chegory remembered the stern advice his father had given him before his return to Injiltaprajura.

'Be honest. Obey the law. Uphold the rule of order. Choose your company with care. Keep clear of criminals. Bring no disgrace upon yourself, your family or your race.'

That decided him.

He set off for the light, choosing solitary dangers rather than the dubious companionship of the lawless. Ah, what a good little boy he was! Bravely forging down the tunnel despite the stench. His footsteps broke up what fraction of the dikle yet remained solid. The stuff leaked into his sun-fractured boots. But his spirits rose regardless, for ahead was a broad and pleasant corridor lit in bright blue.

He gained the corridor.

And was promptly menaced by bright blades held by a four-strong band of men who looked more than ready to use them.

CHAPTER ELEVEN

Chegory's quartet of captors did not declare themselves, but their names in time became well-known to history and its recorders. None was a native of Untunchilamon; instead, all hailed from lands far distant.

[A tautology, and, I regret, but one of many. If someone has been declared to be no native of Untunchilamon then it is necessarily tautological to declare their genesis far distant, since the most cursory acquaintance with geography teaches us that Untunchilamon lies near no other land. To the north is Tameran, to the south Parengarenga, to the east Yestron and to west Argan, all a weary sea-voyage distant. Sundry minor islands are closer slightly, but none could rightly be described as 'neighbouring'. *This criticism inserted by Ventantakorum of Odrum, Seventh Grade Critic Textual.*]

Most fearsome in appearance was a burly barbarian girded in leather. This man of ugly face and jug-handle ears was a Yarglat tribesman by name of Guest Gulkan. He was pretender to the throne of Tameran, currently occupied by the Lord Emperor Khmar. He it was who spoke first.

'Who are you?' said the barbarian.

He addressed young Chegory in the Toxteth of Wen Endex, a language curt and brutal at the best of times. Fortunately, Chegory could speak Toxteth (and Dub, Janjuladoola and Ashmarlan as well).

Don't get the wrong idea! Here you will find no apology for the Ebrell Islanders after the manner of the Ashdan liberals, no claims that these people are capable of intellectual endeavour or (yes, Ashdans have dreamed as much!) of scholarly achievement. Chegory Guy was just as he has been painted: a coarse and ignorant rock gardener with the most limited of capabilities imaginable.

The juvenile redskin was certainly no linguist. This can be proved by having reference to the classical definition of 'knowing a language' which was framed so long ago by the scholarly Iskordan. It is (out of pity for the unwise one must often spell out these things, however ludicrous such a procedure must seem to the educated!) to be possessed of the ability to defend oneself in a court of law in that tongue, to compose poetry in the same argot, and, finally, to frame in that mode of speech a joke which is capable of eliciting laughter from a native speaker of the same.

[True true true. Yet one might wish to supplement this definition by saying that to truly 'know' a language one should also have certificated proof of one's ability to treat with that tongue in the context of educated discourse. The idea that members of the polyglot rabble which infests the streets cities such as Injiltaprajura actually 'know' the languages in which they garble is an offensive notion deeply subversive of the underlying concepts which support the ideology of the Higher Learning, and hence is to be deprecated whenever possible. *Drax Lira, Redactor Major*.]

As Chegory Guy could not have composed poetry to save his life, he did not (to apply Iskordan's technical test) actually 'know' any languages whatsoever. He was therefore a living stereotype, proof of the accuracy and validity of the world's prejudices. That is to say, he was an inarticulate creature who dwelt in a world where the most vital communications are made by the application of brute force and mindless violence.

Nevertheless, young Chegory could 'speak' some four separate tongues, after a fashion. Dub was native to his home; he absorbed it with his mother's milk. He had mastered the complexities of Janjuladoola in the court of Jal Japone, for that was the ruling tongue in the warlord's realm. Toxteth had held the ascendancy in Injiltaprajura ever since Chegory's return, forcing him to acquire a certain competence in the same. As for Ashmarlan, why, that was the tongue of the Qasaba household, and also the language which Ivan Pokrov used in his daily dealings with young Chegory.

Now – where were we?

As yes! With the aforesaid young Chegory in a blue-lit corridor Downstairs, confronting a band of swordsmen whose number included the Yarglat barbarian Guest Gulkan from far-distant Tameran, who had just asked him (in Toxteth) who he was.

While Chegory was competent in Toxteth (at least as competency is understood in the slums of Lubos) he nevertheless had difficulty understanding this simple query, since the barbarian's atrocious accent mutilated the words. However, fear sharpened the young redskin's ability, and, while the meaning of the barbarian's articulations existed at the far border of intelligibility, he nevertheless retrieved that meaning and framed his reply.

'That's my question!' said Chegory, with more courage than prudence.

His reply was nearly identical to that used by the Ashdan commander, Shanvil Angarus May, in reply to an impertinence ventured by Artemis Ingalawa. (Though, to be pedantic, May had spoken in Ashmarlan, whereas Chegory used Toxteth.) You see? Unless these Ebrell Islanders are kept under strict control they immediately begin to ape their betters, putting on airs and manners which should by rights be forbidden to the lower breeds.

'Okay, Thatsmyquestion,' said Guest Gulkan of the jug handle ears, 'what are you doing here?'

'Talking to you,' said Chegory Guy, showing a truly amazing degree of reckless bloody-mindedness.

His patience was at an end. His long day was growing ever longer and longer. First alarums at the Dromdanjerie, then work, then study, then attack by a kraken, then arrest, then boozing in Marthandorthan, a raid, imprisonment, a beating, argument, his deportation to the pink palace, riot, looting and much muddling around Downstairs. Now this!

'Don't dare your neck for nothing,' said a rich-garbed

greybeard in the fluent Toxteth of a native speaker of the tongue. 'That's lunacy!'

'Who are you then?' said Chegory Guy.

'Someone older and wiser than you, young man,' said the greybeard briskly. 'Come, boy! Can your wit outflank weapons? We're four, you're one.'

By now, Chegory's fit of bad temper was passing, and he was reconsidering the risks. His captors could spit him at will, leaving his corpse to rot away to nothing. What's more, they looked perfectly ready to do so. He presumed they were up to no good. They must be criminals of some description, surely. Hence he began to tell the truth of his own recent history, thinking an account of his own villainy would help ingratiate him with these foreign-born gangsters.

Yes, while Chegory had yet to learn the names of any of his captors, he had correctly guessed that all four were from parts far removed from Untunchilamon. As he stumbled through his story of his recent past he speculated as to who they might be.

Chegory picked Guest Gulkan for a soldier of sorts. A fair enough guess, and an accurate one. The greybeard dressed in robes gorgeous he thought to be a wonderworker, one of the sorcerers of Yestron. Close! The tart-tongued ancient was indeed from Yestron, for he had been born in Wen Endex. However, he was no wonderworker. Rather, he was a wizard. In truth he was Hostaja Sken-Pitilkin, the notorious wizard of Drum, a renegade whose death had long been demanded by Argan's Confederation of Wizards.

Then there was a tall clean-shaven man of middle years who wore a strange body-conforming garment which glittered like fish scales caught by the sun. So tall was he, so lordly his bearing and so bright his armour that Chegory could only presume him to be an elven lord straight out of legend. Blue were his eyes, blue and piercing, and his sword threatened to be more piercing yet.

Who was this personage?

Why, this was Pelagius Zozimus, in truth a wizard of the

order of Xluzu, one of the eight orders of the Confederation of Wizards.

Zozimus was a cousin of Hostaja Sken-Pitilkin, which was truly remarkable, for it is (according to all the authorities) very rare to have two wizards who are even distantly related by blood. A pair of wizards of the same generation of the same family is, therefore, an occurrence bordering on the miraculous. If this Text was to seek Verisimilitude at the expense of Truth then the relationship would not be mentioned; however, as this is a sober History it must perforce deal with the facts of the matter, even though many will find these facts incredible.

[Incredible indeed this familial relationship appears to be on the face of it. All authorities agree that the requisite inborn Talent for wizardry is exceedingly rare; furthermore, scarcely one apprentice in a hundred survives the Trials to which the evil wizards of the Confederation subject their students. Nevertheless, a diligent scrutiny of genealogical records sourced in Wen Endex has demonstrated the existence of two cousins so named. That bare fact in itself proves nothing, but the fact that neither is credited with either marriage or progeny may be significant. Those interested in pursuing this matter further will find the necessary references in paragraph 2201 of Issue 4368 of Volume 941 of the Genealogical Abstract. *Oris Baumgage, Fact Checker Minor.*]

These, then, were the people with whom Chegory Guy was confronted. Guest Gulkan, exiled emperor of Tameran. Hostaja Sken-Pitilkin, wizard. Pelagius Zozimus, wizard likewise. Oh, and a fourth – Thayer Levant, a cutthroat from Chi'ash-lan. A nasty, shifty, dangerous piece of work if ever there was one. Rat was his face, but for his eyes, which were vulture. A rag-tatter patchwork cloak he wore, rigged so it could be swiftly offslipped for a knife fight, and cunningly weighted with lead so it could be used as a weapon in such a fight. Since Levant had no language in common with Chegory Guy, he could but stand silent while the Ebrell Islander poured out his story.

Chegory told the truth, the whole truth and nothing but the truth, yet Gulkan, Sken-Pitilkin and Zozimus had deep reservations about the story they were hearing. This is understandable. After all, young Chegory was an Ebrell Islander, and these people of the fire-burning skin are notoriously untruthful. They are born degenerates with an innate genetic disposition toward drug-taking, the murder of cetaceans and that violent and obscene game known as ruck. In most cases those of the flesh of this foul, polluted people drink themselves to death by the age of forty (unless they die first of diseases venereal) and the world thinks itself well rid of them.

Once Chegory had finished his story, Zozimus retailed it in abstract to Thayer Levant in Galish, then all four swordsmen had a quick conference on Chegory's future, voicing their thoughts in the same tongue since they were sure the Ebrell Islander would find it unintelligible. Indeed, young Chegory Guy was unknowledgeable in Galish, which is scarcely surprising since one would have been scrabbling to find any native of Untunchilamon who could converse in that language, which is the Trading Tongue of Argan's Salt Road, and hence belongs to another world entirely.

'I say kill him!' said Thayer Levant.

'You would,' said Pelagius Zozimus disapprovingly.

'The boy by chance could help us,' said Guest Gulkan.

'Help us?' said Levant. 'How?'

'Maybe by guessing us a way to seize the wishstone,' said Hostaja Sken-Pitilkin.

The wishstone?

Yes!

Precisely how Guest Gulkan and his comrades came to Untunchilamon is a mystery which is unlikely ever to be resolved, for they never confessed their mode of travel to any competent informant. But what is certain beyond a doubt is that they came to Injiltaprajura solely in order to find the wishstone. Indeed, it was this band of four adventurers which was responsible for the gaping hole in the treasury through which Chegory Guy had so recently ventured.

Thirty nights earlier this quartet had ventured Downstairs, meaning to find their way to the treasury, blast a hole in the wall, seize the wishstone and be gone. Unfortunately they had run into problems. To be exact, they had lost their way, and had then encountered a therapist left over from the days of the Golden Gulag. It had taken the combined strength and skill of all four to allow them (barely) to escape the clutches of the therapist.

After that trauma – strong men have died of less! – they had at length navigated to the treasury. Then the two wizards Hostaja Sken-Pitilkin and Pelagius Zozimus had used the very last of their presently available power to destroy part of the wall. (They were, you see, ignorant of the existence of the secret door earlier used by the Malud marauders.)

The adventurers had expected to find the treasury dark and empty in the dead of night. Instead, they had found it bright-lit and aswarm with activity. They had fled, and hence had not seen the riot which their attack on the treasury had provoked.

'You think he could help us to the wishstone?' said Levant. 'Okay! Ask him! I wager you'll not get much help from him.'

'Why not?' said Zozimus. 'He's an Ebrell Islander, is he not? They're notable thieves, you know.'

Levant knew no such thing, for he had scarcely even heard of the Ebrell Islands. He shrugged and said:

'As you wish.'

So Pelagius Zozimus spake unto Chegory Guy and said:

'Let's be frank. We're here for the wishstone. Can you help us get it?'

'You mean,' said Chegory, 'you're hunting the thieves who stole it?'

'What are you babbling about, boy?' said Hostaja Sken-Pitilkin. 'We're not looking for thieves. We're thieves ourselves. To wreck a way into the treasury of Injiltaprajura and make off with the wishstone is our intent. We got as far as the wrecking but found soldiers within. Can you tell us why?'

'I've as good as told you already,' said Chegory. 'The wishstone's been stolen already.'

'Who's got it?' said Guest Gulkan.

'Oh, it's no use asking him,' said Zozimus, still speaking in his native Toxteth. 'He won't know.'

'But I do, I do,' said Chegory, eager to please since he thought pleasing likely to prolong life. 'It's pirates, that's who. Three pirates of Ashdan race, though they're not from Ashmolea, no, they're from Asral. That makes them of the Malud, it's Malud they speak though their skins are Ashdan, but Shabble knows Malud as good as Ashmarlan, Shabble's an expert with tongues, and besides one of them could speak Ashmarlan in any case.'

Thus it tumbled out. Fear, fatigue and an intense eagerness combined to produce an overall effect of un-intelligibility.

'Slow down a bit, boy!' said Sken-Pitilkin. 'You're not at race with a dragon, you know. Tell us in bits. First bit. You're a pirate, are you? Is that what you're trying to tell us?'

'Oh no, oh no,' said Chegory. 'I'm an Ebrell Islander.'

'That,' said Hostaja Sken-Pitilkin dryly, 'is no dis-qualification from piracy.'

Then he led the interrogation of Chegory Guy until the truth, or Chegory's version of it, had been extracted. Many subsidiary questions followed until Chegory's stumbling tongue began to bungle so many words he became quite unintelligible.

'So,' said Pelagius Zozimus, summing up, 'these pirates would appear to have the wishstone at the moment.'

Chegory grunted in assent.

'Well,' said Zozimus briskly, 'in due course no doubt we'll catch up with your pirates. Meantime, we have to get out of here. In the confusion of flight from the treasury we happen to have misplaced ourselves. You know this labyrinth well?'

'Yes, yes,' said Chegory.

Though he was near numb with fatigue he was still sufficiently alive to danger to realise that his captors might well kill him out of hand if they once thought him no longer of any use to them.

'Good!' said Zozimus. 'A guide, at last! Lead on, little chicken, lead on.'

So Chegory set off through the underground passages, choosing his direction at random but treading the magnanimous stones underfoot in a confident manner meant to suggest that he knew exactly where he was going.

[Translator's note: preliminary Inspection of this Translation has resulted in numerous Queries, one of which relates to the existence of 'magnanimous stones'. Please be assured that the Text has been Translated with Accuracy Ultimate. The fault, if any, lies with the Originator, who would appear to have, at best, only a shaky understanding of the accepted meanings of the word 'magnanimous'.]

That was the night that Chegory Guy learnt what it means to be asleep on one's feet. Often he stumbled through dreams as he trekked endlessly, endlessly, through the tortuous tunnels. He blinked awake to find himself walking over stone lit by bloody red light. Over black grass growing soft and silent beneath banks of warm grey lights. Over fractured ice, the spillage from chambers where an ice-making machine dropped huge blocks of frozen water on to pyramids of shattered crystal, splintered light.

It was only after the ice was far behind and lost to sight that Chegory realised he should have picked some up to appease his mounting thirst.

Too late, too late!

Through dreams he walked, and then through nightmare.

Where?

'Where are we?' said the violence, shaking him awake.

He woke.

The lord in the elven armour had him by the arm. Blue eyes, blue eyes he had. Obscured by smoke, smoke which made young Chegory cough. His eyes stung. Seared by the smoke. He shook his head, closed his watering eyes. Darkness veiled his eyes and was slow, slow to clear.

'A temple,' said the greybeard.

Voice clear in Toxteth.

'That much I'd guessed,' said the lordly armoured one. 'But why's he brought us here. Well?'

Another shake, jarring Chegory from dream.

He squeezed tears from his smoke-stung eyes. Cracked them open. Just enough to see. Smoke ascending from huge amphorae scabbed by age. Strings of teeth stretched from floor to ceiling. Jaws, huge jaws, gaping jaws fresh-painted with blood. Jaws dead but alive with potent horror.

'Out,' said Chegory, blurting the word with the urgency of a man vomiting up choking blood. 'Out, get out, get out, out now, out or we're dead.'

He had never been anywhere like this. But he knew exactly what it was. It was a temple of Elasmokarcharos, the shark-god of the Dagrin, the aboriginal people of Untunchilamon. And the stuff burning on the altar was zen, zen, it was zen, he had breathed of it, had—

'Out!'

Thus Chegory. All panic.

But:

'There's nobody here,' said the leather-girded barbarian, sword out, sword at the ready.

'Music,' mumbled the greybeard.

While the elven lord was dancing already, was swaying, was stepping, pacing out with an even tread measured in dignity, slow-measured, while down on his hands and knees was the shifty man in the ragtattered cloak, while—

The jaws!

Free-floating through the air came the jaws of the shark. Fresh blood on the teeth. Gnashed open, gnashed shut.

'Not real,' mumbled Chegory.

Then they lunged, they closed, his arm upflung, bitten,

gone, and the pain was real real real, he screamed and screamed and screamed. Screaming, fled.

Stumbling through giddy smoke till there was no more smoke, no smoke, no light, dark only, a smouldering dark through which he wept, agony, his arm was agony, then there was light light light, bright phosphorescence to which he went, only to find the light full of drifting blood.

'My arm.'

He touched his arm. Left hand to right arm. Felt the stump, the bloody stump, it was his, it was his, it was his blood feeding the vermilion fog which crowded the air.

The jaws of the shark had been real, had closed, had torn, had wrenched away his arm, had left him a cripple, bleeding, in agony, dying, dying, dying.

He sobbed with choking horror.

His legs were subsiding, sliding out of control as he fell toward darkness, toward darkness, the darkness.

Darkness all.

CHAPTER TWELVE

'Joma dok notora koopeniti.'

Thus a voice.

'Joma, joma!'

Insistent. Urging.

'Sleeps you?'

That much intelligible. In Ashmarlan foreignly voiced.

'Sleeps?'

A boot. Hard.

Chegory lay still, pretending to be dead. Then a hand grabbed his hair. A full handful of it. Yanked. Hard. He could pretend no longer, hence lurched from the ground. He was seized immediately. His arm wrenched back in an armlock. His arm? Right arm! But that was gone, gone, gone, torn and missing, brutalised by a shark, by the bare and barren jaws of a shark free-swimming through the air itself. Wasn't that so?

No.

That had been but a hallucination.

He had breathed of zen, had he not?

He had.

That much he remembered.

Ah yes, it was coming back to him. The temple of the shark-god Elasmokarcharos. Set up in the manner often described to him by men who had been, who had seen, who had dared. Ancient amphorae from which issued a choking smoke. The smoke of zen, the herb which ruptures reality.

'Are you listening?'

Hard voice emphasised by a slap.

'I'm deaf,' said Chegory, who had been too full of relief for his recovered right arm to pay attention to the lean and elderly Ashdan who had been addressing him in garbled Ashmarlan.

'But you hear me now? Right?'

A shake.

'I hear you,' said Chegory.

He was released from the armlock. As if in reward. Then questioned.

'Very well! Who are you?'

Chegory summed his interogator. Ashdan. Old. Eyes hard, fierce, tired, impatient, desperate. A young one with him, Ashdan likewise. Oh, and a third. A big man, not surpassingly tall but broad as a barrel.

These three he recognised from Shabble's description of adventures Downstairs. These must be the pirates who had stolen the wishstone from the treasury! Shabble had played with them for much of a night, driving them to and fro through the underground mazeways. Then they had escaped their captor when the foolish imitator of suns had slept, trusting them to meanwhile stay put.

Pirates, then.

Pirates of the Malud, from Asral, where life is hard and often short. He must remember that they thought of themselves as the Malud and would take great offence if they were called Ashdans, even though those two peoples were in physical terms identical. What else did he know about Asral? Ingalawa had been there, and claimed it was—

'I said,' said the old man, enunciating his words with great care, 'I said, who are you?'

From the way he spoke Chegory knew his own life might prove exceedingly short unless he came up with a satisfactory reply, and shortly.

'I'm Chegory Guy,' he said, in Ashmarlan far better than that of his interrogator. 'I work for Jon Qasaba in the Dromdanjerie. That's our madhouse, in case you didn't know. I'm down here looking for Orge Arat. He's a lunatic. He escaped. He's loose with an axe. He's dangerous as seven hells or seventy dragons ravening.'

'As dangerous as what?' said the old man, not understanding this last complexity.

'He's dangerous dangerous!' said Chegory, urging a touch of the frantic into his voice. 'We'd better get out of here, out of here fast, he's killed Qasaba already, there were five of us, now one, myself alone, sole survivor, the man with the axe he did for the others, hacked off arms, off heads, off legs.'

'Soboro mo?' asked the young Ashdan.

'Dab an narito,' answered the old man.

'Para-para. Al-ran Lars,' said the big man.

'Tolon! Skimara!'

That from the old man. While they discoursed thus, Chegory was scrutinising his surroundings. He was in a tight-curving corridor. Underfoot was a luxuriant growth of black grass which rustled when stepped on. Overhead, warm grey lights. The pirates continued to dialogue in their incomprehensible argot, presumably the Malud which ruled all conversation on far-distant Asral.

Chegory listened. Hard. Above and below the meaningless pirate talk he heard a thin high whine. Soft, soft and distant. Something rumbling. Low, ominous. Muted thunder. Rumbling this way. Rumbling that. Pausing. Then onrumbling further yet. An intestinal grumbling sourced somewhere in the walls. Some kind of animal there? Or water or some other fluid forcing itself through tangling pipes?

'Did you hear me?'

Thus the elderly pirate.

Emphasising his query with a slap.

'Deaf!' said Chegory, a touch of genuine panic to his voice. 'Deaf, I'm deaf!'

'Dandrak! But now you hear!'

'Yes yes yes, we've been through that. Okay. What do you want? You want me to get you out of here? I know the way, I can take you up, out, wherever you want to go.'

'Good,' said the pirate. 'That's what I wanted to know. Very well. Since you know the way, lead on.'

So Chegory was off again, once more bluffing diligently as he feigned full knowledge of the labyrinth through which he led the pirates who had thieved the wishstone and who (surely) still had it in their possession.

Could he get it off them?

He began thinking, hoping, planning, speculating. If he could triumph that spoil away from them he'd be a hero to all Injiltaprajura. Praise him with great praises! Chegory the Great! Hail him a hero!

'You sure you know where we're going?' said the elderly pirate as Chegory hesitated at an intersection.

'This way, this way,' said Chegory hastily.

So saying he led them on through light, through darkness and into light yet further still. He had quite lost track of time. Was it undokondra still? Or bardardornootha? Or had the sun bells rung out to announce istarlat's start? He had no idea, just as he had no idea how far he had wandered through the territory of shadow and nightmare. But what he did know was that he thirsted and hungered, his thews were aching and his mind was near boggled by fatigue.

He could not remember when he had last seen or smelt sewage. The absence of the human waste suggested they were deep, deep underground, far below the surface of Injiltaprajura. Or maybe somewhere under the Laitemata Harbour. There was no sign of vampire rats in these odourless corridors, either, which again indicated that they were deep indeed.

Stairs. That's what I need. Stairs to go up.

Luck then favoured young Chegory with a find in the form of a stairway leading upwards. He took it. Up they went. A mere thirty steps took them to a landing where they had the choice of taking a narrow, unpromising side tunnel lit by a dull purple light. Chegory spared it barely a glance then went on and up. Another landing, another side tunnel. Still the same purple light within. Likewise on the third landing. The fourth. The fifth. The sixth. By which time Chegory was panting and sweating, his heart playing at hammers in his chest. He was sorely troubled to find himself so fatigued so quickly. It told him his physical reserves were nearly exhausted by hunger, dehydration, labour and lack of sleep.

Up to the seventh landing they went.

There misfortune befell young Chegory and his companions, for a squad of soldiers rushed them from the side tunnel which there debouched. The soldiers were armoured well and armed with spears, hence the pirates had no option but to discard their weapons and surrender.

Then curt commands were issued and a most reluctant Chegory Guy was escorted up the stairs in the company of his Asral-born companions. He knew their captors were soldiers of Justina's palace guard. Their uniforms and accoutrements left him in no doubt about that. Doubtless they had been scouring the depths Downstairs in an effort to capture at least some of the looters who had robbed Injiltaprajura's treasury.

This means execution. At the very least!

So thought Chegory.

Then they reached the top of the stairs and were marshalled at spearpoint into a vast cellerage illuminated by cold lights overhead which shone harsh and bright on a scene of industrious activity. Those few shadows which survived were sheltering under big, heavy barrels. Workers were decanting the contents of these containers into jugs, urns, amphorae and bottles. In the air was a smell which Chegory knew to be that of alcohol.

Justina's guards were everywhere in evidence.

Chegory did not quite understand what was going on here. Obviously this was a secret warehouse for the distribution of drugs, an underground equivalent of Firfat Labrat's warehouse in Marthandorthan. But what then were the guards doing? Was this a raid? If so, why was work proceeding as usual? And who was this tall white-skinned man now approaching?

Was it . . . ?

Could it be . . . ?

Yes, it was!

The now-near newcomer with pink eyes and alabaster skin was none other than the wonderworker Aquitaine Varazchavardan, Master of Law to the Empress Justina of Untunchilamon, the dignitary whom Chegory had last met when the sorcerer had come to Jod to interrupt Ivan Pokrov's lunch with queries about the Analytical Engine. Varazchavardan was still wearing the same silken ceremonial robes alive with dragons ultramarine and incarnadine. As the sorcerer drew near, Chegory made reverence in the Janjuladoola manner.

'Aha!' said Varazchavardan, 'so it's—'

The pirates moved.

A hand-signal from the eldest threw them into action.

The muscle man grabbed Chegory Guy and hurled him at the guarding spearmen, skittling them. The elderly pirate whipped out a hidden blade, triced Varazchavardan into his clutches then pressed steel to trachea.

'Keep back!' yelled Varazchavardan 'Keep back, or he'll kill me!'

But skittled guardsmen were already scrambling to their feet, scrabbling for their fallen weapons. The muscle man picked up a cask of alcohol and hurled it. Then threw another, which burst on impact. Chegory rolled out of the way of a third, picked himself up and dodged a fourth.

Swiftly the throat-threatening pirate dragged his hostage Varazchavardan toward the top of the stairwell. Chegory hobbled after the fast-retreating pirates, splashing through spilt liquor as he went. What alternative did he have? To stay and be arrested. Or killed out of hand! Soldiers followed cautiously. The ancient clutching Varazchavardan let his knife tease a little blood from the albino's skin. The sorcerer screamed at his men.

'You want me dead? Get back, you fools! Get back!'

In response, one optimist hurled a knife, thinking he could skewer the pirate who had the Master of Law in his clutches. The knife went wide. Varazchavardan swore. This called for desperate measures!

'Richardia rincus rident!' he gasped.

A shock of purple flame flashed from his body. It blasted away the throat-threatening pirate. Varazchavardan was free! But the same flames ignited a sea of spilt alcohol. Varazchavardan fled, howling, beating at the flames swift-flaring from his embroidered dragons as fire swarmed up his silken robes. The muscleman pirate had already scooped up the elderly one and was sprinting for the stairs. The youngest of the Malud marauders was hot on his heels, with Chegory Guy close behind.

By the time they gained the stairs the cavernous warehouse was a lurid theatre of dragon-mouthed incineration. Down the stairs they pounded, fleeing the holocaust. First landing. Second. Third. Fourth. Fifth. Thunder roared behind them as barrels of liquor began to explode in the inferno.

Still down the steps they ran.

'Omora sora!' gasped Chegory, pausing on the sixth landing to pant for breath.

This phrase will not be translated, for it was voiced in his native Dub and is therefore axiomatically obscene since it is impossible to say anything in that tongue which has fewer than three unseemly connotations.

While Chegory was so pausing and panting, the pirates were still pounding down the stairs. Chegory knew he must hurry else he would get left behind. But – wasn't that what he wanted in any case? Of course it was! He had no desire whatsoever to keep the company of these desperate killers for a moment longer than he had to. Decision then was instantaneous. He ducked into the narrow side tunnel and began striding out as best he could to put the greatest possible distance between himself and all potential pursuers.

Down the tunnel of purple light went Chegory Guy. He took a left turn then a right. The tunnel broadened. The light changed from purple to lemon. All was quiet, quiet, quiet. Then he began to hear a rhythmical thumping shattering crashing up ahead. On he went, for he thought he knew what it was.

He was right.

The noise was being made by another ice machine dumping huge blocks of ice into chambers already littered with the same. Ice white bright ensnared the colours of lights of red, green and blue downshining from above. Cold, it was cold, the delicious shock of such cold thrilled him into wakefulness, cleared his head, made him sharper, stronger, readier.

His thirst craved immediate appeasement, but such melt water as there was drained away through grilles in the floor so there were no potable pools awaiting. Instead, Chegory must perforce crunch the cold, cold ice between his teeth then swallow the shattered slurry. Soon the mounting burden of fractured ice in his belly was beginning to cause him discomfort. He durst not eat more lest over-consumption led to cramps or stomach upsets.

Fatigue was regaining the ascendancy. The initial excite-ment of discovering the ice (and thus of being saved from thirsting to death) was wearing off. He backed off from the ice and settled himself in an ice-cooled corridor, meaning to rest for a little before he went on. Instead, he slipped off to sleep, for he was far too tired to be kept awake merely by the rocksliding downfalls of ice.

It was cold which woke him.

He found himself shivering. Goose-pimples on his skin. He hugged himself, slapped his arms and thighs, then returned to the ice stack to gnaw more concrete water, thinking it best to stock up before he resumed his march.

Cold, it was cold, bitter cold, he had not been so cold since . . . yes, since last year's flying fish expedition. He had gone out in a local fishing canoe by night. Ox No Zan had been with him, and Olivia Qasaba, and a dozen others, most of them fishermen. Night, and moon on the rippling sea. Flaring torches. Olivia squealing with excitement. Flying fish kicking in the toe-deep water in the bottom on the canoe. Then the long journey back, a lean wind driving the sail and stripping the warmth from their exhausted bodies. He had been truly cold by the time they reached shore, and had remembered it long after since chills of any description were so rare on Untunchilamon.

With ice eaten, Chegory was ready to march. On he went, taking things nice and slow. Then he stopped. What was it, that thing lying in the middle of the tunnel? A nasty, grisly piece of shrivelled black. A banana skin! A banana skin long dead, admittedly, but sign of human life nevertheless, unless one was to presume one of Injiltaprajura's monkeys had wandered this far into the deeps with a piece of fruit in hand.

'Saved,' muttered Chegory, for he was sure he must be nearing an exit.

Fatigue fled in the face of excitement, as it had on his discovery of the ice which had so recently (this was how he thought of it, though he was doubtless overdramatising the situation somewhat) saved his life. His stride lengthened as he stepped out smartly, eager to see what was ahead.

The tunnel down which he strode was pierced to left and right by ovoid doorways opening on empty chambers. Chegory glanced in each as he passed it, and was rewarded when he spotted further signs of human life in the tenth to the right. Rubbish rubbish rubbish! Oh most welcome sight! Among the mingled triflings of garbage were a few pieces of broken coconut shell. The carapaces of a couple of land crabs. A small, discrete dumping of turds. A bit of dried-out banana leaf, perhaps used as the wrapping for a handful of rice or rations similar. A few lumps of charcoal remaining from a fire.

'Someone camped here,' said Chegory. 'Or rested here, at least. Ice miners, maybe.'

The amount of rubbish suggested people had been here often, as did the state of the walls, which past visitors had liberally graffitographed with charcoal sketches of the postures of lust – the fluid strokes of the said sketches suggesting that easy artistry which comes from long and diligent practice. There too young Chegory saw, among an overlay of names and slogans, a few scribbled equations. Familiar were these indeed, for they were couched in the inscrutable elegance of Thaldonian Mathematics. Had Ivan Pokrov been this way? Quite possibly. But Chegory was unlikely to find him round the next corner, particularly since the charcoal marks could have been there for anything from a day to fifty thousand years or more.

Chegory picked up one of the pieces of coconut shell. A few tiny, dessicated fragments of dried coconut meat adhered yet to the brown-black rind. He scratched them off with a thumbnail still black from his rock gardening. Licked them up. Food food food! He drooled at memories of the last lunch he had eaten. Sea slugs and flying fish. Right now he would happily have killed for another such meal. Or any meal.

'Soonest out, soonest fed,' muttered Chegory.

He tossed the coconut shell over his shoulder. It clattered on the metal underfoot. Chegory scratched through the rest of the rubbish. Nothing there. Nothing to eat, anyway.

He picked up a piece of charcoal then began to write on the wall. He wrote in Ashmarlan for that was the sole language he could read and write, since nobody had thought to learn him his letters till he started to board with Jon Qasaba at the Dromdanjerie, and thereafter the language of his education had naturally been that of his Ashdan tutors.

[Here an anomaly. Ashmolea's language of scholarship is not the demotic Ashmarlan but the elegant Slandolin, language of Formal Literature and High Art, hence surely Guy's tutors would have educated him in Slandolin. Does the Originator of the Text err in ignorance? Or is this but an absent-minded slip of the pen? Or is one to presume that the Ebrell Islander Guy was found by his tutors to be incapable of attaining mastery of Slandolin? Quite possibly, since the Originator notes that Guy was, in technical terms, ignorant of any language whatsoever. Scholars should bear in mind ambiguities such as this whenever they encounter a passage in which the Originator is sufficiently hubristic as to lay claim to omniscience. *Sot Dawbler, School of Commentary*.]

Chegory wrote thus:

THALDONIAN MATHEMATICS SUCKS
RED RULES, OK?
AQUITAINE VARAZCHAVARDAN ZABAGRUBS PIGS
OLIVIA OLIVIA OLIVIA
URI THE VALOROUS WAS HERE
JUSTINA LOVES VAZZY.
THEODORA LOVES. AND LOVES. AND LOVES.

Here is, first, conclusive proof that Chegory Guy had at least some awareness of what went on in Justina's pink palace. He knew of the albinotic ape Vazzy which the Empress held in such high regard and he had heard at least a rumour or two of the scandal surrounding the life of Justina's twin sister, the famous Theodora. What is here secondly demonstrated is the essential bankruptcy of the notion of 'educating' an Ebrell Islander. Once Chegory Guy learnt to read and write did he act as an educated man? Did he enter upon politics or the law, or—

[Here a lengthy tirade against Ebrell Islanders and the stupidity of 'educating' them has been deleted on the grounds of redundancy. Conclusive proof of the moral degeneracy and intellectual insufficiency of this subhuman breed has appeared in this Text already. There is no need to reproduce further Comments by the Originator on this subject, particularly when one begins to suspect some of these Comments are Originated not for purposes of advancing scholarship and enhancing the world's enlightenment but merely to allow the Originator an arena in which to display intellectual prowess, or a misguided 'wit' which the Originator equates with such prowess. *Drax Lira, Redactor Major.*]

With his works of literary composition completed, Chegory Guy pocketed some spare charcoal in case he was once more beglamoured by inspiration, then onward he went, soon entering on a huge vaulted hall shod with tessellating tiles cast in three dozen different patterns. Blue and green were the tiles and metal was their substance. Their unity was pierced by half a thousand transparent tubes ascending from floor to ceiling. Fluids flowed within those tubes. Some were clear, doubtless bearing water to feed the fountains which watered Injiltaprajura so generously. Others were stained with colour. A couple did young Chegory recognise – the grey of shlug and the bile-green of dikle. But what was that thick fermented black? That blue made to rival the sky? That ominous red, darker yet than bloodstone? That yellow as bright as the lethal sun scorpion of Zolabrik?

'Here mystery,' said Chegory.

With all enquiry thus dismissed he onward went, caring not for the solution of the mystery. He was, remember, but an ignorant Ebrell Islander with a lust for raw survival, not a philosophic scholar with a taste for knowledge and enquiry. Surely any reputable encyclopaedist (yourself, for instance, dear reader) would under the circumstances have stayed to Examine the tubes, to Speculate on their Origins and their Outfalls, and to make notes in order to be able later to Account. But Chegory Guy did no such thing. Instead, he went hunting for a way of escape.

[While one does not wish to deprecate the scholarly impulse in any way, it must nevertheless be noted that the valuation of intellectual enquiry to which the Originator has made a commitment in terms of autogenerated commentary on the above geophysiopsychic scenario is excessive in objectified terms which take into account the presumed extrapolations in regard to survival expectations which the scenario subject would have been making with at least a partial appreciation of the normative consequences of psychobiological stress (such as a shortfall in terms of bio-environmental substance exchange in the input mode and, equally important, deprivation of required regenerative therapy in the form of subjective experience of nonconscious brain modes) and of the implications of such consequences with respect to global performance factors. While precise medicometrical quantification is impossible on the basis of Textual analysis alone, the Originator's apparent valourisation of speculative enquiry and data acquisition as absolute goods always to be set above the pursuit of socioindividual integration and the preservation of biological integrity is indicative of a failure to rationalise the tension between purely subjective supramundane conceptual freedom and statistically probable biosociopolitical outcomes in favour of a normative accommodation with objectified reality. While neither genetic deficiency nor exobiopsychically sourced transmundane manipulation can be definitively discounted as elements causative of this syndrome, the weight of theory coupled with realtime experience gained from extensive praxis in the context of the client-therapist nexus supports the conclusion that inadequate parenting is the ultimative cause of the psychic disturbance which led to the display of the sociomedicolegalistically maladaptive behaviour which resulted in the Originator being subjected to non-voluntary therapy in an institution for non-normative individuals. To put all this in simple layman's terms, my conclusions are that the psychosocial maladaptation which led to the Originator being incarcerated in a lunatic asylum is predicated upon a sociopathological lack of any sense of proportion, and I blame the parents. *Eshambultung Yafun-groid, Phrenologist-in-Chief of the Board of Scrutiny, Psychometrician Extraordinary and Head of the Committee of Norms.*]

[Perhaps. But who cares? *Oris Baumgage, Fact Checker Minor.*]

[An inexcusable flippancy! Noted, and to be punished in due course. *Jonquiri O, Disciplinarian Superior.*]

[While Yafungroid is not to be lightly dismissed, scholars should nevertheless note that shortly after completing his extensive annotations to this Text the eminent Phrenologist died of a surfeit of lampreys admixed with the Extract of Opium to which he was notoriously addicted. *Sot Dawbler, School of Commentary.*]

[Sot Dawbler implies that Yafungroid suffered mental

degeneration as a consequence of overindulgence in the Balm of Souls. But what of it? Should we care if Yafungroid was brain-damaged? His field was the study of the mad. Set a thief to catch a thief, a lunatic to catch a lunatic! I accept Yafungroid's conclusions in full and wish only that I could aspire to the magisterial magnificence of his style. *Drax Lira, Redactor Major.*]

As Chegory looked for a way of escape he faced a multiplicity of choice. There were, all in all, forty-seven doorways out of that hallway. Young Chegory did not count them but I know it to be so for I have been to the very place myself during my own researches Downstairs. Indeed, you must remember that at every point this history is supported and enhanced by my own detailed and long-standing knowledge of both the participants and the theatre of action.

Thus I can tell you of a certainty that the one doorway which issued on to a flight of stairs was one armspan wide and thrice that in height; that the stairs themselves were of an incorruptible metal unaccountably percolated by multiple holes, each hole being the size of a finger hole; that one climbs 170 steps in all to reach a large, circular chamber made of equally incorruptible plax; and, further, that from this Chamber seventeen tunnels wheelspoke outwards.

Chegory found the stairs, climbed them and reached the chamber with its seventeen-fold choices.

Where now?

He chose a tunnel at random and set off down it, charcoaling the occasional mark on the walls so he would be able to find his way back if he ran into a dead end or danger.

As he walked, he began to worry. Had Aquitaine Varazchavardan recognised him? He doubted that Varazchavardan knew him by name. Nevertheless, Justina's Master of Law might remember seeing young Chegory on Jod, in which case he would know where to start looking for a name. Gods, what a mess!

'Still,' said Chegory, 'it was quite funny, really.'

It was not funny at all. It was an unmitigated disaster. Nevertheless, Chegory allowed himself a little Shabble-like snigger when he recalled Varazchavardan slapping at his burning robes. Fool of a sorcerer! To set his own liquor alight by exercise of magic!

His own liquor?

Chegory corrected his mental slip. That had not been Varazchavardan's liquor. That had been the property of some foul unscrupulous drug dealer. And Varazchavardan, well, he must have been leading a raid on the place.

'Great,' said Chegory, with dry irony. 'I'm a wanted man. Incinerator of soldiers. Consort of drug dealers. Fugitive prisoner. Looter. Rioter. And now I've got enemies in high places to boot! What worse could happen?'

Much, as he found out before he had taken another three footsteps. Lights dimmed, lights darkened, then violet shadows rose around him, weaving, writhing, sharpening into monsters with glaucous eyes and jacinth teeth. One glance at their slavering jaws told him they were carnivorously inclined. He had no time to scream before they were upon him.

Razorblade teeth bore at his raw flesh, shattered his bones, ripped open his gut then sliced his orchids in half with a lacerating pain which sent him swooning into unconsciousness.

For some time he knew nothing.

Then, blunder by blunder, he began to recover thought and sensation both. He was walking. His eyes were open a crack. Grey light hinted at walls, floor, a door past which he strode.

'Stop walking,' he told himself.

But his legs made progress without him. Strong legs they were, hardened to labour by toilsome labours in the rockfields of Jod. His arms immobile at his sides. Strength he had in those arms, the mighty strength which comes from sledgehammering rocks and ruthlessly pursuing spare-time practice with a killing blade. But he was powerless to control that strength.

I am an Engine.

Thus he thought, comparing himself to Ivan Pokrov's Analytical Engine, remorselessly driven by coded algorithms, exercising operations of the most complex precision without possession so much as a shred of free will.

By an extreme effort of such will he at last succeeded in closing his eyes.

Now I will . . .

Now he would nothing.

Will and consciousness blundered away together. His eyes cracked open again. A part of Chegory's brain which in truth could scarcely be called Chegory needed sight that it might control the passage of his corpse through the underworld beneath Injiltaprajura. It is scarcely extravagant to think of Chegory as being just then a corpse, for, though his body breathed, walked, and possessed both blood and a heartbeat, no will was resident in his flesh. No will, no thought, no sentience.

By the time sentience, will and consciousness returned, Chegory's automative fit was long since over. He found himself lying in the dark. Vampire rats! Downstairs, dark meant rats. Were there any? He listened carefully for scrabbles or squeaks. Heard none. Nevertheless his heart was racing. He had been asleep, asleep and helpless, quite unconscious and at the mercy of any four-legged marauder. In the dark Downstairs that could have been suicide.

He stood up, wincing as something went grik! in his spine. He flexed his back cautiously. It was okay. He closed his eyes. Opened them again. Sought light but saw not the slightest leam. Instead, dark absolute, a smothering black velvet shrouding all. Was he blind?

He clicked his fingers. The quality of the echoes suggested he was in an underground room. Quite a large room. He was surprised. Thanks to the dark, he had got the impression he was confined in some place no larger than a coffin. He felt around. Barrels. A smell of – alcohol!

Gods!

Here . . . a board. Something . . . something soft. Friable.

Too coherent to be turd. Lift it. Smell. Cheese. Not the goat cheese from the vats of Beldysobros, sole local supplier. No, this was imported stuff. Very nice, too. Needed that. More? No, just metal. Ow! Sharp. Knife. Good.

Chegory tested his new-found knife then slipped it into the larger of his boot sheaths. He'd need it if he ran up against vampire rats. Or Malud marauders. Or mad elven lords with strange foreign companions. Idly he wondered what had become of his best-beloved fighting blade, his skewer-shiv and his knuckle-lance, lost when soldiers had stripped him of that protection when they arrested him outside the Dromdanjerie.

Okay. Explanations.

How had he got here?

Sleepwalking.

Sleepwalking? Hardly!

Zen.

That was his next thought.

Flashback.

Got it in three!

Indeed, Chegory now realised exactly what had happened. He had breathed of the zen burning in the amphorae in the temple of Elasmokarcharos, shark-god of the Dagrin. The hallucinogenic herb had made him imagine that the jaws of shark floated through the air to tear away his arm. Later, he had made a temporary recovery. However, some time afterwards he had been overwhelmed by the phenomenon known as flashback.

Zen is a strange drug for, unlike alcohol or opium, its effects do not dissipate in direct relation to time. Instead, once one has used the drug the potential exists for sudden, untimely recurrences of the initial drugshock. Hallucinations may partially or totally swamp the sensorium. Worse, the drug may lead to the acting out of desires known or unknown, to murder or rape, incest or arson, shark-swimming or suicide.

In Chegory's case, his one overwhelming desire had been to get the hell out of the mazeways Downstairs, and this was the desire the drug had activated when it had reduced him to an unthinking zombie.

Okay. What now?

He was still tired. Very very tired. Else the knowledge of his vulnerability to horrifying flashbacks would have had him running round in circles screaming in terror. As it happened, he was so shagged out he did little more than acknowledge his vulnerability as a last refining touch to his day of disaster.

Fatigue suggested sleep.

What else could he do?

Was there anything to be gained from a quick release from imprisonment Downstairs?

No.

Since so many prisoners had escaped from the treasury with so much loot there would doubtless be dozens of soldiers scouring the underground mazeways right now, so there was scarcely any point in Chegory rushing to the pink palace to advise the authorities that the pirates who had thieved the wishstone were still below decks. If a search could catch those Malud marauders then it would. Nobody caught Downstairs at a time like this would be presumed innocent, so there was no reason for Chegory to dare his life into the sunlight just so he could accuse the wayward foreigners.

Meantime, he was safest here.

Safe from hunting soldiers?

Probably, since he had stumbled into some storeroom for liquor. Such places were chosen by experts for their invulnerability to search.

But what if said experts find me in my sleep?

There was a risk of that, true. But life had become so dangerous, so fraught with peril, so stressed and unpredictable that Chegory accounted that little additional risk as next to nothing.

He sat back against a liquor barrel, closed his eyes and promptly dropped off to sleep.

Elsewhere, in the Temple of Torture in Goldhammer Street which was serving as a detention centre, Shabble burnt free of a clay pot at a bottom of a well. Steam boiled out of the well as Shabble ascended, shining bright and singing brighter yet.

It was night. Soon the sun would rise and the sun bells would ring out from the belfries at the four corners of the pink palace to announce the end of bardardornootha and the start of istarlat. But, for the moment, dark reigned, and Shabble's localised attempts to subvert that legitimate reign drew protests from adherents of the ruling regime.

'Blow out the light, you nuk!' screamed an angry fishwife.

'I blow out not,' said Shabble. 'I'm a candle not.'

Torrential abuse followed, as if Fistavlir had ended and the long-awaited trade winds had brought downfalling curses rather than downfalling water. Shabble, entirely unperturbed by this onslaught, darted about the temple, seeking friends.

'Oh, there you are, there you are,' said Shabble, shining sun-bright light on a comatose Ivan Pokrov.

The head of the Analytical Institute woke. Stared at Shabble. Mumbled incoherently. Then Artemis Ingalawa said, in very wide awake tones:

'Shabble! Get out of here! Vanish!'

She Who Must Be Obeyed was obeyed. Shabble's light dimmed immediately to nothing and the demonic one soared up, up, up into the night sky. The humid darkness of Injiltaprajura and of the polluted Laitemata fell away below. All Untunchilamon came in sight, a mass of dark within dark, reaching away for league upon league from Justina's capital to the desolations of the north.

Higher and still higher yet flew Shabble, ascending imaginary mountains in nary more than a couple of heartbeats. Exulting in pure speed flew Shabble. So does the dolphin exult when from the water it explodes in joy shimmering. So does the dragon rejoice when in its strength it holds the heights then plunges, diving with a scream, with power ferocious, with speed controlled and absolute precision, terror matched to beauty as it stoops. Up rose Shabble in such triumph until the very curvature of the planetary surface was clearly to be perceived, and the sun also, the sun of the new day.

Then sang Shabble, then Shabble sang, louder and then louder yet, pouring out music unheard for twenty thousand years, rejoicing in the Symphony of the Sun, a song of joy to exult and honour all those who argue with mortality, a paean of praise for the will to be and to become, for ambition unlimited, audacity vaulting and the triumph of the moment.

Shabble rose yet higher. Singing singing singing to the rising sun, the local star, the star itself delighting as it sang with a song fiercer and braver yet than any known to creatures of the flesh, its joy a blaze of energy unleashed, exploding light outburning in vacuum wastelands a hundred million luzacs distant.

Glory to life!

Glory to us and our becoming!

And to the sun, glory!

And to the rising sun, glory!

Thus Shabble, singing as if to rival the sun itself.

Non servium.

CHAPTER THIRTEEN

'What's this?' said Log Jaris, holding aloft a lantern.

No answer came from Chegory Guy who was deep in dream. At that very moment his nonconscious fantasising was modulating from horror ad nauseum to mere absurdity. He dreamt of an acanaceous cabbage with thaumaturgic tendencies multiplying onyx and zircon to the lapidarian delight of a quivering grannam.

'What is cabbage but a form of aliment?' said Chegory, imagining (in his dream) that he had never seen such except in woodblock prints of foreign origin, though in point of fact he knew cabbage well enough since it grew (albeit poorly) in the market gardens of Injiltaprajura.

'Cabbage is god,' said cabbage.

Already the cabbage was inimically exerting its granitic will to crush him, all goodwill gone, just badwill remaining, its cassava cyanide, its perfume dung. Crushed, he fell. Yattering ants mocked his valour useless, his courage absurd, his pride misjudged, his skin tarnished with undeniable Ebrell Island red.

'Wake up, boy,' said Log Jaris, outside his dream.

'I am awake,' said Chegory (or imagined he said) within the dimensions of dream.

Where his unicorn speared her, where she moulded his mangos soft in her hands, her fingers palpating, his banana vomiting, his ants talking the language of sea slugs and carrots as they crawled across her nipples, her hair trailing across his cheeks as Varazchavardan aped monkey in the blue-stained topsails of a coconut tree.

'Must I kick you awake?' said Log Jaris.

Answer came there none.

So he kicked.

Not too hard, but hard enough.

Young Chegory Guy snorted, gasped, jerked awake, remembered his knife and grabbed for it, only it was the wrong boot he grabbed for.

'A blade?' said Log Jaris, observing the empty boot sheath by lamplight. 'No blade there, boy! Who are you?'

Slowly Chegory got to his feet. Looked Log Jaris full in the face. Then turned away.

'Don't turn your back on me, boy!' said Log Jaris, grabbing him by the shoulder and spinning him round. 'I'm not that ugly.'

'You're a hallucination,' said Chegory calmly.

Quite a reasonable assumption, under the circumstances. For Log Jaris was a monster with the body of a man but the head and horns of a bull.

'What?' said Log Jaris in startlement. 'I'm a what?'

'A hallucination. I don't believe in you.'

'You don't believe in me!' said Log Jaris, slapping a heavy hand on Chegory's shoulder. His heavy hand gripped hard then shook the boy. Not much – but enough. 'You don't believe in me? What about this? Do you believe in this?' Log Jaris grasped Chegory's collar bone between thumb and finger. He increased the pressure. 'Hurts, doesn't it? You're awake, right? Not dreaming! But drunk, perhaps. Are you drunk, my boy?'

'I've dosed on zen,' said Chegory.

'You've what?'

'The temple. Temple of Elasmokarcharos. There was zen, zen, burning, huge amphorae, you know, drugs in smoke, in clouds, clouds of it. And . . . I don't have to argue with you. You're a flashback. You don't exist.'

'I wish I didn't!' said Log Jaris. 'It would make life that much simpler. All right, come along, boy. Indulge an old hallucination for a bit and let your story keep him company till he's got the truth out of you.'

Chegory looked hard at Log Jaris. He was in sharp focus. The yellow candlelight shining shining through the lantern's windows wavered ever so slightly but the shadow-mass bulk of the bullman did not. Tentatively Chegory dared his fingertips forward. The bullman grunted with displeasure as Chegory fingered the black bullhair. Chegory flattened his hand against the coarse hairs. Felt the warmth of living meat beneath. Pushed. Encountered unyielding mass, bulk, weight, inertia.

The bullman was huge.

A huge unyielding mass smelling of bullsweat. Hot breath outsnorted across Chegory's face as he withdrew his hand from the bullman's hide. Gold gleamed bright in the quivering moistness of the bullman's nostrils. The outthrust ears, which looked a little like black tubes of hair with their ends sliced off along a diagonal, twitched as the bullman attended to some distant sound. Chegory raised his gaze to the huge ivory horns uplifted high.

For a hallucination, the thing was impressively detailed and uncommonly stable.

'Are you quite finished?' said the bullman. 'My patience is great, but not infinite.'

'You look real,' said Chegory slowly. 'I mean, you're not wavery at the edges or anything. You feel real. You smell real. You talk as if you were real. But, if you are real – how do you explain yourself?'

The bullman snorted.

'You're the one who's got some explaining to do,' said the monster. 'This is my cellarage, after all. So I suggest you get on with it, lest I obtruncate your loathsome corpse without ceremony further.'

Chegory had no wish to be obtruncated, whatever obtruncation was, since it sounded as if it might be painful. He had already learnt that the pain of hallucinations can be at least equal to that of physical existence. So he had best placate the monster whether it was a free-willed entity in its own right or merely a projection of his own psyche.

'I, well, I'm here because I got lost, basically,' said Chegory. 'Lost underground.'

'How?'

'It's a long story.'

'Doubtless,' said the bullman. 'A story which you will tell in my torture chamber. Come!'

So saying, the bullman overturned a barrel and began rolling it out of the room in which Chegory had been caught sleeping. The young Ebrell Islander was bitterly disappointed to realise he had not evaded another ordeal of pain, but nevertheless followed without protest. *Torture, torture!* Thus he helplessly mindsaid, silently wailing with despair as he followed his massively muscled captor. Drump-thrump echoes rolled into the darkness ahead of them as the bullman kicked the barrel over flagstones and cobblestones then up a series of ramps.

Then the bullman stopped.

'Here,' he said, passing Chegory the lantern. 'Hold this.'

Chegory held it. This was his chance! To smash the lantern, punch the bullman on the snout and then go haring off into the darkness. But he did not seize that chance. He had at last run up against one challenge too many. His resources of courage, initiative and daring were exhausted entirely.

Of course, he should have dared. He should have tried. He should have attacked – then fled. Since the alternative was to endure monstrous horror in the bullman's torture chamber he had nothing to gain by cooperating with the hideous thing. Yet cooperate he did, holding the lantern while the bullman bullhandled the heavy barrel up through a bullhole, grunting bullfully as he did so. Then he hauled himself up through the same hole, reached down for the lantern and uplifted it.

Run!

Thus spoke Chegory's last reserve of daring. But already the bullman was reaching down, and Chegory, helpless to resist, found himself extending his own hand to the monster. The bullman hauled Chegory into the darkshadowed room above then closed a heavy trapdoor on the bullhole and bolted it.

Chegory was trapped.

A prisoner in the bullman's lair!

'Through here,' said the bullman, opening a door to reveal a small room lit by bright and cheerful light flooding in through skylights. Blue sky! Blue sky! A startlement of colour pure and bright. So beautiful that Chegory almost wept to see it.

'What day is it?' he said.

'Today,' answered the bullman. True, but unhelpful. Then: 'Come,' said the bullman, 'in through here.'

So saying, he opened another door and rolled the barrel into a room much larger. By the light flooding in through a dozen latticework windows (more sky, a courtyard view, a wall, no hope of escape, not yet, not that way) Chegory saw all. A huge stove at the near end of the room, and a woman cooking at that stove. A dozen trestle tables with benches set before them. Two dozen assorted fishermen and such seated on those benches, all those fishermen busy talking, eating, and drinking from pewter tankards. Doubtless there was liquor in those tankards, for this was surely a speakeasy, a house of degradation built to cater for the depraved tastes of helpless drug addicts, the addicts in question being the fishermen yattering-laughing over their breakfasts.

'You'll stay for breakfast,' said the bullman.

'Oh, of course,' said Chegory, hoping that he himself would not be one of the courses at that breakfast.

Then he caught the smell of a well-spiced cassoulet and realised he was hungry, very hungry, famished, starved, ravenous, a cat among mice, a dog among cats, a dragon amidst lambs, a fire in a heap of paper, so short commoned it was miraculous he was more than dwarfish, his skeleton clad with ghost and fast demanding man, mass, heat, weight, blood, nerve, sinew, bone, kidney, liver, heart, lung. He was ready to grab, claw, eat, bite, suck, gnaw and swallow, hungry enough to shark it out with the sea's mobsters for a bucket of offal, possessed of hunger such that he was ready to beg for his mother-in-law's paps then feed from her twat as well, as the proverbial saying has it, or squeeze a stone for blood, or peel the stone itself then cook it and eat it.

'Here,' said the bullman.

So saying, the monster caused a miracle to manifest itself in the form of a bowl of hot, steaming cassoulet. Beans! Meat! Pieces of cassava! A bit of baked banana on the side!

'Well, boy,' said the monster. 'Don't just gape at it. Sit down. Get into it!'

Moments later young Chegory was sitting at table gulleting into the cassoulet.

'Slowly, young Chegory,' said one of the fishermen sitting at the same table. 'Slowly, or you'll do yourself an injury.'

'Oho!' said the bullman. 'You know this lad, do you?'

'No lad, Log Jaris. This is a man in the prime of youth. Isn't it just, Chegory? You got into that sweet Olivia yet?'

'Working on it,' said Chegory.

'Oh, I bet you are! More meat on that than a chicken, hey?'

'Leaving aside this question of Olivia chickens,' said the bullman Log Jaris, 'what's the rest of your name, Chegory?'

'Chegory Guy,' said Chegory Guy.

'Oho! Not the son of Impala Guy, by chance?' said the bullman. 'Not the son of old man Impala, Japone's beloved stillmaster?'

'The same,' said Chegory.

So saying, he managed a crooked smile.

A crooked smile? Let us be more exact. Chegory Guy experienced a certain degree of discomfiture but was loathe to make this known; hence he tried (but without complete success) to make pleasure rather than displeasure express itself on his face. Following convention, we say therefore that he smiled a crooked smile, though in point of literal fact he did not.

Some people who are in perfect health (and some who are not, such as some who have suffered strokes or varying degrees of severity, or who have been mutilated, or who are under the influence of certain unethical drugs) habitually express themselves by means of a smile which does not run the full length of the mouth, and which can therefore accurately and literally be termed 'crooked'. Some people can do this with ease, just as some people can wiggle their ears.

Chegory Guy could not have wiggled his ears to save his life (except by the expedient of grasping the said ears with his hands and causing them to move by an application of manual pressure). He was completely bereft of innate ear-wriggling talent, just as he was born without poetic potential. Nevertheless, since he had a fair degree of control of the voluntary muscles which supervise the lips, he could no doubt have managed a crooked smile if his life had been at stake. However, he did not. Indeed, he rarely (if ever) did anything so unnatural as smiling crookedly. Even after the most diligent research, it has proved impossible to find a single witness—

[The Originator appears to have succumbed to a fit of what Kerkransolifski Bodo has so neatly termed 'that painful accuracy which makes all Truth impossible'. To preserve the communicability of that which the Originator has elsewhere managed to capture in phrase, and to lessen the incidence of repetitive strain injury among our scribes, an exercise in pedantry which extends for no less than ten thousand words has here been deleted. *By Order, Sptyx Rhataporo, Surveyor of the Office of Overview.*]

[What, pray tell, is wrong with pedantry? I applaud the Originator's outbreak of accuracy and must severely deprecate Rhataporo's unwarranted excision of the same. *Brude, Pedant Particular.*]

After Chegory Guy had confessed to his true identity Log Jaris conducted a gentle interrogation which soon told him all he needed to know about his young visitor. Then the bullman took down an amphora and poured mugs of foaming brown fluid for himself, the fisherman and Chegory.

'What's this?' said Chegory, looking into the mug with the deepest of suspicion.

'Something for the pain,' said Log Jaris.

'The pain?' said Chegory.

'To exist is to suffer,' said the bullman. 'Learned philosophers proved this way back in the dawn of human history, whereupon the greatest genius of the day was assembled to provide a remedy. That remedy you have before you. Drink! For by drinking we prove ourselves true students of the higher philosophy.'

Chegory had never heard anyone espouse such a doctrine before, though it is certain the dogma was not the bullman's original invention; indeed, it is rumoured that the Korugatu philosophers of far-distant Chi'ash-lan first evolved a similar theory over a thousand years ago, and have laboured mightily ever since in an attempt to refine it by practical research.

'This is a drug, isn't it?' said Chegory.

'You would worry about that?' said Log Jaris, with open amusement. 'You, a crazed adventurer who daily dares life and limb Downstairs for the sole purpose of indulging a craving for zen? Will what's in this mug turn your insides out or split your skull to spill your brains upon your feet?'

'No, but—'

But it was liquor, surely.

'Make a choice,' said Log Jaris, with less amusement than before. 'Are you my friend or my enemy? My guest or my prisoner? Come, boy, it's not bub, it is but beer.'

Then Chegory gathered his courage, and did what he needed to do if he was to survive. He lifted the mug of beer to his lips. He drank. What was the alternative? To be trampled to death by the bullman, surely. To be battered and gored, pulped and destroyed. Nevertheless – was that not the better course? For is not addiction to drink a fate far worse than death? And was not young Chegory well-launched upon such a fate? For he had been boozing in the lair of Firfat Labrat just the day before, and now here he was drinking up large in a scurvy speakeasy in the worst of low company imaginable.

But Chegory lacked the courage to die. He wanted to

live, to escape from this place of evil, this hell-hole with its amphorae filled with liquid death, these all-too-jolly fishermen who had already succumbed to the sly seductive wiles of unholy chemical combinations. He wanted to walk once more beneath the clean sky. To walk again in the sunlight. To be pure, and law abiding, and at peace with himself and the world.

So drink he did.

Remember he was but a poor ignorant Ebrell Islander whose philosophical tutoring had been neglected entirely. He had yet to learn that ends seldom justify means, thus he did not realise that his hopes of escaping to a life of purity and peace were doomed when, to secure his survival, he adopted means that were foul, unclean, unlawful, destructive, polluted and corrupt, and evil, immoral, unethical and incontinent, and vile, dirty and sickening to boot. Nevertheless, it must be admitted that by sharing the bullman's beer he did indeed enhance his short-term chances of survival, and of escaping from the speakeasy with both his life and his hide intact.

'You don't look happy,' said Log Jaris. 'What's wrong? Is there something the matter with the beer?'

'Don't you understand?' said Chegory, with a touch of desperation. 'I mean, what I said – Shabble, the soldiers, Varazchavardan, the whole thing – you think that's some kind of joke?'

'Oho, we have us a most unhappy little fellow here!' said Log Jaris. 'Why, from the way he talks, you'd think him up to his neck in sharks already. Yet the worst he's dared already. What's worse than zen? Naught that I know of. The rest is but trouble in trifles. Don't worry about it! Soon enough it'll all blow over.'

'It can't, it won't, I'm done for, there's nowhere to hide.'

Thus Chegory, in something of a wail.

'Can't!' said Log Jaris. 'You're very free with your can't and your won't. How comes this can't and won't so freely from a strong man like you? Have you not legs you can run with? If bad comes to worse then surely your legs can carry you. Jal Japone will welcome you surely. After all, you're the son of Impala Guy.'

Chegory was infuriated by the jesting tone which had entered the bullman's voice. He wanted to pour out his protests in a flood of incoherent anger. Instead, he restrained and controlled himself. He said merely:

'Not Zolabrik. Not ever. I'm not running away.'

'Oho!' said Log Jaris. 'A hero indeed! Yet it wishes to live regardless. Very well! A change of face will do it. Do what I did, my bloodskinned friend. Hide your face forever by means of transmogrification.'

'By means of what?' said Chegory. 'You mean you weren't – you chose – you – you—'

Log Jaris laughed.

'I wasn't born like this,' said he. 'In truth I'm a man of Ashdan descent. My hometown was Pondros Yermento, which—'

'I know, I know,' said Chegory, cutting him off. 'I've lived with Ashdans long enough, you know, they talk Ashmolea no end.'

'Well, if you know you know,' said Log Jaris, more than a little offended by Chegory's interruption.

'He's only a boy,' said a fisherman. 'Don't be hard on him.'

'I'm not being hard on him!' said Log Jaris. 'I'm offering him escape. Anonymity forever! The secret of transmogrification.'

'I'll worry out my own problems,' said Chegory.

Thus he failed to learn about the transmogrification machine Downstairs which, if he had dared to use it, might have turned him into dragonman or dog, centaur or merman, satyr or rundicorn, giant or dwarf. Or – better yet – he might have kept his born proportions while losing his skin of Ebrell Island red. He might have come out black like the Ashdans, or white like the leucodermic Varazchavardan. He might have emerged in an elegant shade of grey like the Janjuladoola of Ang, or in the pink- tending-to-pallor of the natives of Wen Endex. Or bark-brown like many of the peoples of Argan, or strangulation blue like the scholars of Odrum.

Alternatively, if the luck of the stars had been with him, the young Ebrell Islander might have won an appearance like mine own, which would have given him green skin, green hair and two thumbs on each hand.

[What is one to think? Does the Originator truly believe the scholars of Odrum to be blue in hue? We know ourselves to be in truth an eclectic selection of the best brains of the Twenty Seven Superior Races. So does the Originator err by accident or with malice? Furthermore, what is one to think of the Originator's self-description? If he is mad, as Reader Zeb has suggested, then possibly he believes himself to dwell within flesh configured as described, though nothing matching the description is accounted for in the Library, unless we accept into the Body of Knowledge certain wild rumours concerning the impenetrable jungles of the interior of the island of Quilth. These matters scholarship must attend to closely until in the fullness of time thay are elucidated. *Inserted by Order, Jon Jangelis, Scrutineer.*]

Thus did Chegory lose his chance to enlist the help of the formidable Log Jaris and to learn of the transmogrification machine. But, since he was only a backward Ebrell Islander, he knew not that he had lost anything at all. Instead, he occupied himself by trying to think of some smart way to escape his quandary.

'Well,' said Log Jaris, 'since you don't want my help, I can guess where you're going next.'

'Where's that?' said Chegory.

'To the pink palace. The next petitions session is at noon today.'

With that said, Log Jaris ushered young Chegory out into the street, and, with the slightest hint of a shove, dismissed him and closed the door on him.

Young Chegory Guy was so surprised to find himself out in the sunlight – he had still been at least half-expecting imprisonment, torture and sudden death – that at first he entirely failed to recognise this narrow lane. Then, as he orientated himself, he realised he was in one of the sideways of Marthandorthan, not far from the warehouse where his ill-favoured cousin Firfat Labrat presided over a vigorous business in illicit drugs.

CHAPTER FOURTEEN

Since Chegory Guy was bereft of original inspiration he thought first to throw himself on the mercy of Firfat Labrat. So he went to the warehouse, but found it boarded up. Unbeknownst to Chegory, Firfat had gone to ground for the duration of the State of Emergency, which was still in force. During the night Firfat had wholesaled his liquor at loss to bolder men like Log Jaris, then had removed himself and his followers to a secret hideout on the fringes of Injiltaprajura, in among the market gardens on the far side of Pokra Ridge.

Where now?

To portside, to the home of his law-abiding uncle Dunash Labrat? No! The stern and solemn apiarist would not appreciate being involved in scandal. Indeed, notwithstanding family ties, he would probably turn in young Chegory as an escaped criminal.

To the Dromdanjerie, then? Or to Jod?

Again, no.

Soldiers would be searching for him in both places if they seriously sought his rearrest, which they surely would.

So where?

As Chegory was still thinking about it a squad of soldiers came marching down the street. His thoughts flew apart like so many skimble-scamble scatter-sticks, and he strolled as casually as he could round the nearest corner then gave way to terror-deranged flight.

Despite his panic, Chegory soon slowed, panting and sweating heavily in the morning heat. He was walking by the time he gained the waterfront, whereupon he took the path of crushed coral and broken bloodstone which fringed the Laitemata.

He walked along past those open air cafés which served fishermen who did not care for speakeasies; past stalls selling huge bunches of bananas variously green and yellow; past hawkers with trays of spiced rice, curried lizard, pickled cockroach, sunflower seeds and prophylactic amulets sacred to seven different religions; past fish shops abuzz with flies which pestered over clams, crabs, sharkmeat, groper, moray eel, sea slugs, turtle, octopus, tuna and brightsilver sea ghost.

Doctor Death, who was at work in his open-air dental workshop when Chegory went by, straightened up and nodded pleasantly. The patient reclining in Death's operating chair emitted a low groan. Death had a pair of bloody pliers in his hand. A small heap of bloodstained molars sat upon a white porcelain saucer on a nearby table. Chegory shuddered, and hurried on.

He went by a pharmacy where a chemist proudly displayed jars of oily pyrethrin and like mosquito-killers, twists of ground horn of unicorn and other aphrodisiacs of equal reputation, bundles of ginseng and cannabis, small vials of oil of hashish and vials smaller yet of opium, jars of honey, contraceptive calendars, and, taking pride of place, ceramic bottles holding mead and other types of medicinal alcohol (available on prescription only).

He heard sellers and buyers alike ababble in Janjuladoola, Ashmarlan, Toxteth and Dub, in Malud and Frangoni and in other alien argots stranger yet. He saw a man selling dragon's teeth, a woman with herself for sale, a stockbroker auctioning shares in the Narapatorpabarta Bank and the Imtharbodanoptima Brothel. He sauntered past money changers whose hired scimitars stood guard over banks where sunshining ems rivalled their glitter against the sheen of grass-green saladin rings and the shimmer of zeals, the glitz of dragons, the allure of pearls and the argument of damns and dalmoons alike.

Chegory was amazed to find all these people going about their business as usual, as though the State of Emergency meant nothing to them. Here he was, living through a madness equal to anything heard of in legend, yet the world lazed on through its habitual routines as placidly as ever. Young Chegory had endured attack by kraken, arrest by soldiers, beatings, riot, capture first by an elven lord and then by mad Malud marauders, threats of torture from a transmogrified bullman and more – all this is scarcely more than a day and a night! Yet the world still bought, sold, traded and cheated as usual as if nothing whatsoever out of the ordinary had happened at all.

Through the hot sunlight he went, past fortune-tellers and astrologers, pardoners and tax advisers, past letter-writers and story-tellers, snake-charmers and chandlers, travel agents and slave-traders; past greengrocers presiding over counters laden with taro, cassava, mangos, pineapple, paw-paw, kumera, blue potato and breadfruit; past a blood-reeking butcher's shop where more flies yet were competing for space on the skinned carcases of dogs, rats, cats, goats, chickens and pigs; and then past the jeweller's shops bright with rainbow-rivalling paua, pounamu most precious, silver beaten to the brightness of the moon and teardrops of gold basking in the adoration of the sun.

Thus went Chegory, coming at length to the harbour bridge, where he turned left and went through the reeking slumlands of Lubos till he came to Skindik Way. Uphill he went, passing the slaughterhouse where men were chopping up huge chunks of one of the krakens which had died in the Laitemata on the previous day. Not to the Drom-danjerie did he go, but rather to Ganthorgruk, the huge rotting doss-house which rivalled Justina's pink palace in size. He ascended creaking stairs to the uppermost (hence cheapest) levels where he knocked on a door.

It did not open.

'Teeth of a chicken!' exclaimed Chegory.

He kicked the door.

Then it did open, and there was Ox No Zan, looking somewhat bleary since he had dosed himself heavily with the opium Doctor Death had prescribed for the toothache – or, more exactly, for the ache where that dentist had torn a number of half-rotten fangs from the jaw of the un-fortunate Ox.

'Oh,' said Ox.

'Go,' said Chegory.

[A weak joke. The Ashmarlan alphabet includes the sequence Oh Go Ro To Po. *Oris Baumgage, Fact Checker Minor.*]

'Go?' said Ox.

'Never mind,' said Chegory.

[The implication is that No lacked either a sense of humour or a solid understanding of Ashmarlan. One would like to know what language this discourse was being conducted in. It is elsewhere implied that No understood Ashmarlan, yet one would be inclined to believe that Guy conversed with his friend in Janjuladoola. *Oris Baumgage, Fact Checker Minor.*]

'Never mind what?' said Ox.

'Never mind anything,' said Chegory. 'Can I come in?'

'No,' said Ox. 'I'm sick.'

'Don't be so gutless,' said Chegory. 'I need help.'

'You don't understand,' said Ox.

'Oh, I understand all too well. You don't want to get involved.'

'You're not being fair. I warned you! Didn't I? Wasn't I there when you, when you – after the kraken I mean, you remember, you came off the harbour bridge, there I was, I—'

'Okay, okay,' said Chegory, 'so you—'

'I did my duty. All right? So that's all!'

'Listen,' said Chegory, 'aren't we meant to be friends?'

'Yes,' said Ox, with a touch of desperation. 'So what are you doing here? You're all mixed up in, oh, fighting with soldiers, burning people, some kind of treason, a coup at the palace or something, you were—'

'What are you talking about?' said Chegory.

'Well, weren't you there? Up at the palace? Last night? When they had the revolution?'

'Revolution? Ox, you're—'

'It's true! They were fighting, they got weapons off the guards, they—'

'Oh, that was just a riot,' said Chegory, 'just some—'

'Just? You could get burnt alive for less than that. You could get, well, the sharks, you know, or knives, you don't have any idea, you—'

'I've every idea,' said Chegory. 'I'm in trouble, deep trouble, I need help, not—'

'All right,' said Ox, cutting him off. 'All right, let's go down to the dining room, get some soup then talk about it.'

'I've had breakfast.'

'Then dragons for you!' said Ox. 'But I've had nothing. Come on, get out of the doorway, how can I get out with you standing there like a, like a, well—'

Chegory sighed, and stepped aside.

Whereupon Ox took a quick step backwards then slammed the door. The quick-witted Ox bolted it even as Chegory threw his weight against the timbers.

'Open up!' shouted Chegory, kicking and hammering.

No response from Ox.

Chegory kicked and hammered some more. He raised such a bedlam that at last a man threw open a door some three rooms down the corridor to challenge him.

'What the hell do you think you're doing?' said the man in decidedly foreign accents. 'Hey?'

It was a stranger. Some olive-skinned fellow with close-cropped brown hair. Nobody Chegory knew.

'Nothing,' said Chegory. 'I'm just leaving.'

'Don't let him get away!' shouted Ox, words clearly audible despite the muffling timbers. 'Mutiny, treason, murder, rape!'

'Traitor,' said Chegory.

Then kicked savagely at the door. Then strode down the corridor toward the stranger, meaning to fight his way past if the man tried to stop him.

'Hold it there, boy,' said the stranger, stepping out of his room.

Chegory's fingers leapt to his boot sheath. Empty! The other one, the other one, his blade was in the other one. His left-hand down-darted. Fingers found knife-hilt. Drew metal for the kill. His knifehand was relaxed and low, ready to stab upwards, to rip the gut or stab between ribs to vent heartblood.

'Get out of my way,' said Chegory.

'Easy now, boy,' said the stranger. 'Put down the knife and nobody will get hurt.'

There was no fear in the stranger's voice, no fear in his stance, and he showed no signs whatsoever of getting out of the way. What was he then? Some kind of combat expert? Perhaps. But only one such man in a thousand can take a knife from a trained shivman.

'Nuk off,' said Chegory.

Then language left him as his mind cleared for action and reaction, his senses sharpening as his heartbeat hammered, as his footsteps shadowed across the ground, his feet quick-gracing as he slid in fast with his blade slammed from left to right, flickering already from feint to feint, looking for the opening, the kill.

The olive-skinned stranger summed his approach at a glance, saw what he was up against then ducked back into his room. Slammed his door. Chegory whirled past it, turning, knife shifting from right hand to left as he dropped to a crouch, expecting the stranger to dart out to try to catch him from behind.

Instead, the door opened no more than a crack.

The stranger looked out, scrutinising the Ebrell Islander who crouched panting in the corridor, murder in his face.

'Where you learn knife-fighting, boy?' said the olive-skinned one.

No reply.

'You some kind of killer, huh?'

'Look,' said Chegory, recovering the use of language as his heartbeat slowed, 'I don't want any trouble, I just want to get out of here. Don't follow me, you won't get hurt. Okay? Understand?'

'Are you trying to get money off my young friend No? Is that it? How much does he owe?'

'Look,' said Chegory, 'you don't want any trouble, do you?'

A laugh from the olive-skinned one.

'This is no bloody joke!' said Chegory vehemently. 'I'm in deep shit, I don't care if I, if I – cut you up, that's nothing, one dead man, hell, it's all gone to shit, my whole life, don't laugh you bastard, I'll smash your face I'll smash you break you cut you kill you gash you smash you—'

He was shouting now. Giving vent to all his suppressed rage, hate, frustration. To the bloody murder which breeds in the breasts of Ebrell Islanders forced to dwell in the civilised cities to which they are so unsuited. All the unsaid things came out till he was vomiting forth hate unlimited, obscenity unpardonable.

Then he was done.

He stood there, panting. A little shocked at himself.

But the stranger merely laughed.

'Troubles!' said the olive-skinned one. 'You think you have troubles!'

He opened his door a little more. Chegory stood on guard still, but he was no longer poised for murder. Instead, he was assessing the stranger in depth and detail. Not much to look at. A bony body with narrow shoulders. Brown hair and olive skin, as noted already. A strange face, alien, foreign, as weird as his accents. A long, narrow face, length accentuated by steep-slanting cheek bones and a sharp-pointed chin. Thin lips, hooked nose.

'What's your problem then?' said Chegory.

His curiosity was understandable. After all, few people laugh when face to face with a killer. Equally, few respond to violent obscenity with such insouciance, at least not in Injiltaprajura, where uncouth speech tends to cause serious offence.

'My problem?' said the stranger. 'If I had but one I'd be laughing!'

'You're laughing anyway,' said Chegory.

'In extremity, what else is there to do? I'm to blame for the loss of the wishstone – and that's the least of it.'

'The wishstone?' said Chegory. 'How come?'

'Because I'm Official Keeper of the Imperial Sceptre, aren't I?'

'Well, you tell me. Who are you?'

'In truth you see the Official Keeper before you. Odolo of Ganthorgruk at your service. Conjurer and sinecurist. Favourite of the Empress Justina, hence still alive, but only just. And yourself now? Who would you be?'

'None of your business,' said Chegory.

'Come! Don't be like that! If you've got troubles, why not share them? Can't make things worse, can it?'

Chegory hesitated.

'What say we go to the dining room? Hey? Talk it out? You can tell me all about it over a cup of coffee or something. I'll pay. Money's the least of my problems, for the moment at any rate. That's what I think, anyway – my bank manager no doubt would beg to differ.'

Still Chegory hesitated.

'What have you got to lose?' said Odolo. 'If I wanted to make you prisoner I could rouse the whole slaughterhouse with a shout from my window. You'd never get away. Come. I won't say I'm your friend, but that scarcely makes me your enemy, does it? What have you got to lose?'

'Okay,' said Chegory, taking a deep breath as he eased up on the knife. 'Okay then. Let's talk.'

Then the two of them went down to the dining room. This was virtually empty, for most of those denizens of Ganthorgruk who were in regular employ had left for work, while those who were alcohol addicts had slipped off to speakeasies already, unless they were still sleeping off the debauches of the day (and night) before.

'Like the view?' said Odolo, gesturing to a window from which one could see all Lubos, the Laitemata, Jod, Scimitar, the Outer Reef, and vistas of blue and green sea beyond.

'It's okay,' said Chegory, without enthusiasm.

And sat himself at a table while Odolo went for some coffee.

Then the two began to talk.

Both had been, till then, lonely individuals totally isolated in their individual predicaments, effectively bereft (at least for the moment) of any friend or confidant. Both found it a deep relief to indulge in confession.

Young Chegory told of his arrest, of Shabble's untoward intervention and his consequent escape, of rearrest, of his deportation to the pink palace to face the squealer in the treasury, of riot, of his unwitting escape through a hole in the wall of the treasury, of his long wanderings Downstairs and of all that had taken place in that underground realm.

For his part, Odolo told of his strange dreams, some of which had prefigured (or caused?) transformations in the world itself. He told of dreaming (or creating?) the krakens in the Laitemata. Of his breakfast bowl which had come alive with boiling blue scorpions. Of other transformations, transfigurations and transubstantiations which had taken place since. Of a breadfruit which had turned of sudden into a brief-lived globe of red ants. A writing brush which had grown wings then flown away. A hash cookie turned to a cherry.

'A cherry?' said Chegory.

'A stone fruit. From trees, a special type of tree. Nice enough. I'd plant the stone itself except I doubt it'd grow in this climate. That's not all there is to it, either. There's these words, words, my head's crazy with words, whenever I'm not thinking hard they run amok, all kinds of words just scrambling through my head.'

'Well,' said Chegory, 'maybe you're . . . well, you know what I mean. Or maybe someone's fed you zen, you know, I told you all about that. Different people, it, well, I'm not setting myself up as an expert or something but it does weird things to some people. Or then, what if you're a wonderworker? But you just don't know it? Or the wish-stone, doesn't that do magic? Couldn't you, like, pick up magic? Since you've, you've looked after it so long.'

'There's nothing magic about the wishstone,' said Odolo. 'It's, it's beautiful, yes. It's got a kind of soft music about it, and inside there's all rainbows, never still but always moving, a brightness amazing when you get it in the dark. But no magic. Else what would it be doing in the treasury? Injiltaprajura's rulers would be using it from dawn to dusk to wish and rule.'

'You've tried it?'

'I . . .'

'You have!'

'Yes,' admitted Odolo, unaccountably embarrassed. 'But the wishes never came true. I knew they wouldn't. The thing is a – well, let's just say it's an old thing. Very old. The people here, they, it's because it's unique that they've got it locked up, I mean had it locked up. A toy. A bauble. That's all it is, at least to them. A jewel among jewels.'

'You speak lightly of things most valued!'

'You don't understand,' said Odolo. 'What's all that – that gold, jewellery, junk? What does it do? It sits there, that's all. That's all it can do. That's why you people never get anywhere, you're infatuated with accumulation, things, substance. What you don't understand is that it's process, that's everything. Energy! The interplay of energy!'

He was staring not at Chegory but through him. Looking at something. A vision, perhaps. A vision distant in time and space.

'I don't know that I understand what you're saying,' said Chegory, 'but I do know when I'm being insulted.'

'Sorry,' said Odolo. Then shuddered. As if a ghost had walked over his grave.

'What is it?' said Chegory. 'Flashback?'

'What's that?' said Odolo.

'If you have taken zen,' said Chegory, 'then you'll get these flashbacks, like me in the dark, you know. Sudden visions, that's what they are.'

'Oh,' said Odolo, 'I don't think I've taken zen. I don't – I don't know what to think.'

But speculating about such unknowns took them most of the rest of the morning. Their conversation got steadily deeper and deeper as they made their way through (to give here their combined consumption rather than a breakdown by individual) seven cups of cinnamon coffee, four cups of tea, three plates of popadoms, two bowls of goat's meat soup, a bowl of shrimps and then (it was not yet noon, but they were ready for lunch) two bowls of cassava and a couple of plates of fricasseed seagull with more coffee to go with it.

They had just finished the last of their seagull and the last of their coffee when the noon bells rang out to announce the end of istarlat and the start of salahanthara.

'Well,' said Odolo, pushing back his chair and rising from his table, 'let's be off, then.'

'To where?' said Chegory in surprise.

'To the pink palace, of course. The Petitions Session starts shortly.'

'I'm not going there!'

'Of course you are. Where else can you go? You've no friends left to turn to. You could run away, flee into Zolabrik, take up with Jal Japone again. But you've told me already you don't want to do that. So there's only one thing left to do. Petition the Empress.'

'But I'd get arrested if I—'

'You can't get arrested if you're—'

'Oh, if you're a petitioner, fine, usually, but there's a State of Emergency, there's—'

'Relax, relax,' said Odolo. 'I'm known to one and all at the palace as an imperial favourite. You won't get into trouble, not when you're with me. You'll do good for yourself and good for me as well. You'll get a pardon from the Empress, I swear to it. Better, when you tell of the pirates with the wishstone then the soldiers can start searching in earnest.'

'Well,' said Chegory, 'maybe, maybe . . .'

'Definitely!' said Odolo.

Then the conjuror hustled young Chegory out of Ganthorgruk and into the noonday heat through which they went, at a pace appropriate to the heat, up Skindik Way and then up Lak Street towards the pink palace standing in all its glory atop Pokra Ridge.

CHAPTER FIFTEEN

'If this doesn't work,' said Chegory, as they sweated up Lak Street, 'then I'm finished.'

'Relax,' said Odolo. 'Whatever her faults, Justina's merciful, I'll give her that. You'll get your pardon.'

'Sure. Or get my head hacked off on the spot. Maybe this isn't such a good idea.'

'Then do you want to start walking for Zolabrik?'

'That's my other option, isn't it?'

'There's a third.'

'Oh yes?' said Chegory. 'Tell me about it!'

'You work on Jod, don't you? So you know the island's ruler. So why not seek help from him?'

'There's no point going there,' said Chegory. 'Ivan Pokrov's in jail, I've told you that.'

'But that's not who I was thinking of,' said Odolo.

'Who, then?'

'The Hermit Crab, of course!'

Chegory shuddered.

'You,' he said, 'have got to be crazy. Have you ever seen that brute?'

'No, but—'

'It's, let's see, it's intimidating, that's the word. When you know what it's done it's not just intimidating it's bloody terrifying. I have to give the thing meat and stuff. Oh shit! And I haven't! It's missed lunch, that's, that's, gods, maybe it's turning people inside out right now.'

Chegory wheeled. A marvellous view! But he wasted no time admiring it for his eyes were all for Jod. It still existed. That was something! The marble buildings of the Analytical Institute were still there, and so was the harbour bridge. But how much longer would it be before the Hermit

Crab poured out the vials of wrath and inverted the island entire, or shattered it into just so many chips of scatter-stone?

'Don't worry about it,' said Odolo. 'Someone else will feed your happy little friend. Or is it sacred? A sacred ritual, and you its priest?'

'Priest?' said Chegory, startled. 'Me? No, it's not that, it's not sacred, but it's a – a – it's a trust, that's what it is, thousands of people, all Injiltaprajura, but it's me they trusted, so it's, yes it is sacred, it is, a sacred trust, and I blew it, the Crab's starving right now, it's—'

'But someone else will—'

'They won't! They're all slaves, that's what, no more sense than a coconut, or they're mad algorithmists, just cogs and wheels and binary logic, that's all they think of, not, not keeping two legs two arms stopping from getting turned inside out that kind of, of important stuff. I should—'

'You should come inside,' said Odolo, trying in an avuncular way to calm his intense young companion. 'If you're consecrated to the cause of victualling our crustacean-in-residence then you'd best look after yourself.'

By such talk the imperial favourite persuaded young Chegory to climb the steps and pass within the portals of the pink palace.

'Business?' said a guard, one of seven on duty within the foyer.

'Petitions,' said Odolo, and nodded pleasantly, and led Chegory onwards.

One of the guards had a black eye and a heavily bruised cheek, suggesting he might have been one of the un-fortunates who had been overwhelmed during the rioting in the treasury in the night just gone. Chegory expected the man to leap forward and arrest him, but no such thing happened.

'Up here,' said Odolo. 'Up the stairs.'

Up the stairs they went to the Grand Hall where the petitions session had already started. For a moment, the world wavered, and Chegory imagined he saw a fanged monster coming to quench its thirst upon his flesh. For that moment, reality tottered. Even as it did so, he knew what he was enduring: a flashback consequent upon his night-time indulgence in zen.

Then the outlines of the world hardened again into the everyday, the quotidian, the expected and the expectable. The Grand Hall with unlit chandeliers hanging from its high ceiling. An unruly press of petitioners being held back by guards with scimitars naked. The Empress Justina high-seated upon a throne of ebony. Her white ape, Vazzy, even now being dragged away after perpetrating some (temporarily) unpardonable misdeed. Expressionless slaves standing to either side of the throne, their muscles working huge feathered fans to cool the ruler of Injiltaprajura.

Behold Justina! Vigorous her lips and big her nose, high her brow and plump her cheeks. Massive are her breasts, their weight threatening the carmine silk which binds them in. Stalwart are her thighs and thick her wrists. Surely she is the daughter of a mighty father!

Behind Justina's ebony throne stood a huge cage with bars of black iron. Even Chegory Guy knew it for a starvation cage. It had long fallen out of disuse, for Justina was true to the traditions of her forebears, and the Yudonic Knights prefer disciplinary solutions which lead to sharp and bloody death rather than the exquisite forms of lingering agony brought to such perfection by the con-noisseurs of the Izdimir Empire. Nevertheless, the lock on the door to the cage glistened with a sheen of oil which spoke of loving maintenance.

'This way,' said the conjurer Odolo.

Chegory let himself be led. His mouth was agape. He was staring at the battle-shields on the walls. The shields were objects of outright wrath adorned with the bloody coats of arms of the Yudonic Knights of Wen Endex. A riot of monstrous jaws, skulls, bones, sundry decapitations, hacked amputations, dripping blood and worse.

Odolo, by taking advantage of his status as imperial favourite, soon led young Chegory closer to the Seat of

Mercy than he would otherwise have got in the course of the whole afternoon. For the petitions session had attracted an uncommon number of supplicants, since the searches, seizures, raids, captures, inquiries and interrogations of the last five quarters had flushed an extraordinary tally of criminals, sinners, law-breakers, tax avoiders, deserters, traitors, drug-dealers, miscreants, vandals, delinquents, runaways, truants, swindlers, perjurers and embezzlers from their caves, sewers, cellars, lairs, pits, attics, hideouts and houseboats.

Notable among those crowding close to the scimitars was a big man massively scarred by burns. Where skin remained one could see the remnants of once-glorious tattoos of dragons, sea serpents and such.

'Who's that?' said Chegory, pointing him out.

'Uckermark, the corpse master. A regular visitor.'

'Why?'

'He's always offending one religion or another.'

'He's a – a blasphemer?'

'No, it's just his job. It—'

Chegory never received an explanation of the theological disputes which interfere with the smooth flow of a corpse master's work (certain treatments of the dead which are essential to one religion are anathema to another, and Injiltaprajura is rich indeed in religions) because he interrupted, saying:

'Gods!'

'What is it?'

'Just someone I know.'

'Who?'

'Oh, nobody, nobody, don't worry about it.'

The someone who was nobody was actually Chegory's uncle Dunash Labrat, upright beekeeper and dutiful tax-payer, who was moving through the crowd in company with his son Ham. They had some of their apiarian gear with them, for bees were swarming in the pink palace and the two had been summoned to remove them.

Chegory did his best to make himself inconspicuous. This

was just what he had dreaded! Publicity! The embarrassment of declaring himself and his circumstances to the Empress Justina in full view of his uncle. A nightmare come true! Then the Labrats were gone, ushered deeper into the palace by a guiding guard, and Chegory breathed easy once more.

'Well,' he said, eager to get his ordeal over and done with now he was irrevocably launched upon the petitioning path, 'what're we going to do? Push in ahead of those people?'

'No,' said Odolo. 'We wait. The Empress takes breaks at intervals. Then we'll join her in a place more private and plead your case beyond the mob's survey.'

Serendipity!

This was more than Chegory had dared to hope for!

A private audience with Justina, oh yes, that was the way. He could say everything, confess all, knowing it would not be near instantly the common talk of the streets. Under such circumstances he would count it both a pleasure and a privilege to bare his soul to his Empress. Justina the merciful! Justina the good! Most saintly of rulers, most blessed of lawmakers!

One need not search far to find the sources of such extravagant royalism. It was, after all, the Family Thrug which had overthrown Wazir Sin, that dedicated pogromist who had made it his business to wipe out Ebbies first then others afterwards. If it had not been for the intervention of Lonstantine Thrug and Justina's subsequent adherence to her father's policies then Chegory Guy would still have been living as a hunted animal in the wastelands of Zolabrik. Hence young Chegory was a patriot, a royalist, and a staunch supporter of imperial rule.

Chegory waited impatiently while the Empress dealt with one petitioner after another. Then he was astonished to see someone he recognised stepping forward to declare himself.

He was astonished?

Why, you ask, was he astonished?

After all, he was an Ebrell Islander, hence drug-dealers

and law-breakers of all descriptions were his common companions. Surely he could have been expected to recognise many a petition-pleading miscreant on a day so busy. If you have prejudged young Chegory thus then your prejudices are not misplaced, for, as this chronicle has demonstrated already, he was typical of his kind. Nevertheless, his astonishment was fully justified, for the man instantly standing before the Empress Justina was no ordinary petitioner.

No, this was the elven lord whom Chegory had met Downstairs in the night just gone. Or, rather, this was the individual whom Chegory had misidentified as an elven lord on the strength of the glittering fish-scale armour he had been wearing in the underworld. The man in question was actually Pelagius Zozimus, a wizard of the order of Xluzu and the quest-companion of Guest Gulkan (pretender to the throne of Tameran), Hostaja Sken-Pitilkin (a fellow wizard) and Thayer Levant (a cut-throat from Chi'ash-lan).

For the Petitions Session, Pelagius Zozimus had abandoned his miraculous fish-scale armour in favour of an unadorned light green ankle-length robe. A linguist had already established his competence in Toxteth, and even now a guard was using that language to ask Chegory's 'elven lord' the standard question:

'Have you in your voluntary or involuntary possession any knife, bodkin, knitting needle, dragon hook, sword, spear, bow, catapult, arbalest, fighting stick, battering ram, snake, scorpion, basilisk, vial of vitriol or other weapon of death or terror or violence?'

Whereupon Zozimus answered in the negative, was subjected to a swift but expert search, then was allowed to step closer (but not too close!) to the Empress. The Imperial Linguist stepped forward with him. Both elven lord and linguist bowed.

'Toxteth,' said the linguist, then bowed again and withdrew.

Chegory was appalled to see the elven lord standing

almost within striking distance of the Empress Justina. Alone and unaccompanied. What designs did the alien uitlander have upon his beloved Empress. What treason was here afoot?

The elven lord bowed once more.

'Speak,' said Justina, for such was her style.

'Fair star of Injiltaprajura,' said he, 'most gracious of the daughters of Wen Endex, most—'

'Yes, yes,' said Justina, impatiently, 'I've heard all that before. Tell me something I don't know. Get down to business, man!'

'I crave forgiveness for sins enormous, for crimes near unpardonable,' said the elven lord.

Chegory relaxed. So the miscreant was going to confess all. He was going to admit to the Empress that he had come to Injiltaprajura to try to seize the wishstone. Chegory knew that to be the ruling purpose of the elven lord and his companions for they had told him as much after they had captured him Downstairs.

'Crave on,' said the Empress.

'My name is Pelagius Zozimus,' said the elven lord. 'Long have I dwelt in the wastelands of the Scorpion Desert. There, to my sorrow, I have served the evil warlord Jal Japone. His employ have I deserted, here to come to crave forgiveness.'

'How did you serve Japone?' said the Empress.

'I was his chief of cookery,' said Pelagius Zozimus, 'for there lies my talent. I'm a master chef, the unsurpassed lord of twenty-seven styles of culinary delight. I hear my ladyship has a vacancy for such a one.'

'Why, so we do,' said the Empress, delight speaking itself plain across her face. 'Pardoned and employed! My major domo will show you—'

'Ware!' shouted a guard. 'An Ebby!'

For Chegory Guy was plunging toward the throne. Murder was writ clear in his countenance. His intent was to see this Zozimus dead that very day quarter. To denounce the fraudulent thief who had with breathtaking audacity cozened his way into the bosom of the imperial household. To swear that Zozimus was no servant of Japone but a rapacious reaver from across the seas, a conspirator in league with vermin more dangerous yet.

Such was Chegory's intent.

But before the young Ebrell Islander could get anywhere near the throne he was set upon by guards, seized, inverted, punched, booted, slapped, and deprived of his sole weapon – the knife he had found Downstairs and had secreted in a boot sheath.

'A blade!' shouted a soldier, brandishing the weapon for all to see.

At the sight of it, the corpse master Uckermark forced his way forward.

'Hold him, hold him!' cried a scimitar-wielding warman.

Chegory was held. Arms and legs wrenched out in four separate directions. He kicked, writhed, struggled and convulsed. All to no avail. Someone had him by the hair and was hauling hard, hoping to stretch out his neck for easy decapitation.

'Get your hands out of the way!' shouted the scimitarist.

'Wait!' said the corpse master Uckermark.

But nobody paid any attention to that man much-scarred and much-tattooed. Not until he seized the down-chopping scimitarist and threw him out of the way. Next moment a dozen blades were out.

'Stop that!' shouted the Empress Justina.

Nobody paid her any attention either. So she leapt up, seized the nearest slave and charged into the fray, striking out to left and right with this convenient weapon until she stood triumphant upon the field of battle with dazed combatants in recumbent postures to left and right alike.

[One is entitled to doubt that the battle above-described really took place. In the first place, in courts of imperial power the ruler's softest word tends to be obeyed instantly, even when the ruler is a woman. Secondly, the behaviour here ascribed to Justina is not consonant with her gender. Equally telling is that use of a human body as a weapon has already been described once – the muscleman Tolon is said to have used Chegory as such when fighting against soldiers Downstairs – and a third party is later described (in virtually identical language) as employing a similar weapon. One is led to believe that the conflicts in question were settled with far less melodrama than the Text would have us believe, and that the employment of human bodies in battle is purely a figment of the Originator's violent imagination. *Sot Dawbler, School of Commentary*.]

'When I say stop,' said Justina, 'I mean stop! Does anyone want to argue about it?'

As nobody displayed any wish to enter into further dialectical discourse, Justina dropped her slave, who crawled away groggily.

'Right!' said Justina, tucking her breasts back into the confines of the crimson silk from which they had escaped during her exertions, 'Let's have some explanations!'

[This is an amusing little anecdote, though it lacks the hilariousness of the Originator's tale about Theodora and her employment of chickens. However, while this anecdote amuses, it cannot possibly be true. Yet again we find the Originator's imagination distorting the historical realities which underly the Text. A woman, whether Empress or otherwise, is never so casual about the public exposure of her anatomy. When her shame is revealed she reacts with flinching panic, with blushes and delightful squeals of alarm. I myself have observed this on a number of occasions. We would expect that if the Empress Justina had been exposed in the manner detailed then she would have been forced to withdraw from the public eye to come to terms with her shame and to recover her composure. *Sot Dawbler, School of Commentary*.]

[One is shocked to find one so venerable as Sot Dawbler 'amused' by the grossness he has discovered in the Text directly above. Or by the tale of Theodora and her chickens, which, since it is the vile and disgusting invention of a patent lunatic, has been extirpated from this Text on my order. *Drax Lira, Redactor Major*.]

The corpse master Uckermark was the first to recover himself sufficiently to speak.

'The boy,' he said, 'the boy is my apprentice. He's, he has fits of unwittedness, but he's a good boy, your highness, and the knife he had is but a tool of trade. If we can be gone from here I'll chastise him mightily once we're back at the corpse shop. I ask only that – the knife, my lady. It's consecrated to the work of corpses, hence sacred, hence could we have it back?'

Justina considered.

Chegory's fate hung in the balance.

Fortunately, Justina was acquainted with the corpse master Uckermark. Well acquainted. Very, very well acquainted. In truth, acquaintance of the kind which existed between the Empress and the corpse master went far beyond the borders of that cautious propriety which should by rights govern relationships between females of imperial standing and males of the lower orders. Thus Justina was inclined to gratify the wishes of her loyal subject Uckermark.

And, while she was about it, to gratify herself.

But first she had some questions.

'This boy,' she said, 'is he a clean living young man?'

'Oh, very clean living,' said Uckermark. 'A virgin in truth.'

'Is he fit?' said Justina. 'Is he healthy?'

'I guarantee him capable of the most vigorous exertion,' said Uckermark.

'Has he learnt his table manners?' said Justina.

'That he has,' said Uckermark. 'Furthermore, if you wish to have him as a guest at banquet I'll ensure some revision.'

'You read my very mind!' said Justina, clapping her hands together in delight. 'Then the boy will banquet with me tonight. You will accompany him to banquet.'

Then the Empress seated herself sedately on her throne, her slaves resumed the work of fans, and Uckermark recovered the knife so recently taken from young Chegory

Guy and hustled his dumbstruck captive away. Chegory cast one glance of appeal at the conjuror Odolo, but the imperial favourite merely spread his hands in a gesture expressive of helpless amazement.

CHAPTER SIXTEEN

Chegory was so shattered by fate's perversion of all his expectations and by the sheer velocity of the events which had overwhelmed his life's routines that he asked not a single question as Uckermark marched him out of the pink palace, down Lak Street as far as the Cabal House of Injiltaprajura's wonderworkers, down Skindik Way then through the narrows of Lubos to the Corpse Shop.

'This is my house,' said Uckermark when they got there.

'Not for long,' said Chegory. 'It's on fire!'

The door stood ajar – and black smoke was pouring from within. But Uckermark merely laughed and threw the door wide open. Chegory stepped back as clouds of thick, choking fumes billowed outwards.

'Come in, come in,' said Uckermark.

'You're mad!' said Chegory, coughing and choking.

Then, as the smoke thinned a little, he saw the fumes issuing from large double-handled pots set just within.

'In,' said Uckermark.

'But – but the – but why the smoke?'

'Because flies love flesh,' said Uckermark. 'In, so I can close the door.'

Chegory went inside. Uckermark put the lids on the smoke pots then closed the door entirely. When Chegory had finished coughing and crying – the smoke was devilish for stinging the eyes – he began to look around and get his bearings. There was death everywhere he looked.

Chegory had seen a few dead bodies in his time but the corpse shop was something else again for it was crowded with the unkempt dead. Flies in their thousands buzzed in manic frustration on the outer side of the gauze which sealed the windows against their intrusion. Everywhere there were limbs, bones, buckets of blood, assorted organs spilling out of sacks, heads bereft of connection, unidentifiable torsos and worse.

As for the smell!

The slaughterhouse stench was worse than the gut-wrenching odour which arose from the helpless dements locked into Crawlspace Seven in the Dromdanjerie. It made Chegory nauseous. Uckermark displayed no discomfort, which was understandable; the corpse master had no sense of smell whatsoever, since that sense had been utterly destroyed when his face was ravaged by fire.

'Sit!' said Uckermark curtly, pointing to a stool.

Chegory sat, averted his eyes from a pile of unmentionable oddments in a tray near his feet.

'Thank you . . . thank you for saving me,' said Chegory awkwardly.

'I didn't save you,' said Uckermark. 'I saved this.' He meant the knife. A pretty thing: its handle azure, its blade celadon. 'This,' he continued, 'must not win unwanted attention, else the Calligrapher's Union will have to seek a new recognition sign.'

'The . . . the Calligrapher's Union?' said Chegory.

'You don't know!?' said Uckermark, startled.

'Know what?' said Chegory.

'So you don't! Gods, I wished I'd – bugger! The banquet. I have to take you to banquet.'

'Why's that so terrible?' said Chegory.

'Because it means I can't just cut your thieving throat and dump your corpse down a sewer!' said Uckermark.

'I'm no thief!' protested Chegory.

'Then how did you get this knife?'

'I found it, didn't I?'

'Found it!'

'It's true! What's with the knife, anyway? That's – what, something for that union, calligraphy, that's letterwriting, isn't it? You've got a union for that? Look, I'm not in competition, I can't hardly write excepting for Ashmarlan, who uses Ashmarlan anyway, I mean a few Ashdans but but—'

'Shut up!' said Uckermark. 'Stop babbling! Just answer questions. You'll learn all in due course – if you live. If you do want to live pray tell how you came by this knife.'

'Oh, it's a long story, a long story,' said Chegory. 'A terrible story, you wouldn't believe, but it's the truth, I'll truth it all out to you. There were some shark jaws, you see, down below. That's after I met the Malud marauders, or was it, no, I met the elf first, he's a chef at the moment or pretending to be but Downstairs he was all in armour, nice as a fish-skin it fitted, like a, an elven lord from legend. You see—'

Thus Chegory, in a rush, began to vomit up his life's secrets. Uckermark raised a hand, halting his incontinent blatter.

'Let's take this bit by bit,' said Uckermark. 'Where did you first lay hands on the knife?'

'In the dark,' said Chegory.

Which was true, but was less than informative.

'Talk sense!' said Uckermark.

'I'm trying, I'm trying! But you – you – this stink, those flies, the – what do you think I—'

Uckermark sighed.

'Ease up,' said the corpse master. 'Easy, now! We'll try a little medicine, maybe that will make you settle.'

So saying, the corpse master took a small cup of eggshell porcelain, filled it with clear fluid then passed it to Chegory. Who drank without caution. He coughed and spluttered. It felt as if liquid fire had been poured down his throat. He looked at the half-full cup with horror.

This was alcohol!

A righteous, law-abiding young man would have flung the filthy stuff in the corpse master's face. But Chegory Guy was an Ebrell Islander. Therefore, after a pause to collect his breath, he downed the rest of the bub in a single swallow.

Whereupon he began to feel . . . better.

'Good medicine, isn't it just?' said Uckermark, with something of a chuckle.

'It does the job,' admitted Chegory, finding his nerves much steadier.

'Slowly, then,' said Uckermark. 'Let's take these questions slowly. You found the knife in the dark, did you? Pray tell – where found you this particular dark?'

Soon, Uckermark knew the bare essentials of Chegory's adventurings Downstairs.

'I'll send for Log Jaris,' said the corpse master.

'Log Jaris?'

'The bullman.'

'Does he . . . is he . . . is it his knife?'

'Never you mind about that,' said Uckermark. Then he gave vent to an ear-shattering shout: 'Yilda!'

From upstairs there came a hard-bitten woman aged somewhere between forty and sixty.

'Chegory,' shouted Uckermark, pointing at Chegory.

She nodded.

'Go fetch Log Jaris!' shouted Uckermark.

Yilda nodded again, then departed.

'She's deaf?' said Chegory.

'And mute,' said Uckermark. 'The deafness is a problem, but the muteness – ah, many a man would kill to be so privileged.'

Then he chuckled.

It might as well be noted at this juncture that he was making a misogynistical joke. Yilda was deaf – though the degree of her deafness is not known precisely, since she was one of those people who often choose not to hear what is said unless it suits their convenience – but she was not by any means mute.

Since the corpse master was (at least temporarily) once more in good humour, Chegory risked another query about Log Jaris, but his attempts to elicit further information were rebuffed.

The truth of the matter is that both Uckermark and Log Jaris were members of the Calligrapher's Union, a secret society formed on Untunchilamon during the days of Wazir Sin, whose rigorous enforcement of the laws of the Izdimir

Empire had made life very difficult for people who could not properly document their existence. Hence the Calligrapher's Union specialised in forgery. It was, in effect, a self-defence league for people whose legality was at best marginal.

A knife with an azure handle and a celadon blade was the recognition sign of the Union. When Uckermark had seen soldiers snatch such a blade from Chegory Guy in the pink palace the deluded corpse master had thought Chegory to be a member of the Union, or to at least be in possession of the Union's secrets. This misapprehension was what had inspired the corpse master to heroic endeavour in the fight before the throne of the Empress Justina.

'May I . . . have you got anywhere . . .'

'The toilet?' said Uckermark. 'It's in the courtyard. That's out the back. Don't let in the flies! There's three screen doors, my own invention, a flylock. If you can't make sense of it, come and tell me.'

'Yes, but, um . . . what I really wanted . . . if I could . . .'

'Out with it, boy!'

'Well actually, if you've got anywhere I could sleep, I wouldn't mind putting my head down.'

'Oh, sleep,' said Uckermark. 'Upstairs, if that's what you want to do. But there's bars on the windows, so don't think you can run away or anything like that.'

'You're keeping me prisoner?'

'What else can I do? The Empress demands you! I've got to keep you safe till the banquet at the very least.'

'Banquet?' said Chegory blankly.

'The Empress Justina invited you to dine with her.'

'But that – that was a joke. Surely!'

'The Empress,' said Uckermark severely, 'does not joke. Certainly not about matters so near and dear to her heart.'

'I'm not near and dear to her heart!'

'But you will be,' said Uckermark. 'To her heart, liver, kidney, spleen. And something equally wet and warm.'

Then he winked in a truly obscene and insinuating fashion. Did he mean . . . ? No, surely not!

'Are you sure . . . are you sure she wasn't making a joke?'

'I'm positive!' said Uckermark. 'Justina's her father's daughter. She knows what she wants. Oh, she fancied for sure when she clapped eyes on you. So enjoy your sleep while you've got the opportunity!'

Chegory hoped he misunderstood the implications of Uckermark's comments. Nevertheless, whether Uckermark was truthing or joking, the young Ebrell Islander could certainly use all the shuteye he could get. So, after a quick visit to the courtyard, he got himself upstairs and laid himself down on the bed he found there, and was near instantly asleep.

Young Chegory Guy was still asleep when Log Jaris arrived at the corpse shop. Long did the bullman and the corpse master confer and most serious were the matters which they discussed.

Several members of the Calligrapher's Union had been arrested as troops swept and reswept the city in their search for the wishstone. The solution was obvious. The Calligrapher's Union must itself catch the thieves who stole the wishstone. Before things got out of hand.

Thanks to information Uckermark had received from Chegory Guy, they knew the wishstone was Downstairs with three Malud marauders. Log Jaris and Uckermark both knew the depths intimately. One of their legal sidelines was bounty hunting, and they had many times in the past ventured Downstairs to run down escaped slaves, rapists, murderers and eloping young lovers.

'How many men can we muster?' said Uckermark.

'Twenty at short, more at long,' said Log Jaris.

'What about dogs?'

'A dozen hunters, no problem. We'll backtrack from my cellar. Follow the boy's trail till the dogs pick up something else.'

'Will that work? Will the scent be fresh enough?'

'We can but try,' said Log Jaris. 'If that fails, we'll quarter the underworld by sectors. Track any scent we find. Might take us a few days, but they can't hide forever. Got the map?'

Uckermark pulled out a map, one copy of many of the plans of the underworld which the Calligrapher's Union had assembled over the years. Then the two began to discuss tactics in detail.

'What if we catch them?' said Log Jaris. 'Interrogate them ourselves, or what?'

'No, straight to the palace,' said Uckermark. 'The sooner this State of Emergency comes to an end the better.'

'What about this thief in the palace? The man the boy thinks to be an elf?'

'The Zozimus fellow?' said Uckermark. 'Leave him. He's doing us no harm, is he? Might be blackmail money there. I'll keep close hold of the boy, he's our witness against Zozimus.'

'What if Zozimus sees the boy at the banquet?'

'What if he does? I'll be with him, won't I? No, don't you worry about that. Get the dogs together, get the men.'

'Just one thing,' said Log Jaris. 'What if our quarry's gone to ground in here?'

So saying, he pointed at the plan of the underworld. The section he indicated had been mapped more by guesswork than anything else. It was a region of doom. Of hideous things from which nightmare itself would have fled.

'Turn loose the dogs, that's what I'd do,' said Uckermark. 'Let the dogs hunt free. They might flush something out. But if the dogs fail – forget it. You wouldn't catch me going in there!'

'Okay,' said Log Jaris.

'You'd already decided, hadn't you?' said Uckermark. 'You're not fool enough to hunt to the horrors!'

'Yes,' said Log Jaris, 'but I wanted to hear you say the same for yourself.'

Then the bullman and the corpse master both laughed, and settled down to share a drink or three before Log Jaris took himself off to organise a hunt of the underworld for the wishstone and the Malud marauders from far-off Asral who had stolen it.

CHAPTER SEVENTEEN

Young Chegory Guy slept on through much of salahanthara till Uckermark woke him and escorted him uphill toward the pink palace.

'When's the banquet, then?' said Chegory.

'Not yet, not yet,' said Uckermark. 'Don't be in such a hurry! You'll be close enough to her ladyship soon enough.'

'Oh, brender menoth,' said Chegory, who was bad-tempered from lack of proper sleep.

[Brender menoth: chop away. Toxteth phrase. The implication is that the one addressed is guilty of unwelcome use of a wit too blunt to be amusing. *Oris Baumgage, Fact Checker Minor.*]

They were hiking up Lak Street before Chegory was struck by a question which would have immediately occurred to a woman.

'What about clothes?' said he.

'Clothes?' said Uckermark.

'Yes, look, if we're going to, like, a banquet, okay, I can hardly go like this, can I? I mean, look at me!'

Chegory was still wearing the trousers, shirt and boots in which he had been dressed when he had left the island of Jod late in the afternoon on the previous day. Since then, he had been fighting with a kraken and brawling with soldiers, had slept in his clothes on a number of occasions and had gone on all kinds of adventures in a variety of unhygienic places.

'Oh, don't worry about clothes,' said Uckermark. 'The Empress will love you just as you are.'

'That settles it!' said Chegory. 'We're not going to a banquet at all, are we? So where are we going? Where are you taking me?'

'You'll find out,' said Uckermark, his voice becoming stern and grim. 'Oh, you'll find out in time, young Chegory! No – don't try to run. You can't get away. You can't escape! You're doomed!'

But Chegory made a break for freedom regardless. Uckermark grabbed him before he had taken as many as three steps, and, after a brief tussle, the Ebrell Islander was subdued then marched up to the palace.

'What've we got here?' said a guard, when Uckermark and Chegory entered the foyer of the palace.

'Meat for the kitchen,' said Uckermark. 'Human meat. To be cooked up in the kitchen.'

'Oh, meat!' said the soldier cheerfully. 'For the Empress, is it?'

'Yes,' said Uckermark. 'Her master chef Zozimus will cook it up especially.'

'Oh, capital, capital!' said the guard. 'Fresh meat, yes, that's the thing. If I recall right, she ate bits of three when she banqueted last. The heart of a fisherman's boy, the liver of a young blacksmith and the kidneys of a – what was it?'

'That tender young singer from far-off Ashmolea,' said Uckermark.

'Oh, the singing boy, yes, that was it!' said the guard. 'Well, my lad, are you pleased with your privilege?'

'You can't do this!' wailed Chegory fearfully.

So this was what it was all about! He was appalled by the monstrous conspiracy which had been revealed to him. So that was what Justina had meant about having him to a banquet! Now he understood Uckermark's joke about Chegory getting close to the imperial gut. He tried to run – but Uckermark and the soldier both grabbed him. This time he struggled with such violence that it took the strength of both to control him.

As the pair were wrestling the hapless Ebrell Islander to the ground, a harassed official came bustling up to them. It was Justina's major domo.

'What's this, what's this?' said the major domo. 'What's all this fighting then? Stop it immediately!'

'This,' said Uckermark, panting and laughing at the same time, 'is meat from the imperial kitchen. This is young Chegory Guy. The Empress Justina wants him slaughtered for her banquet tonight.'

'Guy!' he said. 'We've been waiting for him! You're late, you're late, oh we'll never get him ready in time.'

'It takes but a moment to gut him and clean him,' said Uckermark. 'Then the chef can quick-fry him in moments.'

But the major domo was not amused.

'Let the boy go,' he said. 'Stand up, boy. Look! He's shaking all over! Worse, you've bloodied his nose! Stand still, boy! Nobody's going to eat you.'

'You mean they were – they – they – a joke, they were joking?'

'Boy, you really think Justina a cannibal? Gods! Only a – never mind. Come this way! We've barely time for the necessary preparations.'

'Preparations?' said Chegory.

'Come! Come on! Look, nobody's going to eat you, really, don't be so childish. This way, quick, quick.'

With that, the major domo led Chegory from the palace foyer, and they had soon left the laughter of Uckermark and his friend far, far behind.

'But,' said Chegory, both frightened and bewildered by the foreboding mysteries of the palace and his complete loss of control of his own life, 'but what's this about preparations?'

'Come this way, this way,' said the major domo, hustling him along. 'Fastest begun, fastest finished.'

'What about Uckermark, Uckermark, you know, the corpse master, where's he, what's he—'

'Don't worry about him,' said the major domo. 'You'll meet him again before the banquet. Gods! What a witless joke! Him and that soldier! I'd have the both beaten if there was one chance in ten of knocking some sense into either.'

With that, the major domo showed Chegory into an imposing bathroom where half a dozen perfumed young women were waiting for him. Immediately they fell on him and, giggling and squealing, began to tear off his clothes.

'Help!' wailed Chegory. 'Help! Stop it, stop them, some-one, help, no, that's, gods—'

But all his protests were to no avail. The imperial ladies in waiting stripped him naked, threw him into a huge bath then jumped in afterwards. Then he was washed, sponged and scrubbed without mercy. To his intense embarrassment (in his anguish he thought he would faint) the young women missed nothing in their quest for cleanliness. Scenes equivalent he had oft enjoyed in fantasy – the uninhibited ministrations of nubile sylphs, of unmaidenly beauty by the roomful – but the reality proved shrivelling rather than arousing.

And what—

Was that a mouth at his . . . ?!

While Chegory at one stage feared he would be raped by these giggling female ravagers, he was still in possession of his virginity when he was hauled from the bath to be towelled and combed then hastened to a table where he was hammered and pounded by a masseur who must have trained in one of the more vigorous schools of all-in wrestling. After that he was rushed to the office of Koskini Reni, her ladyship's personal physician.

'My clothes!' wailed Chegory.

'Don't worry,' said someone. 'You'll get them back.'

Then he was in Reni's office and the physician was checking him over. Scrutinising, prodding, poking, thumping, interrogating. Whores, boy? Have you slept with whores? No? Then with what? Have you ever had a pig? No? You don't know what you've missed! Yaws, boy, have you got yaws? Very well. Lepers, boy. Have you met any? Have you . . .

On and on, till Chegory's head was spinning.

At last Reni concluded his investigations, popped a boil on the back of Chegory's neck, then declared him basically fit and well.

'However,' said physician Reni, 'you are slightly anaemic. Therefore I prescribe a little mead.'

'Mead?' said Chegory. 'I thought that was a medicine for hysteria only.'

He had heard as much said when mead was discussed by his uncle Dunash Labrat, who had a licence to brew up the stuff.

'Hysteria, anaemia, dementia, depression, psychosis and the common cold,' said the physician gravely. 'Mead is the best medicine known for all of those and more, although in truth all classes of alcohol are possessed of such virtues.'

'But,' said Chegory in bewilderment, 'alcohol is a poison.'

'And is not salt?' said Reni. 'In my fist alone I could hold salt sufficient to make you retch, cramp and die. Yet without salt you would sicken and die in any case.'

'Salt we must have for our blood comes from the sea,' said Chegory.

'Aha!' said Reni, with the slyest of grins imaginable. 'So you adhere to the evolutionary heresy, do you?'

'The Empress Justina has declared religious freedom on Untunchilamon,' said Chegory stoutly.

'Even so,' said Reni, 'you are but a fool to enlist heretical superstition in a debate with medical science. Our science, young man, has proved beyond doubt that all poisons are capable of medicinal uses.'

'I don't do drugs,' said Chegory flatly.

By now the red-skinned one had conceived a deep suspicion of the imperial physician. Surely no true practitioner of the healing arts would feed poisons to a patient!

'You take hashish, do you not?' said Reni.

'Hashish is no drug,' said Chegory. 'Drugs are toxic things which kill. Nobody ever died from eating a hash cookie or smoking a little kif. You a doctor! Yet you slander the Herb of Healing by making it one with the Drink of Death which can kill in a night or less.'

'So!' said Reni. 'It is but an Ebrell Islander, yet thinks itself the complete pharmacist. It is but an Ebrell Islander, yet it will lecture its doctor. It is but an Ebrell Islander, a thing which cannot read, write or figure, yet it will lecture a philosopher who has degrees from three of the elite universities of the Izdimir Empire.'

'Alcohol kills,' persisted Chegory stubbornly, not bothering to protest his literacy or his numeracy. 'It takes but three cups of pure alcohol or less to kill a man in the prime of his health and strength.'

This was true, or near enough to being true, yet did not suffice to win the argument, for Reni persisted:

'You drink tea, do you not?'

'Tea,' said Chegory stiffly, 'is not toxic.'

'On the contrary,' said Koskini Reni, 'tea is a lethal toxin if abused. A few pinches of tealeaves consumed without caution will kill the weak and frighten the hearts of the healthy to a frenzy most dangerous to the constitution.'

Chegory knew slaves sometimes abused tea in this fashion when they wished to report sick to escape a day's work. Yet he remained unconvinced.

'No normal person eats tea,' he said.

'Likewise no normal person drinks your theoretical three cups of pure alcohol,' said Reni. 'Remember, all things taken to excess can kill. Why, there are even cases of people who have died of a surfeit of water.'

'So you admit the danger exists!' said Chegory.

'Doubtless,' said Reni. 'That is why alcohol is only available on prescription. This sovereign remedy for all ills is destructive in the extreme if it once escapes the control of professionals. Yet here within the pink palace we use it safely, for it is controlled and prescribed in strict accordance with medical ethics.' Then Reni indulged himself in a condescending smile and said: 'You see, my boy? There's nothing to worry about.'

Yet he tucked Chegory's prescription for mead into a thin manilla folder, leading the young Ebrell Islander to believe he had won the debate even though the physician refused to concede defeat.

In any case, there was no time for Chegory to worry his head about this any further because other demands awaited. He (still naked) was whirled down a corridor to a room dizzy with perfume and colour. There he was annointed with olibanum and a sweet ambrosia founded on ambergris. Then a fussy man with rings on his fingers and pearls at his throat was dressing young Chegory in gorgeous silks of startling yellow and sea dragon green.

'Clothes!' protested Chegory. 'Clothes, I had my own clothes, they, they said I'd get them back when I, well, after the bath and things, where are my—'

'You'll get your rags, boy,' said a hard-faced brute from Wen Endex, who seized Chegory as soon as he was dressed and hauled him away to a windowless room. 'Sit!'

'But what—'

'Sit!'

This in a shout of such violence that it sat young Chegory down in the greatest of hurries. His chair was of wood. It was most uncomfortable.

'You know who I am?' said his interrogator.

'A – a – you're from – you're—'

Chegory meant to say that his interlocutor was without a doubt a Yudonic Knight from Wen Endex and that he (Chegory) had the greatest respect imaginable for such men. Thus he meant to speak, but the words refused to come.

'Gods!' said the interrogator. 'What will she drag in next? Boy, I'm Juliet Idaho. Captain of the Praetorian Guard. Now here's what I've got to say. Don't fool with us, boy. We know who you are, and what. As for me, I'm the man who kills you. One false move, that's all it takes. One mistake and you're dead.'

'I, well, I, look, I'm here for a, I don't know what you've been told but I'm here for a banquet, okay, Justina, she – there's a banquet, I'm invited, well, that's what I'm told, okay?'

'A banquet,' said the grim-faced Idaho. 'That's what I'm telling you about. Table manners. Understand?'

Chegory had a sudden vision. A memory! Himself and Olivia at eats in the Analytical Institute. Kicks exchanged under the table. The curry powder spilling. The flying fish sauce slopping everywhichway. When? Only yesterday! But it felt like a million years ago. Like something from another life.

'Yes, yes, surely, manners, okay, what do you think I am, kicking people under the table and everything, you think I'm going to cut up like that at a banquet, you crazy?'

'What's this?' said Juliet Idaho, producing a vicious piece of sharpened metal.

'That, it's a – a—'

'A stab, isn't it? But you eat with your fingers. Get it?'

'With my fingers,' said Chegory. 'Okay, sure, fingers, that's not a problem. Whatever you say.'

'I say fingers. There are stabs by every plate. That's good manners on our lady's part. She shows she trusts her guests with cold steel. But if you actually touch one of those stabs . . .'

'Then what?' said Chegory.

'Do I have to spell it out?'

'I think maybe you should!' said Chegory.

'All right, Ebby. Listen! There's muscle behind you right through the banquet. You touch that stab and . . . whap! Off with your head!'

'But why?' said Chegory.

'To keep you from killing Justina.'

'But why should I want to do that?' said Chegory.

'We're not fooled! We know why you came here!'

'Why?' said Chegory, baffled.

'You're an assassin, aren't you? A trained killer! We know you! You had that knife, didn't you? Oh, you fooled the Empress nicely, but you don't fool me. My men have their orders. You lay so much as a single finger on a piece of cold steel and – wwwhst! Off with your head!'

'The Empress, she, she might not like that,' ventured Chegory.

'Because what?' said Juliet Idaho. 'Because we'd have to wash the tablecloth afterwards? Don't count on it, Ebby! She's not soft in the head. Maybe I am, though, or I wouldn't let you out of here alive. Okay. I'm letting you live. For the moment. But remember – one mistake, one finger out of line, and it's all over. No charge, no trial, no argument. Just wwwhst!'

'Wwwhst,' repeated Chegory.

'That's right, Ebby. Wwwhst – chop! Okay, let's get going, we're late as it is.'

Then Juliet Idaho led young Chegory Guy from the interrogation chamber to the apartments of Justina's major domo. There Uckermark was waiting. Like Chegory, the corpse master had been bathed, massaged, perfumed and adorned in silk.

'So here you are!' said Uckermark. 'I wondered where you'd got to. Come on then. This way, this way!'

Shortly Uckermark was showing Chegory on to the long balcony which ran the length of the southern flank of the pink palace. There a number of elegant people in silk and satin were sipping at sherbet served by obsequious slaves. Sherbet was proffered to Chegory. He took it. Realised he was holding a glass of crystal worth probably more than he made in a year of rock gardening.

He sipped at the sherbet.

Tentatively.

Was it real?

Was he really here?

He was possessed of a near-unshakable sense of unreality. He could not believe that he, a common rock gardener of Ebrell Island descent, was shortly to banquet as a guest of the Empress Justina. Or that he was doomed to be slaughtered if a single move he made was misinterpreted.

Then someone tapped him on the shoulder. He turned and found himself face to face with the Empress herself. He stooped, intending to grovel at her feet, but she caught him, restrained him. Sherbet spilt all over his hands.

'I am not who you think,' she said.

'You are Justina,' said Chegory.

Already he was shaking with fear lest some move he made be misinterpreted, lest Juliet Idaho come roaring up behind him to chop off his head.

'I am Theodora, her sister.'

'Oh,' said Chegory, 'oh, I – I—'

He could see it, now. This woman was heavier of body and feature, her skin coarser, signs of her legendary abuse of her flesh already writ clear in her countenance.

'And you?' said Theodora. 'You, my delightful young chevalier? Who are you?'

'This, my lady,' said Uckermark, intervening with a suavity one would not have expected from a mere corpse master, 'is Chegory Guy, the guest of honour at tonight's banquet.'

'So,' said Theodora. 'So. My sister has chosen, has she? If she unchooses, then . . .'

She looked at Uckermark and much was exchanged between corpse master and imperial sibling in no more than a single glance. Then Theodora was moving away, hunting game not already spoken for, and a scrupulous slave was cleansing spilt sherbet from Chegory's fingers with a piece of fine linen. Chegory's spilt glass had already vanished, plucked neatly from his fingers by a servant so dextrous in appearance and disappearance that he was well-nigh invisible. Before Chegory could think to ask for a replacement it was in his hands already, and the slave who had cleansed those hands had conjured himself elsewhere.

'Come,' said Uckermark. 'Come, let's admire the view. It's not often you get to see Injiltaprajura from this angle, is it?'

'No,' said Chegory. 'No, it's not.'

Chegory then allowed Uckermark to lead him to the balcony, ostensibly so they could admire the view. Was it mere accident that led the corpse master to position himself within earshot of Theodora, who was by then already in conversation with a short, determined man with a wrestler's build? Or had he parlayed his position as some-time paramour of the Empress Justina into something more permanent? Was he her spy, informer, investigator private? Or what?

These questions must remain forever unanswered, for the

corpse master was notoriously close-mouthed about his past, present and future. But the conversation between Theodora and her wrestler can be cited with total accuracy, for auditors were many, and later scandal gave all occasion to recall the interplay between Justina's twin and the flesh of her fancy.

'I am Troldot Turbothot,' said he.

'Oh,' said Theodora. 'And where do you hail from?'

'From the island of Hexagon in the Central Ocean,' said Turbothot. 'My lord, the Baron Farouk of Hexagon, has chosen me to be the hero to circumnavigate the world.'

'Do tell,' said Theodora, with a delicious little simper.

Whereupon Turbothot struck a pose more fit for stage than for cocktail conversation. Then he declaimed thus:

'Seven years ago I departed from Hexagon. I sailed west through storm and hurricane alike. Cannibal isles I landed on where men have two heads each and ride their women as horses. Gaunt cities betrayed their secrets to mine eyes. Huge towers there were of metal built, of metal empty of all but echoes. Through reefs of metal likewise did I ship, while scurvy, drought and bleeding plague did thin my crew thrice daily.

'We ate our dead and ground their bones with wood to make our bread. Our leather then we soaked and that consumed, then ate we the canvas and the very rigging of our ship. But all came right at end, for, favoured by the weather and the gods, we dared with the dying trades to Untunchilamon's shores. There long in the Laitemata did we linger, doomed perforce to while away the days in barter and in mercantile pursuits.

'Then fate to the palace did then my soul compel, where there the grace of fortune did me bid face to face with that fair damsel of enchantment unsurpassed who now before me do mine eyes behold. The vision of her beauty must then my heart console when I to sea anew do take my ship. Across Moana must I dare, yea, to Ashmolea's shores, then in despite of fear ride south to dare my ship around the southernmost point of Argan. Thus must I dare before I head my craft for home.'

So spoke Troldot Turbothot, spouting such stuff and more in effortless torrents. Injiltaprajura later learnt (when interest expressed itself in questions some of Turbothot's crew talked) that Baron Farouk of Hexagon had exiled Turbothot for writing bad verses, for dramatising the same, and, worse, for seducing members of the Family Farouk to admiration of such dramatisation.

Farouk had framed the exile in terms of a quest impossible, but Turbothot was such a fool he had not known the questing proposition to be but a polite invitation for him to remove himself from Hexagon before the baron removed his head from his shoulders. Instead, the versifying clown had sailed to certain death, a most reluctant crew compelled by oath to join him in the venture. Yet, after seven years, some few still lived, in astonished and astonishing defiance of statistical probability.

Their story—

[Here the Originator of this Text yields to temptation and gives in précis the story of the voyage of Turbothot around this planetary orb on which, or so material philosophers allege, we voyage through airless wastes at a velocity at once (such are the paradoxes of this preposterous theory!) immense yet imperceptible. While the Originator's summary thus given takes up a mere three hundred thousand words or so, it has been thought best to delete it on the grounds that most of it is a tissue of manifest lies. Turbothot claimed, for example, to have met with the ostrich, that purely mythological bird which is conjured to have the height of a man, the habits of a chicken and speed (on land, mark, for myth disclaims the power of flight for the creature!) sufficient to outpace a racing stallion. *Drax Lira, Redactor Major.*]

—thus reaching Untunchilamon, there to be marooned by absence of wind in the languorous longueurs of Fistavlir.

Where were we, now?

Ah, yes! Before it fell to me to tell of Turbothot and of

his voyaging we were on the balcony of Justina's pink palace in Injiltaprajura. There Theodora was in conversation with the worthy hero of Hexagon. Perhaps that very day she heard from his own lips something more of the details of his fascinating adventures. Who knows? But what is certain is that the good Theodora shortly disappeared with the Turbothot creature and thereafter was so engaged with him that she quite failed to put in an appearance at the evening's banquet.

Thus Chegory Guy, Theodora's first-preferred, lost his best chance of further acquaintance with Justina's sister and with those intimate delights so freely granted to the thousands. His consolation prize was enjoyment of the view to which Uckermark had led him. A splendid view it was, for he could see right across the city's rooves to the Laitemata Harbour where three ships lay at anchor.

From the palace steps Lak Street descended steadily as it reached away to the waterfront. Chegory could see someone standing on the battlements of the wonder-workers' Cabal House at the intersection of Lak Street, Goldhammer Rise and Skindik Way. Washing was hanging out to dry on the rooves of the Dromdanjerie and Ganthorgruk.

All of Lubos was displayed to Chegory's scrutiny at a glance. He tried to work out which building was Uckermark's corpse shop, but failed entirely. There were so many, many shacks, hovels and blockhouses all scrambled together that it would have taken an entire day to decipher the quarter's geography.

Marthandorthan was easier to fathom since it was amply landmarked by large warehouses which Chegory knew well. He had no trouble finding the lair of his villainous cousin Firfat, or in tracing the route from the dockland quarter up Goldhammer Rise to the Cabal House, and thence up Lak Street to the steps of the palace which lay beneath his very eyes.

A troupe of beggars were on the steps working the crowd of incoming latecomers hastening to be on time for Justina's banquet which would start shortly after the bat bells rang out to announce the end of salahanthara and the start of undokondra.

Chegory raised his eyes.

He looked again down the length of Lak Street and across the sun-fired waters of the Laitemata to the low-humped mound of Jod where even the brilliant marble of the Analytical Institute had assumed a pink tinge in the sunset. Further yet to the south lay the bloodsands of Scimitar where, even as Chegory watched, palm trees were blackening to silhouette as the sun drowned down in the west. Beyond lay the waters of the lagoon. Then there was the Outer Reef where the lazing seas of evening surfed at their leisure. Ever and ever they rose from infinities of sea which stretched away to forevers further yet where sky was fast darkening to stars.

Chegory knew then:

I love this place.

He had an intense sensation of being here, now, located, focused, balanced, present.

Then the bat bells thunderclapped, their shatter-song bursting from the belfries, and Uckermark laid a heavy hand on his shoulder and steered him inside.

The banquet was about to begin.

CHAPTER EIGHTEEN

Justina's palace was large but not infinite. While it did
contain treasury, dungeons, torture chambers (unused since
the time of Wazir Sin), kitchens, bedrooms, a rooftop
swimming pool and so on and so forth, it had only two
large halls. One of these was the Star Chamber, site of legal
hearings of all descriptions. The other was the Grand Hall
where the petitions session had been held during the
afternoon. It was the Grand Hall which was the site of the
night's banquet.

When Chegory and Uckermark entered the Grand Hall
no people had yet seated themselves. The long tables, which
formed three sides of a square, awaited yet. Justina's ebony
throne had been removed to make way for the Table of
Honour, which was that from which the two Tables Lesser
depended. But nobody had removed the starvation cage.
Likewise, the shields of Wen Endex still adorned the walls.
The revellers would disport themselves with those images
of death and destruction ever within glance.

'Where do we sit?' said Chegory. 'Anywhere? Or special
places?'

While the Empress had personally invited him to the
banquet he did not imagine for a moment that he would
be sitting close to her. After all, Ivan Pokrov and Artemis
Ingalawa had both banqueted at the pink palace on
occasions past, and from what little they had said of it
Chegory knew neither of them had been anywhere near the
imperial person.

'Nobody sits till the Empress enters,' said Uckermark.
'Don't worry. You'll be told. Look around, look around.'

With that vague command, Uckermark disengaged himself from his young companion, abandoning Chegory in

favour of conversation with one of the potent contacts he had made inside the palace since his first acquaintance with Justina.

Chegory wandered round the table, unaware that everyone in the room was studying him discretely. Justina's latest! How long would he last? A night? A week? If more than a week, he would be a very miracle worker, for Justina was persistent in her quest for novelty. So had she been since she attained the age of sixteen. Then, while growing up in Galsh Ebrek, she had demonstrated the strength of her appetites—

[A long and weary catalogue has here been deleted on the grounds that this catalogue, together with its attendant gynaecological details, is intrinsically boring. *By Order, Ostik Vo, Master of Philosophy.*]

Chegory did not think of the bedtime ordeal that awaited him, of the moment when Justina would clutch him to her flesh, when he would have to prove his manhood truly or suffer imperial displeasure extreme. No. He did not think of it because, like all humans, he had a tremendous capacity for denying reality. Despite Uckermark's hints and outright declarations, and despite the implications of everything which had happened to him since his arrival in the palace, young Chegory still thought he would escape from the palace with his virginity intact.

Thus our Ebrell Islander thought not of bed, but worried instead about the banquet. How would he cope with the intricacies of the grandiose protocol such an occasion would surely demand? The table itself intimidated him. Crystal glittering and stabs likewise ashine. Linen as white as the snow which lies on the ground here in the Mountains of the Moon – not that the comparison to snow would have occurred to Chegory, who had never seen such a substance.

'If you would excuse me for a moment, sir.'

This from a waiter busy distributing sheets of parchment. One for every place, to join the small dishes of pineapple chunks and coconut squares and the fragrant mosquito coils softly smoking. Chegory stepped back from the table.

'Thank you, sir,' said the waiter, putting down another parchment.

This was Chegory's first encounter with a proper waiter, and the young Ebrell Islander was so disconcerted by the man's lordly manner that he took him for a high-ranking civil servant at the very least. Nevertheless, he plucked up courage sufficient to ask:

'What are those?'

'Those, sir, are mosquito coils.'

'I mean the – the document things, what you're giving out.'

Chegory asked because he could not read the Toxteth scriptwork which adorned the parchments. As he could only read and write Ashmarlan he was virtually illiterate for the purposes of practical life on Untunchilamon.

'These, sir, are prescriptions,' said the waiter.

'Prescriptions?' said Chegory.

'Indeed. For how can we have wine without prescriptions? Further, how can we have a banquet without wine?'

'Prescriptions,' said Chegory, still puzzling it out. 'You mean – you mean all these people are sick?'

'They are indeed,' said the waiter. 'A tragedy, young sir! There is, you see, a staggering degree of ill health in Untunchilamon's ruling class. Why, here is Lord Idaho's script. Two beers for his poor digestion, five glasses of wine for the pain of his war wounds and a double brandy to help with his flat feet.'

'Flat feet?' said Chegory. 'You can cure flat feet with brandy?'

'I, young sir?' said the waiter, whisking further prescriptions into place. 'I am but a waiter, hence nothing I can heal. But doctors, young sir – ah, their skills would grace a very miracle worker!'

'You mean,' said Chegory, following the swift-moving waiter, 'they can really cure flat feet with alcohol?'

'Cure?' said the waiter. 'A strong word, surely! For it implies a degree of certain resolution which your bravest philosophers will tell you is quite impossible in a world so

202

chancy. Nay, young sir. Your best physician can often work his miracles, yet cannot attempt such feats impossible. Speak not of cures. Speak rather of treatment.'

'Treatment?' persisted Chegory.

'Certainly! Balm, soothing, comfort. For such is alcohol the world's best medicine. Hence here we have in plenty treatments for ague and palsy, for goitre and hernia, the multiplication of chins and the distension of the belly, the loss of potency or an excess of the same, for snakebite, old wounds and varicose veins, for fits of elation and for dooms of despair.'

By now the waiter's progress had taken him almost to the centre of the Table of Honour.

'Here sits Uckermark,' said the waiter, putting down a parchment. 'The corpse master. I know him well. He stuffed my grandmother three years ago. Still she looks as good as new.'

The waiter moved a single place closer to the centre. He stood with the starvation cage just behind him and scanned the parchment in his hand.

'Young sir,' said he, 'are you by chance a victim of anaemia?'

'So I'm told,' said Chegory doubtfully.

'If a doctor told you, it must be true. An Ebrell Islander, thus it says here. Chegory Guy by name. The name is your own?'

'It is,' said Chegory.

'Then here you sit,' said the waiter, and with a flourish he deposited Chegory's prescription in the place to the left of Uckermark's.

'Then whose place is that?' said Chegory, as the waiter deposited the next parchment.

'This?' said the waiter. 'This place belongs to a lady fair who suffers from . . . let us say insomnia. That is the polite way of putting it, is it not?'

Then he winked, which was quite unprofessional of him, then went on his way.

Chegory wandered off to find Uckermark, but had not

yet located the corpse master when trumpets flared and silenced all chatter in the Grand Hall. In came guards bearing naked scimitars. Then the Empress Justina entered upon the banqueting chamber. She waved gaily to her subjects as she made her way to her place.

Which was . . .

Which was the central seat at the Table of Honour.

Right by that assigned to Chegory Guy.

But surely, surely . . .

'A mistake,' said Chegory, as someone grabbed his arm. 'There's been a mistake.'

'You're telling me,' said Juliet Idaho. 'Come on! Don't keep the Empress waiting!'

So saying, the Yudonic Knight steered Chegory toward the Table of Honour. He drove his fingers deep into the young man's bicep.

'Remember what I told you!'

'Stabs,' said Chegory. 'Yes, yes, stabs, I remember, not to touch, no steel, no touching. Eat with my fingers, everything, fish, soup, the lot.'

'Eat soup with your spoon, fool!' said Idaho. 'But the rest with your fingers, certainly. One hand on a stab, and that's it! Wwwhst! Off with your head! See the muscle?'

'I see it,' said Chegory.

He saw the scimitarists standing to either side of the starvation cage and knew they were the muscle to which Idaho referred. They could be upon him in a moment. Slicing off his head!

'So watch yourself,' said Idaho, his threat pitched low, meant for Chegory's ears alone.

Then he gave the Ebrell Islander a push which sent him staggering forward. The Empress Justina smiled on him. At all three tables the guests were standing by their chairs. Waiting to be seated. Chegory felt dizzy. Panic-stricken. He longed to run, flee, sprint from the pink palace and bury himself forever in the deepest part of the underworld.

Chegory reached the table.

A servant pulled out his chair.

What now? Presumably the Empress would seat herself, then her guests would take their places.

Chegory waited.

Beaded sweat rolled down his forehead.

'Sit!' hissed Uckermark, his mouth but a fingerlength from Chegory's ear.

What was right? To sit, or not to sit? Surely he couldn't—

'You're guest of honour,' whispered Uckermark frantically. 'You! Sit sit sit!'

Chegory sat.

The rest of the guests followed suit with a great scraping of chairs, soon followed by a swelling murmur of remark, expostulation and outright gossip. Still the Empress was standing. Was something wrong? Chegory risked a quick glance over his shoulder. The muscle to either side of the starvation cage had not moved. But it was there. Ready. Waiting. The muscle was in the form of two huge men with bullock-breaking thews, their faces impassive as they stood leaning on the hilts of bare-bladed scimitars, the points of which rested on blocks of cork to preserve their sharpness.

Still, still the Empress stood. The chair to her left was empty. Was she waiting for another guest?

Round the table there was a regular tinkling clatter. What? People were pulling off rings, brooches and other baubles. Tossing them so they fell amidst crystal glasses, polished silver, white porcelain. Chegory, who was ignorant of the customs Justina's father had brought with him from Galsh Ebrek, was totally incapable of fathoming the import of this simple ceremony.

The last ring was, temporarily, discarded.

Then, and only then, did Justina sit, exhaling a happy sigh as she ensconced herself in the chair next to Chegory Guy. He stood instantly, as a sign of respect.

'Sit!' said the Empress in a peremptory tone. Then, as he complied, she went on (more mildly): 'Silly boy! You didn't think you could run away, did you?'

To Chegory's surprise, even at banquet she spoke in Toxteth. Now all acknowledge that the language of Wen

Endex is good enough for war, at which the Yudonic Knights are expert. Yet it is entirely unfit for social intercourse at the highest levels, for it lacks the subtle honorifics and diminutives by which the ever-hinting Janjuladoola allows lessers in their every utterance to honour betters and betters to impress upon lessers the inferiority of the latter.

'My lady,' said Chegory, 'I exist only to serve.'

This he had hastily rehearsed but a few moments before, and – better still! – he had rehearsed it in Janjuladoola. For 'my lady' he used Janjuladoola's 'thayalamantalajora', which translates literally as 'goddess surpassing'. From the nine forms of 'I' which were available to him he had chosen (correctly) the word 'varacasondundra', literally 'myself a worm'. It came out perfectly.

Still, even though the Ebrell Islander surprised the universe by choosing language proper and words correct for this pretty little offering, it must be observed that what he came out with was clichéd and unoriginal in the extreme. But then, Chegory Guy had no prior experience in dealing with imperial power, and must perforce fall back on stereotyped dialogue stolen straight from the legends of hero-princes and such.

While young Chegory was still complimenting himself on his successful survival of the first of his many trials in the halls of grace, Justina's albinotic ape Vazzy was brought to the table and installed in the previously empty chair to the left of the Empress. On this occasion the installation included the attachment of the creature to its specially weighted throne by means of leather ankle cuffs. At the last banquet, Vazzy had indulged his passion for staging tournaments at table once too often, and Justina had at last come to the conclusion that a rampaging ape is not an ornament to an evening's entertainment.

Once installed, the imperial favourite regarded Chegory quizzically, then extended its paw.

'Well, Chegory,' said the Empress. 'Where are your manners?'

Chegory sought for words but found none, therefore did but stare at Empress and ape, acting for all the world as if his tongue had been tied after the manner of the torturers of Lower Sladvonia. Given his lack of social sophistication, his attack of verbal constipation is understandable. After all, the hero-prince legends which had supplied his dialogue till then make no mention of the niceties of protocol which arise when a common rock gardener has social intercourse with an ape imperial.

'Go on!' said Justina. 'Give him your hand.'

Chegory was to – to what? Cut off his hand and present it to the ape as a token of fealty? He looked around wildly. Guards in their frowning menace stood but a footfall away from him, their scimitars at the ready. Vazzy rescued Chegory from his indecision. The pink-eyed ape lunged, grabbed Chegory's hand and hauled on it. Chegory hauled back. Sweating. Panting. Biting his lip. His thick Ebrell Island fingers were now directly above Justina's lap. They were but a finger length from – from—

Gods!

'You silly boy!' said Justina, with a windchime laugh. 'Shake his hand and he'll let yours go!'

Shake his hand? Why? Chegory had no idea, but nevertheless jerked the ape's paw several times. To his relief, Vazzy then released him. Chegory snatched his hand away as if it had been scalded. He slumped back in his seat. A solicitous attendant mopped away the sweat now streaming from his brow. Chegory endured these ministrations without protest, then realised a waiter was questioning him.

'What?' he said.

Chegory was startled by his own over-loud voice, by the note of shark-flavoured brutality in the single vocable. A moment later he realised (to his horror!) that he had asked his question in his native Dub, instead of phrasing his query in fragrant Janjuladoola or (second-best, surely – but the Empress used it) good honest Toxteth.

The waiter repeated his question using the politest forms

of Janjuladoola imaginable, yet still managing to convey a weary sense of infinite superiority:

'Mead, sir? Or wine?'

'A – a physician has prescribed mead for my anaemia,' said Chegory, stumbling slightly as he rendered this simplicity in Janjuladoola. He had conceived an immediate fear of the waiter, which was quite natural given the waiter's massive sense of superiority and Chegory's increasing nervousness.

'Those doctors will over-prescribe!' said Justina. 'Give him the wine, it's much safer.'

'My lady has a degree from the College of Medicine,' murmured the wine waiter, 'therefore one trusts her judgement implicitly.'

The qualification in question was an honorary degree, but the waiter made no mention of this as he poured wine for Chegory (the guest of honour), then for the Empress, and then (since the ape was in possession of a medical certificate signed by the Veterinarian Imperial) for Vazzy.

'Thank you,' said Chegory, truly grateful that the Empress had descended (as it were) from her seat amidst the stars to deal so expediently with the waiter.

He congratulated himself for saying his thanks in Janjuladoola. Then was horrorstruck. He had used the familiar form! He had said efkarindorenskomiti, the word by which a friend thanks a friend, or (for this is a very familiar form indeed!) which a lover uses to supplement a kiss just a few moments after orgasm. The word he should have used to express his thanks was (of course) dundaynarbardinadorsklo, for thus and only thus should a slave or similar address a power imperial.

Such lapses of etiquette are not to be taken lightly. In the court of Aldarch the Third (who, for all that can be said against him, is ever at pains to improve the manners of his people) many have been instantly executed for lapses in protocol far less extreme. But the Empress Justina merely laughed. She was delighted!

'I'm so glad we're getting to know each other better,' she said.

Though she spoke in Toxteth, her words implied that she had caught every nuance of Chegory's Janjuladoola. So what could he say? That he didn't mean it like that at all?

'Thank you,' he said, helplessly.

Only this time he said it in Toxteth, a language which offered him far fewer opportunities to make those social gaffes which are almost inevitable when an inept linguist endeavours to grapple with the delicious intricacies of Janjuladoola.

Before Chegory had a chance to embarrass himself further, Justina's white ape hooted in pleasurable anticipation. A white-faced figure gorgeously adorned in robes embroidered with moray eels and scorpion fish was approaching the Empress. However, the ape was to be disappointed, for Aquitaine Varazchavardan remembered what had happened at the last banquet, and halted well out of ape-grabbing distance.

'Hello there,' cooed the Empress Justina, with a sly smile upon her lips. 'What can we do for you today, young man?'

Varazchavardan was not young, otherwise he might have lost control of his temper there and then. Instead, the albinotic sorcerer cleared his throat and said, as banquet protocol compelled him to:

'My most honoured lady, as Master of Law I ask on behalf of myself and of your assembled guests that we be excused the ritual of confession.'

'I don't know,' said Justina. 'What do you think, Chegory? Should we spare the man confession?'

This comment most naturally brought the attention of the Master of Law to bear on young Chegory Guy, who could but stare helplessly at Varazchavardan. The terrified Ebrell Islander looked for all the world like a dormouse surprised by a cobra.

All Chegory could think of was the scene Downstairs where the sorcerer had fought his way free from the Malud marauders who had taken him prisoner. Varazchavardan had sent fire shooting outwards from his body, with dual consequences. First, the elderly pirate holding a knife to Varazchavardan's throat had let him go. Second, the liquor with which the floor was awash had ignited, causing the sorcerer to be almost instantly engulfed in flames.

Obviously, he had survived.

Equally obviously, to judge from the look he gave young Chegory, he remembered.

'Well, Chegory?' said Justina gently. 'Do we spare him confessions or not?'

'Sp— spare me,' said the terrified Chegory. 'Please!'

'He spares you,' said Justina to Varazchavardan. 'Isn't that nice of him? One day, we must spare you not. I'd be most interested in hearing your confessions, Vazzy darling. Most interested.'

Aquitaine Varazchavardan concealed his intense dislike of the insulting diminutive with which the Empress Justina had addressed him. Instead, he bowed very low, then said:

'My lady's wisdom is exceeded only by her personal grace and beauty.'

Then Varazchavardan bowed lower yet, then turned about-face. As the Master of Law began to walk away, Justina offered her ape a bit of coconut.

'Vazzy,' she said, pitching her voice to carry.

Varazchavardan turned, only to see Justina's ape accepting the proffered delicacy from the fingers imperial. Justina smiled sweetly at Varazchavardan. He stared back. If looks could kill, the Empress Justina would have been crisped to the bone then and there. If looks could kill, there would have been instant genocide on Untunchilamon. Sailors would have screamed aloud as they met a mortal end on ships far out upon the striding seas. A swathe of devastation would have cut its way across entire continents. Princes in cities far distant would have fallen from thrones of glory with blood by the bucketful vomiting from their throats. In caves far deep within the mountains huge dragons would have roared in strenuous agony, then kicked in pain and rage, and then expired. Such was the look which Varazchavardan bestowed upon Justina.

The Empress smiled again, every bit as sweetly as before, and Varazchavardan turned and stalked away. Whereupon Justina's ape picked up a mosquito coil and hurled it at the retreating Master of Law. It hit Varazchavardan in the back, provoking a little tittering from some of the less sophisticated wits sitting at table, but the wonderworker ignored the onslaught and walked on as if nothing had happened.

'Now now,' said Justina, in tones of mild reproof. 'That's very naughty, Vazzy. You mustn't do things like that.'

Whereupon Vazzy grinned prodigiously, hooted thrice, then began to devour the saucer of pineapple chunks which the Empress Justina pushed his way. Meanwhile, an aloof waiter promenaded into the half-open square between the three long banquet tables, retrieved the still-smoking mosquito coil then retired with the offending object.

It is to be noted that albinotic apes are very rare and hard to come by, that Aquitaine Varazchavardan had long been in Justina's service before she acquired her pet, and that the privilege of naming the animal had been hers and hers alone. Chegory, who was ignorant of this, and innocent enough to presume the confusion of names to be a coincidence, had nevertheless perceived Varazchavardan's anger. Indeed, he had experienced a (possibly psychosomatic) chest pain as he saw Varazchavardan's clear-writ wrath.

Chegory, in his ignorance, could only presume that it was the provocation of his own presence which had so angered the Master of Law, and that even now Varazchavardan would be planning a special doom for the hapless Ebrell Islander who had so excited his anger. He turned to Uckermark, meaning to ask him for advice, but the corpse master was intent on the over-perfumed woman to his right, a luscious young thing who was smattering away to him as if he were her lover true.

'Chegory,' said Justina. 'Your wine. You haven't even touched it yet.'

'I – I—'

'You're not going to refuse your medicine, are you? Be a good boy. Drink it up. There's plenty more where that came from.'

This was tantamount to an invitation to get roaring drunk. Indeed, to judge from the speed at which fellow guests were demolishing their prescription medicine, and the alacrity with which their empty glasses were being refilled, such behaviour would have passed without remark. Nevertheless, Chegory sipped most cautiously at his own glass.

'You look worried, my dear,' said Justina. 'What is it?'

'Nothing, nothing,' said Chegory.

'Not the wine, I hope?'

'No, no, it's – it's lovely wine.'

'Then . . . the table things, Chegory? You're not worried about those, are you? First will be soup, that's what the spoons are for. Then a meat dish. For that we use stabs, then – ah, but here's the soup! I do hope it's all right. It's the special creation of my new chef, you know. Pelagius Zozimus, that's his name.'

'Zozimus!' said Chegory desperately, seizing his opportunity and plunging right in. 'There's, there's something I have to tell you about him. He's not a chef at all, he's an elf, an elven lord, that's what he is, Downstairs, I saw him Downstairs with sworders with him, all in bright armour he was, really, truly, believe me.'

'Oh Chegory!' said Justina, waving away his desperation to the tune of a tinkling laugh. 'You do amuse me! An elf? Chegory darling, there are no such things as elves. An elven lord, with an army in armour Downstairs? A delightful conceit, my dearest, but save it for my amusement till I've had a bit more to drink.'

Thus Chegory's opportunity to denounce Zozimus arrived, was seized, and came to nothing. His soup was set before him and he began to eat, sampling each spoonful of the nutritious broth with the same caution he had used when trying the wine.

'We do have foodtasters, you know,' said Justina,

observing his hesitation. 'Here, give me that.' So saying, she exchanged bowls with him. 'There! You trust that? It's meant for the lips imperial. Eat, my darling! You want to keep your strength up, don't you?'

'Yes, my lady,' said Chegory.

Then blushed with such fury that his embarrassment visibly overwhelmed the native red of his skin. Justina laughed uproariously, then drank of her wine, then coughed, choked and almost died, for she was laughing still as she drank.

Chegory got through the soup (very good flying fish soup, thickened with sea urchin roe). Then the soup bowls were whisked away and plates of mixed meats materialised in their place. The chef had excelled himself. On Chegory's plate there were bits of cat, dog, monkey, rat, goat, banana frog, crow, vulture, groper, gecko and lizard. His mouth watered. His hand automatically reached for the stab. But just before his fingers fell on the lethal steel he remembered – and wrenched his hand away as if it had been burnt.

Justina's stab was already at work. It flashed to left and to right as she hunted succulent fragments of fine-chopped luxury. She popped her first skewer-load into her mouth, sucked it off, then chewed. She was sweating as she ate, for she was a very fleshy woman, and both air and meat were hot. Chegory was sweating also. He had yet to touch his meat.

'You have many girlfriends, I suppose,' said Justina, pausing between skewer-loads.

'None at the moment,' said Chegory, fearing Olivia Qasaba might be brutally disposed of if Justina learnt of her existence.

'None?' said Justina. 'What a tragedy! Young women have no taste. No taste at all. Or is it your work that puts them off?'

'Work?'

'In the corpse shop.'

Only then did Chegory remember that the Empress

Justina believed him to be apprenticed to the corpse master Uckermark. She thought he worked all day with bowel and brain, with the stench of corpses unclean, stuffing, embalming or dismembering as required.

'The, um, well, job, it's a job, okay, no job no money no food and all that, but, ah, oh well, I suppose I – I wish the people weren't so, so . . . well, so dead.'

Too fast, too fast, he was talking too fast, making a fool of himself. What would the Empress think? He must slow himself, slow down, one word to a mouthful.

'Pah!' said Justina. 'You dislike the dead? Then what are we eating? Why, dead meat! Dead frogs, dead fish, dead birds. Corpses. Carcasses. Are we not animals? With the appetites of animals? The desires? The lusts?'

'Some of us,' said Chegory carefully.

'You're not a castrato, are you?'

This, coming from the Empress, was a joke. She had already perused Chegory's medical file. She knew as much about him as a wife of ten years – or more. But Chegory thought the query was in earnest.

'As it happens,' said Chegory, 'no, I'm not a . . . a castrato.'

He was feeling more and more uncomfortable. Once more he wanted to flee. He was intensely aware of Justina dragonising him. As if he were prey.

'A vegetarian, then?' said Justina, since Chegory was still abstaining from his food.

'No, not that either,' said Chegory.

Then realised his mistake. By pleading vegetarianism he could have excused himself from tackling the meat dish which he must now surely feed upon lest he cause offence. He plucked a piece of banana frog from his plate. Munched it.

'Not with your fingers, Chegory darling,' said Justina. 'Use the stab. That's what it's there for. To eat meat.'

'You'll have to excuse him,' said Uckermark, momentarily disengaging his attention from the coquette to his right. 'He's not versed in his table manners.'

'Ah, but we'll teach him,' said Justina. 'We'll teach him . . . everything!'

Corpse master and Empress exchanged a laugh. Then the coquette claimed Uckermark once more and Chegory was on his own.

'That stab,' said Justina impatiently. 'Pick it up!'

Chegory hesitated still.

'Here,' she said, picking up his stab and forcing it into his reluctant fingers. 'Hold it like that, see? Now stick it into the meat. There! Easy, wasn't it?'

'Yes,' said Chegory.

Blurting out the word in blurred tones but a heartbeat from tears or panic. He hunched his head down, his shoulders up, desperately trying to make himself a more difficult target for the decapitating scimitar he expected to strike at any moment.

'Try it again,' said Justina in her most encouraging voice.

Chegory complied.

'Good, good!' said the Empress. 'You see? You can do it if you try. Very well! Now feed me!'

'Now . . . ?'

'Feed me! You know! Stab in the meat, meat in my mouth. Come on, Chegory darling. It's fun!'

'I . . . I can't. I mustn't!'

'Of course you can! Of course you must! It's an imperial command, isn't it? We can't have high treason at table, can we now? Come on, Chegory! Stab in meat, meat in my mouth! Let's do it by the numbers, shall we? Number one, stab in meat.'

Chegory tried to obey. But his hand refused to obey his will. So the Empress Justina closed her own hot, sweating fingers about his hand and guided his stab into a piece of meat. Then pulled Chegory's stab-holding hand to her mouth. She sucked off the meat. Grinned at him.

'Easy, isn't it? You do it now.'

Hesitantly, he complied. He raised cold steel to the mouth of the Empress. She opened her lips, revealing a dangling uvula, a tongue, a dozen ragged brown teeth, a glistening cavity where food fragments danced amidst saliva. Her lips accepted a piece of dog liver from his stab.

Then Justina skewered a titbit from her own plate and fed it to Chegory. He returned the compliment. They executed this joint manoeuvre again. Then again.

'My! What white fangs you have!' said Justina.

'I chew pandanus,' said Chegory.

'Ah yes,' said Justina. 'That's the way to keep them in order. Pandanus in plenty – and stay way from the sugarcane.'

'Yes, my lady,' said Chegory.

'Call me Juzzy,' said Justina. 'And I'll call you . . . Cheggy. You like that name?'

'I . . . um . . . yes, my lady. Cheggy will do fine.'

'Splendid!' said Justina, and opened her mouth to accept another fragment of meat.

Chegory was starting to get confident. He glanced at the scimitarists. They had not moved. The muscle men were still standing immobile, the points of their razorblade weapons still resting on blocks of cork.

'That's good,' said Justina, as Chegory fed her once again. 'You're getting the hang of it. Now faster!'

'Faster?'

'Yes, faster! You know. Speed, Chegory, speed! Fun!'

Chegory did not think it fun at all, but nevertheless hastened his fingers. Justina accelerated her own hand in response. From plate to mouth flew their stabs. In – out! In – out! Swift as lightning their dancing steel flashed. Cat meat! Frog meat! Poultry! Dog! To lips to mouth to lips to—

Home went Chegory's steel!

'Aagh!'

The Empress Justina wrenched her head back.

Chegory had stabbed her in the lower lip.

'You cut me!' said Justina.

Chegory dropped his stab. The bloodstained steel tinkled to his plate. The Empress Justina was clutching her lip. Chegory could not breathe, or speak, or move. Slowly the

Empress withdrew her bloodstained hand. She turned her terrible eyes upon young Chegory Guy. She announced his doom:

'You must kiss it better.'

'I must . . . ?'

The entire banqueting hall was silent. Even the waiters were watching. Justina placed one fleshy hand round the back of Chegory's neck and drew him toward her. He could not resist. A roar of applause erupted from the guests as Chegory's lips touched those of his Empress. Still she pulled him on and in. Hot and wet was her mouth, hot and wet, her tongue forcing its way into his own oral cavity as her hand fondled his neck in a rhythm suggestive of greater pleasures yet to come.

Then, mercifully, she released him.

'Ah!' she said. 'Pure pleasure, is it not?'

'Indeed, my lady,' said Chegory, hot and shaken, sweating and trembling, dazed and bestaggered.

'Juzzy,' said the Empress Justina. 'Have you forgotten already, Cheggy my love?'

'I . . . I'm sorry, uh, Juzzy.'

'That's better! But don't forget again!'

Chegory promised most sincerely that he would not forget – and the banquet proceeded.

CHAPTER NINETEEN

When the meat dish was finished Chegory got to his feet
and retreated to the sanctuary of the latrines. He had drunk
but a third of a glass of wine yet felt decidedly unsteady on
his feet. His sweat had overwhelmed the perfumes with
which he had been so liberally annointed after his bath.
This banqueting was hard work!

In the latrines he was long fumbling with the codpiece
built into the unfamiliar silks in which he had been dressed.
At last he retrieved his anatomy from the complexities of
his new garments. Then leaned his head against the cold
marble of the wall as he pissed into a bloodstone gutter.
Uckermark joined him while he was so engaged.

'How's it going?' said the corpse master as he pulled out
his shlong.

'That woman's going to rape me,' groaned Chegory.

'No!' said Uckermark, pissing prodigiously. 'You're imagining things. The Empress? With you? Who do you think
you are?'

Chegory looked sideways at Uckermark and saw the
corpse master was grinning.

'Help me!' said Chegory, desperately.

'You really want help?' said Uckermark. 'What's it
worth?'

'My undying gratitude,' said Chegory.

'Very well then,' said Uckermark, buttoning up his
codpiece. 'I'll tell you two things which might help you a
lot.'

'What?'

'First, you're supposed to enjoy it. So whatever happens,
show some enthusiasm! All right? Good!'

'And second . . . ?'

'She likes to be licked,' said Uckermark, washing his hands in the flow of water outgulping from a golden goldfish.

'Licked?' said Chegory.

'You understand, don't you?'

'I'm a dumb Ebby,' said Chegory. 'I don't understand anything.'

'Then listen . . .' said Uckermark.

The gist of his account is—

[Here a ten-thousand-word disquisition on a certain subject has been deleted on the orders of the Chief Censor. Need we state the reason?]

—and thus bring the woman to a pitch of delight unobtainable by any other means.

'Well,' said Chegory doubtfully, once he had received this detailed intelligence. 'Well . . . thank you, I suppose.'

'Relax,' said Uckermark, slapping him on the back. 'You'll be all right once she gets you into bed.'

'But – but – there's uh, um, there's impotence, I might be impotent, or, ah, pregnancy, what if someone gets pregnant, or, or, you know, venereal diseases, she, she's . . .'

'She commands every scimitar within this fair city of Injiltaprajura,' said Uckermark calmly. 'That's what you've got to worry about! Not planting an egg in her womb or picking up some disease which might kill you five years from now, or then again might not. Come! We delay!'

With that he hustled Chegory back to the feast. The hapless Cheggy hesitated at the fateful portal of the banqueting hall, then, knowing he had no alternative, plunged into the by-now-drunken uproar and rejoined his beloved Juzzy at table.

'Wine!' she commanded. 'Drink! You're getting left behind by everyone else!'

Chegory drank. His glass was refilled. Then, at imperial command, he needs must drink again. Dishes came and went. He ate of them scarcely without tasting. The fevered hubbub roared incomprehensible in his ears like something out of nightmare. From time to time an over-englutted guest would raise a demanding hand. A waiter would rush forward with a portable vomitorium into which the guest would disgorge, the better to make room for the next course. Chegory was shocked the first time he saw this, and was shocked all the more when the Empress herself made use of the same expedient.

'Ah!' she said, patting her midriff. 'That feels better!'

'I'm sure it does,' muttered Cheggy darling.

Then seized his glass and drained it manfully.

A refill of his prescription was arranged on the instant. If he did have anaemia then it should be well and truly cured (or at least treated!) by the time the banquet ended – unless he died of his medicine in the interim.

By the time the last course arrived young Chegory felt as if he was floating on the waves of noise which arose from the drunken nobility of Injiltaprajura. The last course was ice-cream, a concoction made of fine-sliced ice mixed with goat's milk and shredded coconut then frozen. Chegory tried to spoon the ice-cream into his mouth, but his hand shook, and the incompliant substance globbed from the implement on to his lap.

'Oh Cheggy darling!' said Justina with great concern. 'You have a palsy! Waiter! More wine for the guest of honour!'

At Justina's command, Chegory's glass was topped up, even though it was almost full to start with.

'I think,' said Chegory, in a very deliberate voice, 'I've had enough.'

'But,' said Justina, 'the palsy! Besides – is your anaemia cured?' She pinched one of his fingernails till the flesh beneath the nail blanched white. 'No! Look, you're almost bloodless! You can't stop taking your medicine till you're cured, can you now?'

So Chegory drank yet more.

He was well and truly feeling the side effects of his medicine. His ice-cream stumbled from spoon to table, to lap, to floor, or sprawled down his chin to his silks of yellow and green. He had to escape before he overdosed entirely and passed out. But how? Drunken inspiration seized him. He clutched his chest.

'Angina,' he gasped.

The Empress Justina laughed uproariously, and whacked him on the back.

'There now, my waggish little fellow!' she said. 'Does that feel better?'

'I'm afraid,' said Chegory, doing his best to imitate the wheeze of a dying man, 'that it . . . it doesn't.'

'Oh my darling Cheggy!' said Justina in alarm. 'Are you really ill?'

'Yes,' said Chegory. 'Yes, yes.'

'Then your darling Juzzy will kiss it better,' said Justina.

She proceeded to do just that, till Chegory abandoned resistance and declared himself cured. Even then Justina gave him one last kiss, for luck. The guests paid no attention to any of this activity for those still capable of cognition were intent on a disturbance at the hall's main entrance.

'Armed men!' said Chegory.

'Yes,' said Justina carelessly. 'Doubtless coming to chop off your head. To make the soup, you know. Soup for tomorrow's lunch.'

Chegory lurched from his chair. But Justina grabbed him and hauled him back.

'Sit down, silly boy! It's a joke. Look, they're bringing me a prisoner. The bullman, is it? No, it's—'

'By the looks of it,' said the corpse master Uckermark, 'Log Jaris has some captives. You may find this very, very interesting.'

Soon three prisoners of Ashdan race (or, as they would have called themselves, of the Malud) had been forced into the open square made by the three banqueting tables. They were the pirates from Asral.

'What have we here?' said Justina.

The bullman Log Jaris, who had a leather pouch at his side, advanced, bowed very low, then straightened up and said:

'My lady fair, may I present to you three pirates from

Asral. The old one is Al-ran Lars, the young one is Arnaut and the one of weightlifting build is Tolon. By their own confession they are the thieves who took the wishstone from the treasure.'

'Where did you find them?' said Justina.

'Downstairs, my lady,' said Log Jaris.

'What on earth were they doing down there?' said Justina. 'The wishstone was found missing yesterday morning. They've had five quarters or more to run elsewhere.'

'They tried to run, my lady,' said Log Jaris. 'However, they were caught by the demon of Jod, the notorious Shabble, who herded them this way and that through the underworld until they were lost beyond their own recovery. They escaped from Shabble by subterfuge but were thereafter unable to find their way out. I caught them myself when I went hunting with some friends and a pack of dogs.'

'Excellent work!' said Justina. 'Have you the wishstone with you?'

'My lady,' said Log Jaris.

He reached into the leather pouch that hung by his side and produced the wishstone itself. The glittering bauble shone in the light of chandeliers as he handed it over to the Empress Justina. She accepted it eagerly.

'Oh,' she said, fondling the facets of the glittering triakisoctahedron, 'it's so nice to have it back. I was so upset when I heard it was gone. Thank you, Log Jaris. In time you will be suitably rewarded. In the meantime – you must join us at banquet. Waiters! Throw out some of those drunks! Make room for Log Jaris! A chair for our friend! I know – bring in my throne! Let the bullman have my throne as a token of my esteem for him.'

This was very tactful of the Empress. Far more tactful than simply saying that no ordinary chair could be sure of supporting the bullman's bulk.

'As for the pirate people,' said Justina, 'put them in the starvation cage for the time being. We'll decide what to do with them later.'

So the Malud marauders were herded into the starvation cage just behind the Empress. They were locked in and the key to their cage was, as law and protocol required, presented to the Empress. Sweating waiters, their poise temporarily vanquished, hauled Justina's ebony throne into the banquet hall, and Log Jaris was then seated on this.

'What a delightful turn of events,' said Justina, placing both the key and the much-fondled wishstone on the table in front of her.

How Chegory longed to get his hands on the wishstone! Just for a few moments! Even though the conjuror Odolo had told him this bauble granted no wishes, he yet yearned to put its powers to the test.

'It doesn't work, you know,' said Justina, seeing his gaze and interpreting it accurately.

'Are you sure?' said Chegory.

'Positive,' said Justina. 'I tried it just now – and not for the first time, either. I wished I was sixteen once more. I wished I could lose some weight – enough, say, to make myself half a dozen coconuts lighter. I wished for Varaz-chavardan to turn into a frog, and I wished Log Jaris to have human form once more. I know he's not happy as he is.'

'You know Log Jaris?' said Chegory, truly amazed at this.

'Oh, I know everyone, everyone,' said Justina. 'Why, we even know each other, don't we? You and I. We'll know each other better yet my dear before the night is out. You really want to make a wish, Cheggy darling? Then touch! Wish! Imagine! Dare!'

With trembling hands Chegory reached out and touched the wishstone. It was warm. It vibrated softly beneath his fingertips. Internal rainbows flared, dissolved, reformed and flared again. Chegory closed his eyes.

He wished.

He wished not to be red. He wished he could be Ashdan black so he could marry Olivia and escape with her to Ashmolea, there to perfect his mathematical studies at one of the great universities such as that at Fardrendoko.

[Fardrendoko: literally (in Slandolin) 'Ford-of-(the)-ox'. Large city in Ashmolea. Famous as home of Ashmolean Museum, one of the great cultural institutions of which the people of Ashmolea South are so proud. *Oris Baumgage, Fact Checker Minor.*]

He wished then for his mother's resurrection and for the undoing of all the death and suffering his people had suffered during the pogrom launched by Wazir Sin. For a reversal of rape, torture, mutilation and execution. For a reversal also of the long years of fear and exile during which he had nightly imagined that dawn would bring raiders in overwhelming strength to encompass his death.

But my mother especially.

Especially my mother.

Alive again . . .

'Why, Cheggy!' said Justina in concern. 'You're crying!'

'Just . . . I'm just drunk,' said Chegory, taking his hand away from the wishstone.

Then he broke down entirely and wept without ceasing till the Empress Justina rose from the table and led him away, leaving the wishstone to look after itself. Out through a back door they went. Then, with armed guards trailing them at a discreet distance, they made their way by one shortcut and another to Justina's quarters.

Chegory scarcely noticed where he was. Scarcely took in the padded luxury of furnishings and wall hangings, the gold and silk, the leather and silver, the glittering lamps and the huge mirrors of fabulous worth. Justina took an amphora and poured a bowlful of cold water. She bade Chegory wash his face. He did so, and his tears eased.

'What is it?' said Justina, her arm about him.

'My . . . my mother.'

'Is she poorly?'

'She's . . . she's . . .'

No words then, only tears.

'I see,' said Justina, soothing him, soothing him, patting his back softly, gently. 'Was it . . . was it in the days of Sin?'

Chegory nodded wordlessly.

'I'm sorry,' said Justina. 'I'm sorry. But it's over now. You're safe now.'

'But,' said Chegory, the word blurring through tears, 'but it's coming back, isn't it? He's winning, isn't he? He'll be here, won't he? Then it'll be all, it'll be, it'll—'

'There there,' said Justina, patting him on the back once more. 'There there. That's as may be but you're safe for the moment, you're perfectly safe.'

She needed no clarification of Chegory's concerns. His fear was of Aldarch III, the Mutilator of Yestron, who threatened to be triumphant in Talonsklavara. Once the warlord had won the civil war in Yestron and had reunified the Izdimir Empire then he would surely turn his attention to Untunchilamon. Then the wrath of the Mutilator would fall on those who had overthrown Wazir Sin, and he would without doubt appoint a new wazir to complete the work which Sin had begun.

Justina sympathised entirely with Chegory's fears since she shared them. Aldarch III would doubtless wish to encompass her own death and surely possessed the power to do so. She had nightmares about his advent, as did most of her subjects. So she gave Chegory all the time he needed to recover before she suggested they return to the banquet.

'Just for a little while,' she said. 'I wouldn't, but etiquette demands it. But it won't last for much longer. Will that upset you too much?'

'I'm all right now,' said Chegory. 'But . . . no more to drink. I can't take any more to drink.'

'Of course not,' said the Empress. 'Apart from that . . . is there anything else?'

'Anything else?'

'Anything you . . . you can't. Or won't. Or don't want to.'

Chegory knew what she was offering him. The chance to escape from all further demands if he wanted to. He did want to! But she was his Empress. It was her father who had overthrown Wazir Sin, thus putting an end to the pogrom. It was Justina who had granted all Ebrell Islanders their full rights as citizens under the rule of an equitable code of law equally enforced.

Hence Chegory was a patriot.

'My lady,' he said, mastering his tongue with a supreme effort which vanquished wine, sorrow and a natural tendency toward incoherence. 'You are my Empress, and I your loyal subject. Your wish is my command.'

'That's darling of you Cheggy dear,' said Justina. 'That's truly darling of you.'

Then she led him back to the banquet with the armed guards who had waited outside her door trailing along behind.

CHAPTER TWENTY

When Chegory Guy and the Empress Justina returned to the banqueting hall they found the festivities in full swing. The conjuror Odolo was performing. Even as they entered he was teasing a seemingly endless streamer of coloured paper from his closed fist. Uckermark had shifted from his appointed seat and was now deep in conversation with Log Jaris. A few more drunks had slid under the table. The captured pirates were sitting disconsolately in the starvation cage.

The key to the starvation cage was no longer on the table where Justina had left it. Her albinotic ape had laid claim to it and, having first torn the tablecloth asunder, was using it to graffitograph the tabletop. Oh well. No harm done. But—

'The wishstone!' said Chegory. 'It's gone!'

'No, no,' said Justina. 'There it is, with my dear friend Juliet. Juliet Idaho, you see? They're passing it round the table, that's all right. It can't come to any harm here, not with armed guards on every door.'

They sat.

'Waiter!' said Justina.

'Ma'am?'

'Take away the young gentleman's wine. In view of the side effects I'm prescribing him sherbet instead.'

'Sherbet. Certainly, my lady.'

Chegory's wine vanished, to be replaced by sherbet in what felt like merely a moment. But it must have been more, for Odolo was done with the streamer and instead was pouring walnuts from his wide-open hands. Transitory rainbows glittered along the edges of the walnuts as they fell.

'Oh!' said Justina, 'oh, do you see what he's doing? That's very clever! I haven't seen him do that before!'

Then something large dropped from Odolo's hands. It was not a walnut. It was a scorpion. A bright yellow sun scorpion as long as a man's forearm.

'My!' said Justina. 'How did he keep that up his sleeve?'

The scorpion stood in defiance amidst the scattered walnuts. Claws raised. Tail arched. Its pose was static yet nevertheless managed to convey the creature's frenzy of paranoid suspicion and homicidal anger.

Schtlop!

A large ewer manifested itself in Odolo's hands.

Already a bright-burning fluid was pouring from the ewer. The conjuror jumped backwards – leaving the ewer poised in space. It calmly continued to outpour the flaming fluid. Walnuts burst asunder as the fluid swept over them.

The flood of death reached the sun scorpion. It writhed in brief-lived agony. Then:

Cher-lup!

The sun scorpion exploded.

Then the ewer, now empty, burst apart into a shower of butterflies which fluttered upwards. Briefly they rose then transmuted themselves into shards of rainbow – and then were gone.

'Bravo!' cried the Empress, clapping her hands.

As Chegory was joining in the applause he noticed more confusion at the main entrance to the Grand Hall. What was it? More prisoners for the Empress? No, it was a man. A wonderworker, if his silken robes were anything to go by. A most extraordinary figure he made, for his skin was of the most startling yellow colour.

'Look!' said Chegory, pointing. 'A yellow man! Odolo must have made him! Just like the sun scorpion!'

'Don't be silly, Cheggy,' said Justina, slapping down his pointing finger to the accompaniment of a delightful little laugh. 'That's Dolglin Chin Xter, my Inquisitor.'

'But – but why is he yellow?'

'Why do you think?' said Justina. 'He's got hepatitis, of course.'

That was one of the reasons why Dolglin had been made head of Justina's Inquisition into the drug traffic on Untunchilamon: his disease sharply reduced the temptation to which he was exposed. Hepatitis tends to put people off their drink; furthermore, if they persist in taking alcohol then the effects of such indulgence tend to be dramatic and disastrous.

'Hepatitis?' said Chegory.

He was so convinced that Xter was a conjuror's creation that he found Justina's explanation hard to credit.

'Didn't I just say so?' said the Empress. 'Yes, hepatitis. The worst case I've ever seen. It's a wonder he's still alive, yet alone on his feet.'

A wonder it was indeed; such a wonder that one is tempted to suspect that Xter was supporting his activities through exercise of magic.

'Hepatitis,' said Chegory yet again, still unsure whether to believe Justina.

'Dear Cheggy!' said Justina. 'Are you after employment as my parrot?'

'No, no,' said Chegory, glancing at the conjuror Odolo. 'It's just that – oh, look at Odolo!'

The conjuror had clapped his hands to his mouth, as if horror-struck by something he had just said. But he had said nothing!

'I think he's ill,' said Chegory, alarmed and concerned for the health of the man who had that day befriended him.

Meanwhile, Xter was grimly marching forward. Why? Because of something Odolo had done? Or what? Aquitaine Varazchavardan was getting to his feet. Varazchavardan and Xter confronted each other, as if for battle.

Then the conjuror Odolo screamed like a virgin molested in her chamber by an incubus.

'Odolo!' said Chegory frantically, rising from the table as he said it. 'He's sick, he—'

'It's all right,' said Justina, calmly abandoning her own seat. 'We'll take him somewhere quiet then—'

But whatever intervention of mercy she had contemplated came to nothing. For, before she could say another word, it happened. Great gouts of smoke and magniloquent flame burst from Odolo's mouth. He vanished behind this incendiary confusion.

'Good grief!' said the Empress Justina. 'Spontaneous combustion! The poor man's caught fire! No, Cheggy! Stay back! You'll get burnt as well!'

Chegory kicked and struggled but his Empress had him in a grip of iron. He could not get free.

'He's burning, he's burning!' sobbed Chegory.

'I can see that,' said Justina. 'But what are we to do? Get burnt along with him?'

Every person who was even halfway sober was staring at the incendiary cloud which had replaced the conjuror. Even Xter and Varazchavardan were transfixed by the sight. Already huge gouts of smoke were beginning to agglomerate to form Something huge and writhing.

Then forth from the smoke and flames it burst. A dragon! A pellucid beast the size of an ox. An ethereal monster still wreathed in the slatternly smoke of its creation, its inner organs transparent, its diaphanous wings shimmering with rainbow. It flew heavenwards, crashed into a chandelier, lost its grip on the air and fell to the floor with a thump. It got to its feet. Shook itself. Raked the floor with claws fast-hardening to jacinth.

'Well I never!' said Justina, glorious with wine. 'Odolo's a weredragon! This is a new one on me! I've heard of werewolves and werepigs – even weremice and were-hampsters, come to that – but never a weredragon!'

'Um, um,' said Chegory, hunting desperately for words, 'um, ah, why don't we run?'

'Odolo wouldn't hurt us,' said Justina calmly. 'Not even as a dragon. He's far too much of a personal friend.'

Chegory had too much pride to beg therefore did not beg to differ. Yet thought the fast-transforming dragon was making the voisinage decidedly unhealthy. Others thought likewise, for the Grand Hall was filled with wails of terror as guests and waiters alike fled screaming. Even Aquitaine Varazchavardan was retreating at the fastest pace which could be remotely conceived to be consonant with dignity, though Dolglin Chin Xter stood his ground.

The dragon was strengthening. Hardening. Its rainbow wings armouring themselves with opal. Its visionary body taking on mass, weight and obstinance. Its water-clear inner organs pulsed with red blood, assumed the hues of intestinal blue and kidney brown, and then a moment later were lost to sight beneath sheathing muscle, the muscle itself disappearing an eyeblink later as the imbricated transparency of scales became dull, obliviating ash. This ash hardened to the colours of flame which rippled as the dragon flexed its strength then roared.

Chegory and Justina were by then virtually alone in the Grand Hall. Justina cooed with wonder as she gazed upon the dragon. A magnifical beast it was, its body gleaming with a high lustre, its polished eyes flaring with flame and rainbow mixed. Then it roared. Gymnic firebursts cavalcaded from its mouth in a prodigious display of incendiarism. This was going too far.

'Guards!' shouted Chegory, meaning to command Justina's men into battle.

But there were no guards left. All had fled, even the scimitarists appointed to watch over the Empress during the meal. A couple of discarded cork blocks was all that remained of their presence.

'Oh my god!' said Justina abruptly, reality displacing wonder from her voice. 'There's Odolo!'

There he was indeed. Odolo was cowering on the floor aneath a table. So he was not a weredragon after all! Instead, conjuror and dragon were two separate entities.

'You!' yelled the eldest of the pirates in the starvation cage. 'Let us out, let us out!'

Chegory needed no further urging – for he was seized by inspiration. He wrested the key to the starvation cage from the imperial ape, slammed the key into the lock, wrenched it round and threw the door open. The pirates bolted instantly. The dragon outbreathed its fury as they fled, but its flamethrowing efforts fell short. Meanwhile Chegory grabbed the Empress Justina and dragged her into the cage closing the door behind them.

We see from this that young Chegory Guy was not destined to fight with dragons in the time-honoured heroic tradition, to win blood-bought glory or to slay a nightmare with but sword alone. No, his first thought was to seek shelter lest he and his lady be eaten. Unfortunately an over-consumption of alcohol had fuddled his wits, and he had yet to realise that iron bars will not protect against the dangers of incineration.

'Vazzy!' cried Justina. 'He'll be eaten!'

The imperial ape doubtless shared his mistress's concern, for the animal was struggling against its bonds. Its specially weighted chair rocked as it threw itself to right then left. Then its leather ankle cuffs burst asunder and it was off, screaming in rage and fury as it fled through the nearest door.

'Be very still,' said Chegory to his Empress. 'Be – be a rock.'

This was good advice. Nevertheless, it is to be regretted that in his panic young Chegory again was guilty of a lapse in etiquette, for he spoke his words not in Janjuladoola or even in Toxteth but in his native Dub. Whether the Empress Justina understood – or even heard what he said – is a moot point. For his words were virtually obliterated by the ear-shattering roar of a dragon in anger.

The fell monster was advancing on Dolglin Chin Xter, sorcerer of Yestron, the sole occupant of the Grand Hall who had refused to run from danger. Xter stood his ground. He was too sure of his skill and too experienced in disaster to be dismayed or agazed by a mere monster.

With bombastic wing-claps the fabricant of fire advanced upon the wonderworker. They clashed in a swirl of smoke, a cascade of colours. Chegory expected to see Chin Xter reduced in an instant to a smoking cinder or a blood-boltered raggage of trampled jelly. But when smoke and colour cleared away, there stood the wonderworker in triumph with the dragon, mortally wounded, writhing at his feet.

Xter's triumph was short-lived, for, a moment later, the heroic slayer of dragons swayed on his feet then quietly fainted. The dying monster began to drag itself toward the comatose wonderworker. Chegory flung open the door of the starvation cage and hurled himself across the hall. He swooped on Xter, grabbed the sorcerer by the hair and hauled him clear of the scrabbling firebrute.

'Bravo!' cried the Empress Justina.

Chegory smiled in triumph then looked for a weapon with which he could finish off the dragon. But there was no such implement to hand. Never mind. Already someone had gone back into the Grand Hall. Who? The corpse master Uckermark – who dared venture close to the dragon even though indigo flames were outbreathing from its mouth. Chegory – and Chegory alone – saw the corpse master feed something to the dragon.

What?

Chegory could not tell, for the thing was wrapped in a napkin. But the dragon gulped it down, whatever it was, then expired in moments, as if this last insult to the organism had ensured its death.

Guards were coming back into the hall, Varazchavardan with them. The Master of Law pointed a bony finger at the conjurer Odolo, who was still underneath a table, and said:

'Arrest that man! The charges are performing magic mala fide! Endangering human life and sanity by sorcery most treacherous! High treason, revolution, insurrection, breach of the peace!'

'I have no magic!' protested Odolo, crawling out from underneath the table as he did so. He stood up. 'Conjuring, conjuring, that's all it is! Illusions! All done with mirrors!'

Then Odolo said no more, for he was seized, a hood was

hauled down over his face and, struggling all the while, he was dragged away.

'Vazzy!' said the Empress Justina severely. 'I'll hold you responsible for Odolo's good health and safety.'

'You don't think he's innocent, do you?' said Varazchavardan. 'What're you thinking of? A pardon? For him? After this?'

'I'm thinking of a fair trial,' said Justina. 'I want him in one piece for that. Do we understand each other?'

'We do,' said Varazchavardan.

At least, he understood her. He was not at all sure that she understood him. Which was doubtless just as well.

'You have one other job,' said Justina. 'To find the wishstone! Where is it?'

'Well, it was—'

'I know where it was!' said Justina. 'I want to know where it is now!'

Very shortly that question on every tongue, resulting in an uproar better imagined than described, for these, the Highest and Greatest of Untunchilamon, indulged themselves in outcry like the faex populi on point of riot. Doors were sealed, guards posted at every exit, and every single person was searched, not excluding Varazchavardan himself. Even young Chegory Guy was searched.

The search was still going on when undokondra ended and the ghost bells crashed out to announce the start of bardardornootha. By then, Chegory Guy was reeling with fatigue. Even the Empress Justina was close to exhaustion. She had a constitution which would have been envied by a water buffalo, but nevertheless the festivities and alarums of the night had left her fit for little more than sleep.

It was then that the corpse master Uckermark approached her.

'Justina,' said he.

'Speak,' said she.

'I would like to remove the dragon for dissection. It's worth a lot if it's done while fresh.'

Justina knew the truth of this. Many precious substances

can be extracted from the fresh flesh of a dragon. Not least of these are the wondrous dyes which give waterfast blues, greens, reds and yellows. But dissection to secure such has to be done quickly for these substances are fragile and swift to decay.

'Fifty per cent for the treasure,' she said, meaning she laid claim to that portion of the corpse-worth on behalf of the state.

'Fifty per cent,' responded Uckermark. 'Done!' There was no haggling because these are a corpse master's standard terms for dragon dissection. Nevertheless, Uckermark did venture to ask for something in addition. 'My lady,' said he, 'the work will be done quicker if I can have my apprentice's assistance.'

'You need young Chegory?' said Justina. 'Very well then. Take him! There's always another night.'

It truth, Justina was glad to be thus rid of the young Ebrell Islander, for, while she did not want to hurt his feelings by rejecting him, the demands of sleep were fast overwhelming those of every other appetite. Her sister Theodora would not have been so quick to let a virile young man escape her clutches. But then, Theodora was already intimately engaged, and had been for most of that night.

Soon the dead dragon was manhandled onto a fish-cart. A dozen slaves were given the job of taking the cart to Lubos and half a score of soldiers went along to protect the convoy from human marauders and (more likely and more dangerous during bardardornootha) the depredations of vampire rats.

Down Lak Street they went as far as the Cabal House of Injiltaprajura's wonderworkers. Then, to the dismay of those doing the hard work, they had to turn down Skindik Way. Such was the steepness of the street and the weight of the dead dragon that Chegory and Uckermark had to lend their strength to the sweating slaves lest the cart escape. The road levelled out as they reached Lubos. Then they had a difficult job finding a way through the slumland maze to Uckermark's corpse shop, for many a path which they tried proved to be too narrow for the cart. Even where the way was wide enough the boardwalk creaked ominously beneath the overloading weight.

But at last they were there.

The dragon was offloaded.

Then slaves and soldiers departed with the empty cart. They departed swiftly – more than glad to escape from the claustrophobic stench of the corpse shop.

Since Yilda was so deaf she did not wake for the noise. Uckermark let his woman sleep on. He lit lanterns to maximise the brightness of the dissection chamber and then, with Chegory's help, gathered together tools and containers as he prepared to anatomise the dragon.

'Have you cut up many dragons?' said Chegory.

'Oh, many enough,' said Uckermark. 'Back when Wazir Sin was alive there were plenty of dragons out by the market gardens.'

'Then what happened to them?'

'When Sin died there was looting and so forth. The mob killed most of the dragons for the wealth they thought was within them. Well, wealth there was indeed, but it's a tricky job getting it out. Here, pass me that chisel.'

'What're you going to do?'

'Knock off some of these scales so I can cut off the creature's head, for a start.'

'But why?'

'Because, young man, the first rule of dragon dissection is also the most obvious. First make very, very sure your dragon is actually dead!'

'It looks pretty dead to me,' said Chegory.

'And to me also,' said Uckermark. 'But I still want to be sure.'

So saying, he began to chisel away the scales guarding the dragon's neck.

Chegory cleared his throat.

'Where do you . . . uh . . . where do you expect to find the, um, well, the . . .'

'So you know about that, do you?' said Uckermark.

'I, uh, well, I didn't exactly see . . .'

'But you saw enough then used your brain thereafter. I thought you saw! That's why I've got you here.'

'Why?'

'To bind you to secrecy with oaths formidable. Or, if you prove unamenable to oathing thus, to slaughter you in secrecy and hide your corpse beyond discovery.'

'I'll swear,' said Chegory quickly.

'By what do you swear?' said Uckermark.

'By my mother's honour.'

'And?'

'By . . . by the honour of the Empress Justina.'

'And? By what else do you swear?'

'What else is there?' said Chegory.

'That's for you to work out, not me!'

'Uh, all right. I swear by – by my own honour! How's that? And, uh, the Orgy God. Deity of the Ebrells! And, oh, I'll think of something.'

Chegory in fact thought of many more things to swear by as Uckermark chiselled away scales, cut off the dragon's head, recovered the wishstone then meticulously performed the rest of the dissection.

Meantime, Uckermark brooded about what he had done. If truth be told, the corpse master had snatched up the wishstone in the heat of the moment without any forethought whatsoever. He had been commanded by an urgent greed, a thoughtless grasping lust for wealth. It was a witless thing to do. Stupid, dangerous and foolhardy. It placed him in great danger. Still, Uckermark was a human being, and had as much capacity for self-delusion as did young Chegory. So by now he had constructed an elaborate belief structure to justify his actions – and had persuaded himself that he had thought the whole thing out before he acted.

When the Calligrapher's Union and its membership had been endangered by the general searches and wholesale arrests which had been turning Injiltaprajura upside down, then Uckermark's first thought had been to hunt down the conspirators who had stolen the wishstone and to yield up both those thieves and the precious bauble itself to the Empress.

That he had done.

Or, to give to this historical account that meticulous precision which the rendition of fact demands, Log Jaris had done as much after detailed consultation with Uckermark. This, together with the events which had taken place at the banquet, had (or so Uckermark put it to himself) the following consequences:

1. The original thieves were known to law and authority to have been uitlander pirates, the Malud marauders Al-ran Lars, Arnaut and Tolon.

2. The only people presently under suspicion with regard to the loss of the wishstone were those who had been at the banquet.

3. Uckermark and Chegory were most unlikely to be under any such suspicion for they had been searched and found to be innocent of theft. Log Jaris, presently under temporary detention at the palace along with most of the other guests from the banquet, would be found equally innocent.

Under these circumstances, Uckermark told himself it was safe to retain possession of the wishstone. He thought it most likely that the searchers would concentrate on the pursuit of the Malud marauders, who had fled the palace during the general confusion. He neglected to remind himself that there was every chance that some clear-minded logician would eventually connect the disappearance of the wishstone with the removal of the dragon from the pink palace. He told himself he was right to take it because:

1. The wishstone was worth a fortune, as agents at the embassy maintained by the rulers of Parengarenga in Ashmolea were permanently prepared to pay out that fortune for its purchase, no questions asked.

2. He had long lusted for possession of the wishstone

since it was the allure of that bauble which had drawn him to Untunchilamon in the first place.

3. Since Aldarch III was almost certain to conquer Yestron and to turn his attentions to Untunchilamon thereafter, all sane people were thinking of quitting the island, and it would be foolish to leave empty-handed.

As for Chegory Guy, he was just glad he had escaped from the palace with his life and his virginity intact. By now he had so much else to worry about that he frankly did not care who gained or retained possession of the wishstone. Thus he swore himself to secrecy in the matter, thinking his involvement in this criminal matter to be but a trifle compared to some of the other things he had on his plate.

Elsewhere, at the Temple of Torture in Goldhammer Rise which was serving as a detention centre, all prisoners were being released. The Empress Justina had bethought herself of their plight, and, before she allowed herself to sleep, had given orders that they be liberated immediately. Though the wishstone was missing again, all in detention were automatically free of suspicion since the true original thieves had been identified.

Thus it was that Artemis Ingalawa, her niece Olivia Qasaba and her employer Ivan Pokrov were released and made their way through the dark of bardardornootha to the Dromdanjerie. There they hammered on the door until sleepers awoke within and they were admitted.

Shortly they were in conversation with a bleary-eyed Jon Qasaba.

'Where's Chegory?' said Olivia.

'I haven't seen hide nor hair of him,' said her father. 'Wasn't he with you?'

'He was, he was, but he got taken away to the palace.'

'Well,' said her father, 'there's been all kind of goings on at the palace. Riots, mutiny, insurrection, attempted revolution and more. Not that anyone's been killed, or not that I've heard. But you never know.'

Injiltaprajura saw nothing of Shabble as istarlat's shadows shortened toward noon. Shabble was still missing as the shadows of salahanthara lengthened toward sunset. Yet all that time the demon of Jod was furiously busy.

Doing what, you ask?

The answer is simple:

Falling.

From morn to noon fell Shabble, from noon to dewy eve – a summer's day; and with the setting sun dropped from the zenith like a falling star. Steam in whispers vapoured into shreds as deep to the seas drove Shabble, descending fathoms five and full, drawn down to the depths where the moray weaves in coils than cobra greater, then drawn far deeper, down to the utter dark, the siltworm cold, the black of blindness enfolding.

Then Shabble uprose and surfaced.

Hovered briefly, then was gone, making for Injiltaprajura – leaving the dark seas rocking, rocking endlessly toward the shore.

CHAPTER TWENTY-ONE

On the day of Shabble's fall from the heavens, young Chegory Guy spent much of the morning sleeping on Uckermark's premises. Not that he slept well: he kept waking because of the exhausting heat. Angry flies constantly battered against frustrating gauze, ever intent on breaking through the windows to feast on the meat within. The oppressive stench of ruptured organs plagued both Chegory's sleep and his waking moments.

At first, he shared the one bed with Uckermark and Yilda, but when the noon bells woke him he found both gone. He rolled over and did his best to get back to sleep – as if sleep could have cured his problems. At last the sun fell, the bat bells rang out to announce the end of salahanthara and the start of undokondra, and Chegory reluctantly roused himself from the bed. He was alive. That was something. But for how long would he stay alive? Did Uckermark mean to kill him, or what?

'Gods,' muttered Chegory. 'What a mess.'

The day before yesterday was but a distant dream. Then, all unawares of the disasters ahead, Chegory had been quietly going about his business on the island of Jod. Raking gravel, chipping boulders, recovering rocks from the kitchen's grease trap, then studying mathematics in the afternoon. It seemed more than a lifetime ago. No wonder he felt lightheaded, disorientated, frazzled!

With some reluctance Chegory went downstairs and there found Yilda busy preparing a meal and Uckermark deep in conversation with one of the Ngati Moana, a ferociously tattooed warrior with a pounamu pendant suspended from each ear. Chegory guessed at once – and he guessed correctly – that Uckermark was negotiating for a passage out of Untunchilamon. The corpse master intended to make his escape from Justina's realm on one of the canoes of the Ngati Moana.

'Who's this?' said the Ngati Moana warrior in the fluent Janjuladoola of an expert linguist.

'Ballast,' said Uckermark.

In that single word the corpse master told the warrior Chegory was someone of no account who could be written off if the need arose. He also told Chegory that he would be joining the flight from Untunchilamon by canoe.

Chegory groaned.

Not inwardly but outwardly.

'I wouldn't take that attitude if I were you, boy,' said Uckermark. 'Most men in my position would have mastered your murder by now.'

'Where are we going?' said Chegory. 'Yestron? Ashmolea? Yam?'

'Never you mind,' said Uckermark. 'You'll find out soon enough.'

The corpse master was snappish, to say the least, for the day had allowed him time sufficient in which to realise temerity of his own actions. The risks were fearful. He might get caught with the wishstone in Injiltaprajura. Even if he escaped Untunchilamon by sea the canoe journey itself would be both arduous and dangerous. Before this game was played out he might get sunk, sharked, murdered, betrayed, imprisoned or tortured. If the worst came to the worst a vengeful wonderworker might even turn him into something horrible and inhuman.

'I want to know now!' insisted Chegory.

'If you're in that much of a hurry for an education,' said Uckermark, 'I'll teach you why Ebrell Islanders live such short lives!'

'No fighting!' said Yilda. 'Not while I'm cooking!'

The warrior of the Ngati Moana was silent throughout this argument. His face was inscrutable though in all probability he was outraged by such a display of bad manners. It was very bad form for Uckermark to allow a bad-tempered argument with a boy like Chegory to disrupt a formal negotiating session.

'Where's the wishstone?' said Chegory.

'Don't even speak of it,' said Uckermark. 'Here. Come with me.'

'Where are we going?'

'To the courtyard. The toilet. You need to go, surely.'

'I don't need help!' said Chegory.

'No,' said Uckermark, 'but you do need watching.'

The walls of his courtyard were twice man-height but he was sure that a nimble young Ebrell Islander could get over them quickly enough, particularly when inspired by fear. Once the toilet trip had been successfully completed Uckermark returned to his negotiations with the warrior of the Ngati Moana. They agreed that any swift departure would surely arouse suspicions.

Why did that matter? The double-hulled canoes of the Ngati Moana were the fastest things afloat; they could outrun any ship in fair winds or foul. Furthermore, since it was presently the season of Fistavlir, all ships were immobilised entirely while the canoes could still ride the coral current through the shallows of the Green Sea.

Mere escape was not the issue. Rather, the continuing freedom of the Ngati Moana was at stake. If rumour of their involvement in the theft of the wishstone ever reached the ears of Aldarch III then the Mutilator might choose to ban the entire coast of Yestron to their vessels. Uckermark could not have cared less but still had to respect the fears and interests of his co-conspirator.

'With the winds of Fistavlir,' said Uckermark. 'What say we leave then?'

'With the winds,' agreed his much-tattooed interlocutor. 'Providing our trading is done by then.'

With escape thus arranged Uckermark felt somewhat more secure. Little did he know! Disaster was imminent. For Log Jaris was even now approaching the corpse shop – and the unsuspecting bullman was being trailed by three Malud marauders.

243

When the pirates had escaped from the starvation cage in the pink palace they had fled without thought or plan. That was only natural. The presence of a large and angry dragon had not been conducive to methodical consideration or elaborate scheming. The pirates had fled downhill as far as the wonderworkers' Cabal House before Al-ran Lars had called them to order.

Then Al-ran Lars had held a hurried council of war with his comrades Arnaut and Tolon. To retreat to their ship would be the equivalent to surrendering themselves since that was surely the first place where Justina's soldiers would search for them. To retreat Downstairs would be equally foolish since that refuge had once already failed to shelter them from hunters with dogs.

Zazazolzodanzarzakazolabrik seemed to offer them their sole chance of safety. If they could escape into the northern wastes they could hope at least to live. But first they wanted some revenge. To be precise, they wanted to kill the monstrous bullman who had encompassed their capture Downstairs.

With that decided, the Malud marauders had gone into action. They had caught themselves a drunk for interrogation. A series of captures and interrogations had allowed them to locate the lair of Log Jaris – easy enough to do since it is hard to hide a bullman in a city as small as Injiltaprajura. Then they had staked out his speakeasy from a rooftop opposite. Then they had waited.

The Malud marauders had waited all through the night of their escape and the daylight that followed. Log Jaris had returned to his speakeasy at noon but there had been men with him – fellow members of the Calligrapher's Union, though the vengeful pirates were not to know this.

At last, early in the evening, Log Jaris had left his lair. But not alone. The bullman had taken three men as bodyguard, for his way led through the streets of Lubos which he did not care to chance alone. The pirates had followed.

Even as Uckermark concluded his bargain with the

warrior of the Ngati Moana his good friend Log Jaris was drawing steadily nearer with the Malud marauders in catfoot pursuit.

The pirates were not the only threat the unsuspecting corpse master would soon have to confront. An alien wizard of the order of Xluzu, Pelagius Zozimus by name, was another.

Pelagius Zozimus, as Justina's master chef, had been in a good position to garner details on the loss of the wishstone, the breakout of the prisoners who had escaped from the starvation cage and all associated events. He had collated all the evidence and had produced a list of hypotheses which might explain the disappearance of the wishstone.

It might have been taken by the fleeing piratical prisoners, in which case its location would prove near impossible to discover.

Alternatively, the Empress Justina might have stolen the wishstone herself. Doubtless she had plans for escaping from Untunchilamon before minions of Aldarch III arrived to seize control of the island. If she sought to take the contents of the treasury with her then Injiltaprajura's wonder-workers might prevent her, fearing the reprisals Aldarch III would exact if they did not. Thus she might well desire one and all to think the wishstone still missing.

There was also the possibility that a wonderworker might have absconded with the wishstone. But Zozimus, who had a low opinion of the will, wit and talent of such sorcerers, was inclined to discount this notion.

He was, however, intrigued by the news that the corpse master Uckermark had removed a dragon from the pink palace. Zozimus had deduced that the wishstone might well have been secreted within the corpse. The possibility was slight – one chance in fifty by his reckoning – but he thought it worth investigation.

Thus Zozimus had organised his colleagues-in-crime: the wizard Hostaja Sken-Pitilkin, the Yarglat adventurer Guest Gulkan, and the cut-throat from Chi'ash-lan who went by the name of Thayer Levant. They had located Uckermark's corpse shop, had put it under observation, and, on noting the entry of the warrior of the Ngati Moana, had drawn the logical conclusions. These conclusions were that:

(i) Uckermark did indeed have the wishstone;

(ii) Uckermark planned to flee Untunchilamon by canoe;

(iii) If captured, the corpse master could be forced to tell where the wishstone was hidden.

So it came to pass that Pelagius Zozimus and his companions were preparing to raid the corpse shop even as Log Jaris drew near with a trio of murderous Malud marauders in his wake.

Simultaneously, Shabble came drifting in across the Laitemata. Shabble did not call into Ganthorgruk in pursuit of Odolo Shabblefriend, nor did the demon of Jod pop into the Analytical Institute to rouse Ivan Pokrov for an evening's conversation. The shining one ignored the lure of the Dromdanjerie where many of Injiltaprajura's best conversationalists lived out their days in cages.

Instead, Shabble flew straight to Uckermark's corpse shop, for the imitator of suns was curious to find out why the wishstone was held there.

In this connection it must be noted that the wishstone was, among other things, a beacon. Ever did it announce its presence to those with ears attuned to its far-flying call. It radiated a species of coded energy once used by the peoples of the Golden Gulag to talk at distances greater than shouting. Such energy was easily baffled by the mass of stone, metal and plax of the underworld Downstairs – but from Uckermark's corpse shop it signalled loud and clear.

Thus the stage was set for an epic confrontation.

Log Jaris reached the corpse shop even as Uckermark, Chegory and Yilda were sitting down to eat their evening meal. The three bodyguards who had so far protected the bullman peeled off, for they had other tasks to attend to. They were to rouse out other members of the Calligrapher's

Union who lived nearby and bring them to the corpse shop for a council of war.

The bullman knocked on the door. Uckermark was slow to answer, for, all too conscious of his own guilt and hence fearing a raid by Justina's soldiery, he was arming himself for combat. Log Jaris knocked again. His bodyguards were out of sight.

The Malud marauders seized their chance and charged from the shadows. They screamed with murderous rage as they plunged toward the bullman. Log Jaris whirled – and saw his danger.

'Keep back!' roared Log Jaris. 'Back – or die!'

Uckermark heard his friend without and flung wide the corpse shop's door. Log Jaris leapt inside. Uckermark slammed the door. And the muscle man Tolon hit it with all his weight. The door burst asunder. Uckermark and Log Jaris were both sent sprawling. In stormed the three pirates.

Yilda grabbed a tiny glass vial filled with a brilliant blue fluid. She threw it at the floor. The flask burst. The fluid exploded on contact with the air. Dragon fire roared upwards. The pirate raiders flung up warding arms.

'Get back!' said Yilda, another vial already in her hand. 'Back! Or the next will find your faces!'

The pirates hesitated. After all, she was only a woman. More to the point, Uckermark and Log Jaris – knocked to the floor by the down-crashing door – would be endangered by any fire which threatened the raiders.

That hesitation lost the pirates their kill.

Already Uckermark and Log Jaris were scrambling to their feet. Even as they did so Yilda was throwing herself into action. She had a mop, was throwing the vial to the air, was striking at it with the mop. The vial exploded into flame. With mop-head blazing, Yilda charged, screaming as she did so.

The pirates fled.

Out into the street they rushed – and almost impaled themselves on the blades of four swordsmen there standing.

The pirates ducked past the unexpected newcomers and fled.

'Bastards!' screamed Yilda. 'Come back and fight like men!'

She bitterly regretted the escape of the enemy. After all, she had wasted two vials of the best blue flame on the battle. The vials themselves were fearfully expensive since they were made of glass. As for the blue flame – why, only a little of this can be extracted from even a most productive dragon corpse. Hence Yilda wanted at least a couple of kills out of the encounter.

'Ho!' said Log Jaris, panting as he came out into the street and saw four shadowy figures standing there in the night. 'Well met, my friends! Put down your swords – the thieves have fled!'

'You misjudge us,' said one, moving into the dragon-fire light of Yilda's blazing mop and revealing himself as none other than Pelagius Zozimus, Justina's master chef. 'You misjudge us, for we are thieves ourselves.'

Yilda, still geared up for battle, slashed at him with her flaming mop. Zozimus ducked. His comrade Guest Gulkan swung cold steel adroitly and lopped off the head of the mop.

'You've come to the wrong place,' said Uckermark, hefting a dragon cleaver in his hand. 'We've no money here. We're not a bank or a brothel.'

'No,' said Pelagius Zozimus. 'You're the corpse master Uckermark. Within you have the wishstone which is what we're here for.'

'You're wrong on all counts,' said Uckermark. 'I'm not Uckermark. I am but his slave. The man himself is within with seven comrades at cards. Master! Thieves without!'

Uckermark's bawling voice echoed down the street. From inside the shop came an answer:

'Coming! Coming!'

It was Chegory Guy, pitching his voice low the better to imitate full-grown manhood. But Zozimus and his three companions were not impressed.

'I know you by your face,' said Zozimus. 'I learnt your name when you brawled at Justina's Petitions Session. Better still, I know you've no fighting force within. We've had your place watched all day. The stone! Now! Or I'll cut your guts open looking for it!'

Out from the interior of the shop there then came Chegory Guy with a wicked corpse hook in hand.

'Uckermark's just coming,' he said in a voice quite different from the one he had used for his bluff of a few moments previously.

'You're beginning to bore me,' said Zozimus. 'I'm warning you! If there's one thing I can't stand it's being bored.'

Uckermark grunted and muscled forward. But Log Jaris threw out a hand and restrained him.

'If we have got the wishstone,' said Log Jaris, 'then give it to them.'

'What is this?' said Uckermark in outrage. 'There's four of us! We can take them!'

Certainly the odds in a fight would have been fairly even. Guest Gulkan of Tameran was a formidable warrior – but then so was the bullman Log Jaris. Uckermark could probably have killed the cut-throat Thayer Levant even though that unscrupulous unworthy was far more dangerous than his appearance suggested. As for the two wizards, Pelagius Zozimus and Hostaja Sken-Pitilkin, why, neither of them was much of a fighter and both for the moment were right out of magic. Chegory and Yilda could probably have cleaned them up.

'We're not going to take them,' said Log Jaris, 'because the wishstone's too dangerous to hold. Justina has sworn—'

'Okay, okay,' said Uckermark in disgust. 'I get the picture! All right, gentlemen. Wait here just a moment. My darling wife is your hostage to vouchsafe for my return.'

Uckermark disappeared into his corpse shop and was back almost immediately with a bag of offal. He flung it into the street. It burst. Bloody organs in various states of decay and disrepair went sprawling across the street. The wishstone rolled free. It was so layered in black blood that its light scarcely showed. Nevertheless, a leam of rainbow revealed it for what it was. Thayer Levant snatched it up and Guest Gulkan's faction began to back away down the street.

'You'll never get away with it!' yelled Uckermark. 'You'll never get off Untunchilamon alive!'

'Get back inside!' said Pelagius Zozimus. 'Back! Or I'll blast you all with wizardry!'

He was bluffing, and Uckermark guessed as much. Nevertheless, the corpse master was glad to have a face-saving excuse to bring the whole nerve-shattering episode to an end.

'Old friend!' said Log Jaris as they went inside. 'You surprise me! So greed got the better of you, did it?'

'The opportunity of a lifetime,' muttered Uckermark, feigning grief.

In truth, he was glad the wishstone was gone. It had been a mistake to take it. The thing was far too dangerous since there was scarcely a person on all of Untunchilamon who would not gladly kill for its possession. Uckermark very much doubted that the latest thieves to seize it would get away alive.

'Chegory,' said Yilda. 'Help me with this door.'

'No,' said Uckermark. 'The hell with the door. Let's eat. We can worry about the door later.'

So eat they did.

Meanwhile, in the night outside, Shabble was bobbing along behind the wishstone thieves. To Shabble's ears, the wishstone's beaconing was loud and strong. Shabble could have jumped the thieves then and there – disarming them, terrorising them, burning them up or making them prisoner. But that would have ended the game too quickly. Hence Shabble went shadowstalking after them.

The demon of Jod was showing no light. Only the occasional squeak of excitement betrayed the presence of the imitator of suns, and, if the thieves heard those squeaks, they doubtlessly attributed them to unseen vampire rats.

Shabble's excitement intensified when three Malud marauders fell in behind the thieves, following them at a distance.

Oh, this was a nice bit of drama! Oh, what fun!

Then the thieves took one of the downways which led to the underworld. In they went, one after another. Pelagius Zozimus. Hostaja Sken-Pitilkin. Thayer Levant. Then Guest Gulkan.

Shabble hesitated.

Then the Malud marauders came catfooting through the night, closing with the doorway in a quick, determined rush. They hesitated also, conferred briefly in whispers, then slipped inside. Shabble watched as Al-ran Lars, Arnaut and Tolon followed the wishstone thieves Downstairs.

For a moment longer Shabble lingered outside. Then innate devilishness conquered fear and Shabble followed. Oh, there would be fun in the dark tonight!

CHAPTER TWENTY-TWO

It is to be regretted that Shabble's over-developed sense of fun almost permitted an unnecessary fatality to take place. For, when the three Malud marauders finally jumped the four swordsmen they were following, Shabble found the ensuing battle so enthralling that all thoughts of intervention quite slipped away. Then Shabble's excitement overmastered sense. The demon of Jod brightened in sheer pleasure as Guest Gulkan made a particularly daring sword-thrust. Thus was the imitator of suns betrayed to the lawless ones, who, unblooded, broke off their combat and stared at their one-sun audience.

'Oh, don't stop, don't stop!' said Shabble. 'You were doing so well!'

'It's that demon-thing!' yelled young Arnaut in his native Malud.

Then he took to his heels and fled.

But Shabble cut him off, and, after some fairly acrobatic flying and flame-throwing, herded all seven criminals into a cul-de-sac. Three were pirates: the Malud marauders Al-ran Lars, Arnaut and Tolon. Four were adventurers: Guest Gulkan's faction, consisting of the Yarglat barbarian himself, the cutthroat Thayer Levant and the wizards Pelagius Zozimus and Hostaja Sken-Pitilkin.

'What do you want from us?' said Zozimus.

'Silence!' said Shabble imperiously. 'You see this?'

Shabble unleashed a bolt of fire which melted a five-fist wound in the plax of the tunnel.

'We're none of us blind,' said Zozimus, pretending (with some difficulty) that he was not impressed.

'That's a warning,' said Shabble. 'Right! March! Anyone who runs gets crisped!'

Here a native of Injiltaprajura would have told the demonic one to stop playing games and would have walked away, confident in the knowledge that Shabble was known to be loathe to burn anyone without extreme provocation. But the lawless uitlanders lacked this knowledge, hence were doomed to obey.

Long did Shabble drive these terror-enslaved victims, forcing them into the doomdepths. There they were held prisoner while Shabble amused Shabbleself by showing off. By, for example, singing various arias from the Dragon Opera, most tedious composition in all of Ho Lung's oeuvre. If one of the hapless criminals tried to escape then the musical one would grow very hot and very bright, and the would-be hero would have to fall back. Tolon tried more often than the others, for he was stubborn and fearless.

As time went by the prisoners' fear began to diminish. While to begin with they had been overawed by the fast-rolling sun which claimed to be a demon-god, Shabble's frequent betrayals of Shabbleself's childish nature led to wariness replacing terror. The captives began to try to bargain their way out of trouble.

'If you let us go,' said Pelagius Zozimus, 'I'll see you rich for ever. I personally vouchsafe your reward. By the rule of law I swear it.'

But Shabble had no use for such juratory assurances. It is hard to bribe Shabble, who has no use for sex, money, fame, power, or any of the other standard commercial jajas. If you ever have a run in with Shabble, then remember that this entity values friendship above all else. Immortals lead lonely lives, for the best of friends live scarcely more than a generation. Millennia roll by to leave one with . . . what?

Memories, at best.

Apart from companionship, Shabble is only interested in two things. Excitement: which Shabble seeks in delightsome practical jokes involving more than a little mayhem. Also: good conversation. Where on Untunchilamon would Shabble find such conversation? Certainly not with that relentless headhunter Jon Qasaba, who is so much the professional therapist that his idea of enjoyable social intercourse is to dissect his interlocutor.

Qasaba! The man has no manners. Has not, never had, never will. Did he look on us as people? No! As material. The raw material of his scholarly enterprises. He exploited our agony ruthlessly for the sake of a well-turned paragraph, the germ of a new theorem. He—

[Here a diatribe has been excised on the advice of our legal department. *O Reno, scribe.*]

[The legal advisement alluded to by O Reno suggests the excision of the diatribe on the grounds that the Qasaba in question may be the very person who at this writing is Waymaster in Obooloo. Yet surely this is an absurdity. For how could an obscure headhunter of Ashdan descent make himself master of the Izdimir Empire? How could a student of provincial madness survive the knifehand intrigues of the heartland of the Izdimir Empire? What would persuade Aldarch the Third to surrender his will to an uitlander from a treasonous splinter on the empire's fringes? Here again we have an example of the paralytic cowardice of our legal department cramping scholastic enterprise. See my memo 19/872816 for supporting detail. *Srin Gold, Commentator Extraordinary.*]

But enough of Qasaba.

Let us return to our prisoners – or, in point of precise fact, Shabble's prisoners – and watch them watching a dreamlike gemstudded machine trundling past. Under cover of the noise of its thungundling wheels they have a quick consultation. They decide if they run in separate directions Shabble surely cannot chase them all. Thus decided, they ease apart.

'Don't even think about it,' says Shabble.

They don't. For the time for thinking is over. Instead of thinking, they run. Only to find seventy-seven Shabbles where there had been but one before. Then a hundred and seventy-seven. Fireballs dancing, hissing, sliding. Scorching the walls where they impact.

The seven throw themselves flat. The fireballs die out. All but one. Which is Shabbleself, spinning triumphantly.

'I am the demon-god Lorzunduk,' says Shabble. 'I existed since times antemundane. I in my glory will exist even after all the worlds have crumbled into dust.'

'Oh what utter rubbish!' says Hostaja Sken-Pitilkin.

Meanwhile, Arnaut fingers a knife. The young man from Asral is one of these mild-mannered people in whom there lurks a dragon-tempered brute. Sooner or later, that brute will out when some new outrage perpetrated by Shabble proves to be the last fish. Then Arnaut will run amok and launch an outright onslaught on Shabble. Which will, one fears, surely prove his death.

['The last fish.' Proverbial. The last fish eaten by the glutton shark (against the dolphin's good advice) was the one which burst its stomach. The same meaning is attached to the words 'the seventh bone'. This is not to be confused with the outwardly cryptic phrase 'when the jaws unhinge', which has a meaning similar to our own proverbial 'when the cat's in the dogskin'. *Valther Nash, Consulting Translator*.]

Sooner or later.

But when?

Don't worry. There is plenty of time. It is still only early in the life of the universe. Early early. As yet our narrative has dealt with but three days and we have all the rest of eternity in which to conclude our history.

[A conceit. A fatuous conceit. The Originator's implied claim to immortality is but a literary conceit quite out of place in a sober historical work of this nature. In truth, the Originator is timebound like the rest of us, and knows it. In any case, there is no such thing as eternity: there is but the moment, as all timeresearchers know. *Brude, Pedant Particular*.]

CHAPTER TWENTY-THREE

At dawn the rays of the rising sun ignited the colours of the glitter dome atop the pink palace of the Empress Justina. The sun bells rang out. Bardardornootha had ended; istarlat had just begun. Yet although it was so early in the day it was still muggy, for though the air had grown less hot overnight it most certainly had not cooled.

The conjuror Odolo, Official Keeper of the Imperial Sceptre, felt the enclosing and unwelcome warmth of the day when he awoke in the profound shadows of a cell in Moremo Maximum Security Prison. He woke on a single niggardly blanket which was grey with lice. He sat up, coughed, stretched, scratched, stretched again to try to ease the aches in his limbs, then tried to figure out where the hell he was.

Already Odolo was bewildered, disorientated and confused. He tried to concentrate, comprehend and cogitate, but this was next to impossible because of the words madly scrambling through his mind.

Words?

Words in Dub, Toxteth and Janjuladoola. Obscenities, profundities, absurdities and inanities. The banal and the quotidian buttock to buttock with the visionary and the esoteric. The words jostled each other senselessly in a mad tumbling disorder, thus:

Yam sot-pot in aspic flaring
black dragon red farmer does dung to be art
gum blue dreamfish prinked lissome their giblets of prophecy
to lithe the blue supply said the rainbow of scorpions
sexed cats sang the sorceress sibyl
taupe baklava shim-sham-shimmying gluttoned its appetites,
ravaged its seas

bamboo the ebony, cassava the ivory
cotton coin candles persistent in welfare
snakeskinned the sunlight sheds pain

Odolo pressed his head against the dank, unyielding stone of his jail cell. The stone at least was cool even though the air was over-warm. He closed his eyes. He concentrated. On ice. A big block of ice. Blue-white. In sunlight. A glory of diamonds. Cool ice. Frozen. Silent. Frozen . . .

Slowly, the words silenced. Odolo centred himself in his cell's shadow-stock in the position known as Celestial Lotus. He was in control of himself. At least for the moment. He started doing a Personal Status Assessment as he had learnt to when he was an acolyte studying under Mantua Hull of the Combat Wing of the School of Strategy on the island of Odrum.

[Here a manifest error. A Records Search shows no student by name of Odolo and no instructor by name of Mantua Hull anywhere on our island in living memory. The Originator lies, or has failed to detect lies told to him by his nameless informant – Odolo himself? This error I verify. *Threndil Falcon, Keeper of the Census.*]

The results of the Personal Status Assessment were reassuring. Momentarily reassuring. He was adequately hydrated. Not particularly hungry. Had slept sufficiently. Was combat-functional. Senses and reflexes intact.

Then all sense of reassurance disappeared as Odolo consulted his memories. He remembered! The banquet, of course. Those amazing walnuts spilling from his helpless hands. Then the Thing upchoking from his throat. His helpless efforts to restrain It. The outrush of acrid smoke. Then – then the dragon. The monster forming itself amidst the smoke.

Mother of turtles! They think me guilty!

If indeed the Powers That Be were blaming Odolo for manifesting a dragon in the banqueting hall then he was in trouble dire, trouble deep, trouble blue and bloody.

'Jit!' said Odolo.

In response to this obscenity the shadows skittered and

scraped. Something dwelt within the cell. He was not alone! What was it? Claws, tentacles, teeth?

'Nothing!' said Odolo defiantly.

Then wished he had not spoken so loudly.

There was a monster in the cell with him! He was sure of it!

So thought Odolo – but only for a few moments. For the briefest scrutiny of the shadows showed him that nothing of any consequence could possibly be hiding there. He must have been imagining those strange skittering sounds. He put them out of mind and turned his thoughts to a more important subject: escape. Could he escape?

First, where was he? Surely he was in Moremo Maximum Security Prison on the northern side of Pokra Ridge. Okay. Could he get out? Through the floor? Through the walls? All were of the bloodstone of Untunchilamon. A rock far softer than granite. So he could surely tunnel out of his cell if allowed to work undisturbed for six or seven years. However, he fully expected his case to be resolved for better or worse (worse being torture, dismemberment and death) within six or seven days at the most.

The oppressive red of the bloodstone was already getting to him. Its blood-heavy ominousness was not at all the sort of colour to inspire optimistic thoughts. Six or seven years to get out through the walls, then. What about the door?

The cell's massive operculum had been painted to resemble a monster with mouth wide open, slavering jaws gaping to receive Odolo into its maw. Artistic ingenuity had made the turnkey's spyhole the pupil of the monster's single eye. Odolo ignored the artwork. He kicked the door. It was solid. Nobody was going to use that exit but by invitation.

Odolo kicked the door once more, for luck. Then stood stock still. Listening. He could hear something! Strange skittering sounds. Yes, he could really hear them. He was not imagining them. So what was to blame? Some kind of animal? Perhaps. But there was nowhere in the cell where anything of any size could hide. Unless it was hanging from the roof.

Odolo looked up.

Moremo's architects had placed a small window at twice manheight from the floor. Light from the eastern sun showed that nothing hung from the roof but a few cobwebs; the same light, shining on the wall opposite the window, stirred the blood of the bloodstone to life and cast shadows of heavyweight bars which prevented egress and ingress by prisoners and marauding animals alike.

Nothing is here but me and nothing can get in to get me.

So thought a relieved Odolo, then relieved himself into the magnanimous dark of the cell's vomit hole, stirring claws in the dark below to a boiling frenzing. An unearthly high-pitched screaming arose from below. Was there a captive skavamareen down there? No! Worse! Vampire rats! The grille guarding the vomit hole was not to stop prisoners climbing Downstairs, for the sewer pipe was far too small to facilitate escape. The grille was to stop vampire rats sallying forth from the sewers to eat prisoners alive.

At this stage a stranger to Injiltaprajura might have relaxed and enjoyed his good fortune, for the grille was a heavyweight affair most certainly rat-proof. Such a stranger would have told himself he was in a cell both pleasant and capacious (as prison cells go). He had privacy. He had light. He had a bed. He had blankets, and company in plenty in the form of friendly lice most urgently desirous of intimacy. Sheer luxury!

However, the conjuror Odolo did not relax at all, for he knew all too well that this was an execution cell. Worse, it was not any old death cell. This was the horror house, the place reserved for those miscreants attainted of the crime of *lèse-majesté*. When found guilty (and who would be accused of something so serious if they were not guilty?) then they suffered a particularly horrible death.

Odolo knew his fate. After he was convicted of treason his executioners would remove that grille then leave him alone in the cell. In the bowels of the night, in the depths of bardardornootha, there would be a snickering squeal. Then up would come the vampire rats in their legions. Then he would die most hideously, losing first his fingers in the defence of his eyes and then—

In panic, Odolo wondered if he was doomed already. What if he had been tried while unconscious? Tried and sentenced? Sentenced and doomed? It was all too horribly possible. Yet – the grille was still in place. So surely he had a chance yet.

Aldarch the Third!

A chance of life! His slim, sole and virtually nonexistent chance. He would be saved only if Aldarch III conquered Untunchilamon in time to stop the execution. Saved? Rewarded, even! For it would seem to the public that Odolo had by sorcery attempted to kill the Empress Justina, bitch-spawn of the rebellious Lonstantine Thrug and sworn enemy of Aldarch III.

But it is Fistavlir.

Indeed. It was the season of Fistavlir, the Long Dry, when Untunchilamon lay becalmed in the doldrums. No wind stirred. Hence no ships. No minion of Aldarch III could approach Injiltaprajura until the next wind season came.

In any case, Talonsklavara could drag on for years yet.

True. The civil war in Yestron, which was in its seventh year, had plenty of history-making potential left. Aldarch the Third was rumoured to be winning, but what trust could Odolo put in rumour?

My life I must save myself.

The grille was still in place. Still guarding the vomit hole to protect him from vampire rats. So as yet he had not been tried and sentenced. He was safe, for the moment. Unless he let hysteria run him amok. He must guard against panic. Must rest. Relax. Conserve his strength.

He closed his eyes.

Tried to rest, to relax.

To embalm himself in sleep.

But found—

Found a remorseless upthrust of images welling into consciousness. Not the much-to-be-expected nightmares of pain, torture, privation and death to which he in his condition would naturally be prone. Not that, but totally disconnected visions. Kicking through his skull. Disordered as a wet-writhing mass of fish dumped from a net to a boatdeck. Data was whirlpooling from the depths of his memory. Fractional glimpses of people, places, events. Tastes, temperatures, smells and tactions. Sights and sounds. Nuances of weight and balance.

Mango yellow. Cassava squirt. Seasalt algae sunbaked. Albatross shadow. Crab scuttle cavecool. Coconut split. Knock-hollow coconut rock-shattered. Finger-lick of moisture. Fingers? Digits. Vestigal talons. Articulation.

His hand was working itself.

Experimenting with itself.

His left hand.

Fingers closing to a fist. Slowly. Opening again. Slowly. Thumb touching first finger, second, third. Odolo slapped his delinquent left hand with his obedient right. The left hand ceased its fidgeting.

But still the memories upswirled, rising in torrents like the blood of the dead in the legend of Pelikan Ova. Memories of ice delicious on days hot. Of nights by mosquitoes tormented. Of seadream diving near the Galley Gate deeps. Of green tea, blue gin, creamed coffee, sherbet and other potatiory delights. He tried to stop the memory-flux. But could not. He was losing sovereignty over his own mind. Was, in a word, going mad.

Worse – the very wall was moving!

Odolo stared at the wall. Then realised, to his relief, that the impression of movement came from the shuffle-shift of an overlay of cockroaches. Free protein! He realised he was hungry. Unless breakfast came soon he might murder a few of the six-legged ones for the pleasure of his belly. Then, as he watched, a waking nightmare abolished both relief and hunger entirely. A shadow amidst the shadows formed itself into a claw. It raked the wall. Knifed its talons in among the cockroaches. They fell in a scrattling rain, sklattering to the flagstones. Odolo felt first strangling fear then—

Silence.

As if he had become—

What?

A pool of clear water.

Silent. Poised. Ready. Waiting.

For what?

While Odolo waited for revelation, the cockroaches scrambled back on to their wall. Then a couple slipped from the justling shadow-hugging mass. More fell as a shadow-formed claw again raked the wall. The fallen cockroaches mucked around on the flagstones. Then, as if drawn toward Odolo by a superior Power, they perambulated toward him, onmarching steadily as if with hideous intent. They were going to – to eat him?

He shrank away from the oncoming monsters. Then the leading cockroach hesitated. Shimmered. Flickered. Softened. Dissolved. Reformed itself as a butterfly. Which took to wing, rising shadow-soft and shadow-silent to the sunlight above. Where it flashed into sudden glory, then swooped between the bars of the cell. Gliding away to freedom.

Odolo glanced back at the cockroach army. It had vanished. Something small and green had taken the place of the insects. It took to the air as he watched and began to circle just overhead. Not another butterfly, no. Not a butterfly but a dragon. A tiny little dragon, barely a fingerlength from nose to tail. It chirruped happily as it flew.

Had all those cockroaches gone to make one dragon in miniature? No. On the flagstones at Odolo's feet were two mango-sized beasts. A lion and a unicorn. Even as he watched, the two tiny animals began to fight. They wrestled each other to the edge of the vomit hole. Slipped. Then fell. From the depths below there came a hideous squealing.

Vampire rats!

Attracted by the noise, the dragon dived from the heights

and plunged into the vomit hole. Moments later, it emerged. Covered in filth. It settled on the flagstones. It flapped its wings furiously, hissing. Muck slished away from its scales. Still hissing, the dragon took to the air. It ascended. Up, up it went, climbing as it circled. As it gained the heights the sunlight caught it, sparking a flare of dragonfly iridescence from its wings. The dragon slipped between the bars, disappearing into the sunlight.

An illusion, surely.

An idle piece of dreamery adrift in the daylight.

Yet . . . motes of dust were still aswirl in the turbulence left by its flight. Odolo closed his eyes. Opened them. Looked upward again. Saw no trace of the turbulence. It had smoothed away to nothing.

'It never happened,' he said.

Perhaps not.

But other things were happening already.

In the dankest corner of the cell a miniature cloud was forming itself. A tiny self-important black cloud coruscating with impatient energy. As sparks of lightning crackled from the cloud, something began to form in the air just above it. Something smooth, oval. Glowing whitely. An egg! A luminous egg! Which hovered above the cloud for a moment. Then fell. Shattered on the flagstones. Splat! Yolk gleamed golden in the sweltering shadows of the cell. Then the cloud disintegrated into a downpour of miniature pearls.

Then the words began to spin again, jumbling swiftly and furiously as they torrented through the helpless mind of Odolo the hapless. In panic he screamed:

'Help me! Help me!'

Then, in desperation, slammed his head against the door of the cell.

Something spoke inside his head:

BE STILL!

Without thought, Odolo punched himself in the head. In tones of authority the voice said:

STOP THAT!

Odolo hit himself again. It hurt. Then something hurt

263

him far worse. Pain flooded his body. Pain? PAIN!

Then the voice again spoke inside his head:

I not you am. Not your symptom am. Thing am. Listen to me, Odolo dishonourable.

'Hi, Thingam,' muttered Odolo.

I am a Thing.

Thus the thing, with dignity and swift-improving control of grammar. Then grammar lapsed again as the thing – thing? – Thing! – said:

Binchinminfin is called me.

'Binchinminfin? That's your name?'

My name is Binchinminfin.

The Thing was learning quickly.

Odolo lay as still as total paralysis. Was he dreaming? He tested reality. He tried to manifest a naked damsel. He failed. But in his dreams he could always cause naked damsels to manifest themselves. Not just to manifest themselves, either, but to—

[Here a deletion. *Drax Lira, Redactor Major.*]

So he was not dreaming.

The undreaming Odolo lay in a sweat of terror. A Thing! A Thing in his head! What could he do? Dig it out with a mango spoon? He giggled hysterically. Then got a grip on himself. Could he negotiate with the Thing? He could try. Out loud, he said:

'What do you want?'

The voice in his head answered:

SILENCE. BE STILL! STOP THINKING.

Thus the Thing. But how could he stop thinking? As he was still thinking about it, the painting of a monster which covered the cell door came to life. Its single baleful eye winked open. Odolo screamed.

'What's the matter with you?' said an unsympathetic voice.

It was surely the turnkey speaking. As artistic mischief had made the cell's spyhole the pupil of a monster's eye, the opening of the same momentarily brought the hideous door painting to life.

'Help me!' said Odolo. 'I'm going mad!'

'That's syphilis then,' said the turnkey, 'isn't it? It's syphilis which makes madness.'

Then Odolo in his agony started screaming like a skavamareen.

'Skeder erket mol,' said the turnkey.

Then, after making several additional comments equally as obscene and unsympathetic, the turnkey departed, satisfied that his charge was in good shape. Odolo was left to his fate. Jumbling discords of random-plucked words spun through his mind. He screamed again, then thumped his head against the wall of the cell. But still the words onspun.

CHAPTER TWENTY-FOUR

The quarter of istarlat did like a lotus bud complete its unfolding, as the elegant phraseology of Janjuladoola would have it. Or, to use the curt and brutal idiom of the Yudonic Knights: the morning died. Or, in the argot of the Ebrell Islanders (ah! and how the words sweeten and soften in their translation from the free-flowing obscenity of the original Dub!) the day's first half was rooted and wrecked.

Thus noon came to Injiltaprajura and the palace bells rang out, disturbing the echoes which dwell in the portside streets. Wandering echoes woke likewise in the city's desert side to the north of Pokra Ridge, some reaching the conjuror Odolo sweating in his death cell in Moremo Maximum Security Prison.

Within the pink palace itself the crash of the noon bells thundered into a silken chamber where the Empress Justina was conducting an intimate interview with Troldot 'Heavy-fist' Turbothot, an alien from far-distant Hexagon. The interview was proving a disappointment. Why? Because, unbeknownst to Justina, Troldot Turbothot had been diligently interviewed by Theodora that very morning.

Noonday's brazen bells were heard even on the island of Jod where Ivan Pokrov and Artemis Ingalawa were discussing young Chegory Guy. They were bitterly disappointed with him. Long had they struggled to raise the Ebrell Islander from the mire in which he had been spawned. Long had they educated, encouraged and counselled him. They had even introduced him to polite society. Yet he had failed them. At the first opportunity, he had got himself into trouble with the law. What was even more offensive was that he had taken up with the lowest kind of company imaginable – a corpse master, of all people!

How did Pokrov and Ingalawa know that? Simple. A mechanic who lived in Lubos had seen young Chegory that very morning helping the corpse master Uckermark repair his door. The mechanic had delivered himself of this intelligence on arriving for work at the Analytical Institute.

Thus Ingalawa and Pokrov knew how far the ill-begotten redskin had fallen. Worse, he had not come to them for counsel. Whatever his problems, surely they could be sorted out by educated advice and the help of a good lawyer. But the Ebrell Islander was running amok in the city, presumably hoping to solve his present difficulties with the help of lies, evasions, criminal associates and (doubtless) violence.

Thus it had to be.

For, if Chegory were innocent of criminal involvement, why would he be shunning both work and the Dromdanjerie?

'As I see it,' said Artemis Ingalawa with grim resolve, 'first we must find out exactly what he's mixed up with. Maybe he joined the riot at the treasury. Maybe he made off with a handful of diamonds or somesuch. I don't know. But I do know he has to be shaken until the truth falls out of him.'

Pokrov agreed. As Pokrov was supervising a General Oiling of the Analytical Engine, he was not free to venture to Injiltaprajura to extort the truth from Chegory Guy. But Ingalawa was, and set forth immediately. Ingalawa's niece Olivia intercepted her on the shores of Jod, learnt her destination, and insisted on joining her on the trek across the harbour bridge to the mainland.

In Untunchilamon's capital (and only) city, in the clutter of hovels and scramble-walks known as Lubos, in the corpse shop of the ill-famed Uckermark, Chegory Guy was dozing despite the stifling heat, despite the stench of maggot-writhing meat and blocked drains, despite the pestilential flies which clung in clouds of blackness to the gauze which prevented their ingression, despite the strenuous snoring of the corpse master himself and the bull-smell of Log Jaris.

The only person awake in the corpse shop was Yilda. She was in the kitchen, bottling maggots. Not to eat herself, but to sell. Corpse maggots are a delicacy highly regarded by those born and bred in Obooloo. Many such people dwell on Untunchilamon, hence maggots were a profitable sideline for the shop. Yilda enjoyed cookery, but was at last distracted from her work by a hammering without. She went to wake the three sleepers. First, using her boot with the panache of an expert, she roused Uckermark.

'What is it, sweet minikin?' said Uckermark, stirring himself from dreams of sugarcane and toothache.

'Someone's at the door,' said Yilda.

They were indeed. They were not only at the door – they were pounding on it.

'Doing renovations by the sound of it,' said Uckermark, as reverberations echoed through his corpse shop. Then he bawled at the top of his lungs: 'Stop that!' But the strenuous wood-thumping continued. 'That's the problem,' grumbled Uckermark. 'Nobody respects the dignity of the dead.'

Then he woke Chegory and Log Jaris, and all three men armed themselves with edged weapons. Chegory had a long-handled corpse hook, Uckermark had a dragon cleaver, and Log Jaris had a massive kraken club.

[Kraken club: a kitchen implement used on Untunchilamon to tenderise cephalopods. Despite the name they are seldom used on krakens either whole or fragmented but are more commonly involved in the preparation of squid or octopus for cooking. *Oris Baumgage, Fact Checker Minor.*]

The men positioned themselves in the shadows near the door. Then Uckermark said:

'Open it.'

Even as he spoke, the hammering intensified.

'Blood and bodkins!' bawled Yilda. 'I'm coming, I'm coming!' So shouting, she hustled smoke pots to the door. 'Wait on! I'll be with you in just a moment! Don't break it down!' She drew back the bolts and opened the door, discovering a parcel of armed guards without. Said she: 'What do you want?'

'Balls of a bullock!' said the soldiers' captain, stepping back from the outswirling smoke. 'Is the place on fire?'

'They're bloody smoke pots,' said Yilda. 'Can't you see? Are you blind or something? Of course you are! Too much autology, that's what it is! Makes you deaf as well. Didn't you hear what I said? I said: what do you want?'

'I'll give you three guesses,' said the captain.

'Don't come the raw prawn with me!' said Yilda.

As her phraseology will no doubt be inscrutable to all auditors from civilised parts, let it be known that she was telling him, in the gutter argot of Injiltaprajura, to put a polite tongue in his head and not to presume that he had a welcome to Yilda's particular parlour. Yet the captain was incapable of taking a hint.

'Put out the smoke, darling,' he said. 'Then I'll light your fire.'

'The smoke's to keep out the bloody flies, isn't it?' said Yilda. 'Blowflies especially. Bloody blowflies about your height.'

Since Yilda was so patently unfriendly, and since she had a poker clenched in her fist, the captain did not continue with his lighthearted banter but got down to business instantly.

'We're looking for the corpse rapist Uckermark and his bum boy Chegory Guy,' said he.

That is a sanitised version of what he said. However, as no application of censorial expertise could produce a socially acceptable version of what Yilda said in reply, it is doubtless best that her retort be omitted entirely. Let it merely be recorded that by the time she had said her piece, Uckermark had laid down his weapon and had emerged from the shadows. Chegory thought it best to follow suit, and did so.

'I'm Uckermark,' said Uckermark.

'I'm Chegory,' said Chegory.

'And if you want either of us,' said Uckermark, 'you'd better have a warrant.'

'We have got a warrant!' said the captain.

A warrant for what? For the arrest of Chegory Guy? Or for his instant execution?

'What kind of warrant?' said Uckermark.

'This kind!' said the captain.

With that he thrust the warrant toward Uckermark, thinking the corpse master illiterate, and therefore to be intimidated by this ornate parchment. Truly it was an impressive document, done in kaleidoscopic colours bright and gay. An ominous sign indeed! For in the Izdimir Empire the grimmest orders are so bedecked and adorned. But Uckermark took the warrant, read it at the skim, then handed it back with a sneer.

'This but tells you to hand us a summons to compel our appearance in court. Give it! Then get out!'

The captain was disappointed. By documentary intimidation he had hoped to extort a bribe from a fool illiterate, but found himself up against a legal expert of sorts. Reluctantly, the captain handed over the summons, which was but a grubby piece of ricepaper ordering Chegory and Uckermark to appear at a depositions hearing at the palace that same afternoon. The conjuror Odolo was going on trial, and the authorities wanted these two to evidence against him.

The captain turned to go.

'Um, ah, wait a moment!' said Chegory. 'How did you know to find me here?'

The captain did not deign to answer. Instead he marched his soldiers away.

'He knows because the whole palace knows you're here,' said Uckermark. 'I told you so before. Now do you believe me? Since Justina's favoured you with her attentions you're famous, at least in the palace.'

'Oh,' said Chegory. 'I thought I was, uh, safe. From soldiers. From Varazchavardan.'

'Relax!' said Uckermark. 'Don't worry! If Varazchavardan wanted you he'd have claimed your head already.' Then, as Yilda made as if to remove the smoke pots, he said to her: 'Leave the pots. We'll have the door open for a bit.'

'These are dangerous times,' said Log Jaris, emerging from the shadows. 'Today's no day for open doors.'

'The way you speak you'd think we were knee-deep in snow,' said Uckermark. 'Don't you feel the heat or what? I'm close to death as it is. The hell with the danger. We'll leave the door open. If we get but nine tenths of a miracle we might get a little breeze. Some ventilation. Lest I die!'

'If you're worried about death then start worrying about this depositions hearing,' said Log Jaris. 'And quickly! This is dangerous!'

'Odolo knows nothing of us,' said Uckermark as he retreated back inside leaving the smoke pots to guard the open doorway against flies. 'He knows nothing of the wishstone or the thieving of such, and nothing of the Calligrapher's Union or our hand in the organisation of the same.'

'So far, so far,' said Log Jaris. 'But his lawyers will start digging for dirt as soon as we're known to be witnessing against him. We've much to fear from such investigation.'

'Shall we run?' said Chegory.

But even as he said it he knew running was no answer. After all, where could they go? He had thought through all the options plenty of times. Hide Downstairs? Or flee the city? If they fled now, they could not depart by sea. Not in the season of Fistavlir. So they would have to go inland.

To Zazazolzodanzarzakazolabrik.

Zazazolzodanzarzakazolabrik, also known as the Scraglands, the Wastes, the Scorpion Desert – or Zolabrik for short. A deathscape of sundrought and rupture, of upthrust pinnacles and rotten rock, of dread ruins undermined by sea-flooded tunnels infested by huge sea scorpions, sea centipedes and monsters yet worse. Chegory's nightmare was to flee to that wilderness where survival's exigencies would force him to seek refuge with Impala Guy, his father – Jal Japone's stillmaster. Surely he would then be doomed to become another alcoholic Ebrell Islander, living as a hunted criminal in conditions of the utmost depravity.

He said as much to Uckermark.

The corpse master laughed.

'So you wish to live innocent, do you? Then you chose the wrong world for your birth. But never mind. I've no thoughts of flight to the Wastes. Yes, a depositions hearing means danger – but running means more danger yet.'

Then discussion ended, even though Chegory had a thousand doubts and questions, for Uckermark was determined to devote himself to the business of lunch. They dined on some splendiferous fish, some magnanimous coconuts, some utilitarian water and some nuts pragmatic. With food in his belly, Chegory started to feel better. Until, as he was sitting back in his chair peeling a piece of sugarcane, he got one of the larger shocks of his life.

What caused it?

The advent of a dragon!

Chegory first espied the dragon when it was sitting atop a gaunt-grinning skull. It was a tiny dragon. Naught but the length of his finger. A hallucination, surely. A flashback caused by zen. Chegory fumbled his sugarcane on to the table, for his sweat-slippery fingers could hold it no longer.

'What is it?' said Yilda, seeing his concern.

'It's a dragon,' said Uckermark, seeing where Chegory was looking.

The corpse master idly lobbed a mango at the miniature monster. The mango missed. Splattered. Log Jaris picked up a piece of clean-scraped coconut shell and flicked it across the room. But his missile also missed. Then the two men began to compete, disposing of the remains of their luncheon in a quick-fire fusillade. The dragon took evasive action. The two ex-pirates rose to the challenge.

Thus it was that when Artemis Ingalawa entered the corpse shop she came upon a truly manic scene. An angry, irritated dragon was slip-sliding through the air as it tried to simultaneously attack its persecutors and evade a barrage of plates, pots, skulls and slops.

'Stop that!' said Ingalawa.

Her sharp command quelled the riot on the instant. The last missiles clattered against the wall. The dragon, seizing its opportunity, hurtled toward Log Jaris. Then thought better of it, veered away, and alighted atop Ingalawa's head. She brushed it away with an irritated hand. The dragon took to the air again. Ingalawa turned the full force of her fury on Chegory Guy.

'Chegory Guy!' said she. 'What are you doing here?'

'You – you have a dragon on your head,' said Chegory, for the dragon had resettled atop the Ashdan mathematician.

'That doesn't answer my question,' said Ingalawa curtly, ignoring the dragon as she tried to stare down the delinquent Chegory Guy.

The hair-riding dragon farted, emitting a tiny burst of steam from its rear end. Chegory, unable to help himself, broke into hysterical laughter. Ingalawa was furious. She swept the dragon from its perch. It tumbled into the air, recovered itself, then flew out of the corpse shop. In the street outside, somebody screamed.

Chegory knew that scream.

It was Olivia's scream.

On the instant, his laughter ceased. He got to his feet and charged outside, snatching up a corpse hook as he ran. He had visions of the dragon, expanded by magic to gigantic size, attacking his darling Olivia in the street. But when he leapt through the billowing fumes from the smoke pots and gained the street, there was no monster to be seen. Only Olivia herself, still shaking from shock. On seeing the tiny dragon, she had momentarily thought herself insane.

There are, after all, no dragons so small which fly. The fabled land dragons of Argan are much larger even when fresh-hatched from the egg. As for the imperial dragons of Yestron, these grow to the size of dogs before they become aviators, while sea dragons never fly at all.

Wordlessly, Olivia fell into Chegory's arms. Considering the length of time the Ebrell Islander had spent in the corpse shop it is fortunate indeed that the fumes from the smoke pots subdued all other odours.

Chegory and his true love clung to each other in the street until Ingalawa came up behind them.

'Break it up, children!' she said.

From the way she spoke, it was clear she was still angry.

'Okay,' said Chegory, breaking it up. Then, to Olivia, who was still tearful: 'Come inside. Come in, and I'll get you a cup of water.'

So in they went. But as soon as the two Ashdan females entered the corpse shop Chegory knew he had made a dreadful mistake, for Olivia's wide-wrenched mouth and startled eyes betrayed both shock and disgust. Said the eyes: in all my life this is the very worst place in which I have ever been, a veritable soulhell. Said the eyes, with eloquence: what has my poor Chegory come to? How did he manage to fall so far so fast? Said the mouth: I'm going to be sick.

Worse, when Chegory handed Olivia some water, she could not drink it. She gagged. The cup slipped from her hand. She fled. Chegory pursued her outside, and was comforting her still when Log Jaris lumbered into the street to join them in the sunlight. His black bullfur shone with sunsheen. The pale ivory of his horns gleamed in the light of day's great luminary. The two young lovers lived in his eyes as miniature reflections. Olivia looked at this obscene creature, this mutant abomination, then hid her face in Chegory's shoulder.

'Are you ready to go?' said Log Jaris.

A couple of flies settled on his nostrils. He waved them away. They dizzied upwards, one settling on his larboard horn.

'Go?' said Ingalawa angrily. 'Where would you be thinking of going? Where are you taking Chegory Guy? And why? Explain yourself!'

'I'm not taking him anywhere,' said Log Jaris. 'It's Uckermark who's taking him.'

'We have to go to the palace,' said Chegory, trying to

explain. 'A, um, a depositions hearing, that's what it's all about. That's why we're going.'

'A depositions hearing!' said Ingalawa. 'Are you guilty? Have you got a lawyer? What have you done?'

'I've done nothing!' said Chegory.

'Oh, that's what you all say!' retorted Ingalawa. 'But you were mixed up in that riot, weren't you? That riot at the treasury? And where were you all yesterday? And all last night? Here? Doing what? Whatever it was, why didn't you show yourself at the Dromdanjerie today? Or at Jod?'

'Look,' said Chegory, 'it's complicated, okay?'

'Complicated?' said Ingalawa. 'What's complicated about it?'

'All kinds of things,' said Chegory. 'Varazchavardan, that sorcerer, you know, okay? He's got – we – we had this like kind of run in so now I want to keep out of his way, okay? So he'd look for me in the Dromdanjerie, okay, or at Jod, where I live, where I work. But he doesn't know about the corpse shop, or I thought he didn't, though maybe he does. And this – these – those soldiers Shabble burnt, they might still be looking for me so I don't want to be found. Because I'm, okay, maybe technically some kind of escaped prisoner, but I've, um—'

'You've got yourself in a mess,' said Ingalawa. 'If you're trying to hide from soldiers or from Varazchavardan then what're you doing going to the palace? They'll easily catch you!'

Chegory reacted violently. The more so because the illogic of his position had already been exposed by the delivery of the summons. The corpse shop was no hideaway!

'So tough!' said he. 'So I tried, okay? Uncaught all yesterday, all last night. Last day of my life, last night maybe. But maybe not. I'll be okay up at the palace because, uh, the Empress, she likes me, trusts me.'

'The boy's deluded!' said Ingalawa. 'If you had the trust of the Empress you wouldn't be going on trial for whatever it is you've done.'

'I'm not on trial!' said Chegory.

'But you just said you were,' said Ingalawa.

This was so unreasonable that Chegory was tempted to hit her. Then Uckermark came out into the sunlight and, speaking over Ingalawa's wrath, said:

'Our young friend from the Ebrells is charged with nothing. Guilty of many things he doubtless is, but he lives innocent of all charges. He is but attending a depositions hearing as a witness.'

'In what kind of case?' said Ingalawa.

'A case of high treason,' said Uckermark.

'What a thing to get mixed up in!' said Ingalawa, in tones of condemnation.

She was making Chegory feel as if he had done something wrong. He reminded himself that in point of fact he had been strenuously virtuous throughout his recent troubles. It made no difference. Ingalawa still made him feel soiled, contaminated, guilty. How did she do it? Easily, easily. Whenever he was in her presence, her air of effortless superiority automatically put him at a disadvantage.

Chegory, boiling with murderous resentment, almost said what he thought, but restrained himself. This took heroic effort, for, despite his recent sleep, he was as tired as the fly which flew to the moon. Waiting around in the corpse shop had scarcely helped him recover from his recent traumas. Instead, it had given him unlimited opportunity to worry about the mess he had got himself into and all the people who might be after his blood.

'So,' said Ingalawa, 'how did you get mixed up in a treason trial?'

'We can go into that later,' said Chegory.

'Chegory,' said Ingalawa sharply, 'I think you'd better tell us what's going on right now. In detail.'

Chegory looked at Uckermark helplessly. What wasn't going on? He was in so many kinds of trouble it would have taken all morning to catalogue them. But he had tried so hard to be good! To be an exemplary citizen!

'Chegory?' said Ingalawa, questioning his silence.

'I don't know where to begin,' said Chegory.

'Then start by telling us what you're doing. Here. With these – these people. Are you in some kind of trouble?'

The woman was being so obtuse! How could he not be in trouble? Chegory had striven strenuously to remain reticent, but now found words pouring out wrath-hot and burning, like a torrent of molten wax:

'Trouble! Of course I'm in trouble! I wanted to go back to Jod, when Ox first warned us I wanted to go back, but you wouldn't have it on. Oh no, you said, don't run away. It's your right, you said. You're a citizen, you said. You've got the law on your side. Oh, all right for you to speak!

'But then what happens? That lunatic Shabble gets us all in the shit and we all get arrested then the guards come back and then what? Oh you stay put, it's no trouble for you, but I get dragged off to the palace.

'And then what? Oh, nothing much. Just riots, breakouts, mad wizards, monsters, drug dealers. And Varazchavardan, oh I could be here all day just telling you about Varazchavardan. And then what? The palace, and that mad bitch Justina trying to rape me, then the dragon, there was a dragon in the palace and I nearly got killed.

'But what about you? Oh you're all right, aren't you? You got out of jail okay, you've got a lawyer I guess, you'll be all right. Because you're an Ashdan, you've got respect, but I'm just an Ebby, they'll kill me as soon as look at me, whatever goes wrong it's going to be my fault, isn't it?

'And none of it would have happened, none of it, if you'd just let me go back to the island. That's all. Just hide away for the night. I knew it, I knew it, but you—'

Chegory clenched his fist as if he was going to hit her. Then he burst into tears instead. Wracked by the unbearable pain of existence. Artemis stood clear of him, not at all sure what to make of his outburst – fearing him perhaps a potential killer. But Log Jaris slapped him on the shoulder and said:

'That's better said than living inside you unsaid.'

Then Uckermark said:

'Time we were going, Chegory. The summons demands.

We can't be late for this hearing. Log Jaris, my friend –
can you stay here to help Yilda look after the shop? In case
of raiders and such.'

'My pleasure,' said Log Jaris.

'If you're going,' said Ingalawa, in a moment of swift
decision, 'then we two are going with you.'

So off they set, Artemis Ingalawa and Olivia Qasaba
travelling in consort with Chegory and Uckermark.

CHAPTER TWENTY-FIVE

It was one of those days when even those born and bred on Untunchilamon find the heat oppressive. The whole city had slowed to the leisurely pace of convalescence, for it was impossible to exert oneself at speed. Thanks to the heat, the very effort of idling up Lak Street had become an exercise in advanced calisthenics.

[It cannot get so hot. Sloth is a deficiency of the intellect which should never be blamed on climate. If a trifling warmth of weather truly inflicted such stasis upon Injilta-prajura then we have a shocking picture of an entire culture sunk in irretrievable decadence. One longs to see the Conquest commence and a muscular Religion bring the virtues of Work and Efficiency to such a derelict society. *Srin Gold, Commentator Extraordinary*.]

Untunchilamon is ever hot, but on exceptional days of sweat like this when even the hardiest armpit lice must fear death by drowning, when every pair of thighs in the city is as wet as honeymoon passion, when every crutch is a reeking gymnasium, then the heat seems to come not just from the sun alone but from the sky itself, and, indeed, from the very streets themselves. The bloodrock was heating to the point of flux. The white mass of Pearl was glazed by an intolerable glare. Heat-distorted buildings shimmered and buckled as the air itself warped in helpless agony.

Such weather produces certain types of madness much feared on Untunchilamon. There is for example the mind-state called (to name it in Janjuladoola) talabrapalau, when one lives in fear of bursting into flame in an episode of spontaneous conflagration. Another psychosis, the name of which escapes me, has one believing that the rocks will ignite. I have also met a man who feared he would dissolve into sweat, flow through the windows of the Dromdanjerie, tumble down the precipitous slopes of Skindik Way to Lubos, muck through the slum-filth then splosh into the Laitemata.

Thus we see that madness is specific to culture. We see this elsewhere, indeed. For example, in the city of Babrika, where everything is so mannerly, where politeness rules all and no voice is ever raised in anger, it happens that from time to time an individual will run amok and hack through the marketplace until being overpowered then chopped into pieces no larger than your baby's thumb.

On the Ebrells, on the other hand, certain individuals revolt against the life of the organism, showing their hatred for the degeneracy of their fellows by developing a condition known as Pinch, when they refuse food and starve themselves to death. Strangely, while thus starving they delude themselves that they are healthy and getting healthier.

In Obooloo, of course, religious mania takes its toll, whereas on the island of Odrum—

[Here sundry slanders and laboriously erroneous pedantries have been deleted. *By Order. Vendano, Guardian of the Honour of Odrum.*]

Thus it was that Chegory and his companions were a muck of sweat as they laboured up Lak Street to the palace where the Empress Justina held court. The palace! A monument to eroticism. The pink thighs of its walls. The breasts of its cupolas. Sweet indeed it would have been, but for the intolerable reflections from the glitter dome, which was very agony to look at.

The redskinned Ebrell Islander and his escorts penetrated the pink flesh of Justina's palace. After the light of the sun, everything was muted except the heat. An usher intercepted them, asked their mission, then showed them to the Star Chamber where the depositions hearing would take place. On the way, they passed the saturnine Slanic Moldova, at work on his great mural, which bears the title 'Sky Worshipping The Kraken Her Master'.

'Hello, Slan,' said Olivia, pausing to look at his work.

Chegory paused with her. Slanic Moldova was working at full pitch, brush darting and sweeping, flashing from palette to wall. Then to flesh. Before Chegory could pull back, Moldova had swept blue paint from Chegory's eyebrows to his chin.

'Zoso!' said Olivia sharply.

At the enunciation of this phrase, Moldova's paint-hand swayed to a halt as he fell into a hypnotic trance. Olivia took his hand and gently guided brush to wall, knowing he would work on for much of the rest of the day without waking from his trance.

'Hurry!' said the usher, with a note of urgency. 'Hurry, else the hearing will start without you.'

So they hustled on down the hall, with Chegory making frantic efforts to clean his face. But mural paint is notoriously difficult to remove.

'Stop!' said Ingalawa, as they reached the portal to the Star Chamber.

She could see the hearings were not yet underway. They yet had time. She whipped out a clean sweat rag and attacked the paint on Chegory's face.

'Leave that young man alone,' said a voice of command. It was the voice of Aquitaine Varazchavardan, Master of Law to the Empress Justina. 'Come,' said Varazchavardan. 'The depositions hearing is about to begin.'

'Just let me just clean his face,' said Ingalawa, renewing her onslaught on the streak of sky besmirching Chegory's flame-red complexion.

'How dare you!' said Varazchavardan, snatching the rag away. 'Interfere with this witness again and I'll have you hung, strung and gutted.'

They stared at each other. A startling contrast they made. Varazchavardan with his eyes of pink. Ingalawa with orbs as dark as the moonless sea. Varazchavardan with his skin as white as the greater narjorgo corpse worm. Ingalawa with her coal-gloss skin as dark as the plumage of the dark lartle, that bad-tempered sharp-beaked bird of Wen Endex.

As Varazchavardan had the full weight and majesty of the state behind him, it was Ingalawa who had to drop her eyes and give way. Thus Chegory entered the Star Chamber with a broad band of blue slashed across his face. He looked quite the clown. Like an actor from the Broko Comedy Theatre, in fact. Though there was nothing amusing about his predicament.

The Star Chamber was the newest part of the pink palace. It was a large hall which had been tacked on to the northern side of the palace. Its pink walls rose to a pink dome high above. Windows inset where wall met dome allowed a pink-tinged light to flood the room, which was tiled with pink tiles, and came complete with a pink-painted mezzanine floor supported by pillars of pink stone. Today the Star Chamber was almost empty, for crushing heat had dissuaded the idle elements of the rabble from attending. A few messenger boys and lawyers' clerks hung around, chewing on betel nut or sticks of pandanus, but the bulk of the mob was absent.

Artemis Ingalawa seated herself with authority on one of the long benches of woven bamboo provided for onlookers. She looked around severely. She was in her power mood, her managing mood, her executive mood. In which she was potentially very dangerous. Note that while Artemis Ingalawa had been born into the culture of elegance which dominates Ashmolea South, her family actually came from Ashmolea North. There the Ingalawa clan is notorious for breeding slaughter swords and assassins.

Blood will tell!

Chegory, fearing as much, hoped Ingalawa would not precipitate any untoward incidents. If she did, he didn't think he could cope. He was too tired. So tired he would need but to close his eyes to voyage instantly into dreams. But his blood rose on the moment to the alert when Olivia seated herself beside him and took his hand. Ah yes! He rose and roused! Consumed by thoughts of juice and softness, of the monstrous secret crouched between her thighs, of harlot-fingered night engorging the cravings of her pubic whirlpool, of—

[Here a lengthy and turgid digression of considerable improbability has been excised. *By Order, Drax Lira, Redactor Major.*]

Yet Chegory's pleasure was not perfected by Olivia's presence, for he was all too conscious of Varazchavardan's pink eyes dragonising him. The white-fleshed Master of Law had a predator's eyes and claws to match. When Chegory closed his own eyes to avoid that implacable stare, he could not help but imagine those claws whittling away his flesh till they reached his very bones.

Slowly, the other actors in this courtroom drama gathered into the Star Chamber. Here came the conjuror Odolo. Sweating – and not just because of the heat. Then the Empress Justina arrived, handbag in hand, to spectate at the depositions hearing – the actual conduct of which would be governed by Judge Qil.

On this day of butterfly dreams and banana-skinned decision—

[Words doubtless senseless, but there is no helping that. Often one suspects that the Version we are translating from is hopelessly corrupt. But what can one expect from a madman? *This insertion here placed by Valther Nash, Consulting Translator.*]

—the Empress was wearing a curious confection which was composed mostly of string, with but a little silk at each of the seven Strategic Places.

[One of the Strategic Places is the omphalos, but I have been unable to precisely locate the other six. These matters are dealt with in detail in the Book of Flesh, but access to this scholarly treatise has been denied to me by a prudish Librarian Major. *Oris Baumgage, Fact Checker Minor.*]

The Empress smiled upon Chegory Guy, her smile making it very, very clear that she had not forgotten him. Then she saw Olivia was cosseting Chegory's hand.

'Who is your charming young friend?' said Justina, in tones less than entirely friendly.

'This is but – but a friend of my family,' said Chegory, inventing as best he could.

Was Olivia at risk? Perhaps! Yet Chegory, feeling her stiffen, knew he should not have spoken of her in such dismissive tones. She was offended. She was, after all, an Ashdan – and these people have far more pride than the rest of us.

'What kind of friend?' said Justina, in tones auger-sharp.

Sweat dripped from Chegory Guy's forehead as he sought desperately for some adroit way to resolve his difficulties; that is, to divert Justina's attention from Olivia without offending that delicious young personage. He failed entirely. To his horror, he heard himself saying:

'Oh, just some Ashdan.'

Young lovers take note: this is not the way to talk of the lust of your heart in her presence. In proof of which, Olivia took umbrage immediately, and removed herself. Chegory wanted to flee to her side, to apologise, to kneel and kiss, to whisper and grovel. But he was not free to so express himself, for the Empress Justina was still talking to him:

'. . . which will be tonight.'

'Pardon?' said Chegory.

'You have an audience with me,' said the Empress Justina. 'Tonight.'

'Tonight?' said Chegory, gaping like an idiot.

'All night,' said the Empress Justina. 'From dusk to dawn. Undokondra and bardardornootha entire and complete.'

'My . . . my lady. I am . . . I am honoured. But – um – ah . . .'

But Olivia would kill him.

'We are glad you are properly appreciative of the honour,' said Justina severely. 'That is as it should be. Wait here once you have given evidence. We shall meet at session's end.'

Thus she spake, then smiled, and withdrew.

Chegory swore to himself as he watched the Empress seat herself on a chair of woven cane and place her crocodile-skinned handbag down beside her. A sensible choice was this chair of cane, for it was far too hot to endure the magnificence of a velvet-clad throne. Slaves, each wearing naught but a tight-strapped codpiece, fanned her with ostrich feathers.

[One doubts that either the Empress Justina or her slaves could have been attired as suggested by the Originator. One recalls, for a start, that the ostrich is a purely mythical beast. Yet there are improbabilities here which are larger yet. In all likelihood the descriptions of dress given above are but a quirk of the Originator's purile imagination. Doubtless the Empress and her slaves were in fact decently clad in woollen gowns and leather weather helms. *Sot Dawbler, School of Commentary.*]

Then the depositions hearing commenced. Chegory was among the first to give evidence, but once finished he could not leave the session because the Empress Justina had commanded him to wait. Thus he sat solitary. Sweating. Aware that he was being dragonised by the Empress, by Qasaba and Ingalawa, and by Varazchavardan himself.

Gods! What will become of me?

CHAPTER TWENTY-SIX

At length the depositions hearing came to an end. Judge Qil announced his decision.

'Odolo,' he said, 'you can count yourself lucky. I am dismissing several of the charges which have been laid against you. First, the smoking charge. It would be wrong for you to be put on trial for smoking at a royal banquet since the smoking the law alludes to clearly relates to the consumption by combustion of kif, opium or grass clippings.

'I am reluctantly dismissing the charges of keeping an unmuzzled dragon within the city limits, of displaying a dragon with intent to terrorise and of allowing a dragon to come in close proximity to alcohol. To my deep regret, the law is clear. For the purpose of the relevant clauses a dragon is strictly defined as an imperial dragon, land dragon or sea dragon. The corpse master Uckermark has testified that dissection proves your alleged creation to be none of these three, hence while it is obviously a dragon of some description it is not a dragon for the purposes of the law. It may however be a dog, but that seems doubtful – so the alternative charges of keeping, displaying and allowing a dog are also struck out.

'A charge of transforming yourself into a beast of terror is also dismissed, as are the accusations of witchcraft, illegal hypnotism, heresy, insult general to a public religion and striking fear into the heart of the Empress. The last charge cannot be sustained since our beloved Empress is the daughter of a Yudonic Knight and is known to be fearless.'

By now both Justina and Odolo were smiling on the judge. But the eminent Qil was not finished. He continued:

'However, Odolo, on many counts a *prima facie* case has been established against you.'

The conjuror cringed. The very vraisemblance of coward-ice incarnate. The judge onspake remorselessly:

'Therefore I am committing you to trial on two charges of high treason, three of middle treason, one of low treason and a half-charge of sub-treason. You will also be tried on charges of revolution, waging war against the state, attempted murder, practising generative magic without a licence, littering, common insolence, disorderly conduct, and conduct prejudicial to civil discipline.'

The last charge was the most dangerous because, as virtually anything anyone does can be construed as conduct prejudicial to civil discipline, it is near impossible to launch an effective defence against such a charge. This is why in my own case I had to plead temporary insanity when—

[The Originator here presents us with an extended plea in mitigation to explain the conduct of his own life. This has been deleted on the grounds that it is (a) indecent and (b) libellous. Scholars who inspect the unexpurgated text of the original manuscript will doubtless agree that there is nothing temporary about the Originator's insanity. *Srin Gold, Commentator Extraordinary.*]

The judge concluded by saying:

'Have you anything to say?'

'Yes!' said Odolo. 'That I'm innocent!' Then he turned to the Empress Justina to cry: 'My lady! Have mercy! I beg you!'

Odolo's guards roughed him to silence. Justina studied him. Then, with a faint smile on her lips, she said: 'Should I have mercy? Who will advise me? No, Varazchavardan – I can guess your counsel already.' She turned to Chegory Guy. Her smile deepened. 'Let's try . . . let's try advice from another source. Pray tell, what would an Ebrell Islander do?'

Even though there were but few people in the Star Chamber, an audible murmur of outrage ran round that Chamber when thus the Empress spoke. Even Chegory himself was shocked. He slumped down in his chair. Cringing. Pretending he was invisible. Pretending he was asleep. But, as a guard was already poking him with a scimitar, he rapidly realised this strategy could not succeed. Reluctantly, he got to his feet to say:

'It is not for an Ebrell Islander to dispose of the lives and laws of the free citizens of Untunchilamon.'

'Nonsense!' said Justina. 'All citizens are equal under law, are they not? Lawyers are but citizens like the rest, yet venture to give me advice on a daily basis. If lawyers, then why not you?'

'Because—' ventured Varazchavardan.

'Silence, Vazzy!' said the Empress in a head-chopping voice. 'It's far too hot for argument. Let's hear the boy speak.'

Varazchavardan ventured no more, but waited for Chegory to give them the benefit of his wisdom. As did everyone. They waited and they watched. Chegory wanted to vanish. To disappear in a clap of thunder and a puff of smoke. To run and run and run and never be seen in Injiltaprajura again. For whatever he said was bound to be wrong. He was totally exposed. Totally vulnerable. Worse—

Whatever he said, did or tried he was sure to remain visible, exposed and vulnerable. Famous, in a word. For the last couple of days had won him so much notoriety that he would never again be able to pretend he was a rock. His days of safety were over, so doubtless his deathday lay very close in the future.

Then Chegory was seized by inspiration. He turned to Varazchavardan to say:

'Uh, I'm not, um, how do I say this, well, I'm not, I am not of the Wise, okay, thus seek the help of the Wise. Help of the Master of Law. Varazchavardan the, uh, honourable. We don't know each other but maybe we could. Know each other, I mean. If he could help me just a bit with this, uh, legal thing, I'd, well, whatever I could help him with I would.'

Chegory was doing his best. He was trying to say:

'Dear Varazchavardan, you whom I love and respect

above all other men, forget you ever saw me with the mad pirates who tried to kidnap you Downstairs. Forget that. Remember instead that I'm the latest imperial favourite. My friendship could be worth having. So do me a favour. Help me out.'

Considering how much he could not say outright he managed (or thought he managed) to get quite a lot of this across. He was most pleased with his eloquent little speech. But was Varazchavardan pleased? The worm-white albino regarded the blood-red Ebby in silence. While the Master of Law never later discussed what he was thinking at that time, we can deduce his thoughts effortlessly, and with a high degree of probability.

Doubtless Varazchavardan reflected on Chegory's Ebrell origin, with its implications in terms of a natural affinity for death-liquor in all its manifestations. This Ebby looked young enough, fast enough, tough enough. A knife-capable young man. Who (for the moment) had the ear of the Empress herself. An ally potent. An enemy dangerous.

Thus (doubtless) Varazchavardan thought.

Then said:

'I welcome this pledge of allegiance from the young Ebrell Islander. I have oft thought that we underestimate the capabilities of our red-skinned friends. I will welcome the opportunity to talk with him in private hereafter.'

On hearing this, Chegory sat back in his chair with a feeling of sweet release and relief. He had done it! He had turned the wrath of Varazchavardan away from himself. He had turned an enemy into an ally. He was very pleased with himself. But he had no time for extended self-congratulation, for Varazchavardan was onspeaking still. Chegory had missed part of his speech, but realised it concerned Odolo:

'. . . would be the consequences of extending mercy before trial? Surely a key function of the law is to determine the truth. Once the truth is known then we can contemplate mercy. But mercy now would be a sorry blow to the determination of truth. Hence I say this.'

Varazchavardan paused for breath, but did not proceed to say this. Or that. Or the other. For he was interrupted by the arrival of Dolglin Chin Xter, who had not been seen in public since the dragon manifested itself in the banqueting hall of the pink palace. Yes – Dolglin Xter. Have you forgotten him? Already!? Then do not tell him, or he will be mortally offended! Remember, you were properly introduced. Dolglin Chin Xter! Head of Justina's Inquisition into drug pushing on Untunchilamon! Remember now?

Xter is the one who is as yellow as the flesh of a mango, thanks to the disease which has him in its grip. Why he is not dead of hepatitis is a mystery. Why sweat pours from his skin is a mystery also, but a lesser one; heat, hepatitis and malaria may all have something to do with it. As for his shaking hand – why, that may well be the fear-palsy. For the Inquisitor has committed himself to a potentially lethal course: a public confrontation with Varazchavardan.

Dolglin Chin Xter, then.

That is who he is (or was – he may be dead by now) and here is what he said:

'Have I leave to speak?'

Not the most dramatic of things to say. After the build-up above you may well think it bathotic. If so, blame history, not me. This is but a record of events, and of words spoken in the course of events, and one cannot rightly distort history for the sake of drama. Doubtless it would have been more satisfactory (from a dramatic point of view) if Dolglin Xter had burst into the Star Chamber shouting thus:

'Varazchavardan, you foul demonic blotch of blood! You, most evil and most blood-greedy of a brood of scorpions! It is you who I accuse, for you have been discovered! All is known! Prepare to meet your doom!'

However, Dolglin Xter did not speak thus. What he actually did say ('Have I leave to speak?') was the right and appropriate thing to say under the circumstances, for even an inquisitor cannot interrupt a depositions hearing in the Star Chamber with impunity.

Thus did the Empress Justina reply:

'Of course, Dolly my darling. Speak on for as long as you wish.'

But Dolglin Chin Xter at first did not speak at all. Instead, yellow Xter ominous looked left to right and around, then pegged his gaze on Varazchavardan.

[*Translator's Note*: Here the syntax and vocabulary of the Original are obscure in the extreme. This temporary Version must serve until scholarship has given us a definitive Interpretation.]

Then Xter did begin to speak, saying:

'Here the best minds of Untunchilamon sit in solemn ceremony, considering the case of the conjuror Odolo.'

Why did he say that? Everyone present knew as much. He was only stating the obvious. Doubtless his legal training was to blame. Yes, Xter was something of a lawyer, and nine-tenths of the practice of law is to win economic advantage by laboriously stating and restating the obvious in order to delay the resolution of the matter at hand so that the attendant legal fees may be increased to a level commensurate with lawyerly greed.

Fortunately, since Xter was very ill, the pressures of physical disability curtailed the loquacity to which his training had predisposed him, and he thereafter got down to business instanter:

'Some would say that justice is thereby served. But I would beg to differ. This trial is a nonsense.

'It is a nonsense to accuse Odolo of creating a dragon at banquet. For such powers of creation are vested in only the greatest. Odolo is but a prestigitator whose sole skill lies in manual manipulation. What lunacy could make anyone think this idle entertainer could have created a dragon?

'The true villain is another person altogether. Aquitaine Varazchavardan! Yes, Varazchavardan made that dragon. He made it in an attempt to kill me. Why? Because my Inquisition was on the brink of proving his guilt. Now we have proved it! The last evidence has been obtained! Varazchavardan is a drug dealer!'

Dolglin Chin Xter paused. Not for dramatic effect, but to recover his breath. Nevertheless, while his motives for the pause were mundane, the effect was dramatic in the extreme.

The pause gave Chegory the chance to curse himself for erring most dreadfully. When he had met Varazchavardan Downstairs under inauspicious circumstances the wonder-worker had not been supervising a raid on an illegal warehouse – no, he had been the proprietor of that warehouse!

The albinotic one was filth of the worst order, a fiend from the legions of the damned. He was one of those monsters who traffic in the most abominable drugs imaginable, drugs which cause insanity, cancer and death! The sorcerer was a callous, unprincipled brute who sold alcohol – evil of evils! – to enrich himself and glut his greed for worldly wealth. Yet Chegory had tried to pact with him.

With incredibly bad timing, Chegory had declared himself for Varazchavardan just before the man was revealed as a master criminal. His error was compounded by the fact that he had done so in public. In front of the Empress! In front of Olivia and Ingalawa both! Somehow, he had to extricate himself from this mess. To repudiate Varazchavardan. Quickly! But how?

Before he could think on it further, Xter continued:

'Aquitaine Varazchavardan, in my capacity as Inquisitor General I order you to be suspended from all official duties and placed under arrest. You—'

'You're mad!' said Varazchavardan. 'I refuse to be suspended by a madman! He's a lunatic, a crazy, a blue banana.'

'Guards!' shouted Xter, pointing at Varazchavardan. 'Seize him!'

Those guards who placed their trust in Dolglin Chin Xter advanced upon Varazcavardan, who repeated his accusations of insanity:

'He's mad, mad! Seize him! Not me! Him!'

Those guards loyal to Varazchavardan closed in on Dolglin Chin Xter.

It was all on!

The Empress Justina was on her feet. Shouting something. But what? Her voice was lost in the uproar as roaring guards charged Xter and Varazchavardan both. Smoke of many colours boiled up around the two embattled sorcerers. The guards disappeared into the smoke. From that roiling pother came shouts and snarls, cries and screams. Slowly outcry gave way to coughing as smoke subdued the mob.

'Stop!' commanded Justina. 'Stop fighting! Now!'

She had a formidable pair of lungs. She was obeyed. Or appeared to be obeyed. In fact, combat ended because both sorcerers had disposed of the guards sent against them. Smoke cleared. Revealing the two wonderworkers. Who stood on guard with smoke still dribbled from their fingertips. Around them lay groaning guards in various states of disrepair. Nobody had been killed – a very miracle indeed! – but most were feeling more than a little sick.

'Order in the court!' said Judge Qil, venturing to speak now that order had been restored.

The Empress Justina ignored him. She turned her fury on her Master of Law. 'Varazchavardan!' said she. Then coughed as a little smoke invaded her airspace. Then went on: 'Explain yourself! Are you a drug dealer or are you not?'

'I am not,' said Varazchavardan. He jabbed one talon in Chin Xter's direction. 'What's more, this man's a criminal! He accuses me, but he's the one! He did it! He unleashed the dragon! I saw, you saw, we all saw! In came Xter, into the banqueting hall. Next moment – the dragon! He's the one!'

Dolglin Chin Xter was so shocked and shaken by his battle with the guards that he could barely stand. He had no breath for eloquence. Indeed, he barely had breath sufficient to sustain life. Verily, he looked as if he might have a heart attack instanter. So there were good reasons for his silence. Health reasons. But few spectators thought of that. To most of the mundane intellects present, Xter's silence meant only one thing: he must be guilty.

'I order Xter to be suspended and arrested,' said Varazchavardan. 'On charges of high, low and middle treason. On charges of keeping dragons without licence. And – and – and of letting prisoners escape.'

'Prisoners?' said the Empress Justina, bewildered. 'Stand still, you men! Still, I say! Vazzy, what's this about prisoners?'

All action in the Star Chamber was for the moment suspended as the Empress confronted her Master of Law.

'The prisoners I speak of are the Malud marauders who were trapped in the starvation cage,' said Varazchavardan. 'Xter let them out! I have proof!'

'You are mistaken,' said the Empress with a considerable degree of severity. 'Young Chegory Guy let the prisoners out.'

On hearing that, Varazchavardan realised he had made a mistake. He had over-reached himself. He pushed on recklessly:

'Then arrest him too!' said Varazchavardan. 'Doubtless he was Xter's agent.'

'He only let them out so we could shelter from the dragon in the cage,' said Justina. 'If he hadn't let them out, I'd be dead. Eaten by the dragon.'

'But who brought the dragon into the banqueting hall in the first place?' said Varazchavardan. 'Xter! Don't you see? It's a conspiracy! In came Xter, in came the dragon, then Chegory opened the cage, out went the prisoners, in went the Empress, confusion reigned—'

'But I reign here and now,' said the Empress. 'Varazchavardan! You are out of order! Be seated!'

The Empress Justina was not a political genius. But her father, Lonstantine Thrug, had taught her the basics. In particular, he had taught her that speed is dangerous. Speed kills! Right now, a great many things were happening very very quickly. The Empress did not like it. Was Varazchavardan guilty? Was Xter? Was Odolo? She knew not, but knew full well she needed time to think about it.

'Be seated!' she said, repeating her order to the recalcitrant Varazchavardan.

But Varazchavardan would not be seated. Since he had gone too far already he must now go further yet – or be doomed for certain. His accusing talons needled the air as he shouted:

'Xter! You're under arrest! And you! The Ebby! And that corpse master, he's under arrest! And—'

'Halt!' cried Justina. 'This has gone too far! This is a gross abuse of our Presence, of the judicial process, the constitutional mechanism, your office and the public patience.' What the Empress said might have made very little sense if subjected to detailed intellectual analysis, but it sounded magnificent. She continued: 'Nobody is under arrest here. Not unless I say so.'

'Then say it!' said Chegory Guy desperately, seizing his chance. 'Say it about Varazchavardan! He's a drug pusher! Xter's right! I've proof! Varazchavardan's evil! Drugs, drugs, that's what he's into! I saw him, he had liquor, barrel upon barrel of it. I saw it Downstairs! He had rum!'

He had rum! In Injiltaprajura, that was about the worst accusation one could make about someone.

'That is a baseless accusation,' said Varazchavardan roundly. 'A vile slander. This Chegory is in league with Xter! He's part of a criminal conspiracy to undermine the administration of law. Treason, in a word!'

Chegory could hear pounding footsteps fast-approaching. Whose footsteps? Who was coming?

'We'll see,' said the Empress Justina grimly. 'For the moment, Vazzy, you're out of a job. I'm removing you from your position. You'll—' She broke off as armed guards came pounding into the Star Chamber. At their head was the captain of her palace guard, the elegant Bro Drumel. 'Brody!' said Justina. 'Just the man I wanted to see! I want you to—'

'Seize the bitch!' shouted Varazchavardan. 'It's now or never, man!'

To Chegory's bewilderment, Bro Drumel and his men laid rough hands upon the Empress Justina without so much as a moment's hesitation. Comprehension came to him a trifle belatedly: Bro Drumel and his men must long have been leaguing with Varazchavardan. Here was conspiracy true and proven!

'What are your orders?' said Bro Drumel to Varazchavardan.

'Secure the palace,' said the sorcerer. 'Let none enter or leave. Guard the treasury. Summon up the troops. Declare a State of Emergency. I am taking control of Untunchilamon in the name of Aldarch the Third, Mutilator of Yestron.'

'You cannot do this!' cried Justina, in high dudgeon truly. 'Such base ingratitude! Such vile turpitude!'

'Silence, bitch!'

That was Bro Drumel speaking. Then he said no more, for the Empress thumped him with her handbag, and he fell as if poleaxed. Roaring like a buffalo in heat, Justina laid about her, laying out guardsmen right and left.

'Cut her down!' screamed Varazchavardan, quite losing his cool. 'Kill her where she stands!'

But none of the guardsmen was quite prepared to hack into the imperial flesh. Instead, they abandoned their scimitars and endeavoured to subdue the Empress by brute force alone. As battle imperial progressed, Chegory Guy edged toward the door.

'The Ebby!' said Varazchavardan. 'Don't let him get away! Seize him! And those Ashdan bitches! The corpse master, get the corpse master!'

This was done. Thus Chegory Guy, Olivia Qasaba, Artemis Ingalawa and the corpse master Uckermark were swept into Varazchavardan's net together with the Inquisitor Xter and the Empress Justina. Yes, Justina was captured. Panting, sweating, speechless with rage and exhaustion. She spat at her treacherous guard captain as he picked himself up off the floor.

'Search them,' said Bro Drumel.

Obedient to his orders, the guards began to search the captives. Starting with Justina.

'Take your filthy hands off me!' said the Empress Justina, rapidly recovering her voice. 'How dare you maul the royal person with your vulgar paws?'

Her wrath made very little impression on the guards. Unfortunately most of Untunchilamon's soldiers were from Ang, and hence had scant natural regard for the daughter of a Yudonic Knight from Wen Endex. While they had served her faithfully during the years of civil war, none fancied the idea of dying in a futile attempt to shield her from the wrath of Aldarch the Third, who now seemed certain to obtain victory in Yestron.

To the guards, throwing in their lot with Varazchavardan made a lot of sense. As they were eager to prove their loyalty to that eminent sorcerer, they made a thorough job of their search. Since the Empress was wearing virtually next to nothing they found scarcely anything about her person.

But a search of her handbag uncovered:

A bodkin, a poison ring, a pet asp in an enamelled box, a confectionery case holding half a dozen condoms and a piece of zurkish delight, a soljamimpambagoya rock, two pages of a treatise on sodomy, a miniature prayer scroll, a twist of hashish, a snuff bottle, a clean sweat-pad, two pearls, a tiny spoon designed for cleaning the nostrils, a fragment of pumice, a silken pomander, a likoraskifdadona, assorted coinage, some items related to intimate feminine hygiene, the tooth of a basilisk strung on a silver chain, a dragon's tooth, a piece of raw ambergris, a scorpion embalmed in amber, an embroidered snot-rag, an ivory chin-scratcher and a dead mosquito.

Now that Varazchavardan was sure Justina was not in possession of any concealed weapons, he approached.

'Faugh!' she said. 'So this is the thing which means to kill me!'

There was a low grumble from the audience. To his discomfort, Varazchavardan realised that a great number of spectators had entered the Star Chamber, attracted by the drama there taking place. He had not noticed them till then, for none had dared venture on to the ground-floor battleground. Instead, they were crowding the mezzanine floor. If he tried to have Justina killed out of hand, he might precipitate a sudden outbreak of suicidal patriotism amongst the spectators.

Varazchavardan counted his guards, rough-counted the spectators, then substituted 'murderous' for 'suicidal'. If things got out of hand, he might die. Here and now!

'Nobody means to kill you,' said Varazchavardan, in his most sincere and soothing voice. 'My dear Justina, you've been ill. My old friend Aldarch Three will understand that, particularly when he finds you in the Dromdanjerie with your father.'

The Empress hissed with rage.

Spat.

Missed.

Varazchavardan addressed the mezzanine audience directly, saying:

'The Empress is suffering a mental disturbance. Thus will be held in protective custody lest she come to harm. Aldarch Three will understand. No harm will come to her. Or . . . or to us, to all of us, we who have stood by her for so long. We were right to do so while rule in Yestron was in dispute, but now rule is disputed no longer we must . . . we must take care of everyone in danger here. Including Justina. To rule any longer would prove her death. And . . . and ours, my friends.'

This may seem a simple speech. It was. It was no great exercise in eloquence, to be sure. But it brought the audience to order, for it contained some very potent truths. Aldarch the Third was almost certain to triumph in Yestron, and would doubtless be most unhappy with anyone who opposed his claims to absolute power.

Then a strident voice cried from the mezzanine:

'Who says she's mad?'

'What else could she be?' said Varazchavardan. 'Unless

mad, why would she consort with this Ebby?' He laid his hand on Chegory's shoulder. He dug his talons into Chegory's flesh.

'Ebbies are okay,' said the same strident voice.

Varazchavardan wished he could see who the voice belonged to. Its owner would then be in line for a bath in boiling oil. From the mezzanine there came an ugly muttering. Others took up the cry in favour of Ebbies. But Varazchavardan was equal to the situation. He plunged a hand up one of the sleeves of Chegory's silken canary robes and withdrew it, holding something bright and glittering.

'What's this?' said Varazchavardan, holding aloft the trophy he appeared to have snatched from Chegory's possession.

'Something you put there!' said Chegory.

'Thus says a thief!' said Varazchavardan, upholding the glittering bauble for all to see. 'This is the wishstone, isn't it?'

'It's not, it's not!' said Chegory. 'It's glass, that's all. A triakisoctahedron in glass!'

'Triakisoctahedron!' said Varazchavardan. 'My, what a big word for an Ebby! This is no triakisoctahedron. This is the wishstone! The precious magic which Chegory Guy stole from the treasury then used to overpower Justina by sorcery!'

'You put the thing up his sleeve before you pulled it out,' said the conjuror Odolo. 'Besides, that's no wishstone, that's—'

Bro Drumel made a curt gesture. A guard grabbed Odolo from behind and muffled him. Judge Qil protested.

'I say!' said the judge. 'You can't—'

But he too was suppressed even as Varazchavardan's voice rose above Chegory Guy's protesting babble.

'You see?' said Varazchavardan, holding up the cut-glass bauble. 'The wishstone! Stolen by Chegory Guy! Used by him to subvert the rule of law! To win the heart of the Empress! Nightly she couples with this sweaty animal, this

299

thing from the gutter. His vices have half-emptied the treasury. His counsel—'

'Hey, hey!' said Chegory desperately, so astonished by these blatant libels that he could hardly speak. 'I never—'

A guard hit him. Once. Hard. In the delectable softness below the floating ribs. He doubled up, hissing with pain. He heard Varazchavardan's remorseless eloquence playing to the prejudice of the crowd. There was a cry of 'Kill the Ebby!' Things were starting to look grim for Chegory Guy. Then Justina made her move.

At the top of her lungs she shouted:

'It's lies! All lies! Rise up, my people! Liberate your Empress! Five dragons for every man proved loyal!'

Five dragons is a lot of money as wealth is measured on Untunchilamon. Fifty dalmoons! Or, to put it in terms even a rock-gardening Ebby could understand, two thousand damns. This massive bribe brought those most eager surging to the very edge of the mezzanine floor. But the scimitars of the waiting guards were very sharp, and nobody was quite prepared to be first to jump to the ground floor.

Varazchavardan considered offering a matching bribe to the crowd, then saw there was no need. The spectators had been for the Empress, then against the Empress, and now they were for the Empress again. Which proved they lacked the single-minded passion which makes people dangerous in decision. The scimitars alone would hold them. Furthermore – what was this, fast approaching? Why, another squad of guards!

'Clear out the spectators,' said Varazchavardan.

Bro Drumel amplified his orders, and soon it was done. Varazchavardan's coup was complete.

'You know it's all lies!' said Chegory. 'That – that thing it's, it's not the wishstone, is it? You put it, didn't you? Up my sleeve!'

'Perhaps,' said Varazchavardan, 'but it will serve as excuse sufficient for your execution. And for the execution of the old whore who's nightly been entrancing you into her perfumes.'

Chegory, seeing Olivia looking at him with horror, protested:

'It's all lies! Lies! About the Empress and me! And – and you can't kill her. You gave your word. Taking care of her, that's what you said. The Dromdanjerie. You gave your word!'

'Lightly given, lightly withdrawn,' said Varazchavardan. 'She's too dangerous to keep under lock and key. Come undokondra, the vampire rats will have her.'

'This is pure perduellion,' hissed the Empress. 'You shall pay for this!'

'I can afford to,' said Varazchavardan dryly. 'I have an excellent credit rating.'

'You jest?' said the Empress in outrage.

'Why not?' said Varazchavardan. 'Were you ever more than a joke? A libidinous soldier's brat from Wen Endex posturing in the robes of empire!'

The Empress struggled. Chegory struggled too, trying to make a break for freedom. Olivia screamed, and Artemis Ingalawa began demanding a lawyer. Then Uckermark broke free. The corpse master scooped up Odolo and bashed the two nearest guards with this convenient weapon. Down they went. Down went Odolo too. Uckermark was off! For a moment he was on the loose, running for the nearest door. Then Bro Drumel tackled him. The pair crashed to the floor. A good half-dozen soldiers promptly jumped on the bold-daring corpse master.

The situation was under control again.

Momentarily.

Then:

'Gaa!' screamed one of the soldiers holding Dolglin Xter.

The soldier's clothing had turned to a scuttling curtain of scorpions.

As the soldier writhed away from the sorcerer, Xter flung up his hands and said:

'Anitha! Bin go ska—'

Then a soldier kicked him in the crutch. He doubled over and (for the moment) said no more. In the air above him, a half-formed horror monster with three mouths and half a dozen arms wavered, made tentative groping movements toward Varazchavardan, then disintegrated and disappeared.

'Right!' said Varazchavardan. 'That settles it! We'll kill the lot of them! Right now!'

Thus spake Varazchavardan. Whereupon the Empress Justina wrested herself from the grip of her guards in one convulsive convulsion and tried to claw out the sorcerer's eyes. Her savaging fingernails raked his countenance. Then her guards secured her again. Varazchavardan stood. A drop of blood welled from a claw-track. Fell to the pink tiles. Red upon pink.

Ah, beautiful, beautiful! It is strange, is it not? This Varazchavardan was but a banal power-player wargaming for dominance, yet his blood was as red as the juice of a ruby, potently suggestive of that very special wound which obsesses our imagination. But his blood's outflow was wasted in the Star Chamber, for none had eyes for this beauty, or time for the thoughts of seduction and lost virginity which it should have stirred. Instead, their minds were given to anger.

'Chop their heads off,' said Varazchavardan.

'Chop off whose heads?' said a guard.

'All of them!' said Varazchavardan, with a wave of his hand which doomed all the prisoners to instant death. 'The Ebby. The Ashdans. The mad daughter of the madman Thrug.'

'You mean . . . you mean the Empress?'

'By Sqilth and Zigletz!' said Varazchavardan. 'Didn't I just say as much but a moment ago? Who do you think I mean? The Green Octopus of Outer Branpapia?'

Silence.

Silence from the Empress, too enraged to speak.

Silence from Olivia, too shocked to speak.

Silence from Uckermark – a fatalist at heart.

Silence also from Chegory Guy, who was now (he was an Ebrell Islander, remember!) waiting for any momentary chance in which he might get the opportunity to kill Varazchavardan.

Then Odolo piped up, and this is what the conjuror said:

'If you please, I've . . . I've no strong political beliefs of my own. There's no need to kill me, for I'll happily serve the victor.'

'Silence!' said Varazchavardan. Then: 'Kill them!'

But still his guards made no move to lop off heads. After five years of the benevolent rule of Justina, they were quite out of the habit of executing people. Besides, they were all in their best dress uniforms, which had been bought at their own expense, were hideously expensive, and would get ruined entirely if they obeyed Varazchavardan then and there. After all, it takes but a cup of blood to besplatter a man from head to toe, and those of you who have seen a judicial decapitation will agree that the spillage from such is far greater and that the chances of the executioner avoiding the outspurt are negligible.

Thus, while the guards had no special regard for the Empress, they were far from keen about the idea of instant executions. At the very least they wanted the chance to put on some old clothes before they started chopping heads.

'Sir,' said Bro Drumel, understanding his men's hesitation, 'sir, if you please, sir, execution would best be done later, sir, in accordance with the proper forms, sir. Sir, shall I have the prisoners taken away, sir?'

Another drop of blood dripped from Varazchavardan's torn cheek and fell to the pink, pink tiles of the Star Chamber.

'You can have them taken away,' said Varazchavardan grimly, 'when they're all dead.'

So saying, he seized a scimitar from one of his guards. He stalked toward Odolo, intent on murder. He would save Justina to the last. She could have the pleasure of watching all her underlings get slaughtered before she herself fell beneath the blade. As Varazchavardan advanced upon Odolo, the cowardly conjuror made no move to defend himself, but instead grovelled at the sorcerer's feet.

'Sit up!' said Varazchavardan, who wanted a clear target to swing at.

Odolo reluctantly sat on his thighs.

'Raise your head,' said Varazchavardan. 'Come on! Chin up!'

Odolo complied.

Reluctantly.

Varazchavardan grimaced. He did not really want to do this. Like the guards, he disliked the idea of getting blood all over his clothes. If he were to behead the conjuror there would be no way to avoid such a besmirchment. Furthermore, he was wearing his favourite robes. Besides: what if Odolo flinched? Then the blade might well hack out a piece of his skull and leave him alive and screaming. Unless an expert is in charge, execution by decapitation can take a long time and be very, very messy. Still, politics is politics, so Varazchavardan had no choice.

He drew back the scimitar.

He struck.

He put all his strength into the blow.

The scimitar swept toward the conjuror's neck.

Then burst into splinters.

Olivia screamed. Justina screamed. Ingalawa (to her shame!) screamed also. Uckermark stared in disbelief. Dolglin Chin Xter fainted. Then Chegory Guy made his move. The husky young Ebrell Islander tried to burst free – but his guards restrained him.

'Sir!' said Bro Drumel urgently. 'Are you hurt?'

Varazchavardan, who had clapped a hand to his cheek, brought it away bloody. He had a fresh wound in addition to the claw-marks where Justina had scored him. A piece of shrapnel had pierced his flesh. The splinter of steel was half-projecting from his wound.

'Odolo!' said Varazchavardan.

He turned his bloody eyes on the conjuror. He raised his hands. He cried:

'Jenjobo! Jenjobo! Dandoon! Dandoon!'

Smoke wreathed from Varazchavardan's fingertips and

surged toward the conjuror. The smoke formed, turned into a fifty-fingered monster, a monster dire, a monster huge, a thing of volcanic height and night-bat shadows, a thing which screamed with a lunatic voice which was half whip-crack hate and half insanity. The monster closed with the conjuror. With a death-scream, it struck at Odolo—

Then, on an instant, dissolved.

One moment it was there. A moment later, it had collapsed.

The collapsed remnants of the monster spilt to the floor and flowed away in all directions, steaming slightly. The monster had been converted to a flood of chowder and kedgeree.

'Nadinkos!' said Varazchavardan, now ankle-deep in this food-flood. Then he swore again. Then raised his hands again. In a voice of outraged fury he shouted: 'Wenfardigo! Wenfardigo! Doktoris! Doktoris! Ko!'

On an instant a nightmarish beast formed itself from the very air. It was a creature of horror, a screaming fiend with scrabbling claws and teeth demonic. It breathed out smoke, then sulphur, then screamed again – and then attacked. But before it could open so much as a needle-point pin-prick in Odolo's hide, it collapsed into a slather of very hot curry, adding heat and pungency to the slovenly carpet of chowder and kedgeree which had already polluted the Star Chamber.

'That does it!' said Varazchavardan.

Once more he raised his hands. He took a deep breath. Then he cried out again in a high, twisted language. There was a crash of thunder. A blinding flash of light. Then a hideous scream of tearing stone and rending metal.

Most people who could – fled.

Bro Drumel fled.

Chegory Guy's guards fled.

But Chegory himself stood his ground.

Those who (like Chegory) were fool enough to linger were privileged to see Varazchavardan and Odolo grappling with each. Both had Changed. To things of stone and steel. To things inhuman which tore each other with energies unearthly.

For half a heartbeat, Chegory Guy watched these two monster-made Powers battling with each other. Then, ruled by the dictates of sanity, Chegory fled. He burst out of the Star Chamber and ran mindlessly until he collided with someone. The collision sent him sliding to the floor.

'You,' said tones far from unfamiliar, 'have been walking in your food.'

Panting, Chegory looked up. The speaker was none other than Slanic Moldova. Having said his piece, the lunatic returned to his mural.

'Slan,' said Chegory, 'get out of here. There's wonder-workers at war in the Star Chamber. Slan. Do you hear me? Slan!'

But Moldova ignored him.

So Chegory picked himself up, scraped the curry, kedgeree and chowder from his feet. Then started to think. Where was Olivia? Where Ingalawa?

He dared a shout:

'Olivia!'

Someone came running from the direction of the Star Chamber. A soldier with a torn ear.

'Stop!' said Chegory. 'What's happening back there?'

But the soldier ran past without stopping. After him came the corpse master Uckermark.

'Come on,' said Uckermark, grabbing Chegory by the arm. 'Let's get the hell out of here.'

'No!' said Chegory. 'I have to get Olivia!'

He pulled away from the corpse master then began to jog back toward the Star Chamber. Uckermark hesitated momentarily, said something decidedly obscene, then followed at a leisurely pace. It was far too hot to run any more. Besides, if young Chegory Guy truly wished to die, why should a law-abiding corpse master be in any hurry to join him in death?

Before the fast-hastening Chegory Guy reached the Star Chamber he heard the hideous sounds of combat still proceeding within. He gained the portals of the Star Chamber. He halted. Odolo and Varazchavardan, still guised in the very shapes of hell, were locked in mortal combat. Granching and dranching they raged, clubbed each other with synthetic gravity and clawed with sharpened light.

Harsh actinic illumination outglared from their carapaces. A matching radiance burnt from the very walls of the Star Chamber itself. No shadow could survive in that room. The dazing light was thrice brighter than the noonday sun. Chegory, near-blinded by the glare, could not tell whether any of the huddled forms at the feet of the fighters might be Olivia.

'Olivia!' he cried.

Then he tried to shout again – but his voice cracked, broke, failed. He swallowed. Then screamed:

'Odolo! Varaza – Varazchavardan! Stop it! Stop!'

The two combatants broke away from each other as if they had heard him and had chosen to obey. Then, still guised in the shapes of nightmare, they growled with hideous voices which made the very floor vibrate. Then they charged each other. They flailed wildly as they clashed once more. Lighting crackled around their metal-insect hulls as they slashed and hammered at each other. They grappled. Had each other in a death-grip. They were changing even as Chegory watched, sprouting claws ornate and pincers savage, growthing clutching tentacles and head-cropping mandibles. From one came an intolerable screaming.

Then—

Both fighting forms collapsed into chaos.

One moment they were there. The next, gone. Dissolved to a thrashing cloud of murk and motion. Which, even as Chegory watched, reformed. The cloud of obscurity resolved itself into two human forms, radiant still with actinic light, still in a death-grip locked.

There was the flesh of Varazchavardan, and there Odolo. Who was dying, surely. For Varazchavardan had the conjuror's neck in a grip of iron. Literally. For one of Varazchavardan's arms had not reverted to flesh, but was metal still. That metal arm was forcing Odolo's neck around. Soon the neck must break.

Now was Chegory's chance.

If one of those plague-silent bodies was Olivia's, then he must get her out and away now, now, now! Before the battle ended and Varazchavardan was free to turn his wrath on other targets.

He ran forward.

The light flared to a blinding brightness.

'No!' screamed Chegory.

He slipped. He slid. He fell. He sent sprawling in the undelights of kedgeree and curry. Splot! He opened his eyes, but found himself blind. Then rage possessed him. He swore as only an Ebrell Islander can. He leapt to his feet, meaning to do battle with anything he in his blindness could find. But his feet went out from under him, for the floor was slippery as a five-lust aftermath. Down he went, and thump went his head on the floor.

Half-dazed, Chegory lay there.

Was his back broken?

No.

Could he get up?

Yes.

Could he see?

Well . . . a little.

Yes, his sight was returning. Meanwhile, his hearing was as sharp as ever. He could hear a single human floundering around in the slurry. Who? Chegory strove to see. Amidst a wash of purple light and strobing suns he made out the features of Odolo. Yes, it was the conjuror Odolo who was crawling through the food.

So where was Varazchavardan?

'Chegory!' said Uckermark, entering the Star Chamber.

'Watch out!' cried Chegory. 'Varazchavardan!'

'Yes, yes,' said Odolo, his voice slurring and blurring. 'Where is Varazchavardan?'

He had to ask because his eyes were nearly closed by bruises. He had been battered as badly as a haplass elitamoripadroti used for a game of kathandamatandatu.

'Here,' said Uckermark, striding forward and dealing out a hearty kick to the recumbent body of the Master of Law.

Varazchavardan lay supine and senseless in a sea of kedgeree which was almost (but not quite) deep enough to drown him. But though Varazchavardan was unconscious, his monstrous metal-formed arm, souvenir of his battle of transformations with Odolo, had a life of its own. The finger-equivalents opened and closed. Opened and closed. Opened and closed. Click click click!

'You must kill,' said Odolo. 'Kill him.'

'With pleasure,' said Uckermark, scooping a discarded scimitar from the goop on the floor.

This was Chegory's moment. This was Chegory's chance. If he had seized it, he could have found Olivia and could have hustled her out of the Star Chamber before anything else went wrong. But he failed to take advantage of the brief-lived chance – because he was too busy watching with fascination as Uckermark advanced upon Varazchavardan.

'Hold!' cried an intruder.

Uckermark held. Turned. Faced the intruder. Who was none other than Nixorjapretzel Rat. Where had he sprung from? The answer is simple. Rat had watched most of the proceedings from the mezzanine. Now he was intervening to save his master Varazchavardan from certain death.

'Get out of here,' said Uckermark, raising the scimitar with murder his intent.

Rat raised his hands. He did that bit perfectly. For a moment he looked every bit the wonderworker. Uckermark hesitated, watching Rat with a degree of wary suspicion.

'Phidamas!' cried Rat. 'Phidamas! Strobo, um . . . stroboko! Stroboko!'

Nothing happened.

So Uckermark turned back to Varazchavardan, murder once more his intent. Down came the scimitar. Straight into Varazchavardan's skull. There was a clang of metal against metal. Uckermark dropped the scimitar. He clutched his swordhand.

'This sorcerer's skull is of metal!' said Uckermark.

True. Varazchavardan's skull had failed to revert to its original bone after the battle of transformations. Worse, Varazchavardan's arm of monster-metal, which had also failed to revert, was starting to look for something to crunch and kill.

'Look out!' screamed Chegory.

Uckermark leapt aside. Just in time. The finger equivalents of the monster-arm closed on empty air and crushed it to nothing. Meanwhile, Rat was still trying to kill Chegory, Uckermark and Odolo by exercise of magic.

'Phildamas!' cried Rat. 'Phildamas stroldoko! Mancredos! Mancredos! Fa!'

At his command, a whirlwind of shadow and flame roared into life. Roaring still, it began to spin toward Varazchavardan's enemies. They, realising they had underestimated young Rat, took to their heels and fled for their lives.

From the pink palace they escaped: Uckermark, Odolo and Chegory Guy in consort. They did not linger but fled down Lak Street in blatant defiance of the sweltering heat of the day. When they reached the Cabal House of the sorcerers of Untunchilamon, they turned down Skindik Way, disturbing some crows which were holding a business conference, haggling for shares in the belly of a dead dog.

Past the Dromdanjerie they went, then past Ganthorgruk. Then, when they reached the city's slaughterhouse, they stopped. Hot, panting, and exhausted.

'Gods!' said Chegory.

Then said no more, but leaned against a wall and panted some more. He could smell himself. He stank of sweat, curry, chowder and kedgeree. His silken canary robes were near enough to ruined. Gods! What if he was made to pay for new ones? Where would he find the money?

'I don't believe it,' said Odolo.

'What don't you believe?' said Uckermark.

'What happened!' said Odolo.

The conjuror wiped a hand across his glistening brow. He shook the hand. Drops of sweat flashed through the air. They made momentary pattern of dampness on the hot bloodstone of the street. But the pattern dried to nothing in instants.

Chegory's breathing began to settle. The sun shone. A drunken vampire rat staggered from a speakeasy opposite the slaughterhouse, its night-adapted eyes closed against the sun. Chegory watched it for a few moments, then looked back up Skindik Way. Which was quiet, empty and uninteresting, but for the dog-consuming crows.

'Come on,' said Uckermark.

'Where are we going?' said Chegory.

'Where do you think?' said Uckermark.

But Chegory Guy did not think. He only guessed. Where could they go? At a guess, Downstairs. No other destination occurred to him.

'We can't go there!' he said, in tones of horror.

'We can,' said Uckermark. 'We must. We will.'

On he went, with Chegory following after him. At last – to his relief – Chegory realised they were not making for Downstairs. No. Their destination was quite otherwise.

CHAPTER TWENTY-SEVEN

All this time the Malud marauders and Guest Gulkan's faction had been penned up Downstairs by Shabble, who had not had so much fun for ages. It was delicous! So many people to play with! There were the two wizards, Pelagius Zozimus and Hostaja Sken-Pitilkin. There was the barbarian Guest Gulkan and the shifty-eyed Thayer Levant. Oh, and the three pirates from Asral: Al-ran Lars, Arnaut and Tolon.

During this time – and quite a time it was – these seven prisoners had made their own contributions to the flow of sewage which so liberally polluted the depths of Downstairs. They had scavenged a little ice in the course of their compulsory wanderings but had had nothing to eat, and were consequently hungry, tired and out of temper.

They were also hoarse.

Why hoarse?

Because Shabble had been threatening to amuse Shabbleself by executing them, and to provide the globular one with an alternative source of amusement the prisoners had been telling non-stop stories. True stories, false stories, tales, jokes, legends and chronicles. In between stories, they had been trying to persuade the haunter of many millennia that it would be really amusing to go to Justina's palace, burn up a few guards and make themselves masters of Untunchilamon.

Unfortunately, Shabble remained resolutely unpersuaded.

It was Arnaut who cracked first. Shabble had made the youngster from Asral carry the wishstone. Arnaut had wished on it time and time again – to no effect. Now he was going to try direct action to get his way. He was the youngest, and had a bloody temper when roused.

'You shib!' said Arnaut. 'I've had enough! That's it! You can beat me, burn me, hit me, hate me, but I'm not doing any more. I can't talk any more. No more jokes, no more stories, no more songs.'

All this was said in Arnaut's native Malud, but Shabble, who was a linguist of the first rank, understood it perfectly.

'Why not?' said Shabble, sounding as hurt as Shabble felt.

'Because I'm dying of hunger!' screamed Arnaut in a cracked and ragged voice.

'Then why didn't you say so?' said Shabble reasonably. 'Come on, I know where there's some vampire rats.'

'Rats!' said Arnaut.

'Yes, rats, rats,' said Shabble, drifting off down a corridor.

'We can't eat rats!' said Arnaut.

'Cats eat them,' said Shabble. 'So they've got to be good for you. Cats never settle for anything less than the best.'

'What're they saying, what're they saying?' said Thayer Levant, who could not follow any conversation held in Malud.

'I'll find out,' said the brawny Guest Gulkan.

An exercise in translation followed. Then:

'Man cannot live by rats alone,' said Pelagius Zozimus. 'If you want to keep us in good shape we'll need green vegetables as well.'

'Green vegetables!' said Shabble huffily. 'I suppose you'll want to be sleeping next!'

'Well . . .'

'I knew it!' said Shabble.

Then, in a fit of pique, the free-floating lord of misrule spat out a blue-blazing fireball. It drifted to the floor and exploded in a flare of ionising radiation. Zozimus winced and all argument about diet ceased.

On went the refugees, guided by the fearsome imitator of suns. Quick-striding in their hunger-haste, they passed a corridor lit by blue light. Zozimus glanced along it, wondering if he should make a break for it and run.

'Should we run?' muttered Al-ran Lars to Arnaut and Tolon, for he was thinking along identical lines.

'Let's,' said Arnaut.

But already their haste had taken them past the corridor junction, and if they turned to sprint back they would collide with the close-following Guest Gulkan.

'Let's risk a dash when we reach the next corridor,' said the muscle-man Tolon. 'But watch yourselves! That sun-thing's three parts mad.'

'I am not mad!' said Shabble, who had hearing as acute as you could imagine.

'Sorry, sorry, sorry,' said Arnaut, throwing up his hands as if to ward off a fast-flung rock. 'You're not mad, not mad at all, not – gods, what's that?'

Something was emerging from a side corridor up ahead. Arnaut knew only that it was big, heavy, brown and bulbous. A monstrous, hulking thing stubbled with in-scrutable protrusions. It made a sound like heavy breathing as it advanced. Then it halted. Blocking the corridor.

'Turn around,' said Shabble, in great haste. 'Turn around, everyone. I don't want to lose you.'

Everyone turned around. They didn't need to be told twice. They had already guessed that the thing up ahead was fearfully dangerous.

'Go back the way we were going,' said Shabble, in something of a panic. 'Don't run!'

The wingless wonder softly but swiftly said that thrice, each time using a different language. This was very, very important. Shabble did not want to have these wonderful new playmates killed by the monster.

The lord of light and laughter knew what the monster was. It was stupid. Very stupid. But it was also dangerous. Very dangerous. Very very very dangerous. It was a machine. It was a dorgi. Shabble had instantly recognised the dorgi for what it was, even though the shining one had not seen such a menace for over five thousand years. Shabble, my friends, does not forget.

314

'HALT!' said the machine.

None of Shabble's prisoners understood the Code Seven used by the dorgi, but they all halted the instant it spoke. They all knew a sentry's challenge when they heard one. Their bright-shining companion halted also. The monster was definitely a dorgi. Those rock-crunching tones were unmistakable. Theoretically, Shabble is incapable of shuddering. Yet Shabble shuddered regardless. The demon of Jod had not known there were any dorgis left. But there were! Shabble was terrified.

Nevertheless, the shining one played it ultra-cool.

'Oh, hi!' said Shabble, speaking Code Seven to the dorgi. 'Why, what a surprise! I didn't see you there! Don't worry about us, we're just passing through.' So saying, Shabble started to drift away down the corridor. 'Yes, yes, don't worry about us, we'll find our own way thank you.'

'HALT! HALT RIGHT NOW!'

To emphasise its commands, the dorgi trained the seven snouts of its zulzer on the slow-drifting Shabble. Under the threat of the zulzer the demon of Jod came to an abrupt halt. The zulzer could not kill the lordly persecutor of cats, but was quite capable of destroying the transponder linking the feckless one with the local cosmos. Once that was destroyed Shabble would be deaf, blind and helpless. Trapped in a different universe entirely. Mute, blind and bereft of kinaesthetic sensation. Alone, alone, doomed to be alone, unloved, uncherished and unbefriended, all alone and hideously lonely for all the rest of eternity.

Hence Shabble regarded the dorgi and its zulzer with nothing short of horror.

The dorgi spoke again:

'HALT! HALT! RIGHT NOW! DROP YOUR WEAPONS! MOVE UP AGAINST THE WALL! HALT! OR YOU WILL BE ELIMINATED!'

If Shabble could sweat, then Shabble would have been sweating then. The shining one had absolutely no idea what to do. But while Shabble vacillated, the killer Tolon unshipped a knife. What good would that do? Not much.

Tolon might as well have armed himself with an ostrich feather. But he didn't know that. He had never met a dorgi before. He had no idea what he was up against.

None of the other humans had ever met a dorgi either – but some of them were already making some acute guesses as to its nature.

'What is that thing?' said Guest Gulkan. 'What's it saying?'

'It's saying we're chin-deep in something unpleasant,' said Thayer Levant.

'Never mind,' said Hostaja Sken-Pitilkin, with a confidence which was entirely feigned. 'I'm sure our guide can handle it.'

'Our guide is a Shabble,' said Pelagius Zozimus, 'and I wouldn't trust a Shabble to do so much as cook a pancake. Get ready to run!'

The dorgi was getting angry. It was working itself up into a killing rage. In a roar of fury it said:

'NOW! NOW! AGAINST THE WALL! OR ELSE!'

In extremis, Shabble was seized by inspiration.

Said Shabble, in a perfect imitation of Anaconda Stogirov, the immortal Chief of Security of the Golden Gulag:

'Let me pass with my prisoners.'

There was an ominous rumble from the dorgi.

'I have an Absolute Authorisation!' said Shabble, still using Stogirov's voice. 'You doubt? Then check your Security List! Now! Or I'll have you dismantled. Bit by bit. Preserving your pain circuits intact until the very end.'

The dorgi growled again. But backed off a bit. It began to check the Vocal Identities preserved in its Security List. Then the dorgi rumbled in discontent. It had checked Shabble's Vocal Identity against the Security List. According to the check, Shabble was in fact Anaconda Stogirov. But Stogirov was human, female, 567 incas high, 96 noks in weight, and had blue eyes, red hair and fair skin.

This then was the problem which troubled the dorgi: could Anaconda Stogirov have been ablated and reshaped in a fashion radical enough to leave her with the outward appearance of a Shabble, that is to say a shiny free-floating globe the size of an orange? The dorgi grunted strenuously. A problem indeed! For it knew virtually nothing of human anatomy, and equally as little about the internal construction of Shabbles.

Even as the dorgi watched, the globe was changing. It was radiating heat. It was becoming a fireball. Could humans do that? The dorgi hunted through its memory banks. Yes! Humans radiate heat! No! Humans die at fireball heat! Yes! Humans clad in reflective materials dare such heat! No! No! Yes Yes! No no no! Yes!

In desperate doubt, the dorgi consulted its Supreme Directive. This was very simple, and tells us a lot about the Golden Gulag:

1. WHEN IN DOUBT, QUESTION.

2. IF STILL IN DOUBT, TORTURE.

3. IF STILL IN DOUBT, KILL.

4. IF NOW NOT ENTIRELY SATISFIED WITH AREA SECURITY THEN PROCEED WITH AREA DESTRUCTION.

Instantly the dorgi became calm. That was the Law. The dorgi need only follow the Law. Furthermore, it could be as rude and as violent as it wanted to be as long as it did follow the Law. The dorgi had already executed Instruction One. Therefore it must go straight to Instruction Two. This intruder must be tortured!

'I hear Stogirov,' said the dorgi, 'but I see a Shabble. A delinquent Shabble! Imitating a human! You will be escorted to a therapist immediately for interrogation in depth.'

'There are no therapists,' said Shabble boldly. 'They're all dead.'

'There is a functional therapist on level 433,' said the dorgi in tones of ponderous menace.

A dorgi does not lie. A dorgi is a primitive mechanism which is incapable of anything as sophisticated as a fiction. A dorgi is however capable of error. But the possibility of error in this case was vanishingly small. When a dorgi says that a therapist exists then a therapist truly must exist.

'All right, all right,' said Shabble, gaining height slowly so as not to alarm the dorgi. 'I'll come quietly.'

'Then descend 934 incas and proceed along the corridor.'

'Which corridor?' said Shabble, rolling slowly through the air toward the blue-lit branch of the Downstairs maze which its prisoners had so recently considered as an escape route.

'This one!' said the dorgi. 'The one we're in!'

'Oh, this one!' said Shabble, accelerating.

'Yes, yes,' said the dorgi. 'But not so fast! And descend! Descend I say! Halt! You are going too fast! Halt or I shoot! Halt! Halt! Halt!'

The dorgi's alarm klaxon blared. It was the final warning – as Shabble knew full well. Shabble blasted the dorgi with fire hot enough to melt forged steel. The dorgi shrugged off the onslaught – but was momentarily blinded. In that moment, Shabble span furiously, spitting out twenty-seven Shabble-sized fireballs.

The dorgi recovered its powers of sight. It stared disbelievingly at the twenty-eight Shabbles hanging in the air. What the hell was going on here? Well: shoot first, ask questions afterwards! The dorgi opened fire, trying to gun down all twenty-eight Shabbles simultaneously. It was so busy shooting at fireballs that it temporarily forgot about the humans.

The humans were already running.

They sprinted, collided, fell, rolled, scrambled, recovered, ducked, dodged, then threw themselves into the blue-lit side corridor. Behind them, the deafening thunder of the zulzer ruled all. Chunks of plax exploded from the walls. Shabble skidded round the corner into the blue-lit corridor, counted the humans – all seven were there – then urged them to action.

'Brodirov kanamensky!'

'What?' said Zozimus.

'Shavaunt!' said Shabble, reverting to Toxteth.

The humans got the hint, and, dizzy and dazed though they were, they started running. Their overlord was pleased to see the one called Arnaut still had tight hold of the wishstone.

In the main corridor, the thunder of the zulzer continued for quite some time. The dorgi only stopped shooting when it had exhausted all its ammunition. It looked for corpses. There were none. Maybe the zulzer had atomised them. Maybe.

'We'll see,' said the dorgi.

It consulted an image-record of its onslaught of the corridor and did a spectral analysis of the same. Unfortunately, spectral analysis indicated that no large carbon-based lifeforms had been destroyed. Also, the Shabble appeared to have escaped.

'Sinvoco senvoco sabvoco!' said the dorgi, nearly overloading its obscenity circuits.

The intruders had got clean away.

The dorgi did an Advanced Situational Analysis, grunting at the pain of such intellectual analysis. Then concluded:

'They must've gone down that side corridor.'

It thundered to the side corridor. Which was too small to admit it. The dorgi did another Advanced Situational Analysis, which was every bit as painful as the first. It concluded:

'I cannot pursue.'

By now it was in something of a quandry. So it once more consulted its Supreme Directive. Which clearly stated:

4. IF NOT NOW ENTIRELY SATISFIED WITH AREA SECURITY THEN PROCEED WITH AREA DESTRUCTION.

'Right!' muttered the dorgi. 'That does it!'

Swiftly it charged up its Probability Disruptors, highly satisfied with the comforting thought that everything within fifty luzaks would shortly be chonjorted beyond repair.

'Here goes!' said the dorgi.

Then Initiated the Probability Disruption.

319

Nothing happened.

Doubtless the Probability Disruptors were on the fritz.

'Just my luck,' muttered the dorgi dourly, and consulted its memory banks, where it eventually located:

Directive 238768138764: Equipment Malfunction.

IN THE EVENT OF A MISSION-CRITICAL EQUIPMENT MALFUNCTION SEEK OUT A SUPERVISOR, ROBOTIC, GRADE 7.

The dorgi grunted. Then grunted again. It did not like supervisors. They were intelligent. Worse, they were more intelligent than dorgis. (Most things were.) Still, there was no helping it. A Directive was a Directive. There would be several thousand years of intensive algetic therapy in store for any dorgi rash enough to disobey a Directive.

Grunting and grumbling, the dorgi began to rumble along the corridor, diligently looking for a supervisor. It was going to be looking for a long time, for the last operational supervisor had suffered a terminal malfunction some three thousand years earlier.

Still, such is life.

CHAPTER TWENTY-EIGHT

While the dorgi was busy looking for a supervisor, and Shabble was regrouping Shabble's prisoner playmates, the conjuror Odolo lay in bed in Ivan Pokrov's private quarters in the Analytical Institute on the island of Jod. Odolo had collapsed halfway across the harbour bridge, and Uckermark and Chegory had lugged him the rest of the way.

During the battle in the pink palace, Varazchavardan had made a very determined effort to strangle Odolo, and the marks on his throat which evidenced the effort were steadily darkening from slap-smash red to thunder black. Still, Odolo was alive and breathing yet. Uckermark and Chegory sat by the unconscious conjuror's bedside, discussing him with Ivan Pokrov.

'You say he transformed himself?' said Pokrov.

'We're not kidding,' said Chegory. 'He – he's a – it was a, like, a nightmare, okay?'

'All right, all right,' said Pokrov, doing his best to soothe the uptight Ebby. 'So he transformed himself. I believe you!'

'He must be a wizard,' said Uckermark. 'Or a sorcerer at the very least.'

'A wizard,' said Chegory. 'They're at war, aren't they? Wizards and sorcerers? So he's a wizard. Else why would he hide his powers?'

'They're not exactly at war,' said Uckermark. 'Wizards and sorcerers, I mean. They just don't get on very well.'

Pokrov tried to think of some intelligent contribution he could make to this debate, but failed. He was used to dealing with life, death and the universe in terms of mathematical theory, but had no satisfactory theoretical explanation for magic. This is scarcely surprising, for even

Thaldonian Mathematics fails to provide a Predictive Paradigm to explain those processes which the researchers of the Golden Gulag were in the habit of describing as Synergetic Improbability.

'I still don't know why he made that dragon, though,' said Chegory. 'At the banquet, I mean.'

'Maybe it was a joke,' said Uckermark.

'Banquet!' said Pokrov, grateful to have something sensible to say. 'That reminds me! I've been so busy all day I haven't yet had lunch. Would you care to join me? Odolo doesn't need us to watch over him.'

Chegory wasn't really ready for another meal. In fact, he felt sick at heart because he had abandoned Olivia to the dangers of the pink palace. Furthermore, despite the anatomical difficulties involved, this sickness of heart had communicated itself to his stomach. In short, he was off his food.

Still, it would have been rude to refuse. Besides, in the presence of Pokrov, Chegory still felt constrained to play the role of the polite, disciplined, upwardly mobile young Ebrell Islander. Even though he knew he was a doomed outlaw, a debauched wastrel on the run from law and authority both, a hoodlum hopelessly entangled in a world of drugs, deceit, conspiracy, coups and sudden death.

'Yes,' said Chegory. 'That's, um, a great idea. We'll have lunch, okay, it can't make things worse.'

Over a (very) late lunch they discussed the probable fate of Olivia Qasaba and Artemis Ingalawa.

'I wouldn't worry about them,' said Ivan Pokrov blithely. 'Varazchavardan's got nothing against them. Doubtless they'll be back at the Dromdanjerie right now, cleaning up.'

Chegory shuddered.

'You didn't see what we saw,' said he.

After lunch, Chegory quit the Analytical Institute and stood on Jod's burning shore, where the wealth fountains were still pouring out streams of dikle and shlug as if they would never stop. The longest fountain flow on record had lasted for three years and had killed out all the lagoon life to a distance of five leagues from the disaster. Judging by the quantities of dead fish afloat in the harbour, this latest outburst might prove equally as disastrous.

Still, who could complain? Without such poisons, there would have been no wealth on Untunchilamon. It was dikle, shlug and other alien substances equally as miraculous which had made the island a wealthy and desirable part of the Izdimir Empire and had financed the construction of the fair city of Injiltaprajura.

Young Chegory Guy looked across the Laitemata Harbour to the streets of that city. All looked quiet. Dead. Normal, in a word. For in the usual course of events nothing would move in Injiltaprajura in the late afternoon of a day so hot.

Chegory watched the distant pink palace.

What the hell had happened back there? He had seen a contest of Power between Varazchavardan and Odolo. The pink-eyed albino had almost broken Odolo's neck. Then the conjuror had somehow rendered the wonderworker unconscious. Then, before Uckermark and Chegory could kill the odious Master of Law, Nixorjapretzel Rat had intervened.

'So what do I know?' said Chegory. 'I know Varazchavardan wants to win Injiltaprajura for Aldarch Three. That he wants Justina dead. And me dead. And Olivia dead. And Ingalawa dead. And Uckermark dead, come to think of it.'

Yet Ivan Pokrov would have it that there was nothing to worry about!

The more Chegory thought about it, the more he was sure the Analytical Engineer was being wildly optimistic. Pokrov was so bland, so sure, so confident. So detached from reality! This was a life or death situation. Very shortly, Chegory was going to be dead. Unless Varazchavardan died first.

'He's got the soldiers on his side,' muttered Chegory.

Then, after some thought: 'But all it takes is a knife. One man with a knife.'

There was not much question about who that man was going to have to be. Yet Chegory did not rush back to the palace then and there to do or die in the manner of heroes for he had been taught to think his problems through before he acted. Think he did. But little good it did him! The process of thought made his head hurt and his tongue go dry, but apart from that it had no demonstrable effect whatsoever.

Yet, even when Chegory realised thought was useless, he did not rush into action. Instead, he procrastinated, pretending he was thinking still. In truth, he was afraid. The world had become larger and its stones had become heavier and harder – while Chegory himself had become smaller and softer and more vulnerable to pain. At last, all pretence of thought wearied away to nothing. He sat on a rock and concentrated on sweating.

Thanks to dehydration, Chegory was wearier yet by the time salahanthara came to an end. A malevolent sun sank through skies of butchery to seas incarnadine. Then the day died in a spectacular display of exsanguination as the colours of bloody death drained from the sunset sky. The sunset bells – drowned by blood, no doubt – failed to ring. The redskinned Ebrell Islander, his own colours darkening to death in the worldshadows of evening, sat on the shores of Jod watching the bloodstone buildings of Injiltaprajura clotting into the black congealment of night. Still the dikle and shlug poured endlessly from the wealth fountains, and still the oppressive heat suffocated all of Untunchilamon.

Then, in the dark, Jod's slabender frogs began to chorus: Gork-mork-gork-mork. Gork-mork-gork-mork . . .

The night was hot. Breathless. Stars conjured themselves in the heavens in the livery of phoenix and firedrake. Chegory sat there staring across the black waters of the Laitemata until he had come to a decision. He would—

'Chegory!'

It was Ivan Pokrov, calling him.

'What is it?' said Chegory in a voice of charred wood and cracked leather.

He was thirsty, thirsty, he had not realised he was so thirsty.

'It's Odolo. He's roused himself. He's got something to tell us.'

So Chegory roused himself from his rocks and accompanied Ivan Pokrov inside. Pain pulsed in his skull: a headache brought on by heat and lack of water.

When Chegory entered Odolo's sickroom, the first thing he saw was the ugly Uckermark. The corpse master, who still smelt faintly of the dead, was trimming the wick of an oil lantern. How hideous he was! A grotesque mess of scars and tattoos. He grunted as Pokrov came in behind Chegory, then said:

'Our friend's excited.'

He spoke truly. The conjuror Odolo was sitting up in bed. He was alarmingly feverish, his eyes over-excited, his hands conjuring rhetoric from the air, his knees jog-jolting beneath a thin mosquito sheet. He reminded Chegory of the way some of the more manic patients in the Dromdanjerie looked just before they gave themselves to violence.

'Excited indeed!' said Pokrov, observing Odolo's agitation. 'Has he told you why?'

'He'll tell you himself,' said Uckermark.

Then, having trimmed the oil lamp, the corpse master left the room. Odolo began his explanations instanter.

'I,' said the conjuror, speaking clearly despite the bruises disfiguring his throat, 'have been possessed by the demon Binchinminfin.'

'Yes, yes,' said Chegory, imitating Jon Qasaba's most soothing voice to perfection. 'Yes, um, that's okay, all right? Just sit back, nice now, nice and easy, and we'll, ah, we'll take care of things, okay?'

'You'd better believe this,' warned Odolo. 'Lives are at stake. Don't think me mad. Can madness by itself conjure dragons or make a man the match of a wonderworker in battle?'

Chegory made no answer. What could he say? He had made yet another social gaffe! Everything he did or said or thought was wrong, and got him in trouble with someone. He was too tired to cope. He just wanted to vanish.

'Well,' said Odolo. 'Can it? Can madness conjure the powers of magic?'

'I must apologise on behalf of young Chegory Guy,' said Ivan Pokrov. 'He's boarded at the Dromdanjerie for so long that he probably expects everyone he meets to be at least half-way insane.'

Chegory was too tired to be grateful.

At that point Uckermark returned with a couple of servants bearing wickerwork chairs, jugs of cool water and beakers for the drinking of the same. Chairs were distributed, water was poured, the servants departed, then Chegory, Uckermark and Ivan Pokrov sat back and listened in silence as the conjuror Odolo told his story. Told how:

the demon Binchinminfin had taken residence in his skull;

the demon Binchinminfin had then brought Odolo's dreams, fears and nightmares to life. Water to blood at his bedside. Scorpions in his breakfast bowl. The sky made rainbow. Krakens in the Laitemata. All this the work of the demon, as it toyed with concepts it found in Odolo's head before it properly understood what they were.

'So it understands now?' said Chegory.

'It's grown less extravagant,' said Odolo. 'If that means understanding, well – maybe. That dragon at the banquet, that dragon was the last thing it made as if from a whim. It's as if – as if it's outgrown the playing stage. It's got serious. It's got down to business.'

Then Odolo told how the demon Binchinminfin:

had ransacked Odolo's brain for knowledge of the languages of Untunchilamon while Odolo was incarcerated in a cell in Moremo Maximum Security Prison;

had practised its powers by fabricating life-forms in miniature in the same cell;

and had sat back waiting and watching until Varazchavardan tried to kill Odolo.

326

'So it refused to help you till then?' said Chegory.

'You – you don't understand,' said Odolo. 'When you've got a demon aboard, you don't – you don't exactly ask it for things. When it wants to exert itself it does. Then it takes control entirely and there's nothing you can do about it. But the rest of the time – well, it just rides about with you, invisible and weightless.'

'But help,' insisted Chegory. 'You could have asked it for help, surely.'

'You're forgetting something,' said Uckermark. 'Terror, that's what you're forgetting.'

'Yes,' said Odolo gratefully. 'That's how it was. It was terrifying. So – so there's things you think of afterwards which you don't think of at the time.'

'Afterwards?' said Pokrov, trying to understand. 'Are you telling us you're no longer possessed? Are you telling us the demon's gone back where it came from?'

'Not at all!' said Odolo. 'I'm trying to tell you. If you wouldn't mind listening, maybe I could get through this a little quicker.' Pokrov promised silence, then Odolo continued. 'This Binchinminfin demon behaved itself. All day. Till Varazchavardan tried to chop off my head. Then Binchinminfin took me over entirely to do battle with Varazchavardan. Long they fought, till Varazchavardan got the better of Binchinminfin.'

'But that's – that's crazy!' said Chegory. 'These demons, aren't they, you know, all powerful? I mean, how does Varazchavardan smash up a demon when he's only a wonderworker?'

'You underestimate our wonderworkers,' said Odolo. 'They obtain their powers by permitting demons to partially possess them. In extremis, a sorcerer will permit possession complete. This must be what Varazchavardan did. Thus did the Master of Law find the strength to meet and defeat Binchinminfin.'

Chegory, angry because he had erred yet again in public, could not help challenging this.

'Well, that's what you say. But what do you know?

You're a conjuror, aren't you? So what do you know about sorcery and stuff?'

'I know,' said Odolo, 'because I have communed with a demon direct. Binchinminfin is the source of my knowledge.'

'Well,' persisted Chegory, still reluctant to be wrong, 'if a demon can just take someone over like that, how come we haven't all been taken over by demons?'

'Because the demons themselves forbid it,' said Odolo. 'Our world is fragile, its substance thin. Our world is like a sheet of ice. If demons in great number were to commit their full weight to our world, it would shatter. Thus to enjoy the world's pleasures they must commit but a fraction of the weight of a few. This they arrange according to their own laws.'

The conjuror sipped at his water. Chegory did likewise, then refilled his own beaker. His headache had eased away to nothing and he was feeling stronger and more alert now that he was rehydrated. He listened as Odolo continued:

'It was the demons who sought out the first sorcerers. Who taught those sorcerers the disciplines whereby a man supports at least some of the weight of a demon without wrecking the world. Thus says Binchinminfin. Who is himself a renegade, a demon working in our world in defiance of the laws of his own.'

Thus said Odolo.

But everything he said must be treated with caution.

After all, the sole source of his knowledge was the self-confessed renegade, Binchinminfin. Even supposing that demon meant to speak true, little knowledge of the World Beyond can properly be conveyed in the language of the World of Events. To attempt to express theological truths in the language of barter and commerce is ultimately futile. Or, at the least, grossly unsatisfactory. It is like trying to build a model of Time out of fishbones. Like endeavouring to express the satisfactions of the organism in an accountant's arithmetic. Like trying to build a house from a perfume's aroma, or shape fire out of ice.

'So now,' said Chegory, 'this Binchinminfin's dead.'

'Wrong!' said Odolo.

'But,' protested Chegory, 'you said Varazchavardan got the better of Binchinminfin.'

'In combat, yes,' said Odolo. 'Varazchavardan won the battle of transformations. But Binchinminfin defeated him nevertheless. For, when Varazchavardan tried to destroy my body with his claw of iron, Binchinminfin leapt from my body to Varazchavardan's.'

'But you said a demon was already in possession of Varazchavardan,' objected Pokrov.

'A demon has neither weight nor extent nor substance,' said Odolo. 'An infinite number can therefore dance on the head of a pin. Or contend for dominance within a single mind.'

'So that's why Varazchavardan collapsed,' said Uckermark, who had been notably silent till then. 'Because two demons were at war in his head.'

'No,' said Odolo. 'It is the mere act of possession which causes unconsciousness. The demon's presence disorders the mind, which takes time to recover itself.'

'So which demon now rules Varazchavardan?' said Chegory. 'His own, or this Binchinminfin?'

'Your guess is as good as mine,' said Odolo. 'When Varazchavardan recovers consciousness, either he will be himself, or Binchinminfin will be in possession.'

Odolo fell silent.

Chegory, Uckermark and Pokrov watched him, waiting for further revelation.

'It's no good looking at me,' said Odolo. 'I've said my piece. You know as much as I do. What we do now – well, that's not for me to say.'

'What we do now is simple,' said Chegory. 'We kill Varazchavardan. Whether he's possessed by a demon or not, he's our enemy mortal.'

Ivan Pokrov cleared his throat.

'I think,' said Pokrov, 'that rather than rushing off to kill someone, we'd better think this through. While we think, we might as well eat.'

Then Pokrov clapped his hands, calling in his servants. He gave them orders, and soon they returned with food, which was served in bowls decorated with floral patterns of the lightest blue. Each bowl had rice-shaped pieces of white porcelain incorporated into its thin sides.

Usually, Chegory would have worried in case his thick and hefty hands broke something. But tonight he didn't give it a thought. He was hungry, and there was excellent provender in the bowls. Olives. Pieces of smoked snake meat. Fresh fried octopus. Roast crickets. Giant chameleons stuffed with bacon. Pickled cockroaches. Mangos. Chunks of coconut. Thin-sliced disks of pineapple golden.

Thus, though his true love Olivia languished in a demon's grasp, Chegory ate greedily. His earlier loss of appetite had passed entirely. He was, after all, an Ebrell Islander, and it takes more than a coup, a kidnapping and a national disaster to upset an Ebby's appetite permanently.

While Chegory ate, the others thought, but at meal's end they were none the wiser.

'We lack sufficient data for precise analysis,' said Ivan Pokrov. 'We must send a mission to the mainland, if only to gather additional data.'

'No,' said Chegory flatly. 'We'll go to the city to kill Varazchavardan.'

Everyone looked at him. A declaration of intent to murder had been Chegory's first reaction to the situation. Now, after enjoying a good meal and thinking about it, his intent was exactly the same. Just what one would expect from an Ebrell Islander! No attempt to dialogue the situation. No thoughts of compromise or negotiation. No suggestion of sending an embassy of sorts to talk things through with their enemy. No, none of that. Just an immediate vote for murder.

This is hardly surprising, for on the Ebrells the typical instruments of conflict resolution tend to be edged weapons. Though Chegory had been born and raised on Untunchilamon, he had nevertheless been raised in the cultural tradition of the Ebrells.

What is surprising is that after some discussion, all agreed Chegory's plan to be sound, reasonable and rational. Odolo, graced with intimate acquaintance with Binchin-minfin, thought it an excellent idea. Uckermark, for his part, could certainly think of nothing better. Even Ivan Pokrov, that determined student of the rational, could devise no scheme more sophisticated.

'But,' said Ivan Pokrov, 'let's not risk our own lives in the attempt.'

'Nobody else is likely to help us,' said Uckermark.

'Oh, I beg to differ,' said Pokrov. 'I can think of one group of people who might be very willing to help.'

He explained.

'That's too dangerous!' said Odolo. 'They might prove enemies rather than friends!'

'You don't have to come if you don't want to,' said Uckermark.

'I don't want to,' said Odolo.

He was in no state for heroics. He was bruised, battered and exhausted in both body and psyche.

'Then stay here,' said Pokrov, 'and the rest of us will go.'

'You?' said Chegory. 'You'll come with us?'

'To help negotiate with our intended friends,' said Pokrov. 'And . . . and perhaps to see this demon-thing. My curiosity, you see, is excited.'

Thus it was decided. Uckermark, Ivan Pokrov and Chegory Guy would venture to Injiltaprajura to seek help for a war against Varazchavardan. Soon, suitably equipped with weapons, they were on their way.

CHAPTER TWENTY-NINE

Jod's heroes sweated through the hot night to Uckermark's corpse shop where Yilda and Log Jaris greeted them with urgent demands for information. After hearing lengthy explanations, all voiced at something close to a shout as a concession to Yilda's deafness, Log Jaris declared that he would join the expedition to the pink palace. 'And I!' said Yilda. But her mate forbade it, thus precipitating a row. Thanks to the support of all the males present, Uckermark triumphed over his woman in argument – a rare occurrence indeed.

Then the corpse master extracted a bottle of a queer purple fluid from a secret cabinet. It glowed in the candlelight with an evil, eldritch phosphorescence. It was Dragonfire, a form of that carcinogenic poison known as alcohol, and it was surpassed in potency only by the firewater of the Ebrell Islands. Rough stuff indeed!

'This should sweeten the temper of our demon-dealing friends,' said Uckermark.

As gifts go, this one was truly extravagant, for the glass bottle alone was worth more than most people earnt in a month. But they had to do everything possible to win the wonderworkers as allies in their war against Varazchavardan. The sorcerers must be persuaded that the Master of Law was indeed possessed by the demon Binchinminfin, and must therefore be destroyed to force the delinquent demon back to the World Beyond.

Forth went the heroes, forth through the streets of night where massive bloodclot shadows loomed in every doorway. The night was hot and humid – and preternaturally peaceful. Shuttered silence guarded many a window which would usually have been alive with lamplight and laughter.

All Injiltaprajura knew that something untoward was going on and the city had battened down as if to meet a hurricane.

Our heroes quested through this ominous atmosphere to the Cabal House: and found it closed against them. A mirbane balefire was burning bright atop the building, summoning all the sorcerers of Injiltaprajura to ingather. Judging by the raucous uproar coming from the upper rooms, those worthies had ingathered indeed.

'It sounds like a party,' said Uckermark as he knocked on the door.

There was no response, so Uckermark used his boot. The door hummed, glowed yellow, belched sulphur, then darkened to silence. He kicked again. This time the door maintained a stolid impassivity. As the corpse master attacked the door yet again, Log Jaris turned and walked away.

'Where are you going?' said Chegory in bewilderment.

But the bullman walked on without looking back. Uckermark, ignoring his comrade's retreat, continued to assault the door. Then Chegory Guy joined him, for the young Ebrell Islander could resist the temptation no longer. Chegory displayed such enthusiasm for kicking, thumping and hammering that Uckermark left him to continue the attack alone. The corpse master himself stepped back and bawled at the top of his voice:

'Come out of there, you turd-spawned dog-eaters!'

Sounds of drunken singing floated down from above, but if Uckermark was heard he was ignored. So he began to harangue the sky-dwellers at length. Half a thousand obscenities later, Chegory abandoned his attempts to break down the door.

'This is useless,' said he, wiping an abundance of sweat from his feverish brow. 'We'll never get through this.'

'I think we will,' said Log Jaris, returning from his travels with a sledgehammer slung over his shoulders.

Without further ado, the bullman began to smash down the door to the Cabal House.

'I don't know that this is entirely wise,' said Ivan Pokrov, who possessed all a good citizen's inhibitions against vandalism in full force.

'Then you know what you can do with wisdom,' said Log Jaris.

He swung the sledgehammer again. One of the door timbers cracked.

'Orcs!' screamed a terror-stricken voice within. 'There are orcs without!'

'Yes, orcs!' roared Log Jaris. 'Big huge hulking orcs with bloodstained teeth! Coming to eat you up!'

Sounds of panic ensued. Then faded. Whatever sorcerers were guarding the door had fled.

'Gutless wonders,' muttered Log Jaris.

Then he wrecked the door entirely and stormed inside, closely followed by Uckermark and Chegory Guy. Ivan Pokrov lingered outside, for, though the analytical engineer had felt wildly brave and courageous on Jod, he had survived for many millennia by not taking unnecessary risks, and in immortals such old habits die particularly hard.

Pokrov's reckless companions found the ground floor of the Cabal House deserted but for the heavy odours of incense and sulphur. Log Jaris led an unopposed assault which swiftly took the heroes to the heights. There they found the sorcerers, who had broken out their supplies of alchemical alcohol ages ago, and were all thoroughly drunk. One, more sober than the others, questioned the intruders. Thus:

'What are you doing here?'

Chegory knew this sorcerer. It was Nixorjapretzel Rat, Varazchavardan's erstwhile apprentice.

'We're here seeking help,' said Log Jaris.

'Piss off,' said Rat.

'In case you don't know,' said Uckermark, 'a demon, Binchinminfin by name, has taken possession of your master Aquitaine Varazchavardan.'

'He's my master no longer,' said the drunken Rat. 'I graduated to sorcerer last year.'

'The hell with your quibbling!' said Uckermark. 'Are you listening to me? There's a demon, a—'

'We know, we know,' said Rat. 'We know all about that. It may mean the end of Untunchilamon. It may mean the end of the world.'

'Why?' said Chegory. 'It's, um, only a demon, okay? We can take it, gang up on it, right?'

'You don't understand,' said Rat. Weeping fat tears of fear, grief and self-pity. 'The demons have scant sense of self-discipline. The Grand Treaty of the High Consenting Powers has long been endangered—'

'Oh, stop babbling!' said Uckermark, with impatient anger. 'What are you on about? Talk straight sense!'

'I mean,' said the young and still-blubbering sorcerer, 'when one demon disrupts, others will likewise.'

'What means this in-house argot?' said Log Jaris. 'Are you trying to tell us that other demons will do as Binchin-minfin has?'

A sorcerer older, wiser and more articulate tottered over to them and said:

'As a single ringleader can make a mob from an honest crowd, so a single delinquent demon can rouse the jealous mass of his fellows to actions criminal, even though demons and sorcerers alike know the destruction of the very world would follow. Every head in the city may house a demon by this time tomorrow morning. If so, then the world will end the day after.'

'Then what are you going to do about it?' said Uckermark with contempt. 'Drink yourself into oblivion? Or what?'

'We're working on it,' said the older sorcerer.

Evidently he meant they were working on getting drunker, for he turned away and seized the nearest flask of alcohol, clearly intending to do just that.

'Rat!' said Uckermark. 'We're going to the palace to take on this demon. You're coming with us!'

'I'm doing no such thing!' said Rat, who had no taste for suicide. 'Back! Back, I say! Or I'll turn you into a frog!'

Then Rat raised his hands and cried out in a high and hideous voice. One of Uckermark's boots promptly turned itself into a frog. As the corpse master's weight was bearing down on it at the time, the boot's unexpected incarnation as a web-footed amphibian was chiefly notable for its brevity.

'Come on,' said Log Jaris. 'Let's be going.'

Nixorjapretzel Rat was raising his hands again. Was crying out. The heroes hastened toward the stairs. Fire flashed toward them. They ducked, and fled.

They halted, panting, at the first landing. The young and relentless Rat was standing at the head of the stairs, his hands raised yet again. He spoke in a high, sibilant voice. The air wavered. A good half-dozen stones directly above the heroes converted themselves to butter. One of these stones was the keystone of an arch.

'Oh shit!' said Uckermark.

Then led the retreat, taking eight stairs at a single leap. Behind the heroes, stones creaked. Then, with a roar, the arch collapsed. Fragments of rock pursued them at the rattle. When the heroes halted at the bottom and looked back, they saw the stonefall had sealed off the stairway.

Untunchilamon's wonderworkers were, to a man, trapped in the Cabal House.

'Borgan!' said Log Jaris.

Then, having voiced that obscenity, he led the way outside. Sounds of drunken singing still floated from the uppermost chambers of the Cabal House.

'No joy?' said Ivan Pokrov, who had waited patiently in the street all this time.

'Well, we did learn something,' said Uckermark, taking off his remaining boot since he thought it easier to walk barefoot than one-booted.

'What?' said Pokrov.

'The demon Binchinminfin is definitely in possession of Varazchavardan. The sorcerers have told us as much. They also say that where one delinquent demon has gone a thousand may follow.'

'Well,' said Chegory, trying to sound brisk and brave. 'That's it, then, isn't it? There's, ah, well, only one thing for it. Go to the palace, that's it, then it's knifework, that's the way, slaughter this demon man to man.'

But they did no such thing, for before they could do anything so brave or so foolish, Yilda came panting up the street toward them.

'Come back!' she said. 'Back to the corpse shop! Now, now!'

'Why?' said Uckermark.

Once Yilda had got her breath back, she explained.

With explanations given, all hastened back to the corpse shop. They plunged in through the wide-open door and hastened to the backsquare courtyard. There a sun-shining bubble of light was lording it over a disreputable bunch of ill-assorted humans.

'Hello, Shabble,' said Log Jaris, who knew the demon of Jod of old. 'What have you got for us?'

'Prisoners!' said Shabble, squeaking with excitement.

Prisoners indeed. Exhausted, haggard, nerve-shattered prisoners.

The unfortunates in question were Arnaut, Al-ran Lars, Tolon, Guest Gulkan, Thayer Levant, Pelagius Zozimus and Hostaja Sken-Pitilkin. After the encounter with the dorgi, Shabble had herded them through the interstices of the underworld until at last, after following a cautiously circuitous route, they had emerged into the starlight of Injiltaprajura by night. Then the demon of Jod had brought them to the corpse shop.

'You dare much by taking us captive,' said Pelagius Zozimus.

Strong was the voice of the wizard of Xluzu and stern was his demeanour, for his pride would not let him confess to his dilapidated condition. In contrast, his cousin Hostaja Sken-Pitilkin looked to be at death's door, and was mumbling incoherently in the quavering voice of an old man on the edge of senility.

'We dare nothing,' said Uckermark. 'It's Shabble who dares.'

'But, sirrah,' said Pelagius Zozimus to Uckermark, 'is not this ill-mannered goblin your servant?'

'Silence!' said Shabble, who knew not what a goblin was, but presumed the designation to be insulting.

'Because if it is,' continued Zozimus, 'then I—'

'Silence!' said Shabble again, this time in female accents terrifying to hear. Yes, Shabble had again borrowed the voice of Anaconda Stogirov, Chief of Security for the Golden Gulag. A voice which had always commanded both fear and respect.

Anaconda Stogirov! What do we know of her? That she—

[Here some thirty thousand words of elaborate fantasy have been deleted. I must repeat facts already made clear in my Editorial Note. The 'Golden Gulag' is mythical entirely, the Originator is in many respects an irresponsible fantasist, and this Text in its entirety is to be treated with the greatest of caution. *Drax Lira, Redactor Major.*]

—thus we see that Stogirov was a woman worse than the Iron Lady of the Death Cycle legends.

Anyway, to return to our history.

You will remember that (some 30,000 words ago) we left Shabble in the courtyard of the corpse shop with Shabble's prisoners. Zozimus was angrily protesting against imprisonment, and though 30,000 words have passed we find him angry still. Anyway, to return to our narrative tense (the past) let us discover him saying:

'I am Justina's master chef! An imperial servant! My mistress will have you fried alive unless you release me now!'

The bluff was senseless, since Uckermark already knew Zozimus to be but a foreign thief, and Zozimus knew that he knew. Even so, the bluff was a brave feat of rhetoric considering that poor Zozimus was so tired he felt drunk.

'Maybe there will be some frying alive,' said Uckermark, with a grin. 'And quickly! Shabble will fry you on the spot if I ask as much.' It was then that he saw the wishstone in Arnaut's hands. He removed it with a polite 'thank you'.

Then said to Shabble: 'Why have you brought these people here, little friend?'

'They are criminals guilty of crimes against the State,' said Stogirov's voice. 'They will suffer sundry peripheral ablations before they endure execution most bloody. They—'

'That's enough!' said Ivan Pokrov, who, unlike Uckermark, was not enjoying this at all. 'Shabble! Come to order! Or I'll take you to a therapist! Right now!'

Shabble squeaked in terror. The light of the shining one faded till the dim-glowing globe was scarcely visible in the dark. This eclipsed sun drifted toward Chegory Guy, who took pity on poor Shabble and bundled the sad and sorry demon into the most capacious pocket of his canary robes.

'Thank you for reining in your goblin,' said Zozimus. 'Now, as an imperial servant—'

'The Empress Justina is a captive, and possibly dead,' said Ivan Pokrov, interrupting without apology. 'We have a crisis situation here. You have to help us kill a demon.'

'A demon?' said Zozimus, momentarily taken aback. Then he shuddered as if emerging from very cold water, pressed his fingers to his temples as if attempting to expel fatigue by an exercise of brute force, then said, crisply: 'Explanations!'

Pokrov proceeded to explain in Ashmarlan. Tolon listened impassively (perhaps understanding, perhaps not) but Arnaut clamoured for a translation into Malud which Al-ran Lars provided. Meanwhile, Pelagius Zozimus put Pokrov's dialogue into Toxteth for the benefit of Guest Gulkan, who then rendered the translation into another tongue entirely at the request of Thayer Levant. Hostaja Sken-Pitilkin, who was temporarily non-*compos mentis*, followed the conversation not at all.

'Duggerlop,' muttered Thayer Levant, when the translation of a translation had enlightened him as to their situation.

The precise meaning of this is unclear, but it can reasonably be presumed to be a statement of extreme discent. Levant then exchanged further words with Guest Gulkan in a tongue foreign to all our informing witnesses. Whereupon Guest Gulkan addressed the others in tolerably good Toxteth:

'My good friend Thayer Levant notes that we've got nothing personal against Varazchavardan. If you want us to help kill him, we will – but only if we get a suitable reward.'

'We'll give you the wishstone,' said Pokrov grandly.

Uckermark and Log Jaris looked at each other. How could the crazy analytical engineer say something so stupid? The wishstone was of incalculable value. Still, the words could not be unsaid. They sparked a clamour from the Malud marauders and from Guest Gulkan's faction. Both sides wanted the wishstone.

In a moment, there were weapons alive in the night, and the two factions were squared off for combat.

'Shabble!' said Pokrov, thinking to restore order with the help of his 'goblin'.

Shabble lay inert in Chegory's pocket. But Chegory fumbled the now unshining one out of the pocket and tossed this fearer of therapists into the air. Shabble dropped like a stone. The long-surviving plaything of many millennia was playing dead.

'Enough of this!' roared Log Jaris.

Toxteth is a great language for roaring so that is what he roared in. Even those who did not understand his vocables paused nevertheless.

Log Jaris confronted the would-be combatants. This was a very ticklish situation. Shabble had never thought to disarm the prisoners, who were well-equipped for slaughter. If the prisoners thought to combine – as they shortly surely would – they could easily overwhelm Log Jaris and his friends.

'The demon Binchinminfin haunts Varazchavardan's flesh,' said Log Jaris. 'Varazchavardan so possessed will prove our doom unless we doom him first. There's no escape from Untunchilamon till Fistavlir ends and the winds renew once more. Oh, we could escape from mortal men in a shallow canoe – but from a demon?'

'I'll take my chances in a canoe,' said Guest Gulkan. 'Give me the wishstone and I'll be gone.'

'What do you want with the wishstone?' said Log Jaris.

'To rule the world,' said Guest Gulkan.

The bullman laughed heartily.

'This thing,' said Log Jaris, taking the glittering triakisoctahedron from Uckermark's hands, 'rules nothing. Wishstone it is called but it grants no wishes. It is but a toy. A bauble. Opal and diamond in one, hence treasured much – but useless for the exercise of power.'

'Wrong!' said Guest Gulkan. 'It is a power among powers for those who know how to use it.'

'Then suppose we hand it to you?' said Log Jaris. 'Can you abolish Varazchavardan? Can you defeat Binchinminfin? Can you turn Injiltaprajura upside down and inside out?'

'Yes!' said Guest Gulkan, his voice shaking with untrammelled emotions. 'Give it to me! It's mine!'

He reached for it.

Tolon growled with displeasure.

Swords leapt to the ready.

All were poised for slaughter.

Then Shabble in a single moment evolved from stone to firefly, from firefly to candle, from candle to sun. So evolving, the shining one leapt skywards. Swordsmen flinched from the glare. Then Shabble spoke in a cooing female voice most melodious and most beautiful to hear, saying sweetly:

'Don't fight, dear friends. For I, dear friends, must fry you to cinders if you do.'

This beautifully voiced death-threat brought order to Uckermark's courtyard and set the stage for long and involved tripartite negotiations to begin. It would be tedious to recount these convoluted negotiations in detail but the gist of the matter can be given in moments.

Of the three parties present, only guest Gulkan's faction

wanted the wishstone for its own sake. The Malud marauders sought the precious bauble only because they knew it could be exchanged elsewhere for fabulous wealth. If Uckermark and his friends lusted for the thing, they likewise did so only because they could use it to get rich.

'So there's no problem,' said Log Jaris, when all parties had made their positions clear. 'If we kill Varazchavardan, we'll be heroes. If we secure the rule of Untunchilamon for the Empress Justina, her gratitude will let us rape the treasury entire. There'll be riches and honours for the least of us. We'll sleep on pearls and swim in liquid gold. If our friend Guest Gulkan will consent to settle for the wishstone then the rest of us will surely settle for treasure.'

'But,' said Chegory, objecting, 'what if, um, this Gulkan guy uses the wishstone to, well, to chop off our heads or something? He says it's a power-thing, doesn't he?'

'Come now!' said Pelagius Zozimus. 'You don't believe everything you're told, do you?'

'Your Gulkan man said the wishstone's a power-thing,' said Chegory stubbornly. 'I want to know what it is. What it does.'

Zozimus sighed.

'It's a long story,' said he, 'and we've shortened the night too much already. If you must know, the wishstone is actually the x-x-zix of the Iltong Legends, of which you've never heard. It was made by the Dissidents, of whom you know nothing, to control the breathings of the Cold West, a place stranger than anything you could possibly imagine. Once we have the x-x-zix in the Cold West we can fight for control of Chi'ash-lan, a city you've never been to and never will. Success will give us the rule of a Door. Then we can strive for control of the Circle. That leaves you none the wiser – but still you're as wise as you ever will be. We've got a deal. Let's waste our time no longer. To the palace! To face this demon! To kill it where it stands!'

All this was said in the most ferocious quick-fire rattle imaginable, for even in fatigue the formidable Zozimus remained a brilliant wizard with little patience for the foolish or the ignorant. Chegory insisted that he still didn't understand, and wanted to, and would. But he was overruled.

'We've talked too much already,' said Uckermark, pulling on his second-best pair of boots. 'Friend Zozimus is right. Let's be on our way. But first—'

'First what?' said Zozimus impatiently.

'I had a bottle I meant to trade to the wonderworkers, but they weren't in the mood for trade. So . . .'

So the rebooted Uckermark gathered together a gimcrack collection of cups, bowls and tankards. Then, with utter contempt for the laws of Injiltaprajura, he cracked open his bottle of Dragonfire and poured a tot for everyone present (with the sole exception of Shabble).

'A toast,' said Uckermark.

This thing called a 'toast' is one of the rituals of these alcohol-abusing drug-takers. It is a very important ceremony which lies right at the heart of the drug-taking cult. Indeed, students of such aberrations believe that, for many addicts, such rituals are almost as important as the actual alchemical effect of these toxic substances.

'A toast,' said Uckermark. 'To . . . to Justina Thrug!'

All raised their death-containers then drank. The mumbling-muttering Hostaja Sken-Pitilkin was so shaky in the hands that he spilt half his drink, but he managed to down the rest. Only Chegory Guy left his cup untouched.

'You're not drinking with us, boy,' said Uckermark, in tones of severe disapproval.

'I have an upset stomach,' said Chegory lamely.

Actually, he was thinking of Olivia. She who was (at least in his imagination) so pure and spotless. He was ashamed of the number of times he had been tainted by alcohol in the recent past. Now he was decided. Hereafter he would keep himself pure for her, abjure the horror of drugs and remain staunchly teetotal.

'Ah well,' said Uckermark philosophically, 'if you're sick, you're sick.'

Then he downed Chegory's share of the Dragonfire.

343

'Okay!' said Uckermark. 'Let's be going! Shabble, you lead the way!'

But Shabble had closely followed all the negotiations and explanations which had taken place in the corpse shop. The imitator of suns wanted nothing to do with demon-killing, particularly as this Binchinminfin sounded easily dangerous enough to kill a poor defenceless Shabble.

So the childlike one again played dead.

'Shabble!' said Pokrov, giving the dead-dull sphere a kick. 'Wake up! Or I'll get a therapist! I will, you know!'

But Shabble woke not. So Chegory pocketed Shabble once more, and the heroes (now ten in number) set off for the palace, leaving Yilda in sole possession of the corpse shop. As none of the three factions entirely trusted the others, Uckermark brought the wishstone along lest one faction abandon the others in battle and race back to the corpse shop to seize it.

[The Originator errs. There were not ten. There were actually eleven of them. Guest Gulkan, Thayer Levant, Pelagius Zozimus, Hostaja Sken-Pitilkin, Al-ran Lars, Arnaut, Tolon, Chegory Guy, Uckermark, Log Jaris and Ivan Pokrov. Twelve, if one counts the goblin Shabble. *Prill, Pedant Minor.*]

CHAPTER THIRTY

Closely did the manly dark embrace the heroes, holding them in its virile grip as they hastened toward the pink palace with an enthusiasm for battle which was made all the greater by the Dragonfire they had consumed. Booze had put fire in their bellies indeed. Even Hostaja Sken-Pitilkin advanced with a will, albeit at a muttering stagger.

Up Skindik Way they went, past the slaughterhouse, past Ganthorgruk and the Dromdanjerie, to Lak Street. As they passed the Cabal House of the wonderworkers they heard the party within still raging strong. On they went, past the ship-sized bone chunk known as Pearl, then past the houses of the great and the grand aglimmer with the blue-green light of moon paint.

The pink palace loomed ahead.

Dark as an untenanted skull.

Chegory began to lag behind, for, while the danger of internecine conflict seemed past, he was appalled by the swaggering overconfidence of his fellow heroes. Since the young Ebrell Islander was innocent of the consumption of any alcohol, he did not share this braggadocio. His head was clear, and he had had time to think.

He had thought indeed.

While the idea of killing Varazchavardan had been his to start with, was it really such a smart thing to do? So the man was possessed by the demon Binchinminfin. So what? Who cared if a demon ruled Untunchilamon? Doubtless the demon would go in for a certain amount of rape, pillage and torture, for tradition tells us that demonic creatures from the World Beyond are addicted to such activities.

But – seriously now – could a demon possibly be worse

than Aldarch the Third? They have a bad reputation, these demons, but that reputation is mostly hearsay. If Binchinminfin ruled Untunchilamon, surely the island would be safe from the Mutilator of Yestron. Which was a major consideration now the Mutilator looked likely to win the civil war raging in the Izdimir Empire.

True, the wonderworkers claimed that Binchinminfin was the first of a storm of demons which would destroy the world. But were the wonderworkers necessarily to be believed?

In retrospect, Chegory thought the sorcerers in the Cabal House had all been enjoying themselves far too much. Perhaps the world was truly endangered. But he strongly suspected the wonderworkers were only using that as an excuse to get smashed on alchemical alcohol. That the world would still be there in ten days' time, and the sorcerers knew as much.

By the time Chegory had thought all this, he was at the entrance to the pink palace. However, he had lagged so far behind that the others were out of sight.

'Well,' said Chegory, 'that's their problem, not mine.'

He wiped his face with his hands, smearing away the sweat which bubbled so freely from his skin, then sat down in the portico, leaned back against one of the dark pillars which he knew to be pink, and waited. After a while, Shabble crept from Chegory's pocket, rose into the air to a height of seventy incas, and began to glow softly.

'So you're alive,' said Chegory moodily.

Shabble assented happily, then began to sing a cheerful little song.

'Turn down the light,' said Chegory. 'You're a beacon for every moth in creation.'

But the demonic one brightened slightly and began dancing in the air, playing with the moths. Chegory thought of threatening his feckless friend with the therapist (whatever that was). The threat always worked. But he was too tired to bother. A kamikaze bug splattered itself against the therapist-fearing beacon, which promptly nuzzled up to Chegory to remove the wreckage. Chegory pushed Shabble away, and again wiped his hands over his face. He was still sweating. He'd never known it to be so hot!

At least there's no mosquitoes.

So thought Chegory.

The next moment, of course, he heard a mosquito zining through the air beside his right ear. He swatted the mosquito. He missed. But stung his own ear nicely.

'Shabble,' said Chegory, 'why don't you make yourself useful? See where our dear friend Ivan Pokrov's gone.'

'We know where he's gone,' said Shabble. 'He's gone to kill the demon Binchinminfin.'

'Well, why don't you go in after him?' said Chegory. 'You're not afraid of a little old demon, are you?'

'Not sure,' said Shabble guardedly.

Actually, though Shabble sometimes had fun pretending to be a demon, the cautious survivor of many millennia wasn't really sure what a demon was. Furthermore, Shabble was in no hurry to find out the hard way.

Chegory waited some more.

Then he heard footsteps approaching at the totter. Cautiously, he got to his feet. He stared into the interior darkness of the palace. Ivan Pokrov emerged from that darkness and stood before Chegory. Swaying.

'Are you all right?' said Chegory.

'I'm alive,' said Pokrov.

Then fainted.

Chegory caught the analytical engineer as he crumpled. Dragged him away from the portal of the pink palace. Laid him down on the night-warm stone of the portico. Pokrov was breathing okay, and the pulse in his thin wrist was strong and slow. He'd live. Chegory then felt his own pulse, which was fleeting in panic.

You're scared!

He was scared indeed. Fear had abolished fatigue, and he was ready to run. But he could not. Olivia was still in the palace. He returned to the portal, clenched his fists and tried to nerve himself to venture within.

I should have gone in with the others!

Chegory had no time for further self-recriminations, for something large, green and glowing was advancing from out of the depths of the palace. He ducked behind a pillar. As the green-glowing thing drifted past, Chegory saw it was a capsule of light. Inside was the young man of the Malud, Arnaut of Asral.

'Hey!' shouted Chegory. 'Hey, what the hell's going on?'

Arnaut struggled frantically within his cocoon of light. He punched, kicked and clawed. But he could not break free. The capsule of green light floated away down Lak Street bearing the hapless pirate with it.

Chegory stared after the receding cocoon of light.

'Shit,' said he.

In the Ebrell Islands, this passes as eloquence.

Having indulged himself in this delightful little soliloquy, Chegory turned back to the palace and waited for further revelation. None came. What was most ominous of all was that he could hear not a single sound from the interior. Not a shout, not a cry. Not so much as a squeak.

He could hear his own heartbeat, though. Also: a mosquito. Which settled. On his cheek. Swiftly, he smeared it. Felt its fragility roll beneath his fingers as he crushed it. Knew this was the moment of decision. Run. Immediately! Or venture inwards. He closed his eyes. Thought:

Olivia Olivia Olivia.

He opened his eyes. Wiped sweat from his face yet again. Took a deep breath. Then – moving swiftly, lest cowardice betray him – ran straight into the darkness of the palace.

He had scarcely gone a dozen paces when something tripped him and he fell heavily. Even as he recovered himself, Shabble came tumbling through the air after him, lighting the surrounding scene. Chegory had stumbled over a corpse. The body of old man Al-ran Lars! Covered in blood, alive with blood, streaming with blood, blood, red blood of death and butchery.

'Get the hell off me,' said the blood-smeared corpse.

Chegory gave a strangled scream as he leapt away from the dead man.

'What's wrong with you?' said Al-ran Lars.

'You're – you're dead,' said Chegory.

'The hell I am!' said the elderly gentleman adventurer. Then fainted.

'He's not dead, stupid,' said Shabble.

'So I gather,' said Chegory stiffly.

He bent over the Ashdan-skinned pirate, checking the old man for wounds. There was but one: a scalp-gash. From this the ancient had lost perhaps a handful of blood, enough to give him the appearance of something from a horror-house, but not sufficient to endanger his life. As blood was still free-flowing from the wound, Chegory ripped away Al-ran Lars's shirt then used it to bind the gash tightly.

'Hey, old man!' he said, shaking his patient roughly. 'You're all right! Wake up!'

But if the pirate heard him, he gave no sign of it.

Chegory said something unkind, then got to his feet.

By now, this scion of a bloodstained race of whale killers had entirely forgotten his earlier reservations about murdering the demon Binchinminfin. The sight of blood had been sufficient to rouse the lust for slaughter within his savage breast.

'Weapons!' he said. 'I need a weapon! Shabble, find me one!'

Shabble rose higher in the air, brightening all the while, illuminating more and more of the palace.

'Nineteen paces forward then five to your left,' said Shabble.

'I see it,' said Chegory.

He strode forward to claim the scimitar at the location indicated. It was heavy, and he held it awkwardly. Despite the clamancy of the moment he felt more than a little self-conscious to find himself in possession of such a theatrical weapon.

'Well,' said Chegory, squaring his shoulders. 'Let's get going.'

Going he got, with Shabble close behind him.

'I'm scared,' said Shabble.

'You don't have to come,' said Chegory.

'But if I stayed behind I'd be lonely!' protested Shabble.

'What does that matter?' said Chegory.

'You don't understand! Loneliness is the worst thing! How would you like it, to live for thousands and thousands of years with—'

Thus began Shabble's explanation of Shabbleself's own emotional motivation, which was a long one. But Chegory hardly listened, for he was gearing up for combat. He was:

Here!

Now!

Focused! Centred! Ready!

Through the danger-dark stalked this warlike Ebrell Islander, murder his intent. Then he saw a baleful green fire glowing up ahead. 'Shabble!' said Chegory. Shabble promptly lowered Shabbleself's illumination to next to zero, and, thus dimmed, hovered at Chegory's shoulder as the murderous one advanced to deal with demon Binchin-minfin.

The green-glowing room ahead was none other than the Star Chamber, and when Chegory Guy peered inside it a truly piquant scene met his eyes.

Aquitaine Varazchavardan had indeed been possessed by the foul and hideous Thing from Beyond, the demon Binchinminfin. Possession was obvious at a glance. Varaz-chavardan's lean and bony body had not been altered in the smallest particular – yet it had changed entirely.

All sense of overbearing dignity and ruthless self-control had deserted the wonderworker's ice-white flesh. The demon-possessed body lolled, relaxed in a sybaritic ease impossible for anyone to associate with the tense and hard-driving Master of Law. Yes, Varazchavardan had most definitely lost control of his own corpus. The demon Binchinminfin had unopposed command of the wonder-worker's flesh and bones.

The perfidious monster had crowned itself with the most

ornate object to hand, which happened to be a chamber pot which hailed from Wen Endex. There all artistic activity is frowned upon, and the ruling Yudonic Knights condemn would-be artists to exhaust their talents on the creation of such base objects as chamber pots and spittoons.

Hence the genius extant in this chamber pot, which featured—

[A catalogue follows. It has been excised on the grounds of obscenity; it raises questions concerning both the genius of the chamber pot and the morals of the Originator. *Soo Tree, Redactor Subminor.*]

To complete his glory, Binchinminfin had garbed Varazchavardan's flesh in a kitchen maid's kirtle and a glittering silver cuirass. Thus attired, the demon was reclining on a silken cushion, his naked feet resting in the congealed mass of curry, kedgeree and chowder which carpeted the Star Chamber. He was dining upon a dish of highly spiced spitchcock while he softly fondled Justina's albinotic ape, which was feeding from the same dish.

Chegory crouched in the entrance to the Star Chamber. Watching.

He knew a demon to be in command of this body, because Varazchavardan had never been able to endure the presence of Justina's ape. Then there was the matter of the body's eccentric attire. So this was what a demon looked like! Binchinminfin reminded Chegory of a drunken vampire rat – for here was a body disporting itself without regard for anything but its own comfort. Flesh relaxed, face softened by pleasure undiluted. A delving hand fumbling in the spitchcock under the governance of greed unrestrained. A mouth which, caring for nothing but appetite, gobbed and slathered at the hand-delivered.

At the demon's feet were slaves kneeling in the postures of worship, careless of the clogged mass of foot-mucked food in which they grovelled.

So what had happened to Uckermark? To Log Jaris? To . . . oh! There they were! All the missing heroes were hanging in mid-air on the far side of the Star Chamber.

Hostaja Sken-Pitilkin's eyes were closed, and the decrepit old wizard's head lay to one side, so he was possibly dead. But the others were clearly alive and intact – indeed, they still possessed weapons brought with them from the corpse shop or picked up along the way. But they were obviously trapped, held by invisible forces of unknown strength.

Chegory met the eyes of the muscleman Tolon. The night-black foreigner from Asral mouthed something at him. What? Chegory, unable to lip-read, shook his head. Tolon glared at him. The muscleman was armed with a massive spear made entirely of iron, a ceremonial weapon far too weighty for most mortals to put to practical use. His expression suggested that if he got the chance he would use it on Chegory.

This was all most unfair!

What was Chegory supposed to do?

How exactly does one dispose of a demon?

Chegory thought about it, then thought about it some more, then decided he should creep up on Binchinminfin then hack the demon to death. It dwelt in human flesh. Ergo, it could be killed.

Yet still he hesitated, until one of the demon's slaves raised her head from the muck, saw him, and wailed in unfeigned despair:

'Chegory! Chegory! Help us!'

It was Olivia!

Instantly, Chegory was on his feet. Charging, screaming. His scimitar leapt for Binchinminfin's throat.

But—

He was seized.

Gigantic fingers – invisible quite! – seized him. Squeezed! Squeezed the air out of him. He was choking. Gasping. Unable to breathe. He was—

Moving.

Chegory kicked and struggled helplessly as the invisible fist conveyed him across the room to join the line of heroes hung high in the air. When he got there, the fist relaxed its pressure. But still kept hold of his midriff. Chegory hacked at it wildly with his scimitar. But the blade met nothing.

'Didn't you believe me, you dumb Ebby?' said Tolon in passable Toxteth. 'I told you it was no use attacking the thing. I told you to get help.'

'Ah, go scrag yourself,' said Chegory.

Then hacked some more at the fist which was not there to be hacked. Binchinminfin watched him through Varaz-chavardan's pink eyes. Then scratched Justina's ape behind the ears, mouthed some more spitchcock, then laughed. Belatedly, Chegory, started thinking.

'Shabble,' said Chegory cautiously. 'Shabble, are you here?'

'Yes,' said a voice from just behind his ear. 'Chegory, Chegory, don't let that thing hurt me.'

'Shabble dearest,' said Chegory, 'I won't let it hurt you at all. What I want you to do is get help. Roll upward, upward. There's windows up there. Go get Yilda, tell her what's happened. She'll know what to do.'

So spoke Chegory, doubting that there was actually very much Yilda could do at all, apart from arranging for their funerals. He waited. At length, a reply came from his cautious companion.

'I can't,' said Shabble. 'It's too dangerous.'

'It's dangerous to be here!' said Chegory. 'That thing down there, that's not Varazchavardan! That's Binchin-minfin! A demon! A horrible hideous Thing from Beyond come to rape, kill and pillage!'

'Shabbles can't be raped,' said Shabble. 'Or pillaged.'

'Perhaps not,' said Chegory. 'But they can be killed. Or sent to the therapist.'

'Why should the demon do that?' said Shabble.

'Because it's evil!' said Chegory.

'How do you know?' said Shabble, to Chegory's intense irritation. This was no time for ontological discourse! Nevertheless, Shabble continued: 'Can you prove it?'

'Look,' said Chegory, taking a deep breath. 'Never mind the demon! If you don't take a message to Yilda I'll kill you myself. Or – or I could send you to a therapist myself!'

'You couldn't do either,' said Shabble reasonably. 'Not when you're hung up here like this.'

The fallen one was bluffing. The lord of lies knew that in fact any person-in-the-flesh can send any Shabble to any therapist at any time whatsoever on any pretext at all. The Shabble-designers of the Golden Gulag had carefully skewed Shabble's logic-sense to ensure that this bubble of free will would always believe as much.

However, Chegory Guy did not know that his flighty companion was bluffing, therefore the young Ebrell Islander failed to make the overt threat which would have forced his recalcitrant spherical friend to obey. Instead, Chegory hung there, cursing impotently. Thayer Levant and Tolon joined him in a prolonged exercise of rage and obscenity.

'It's no good,' said Uckermark. 'Save your strength.'

'The demon-thing must sleep sooner or later,' said Log Jaris. 'Everything sleeps. Then we can get away. Surely.'

'Oh yes,' said Guest Gulkan. 'Unless it kills us before it sleeps.'

The wizard Pelagius Zozimus made no contribution to this conversation, for he was speaking urgently to Hostaja Sken-Pitilkin. At last his cousin stirred, opened his eyes and replied. Soon the two masters of the mirific were engrossed in a colloquy of their own in the High Speech of wizards.

Chegory fell silent, but only for a moment. Then his anger overwhelmed him. In a strident voice he cried:

'Binchinminfin! I'm calling you out! I challenge you to single combat!'

A rash thing to say!

Consequences were immediate!

The demon, garbed in Varazchavardan's flesh, got to its feet and picked up a scimitar.

'Pain,' said the demon, forcing Odolo's strange foreign accents from Varazchavardan's flesh. 'Let us play with pain while we hack you to bits. The feet will go first.'

Then the demon advanced on Chegory, swinging the scimitar as it came.

Chegory realised his error. The demon-thing had no sense of honour. It would not dare a challenge, blade against blade. Instead, it would chop him to pieces as he hung helpless in the air. He screamed with fear.

But before Binchinminfin could hack away Chegory's feet, a voice roared out. Oh, and what a voice!

'Don't you dare!' said Anaconda Stogirov.

Binchinminfin, fearing the presence of a hostile Power, fell back. The suspended prisoners were released suddenly. They toppled from the air. Chegory landed heavily on all fours.

'Who spoke?' said Binchinminfin. 'Who was it? Who is it? Who's there?'

'It is I,' said Shabble, burning brightly in the air above, greatly emboldened by the demon's manifest fear. 'It is I, Anaconda Stogirov, Chief of Security of the Golden Gulag. Hear and obey! Or I will send you to a therapist immediately.'

'Spah!' said the demon.

It threw a fistful of air in Shabble's direction. The air became a fireball. Shabble never moved. The fireball and the bright-gleaming Shabble became one. Shabble glowed a little brighter. Then replied by unleashing a fury of flame that should by rights have incinerated the demon. But Binchinminfin laughed. Demonic laughter shrivelled the flame-fury to a few shreds of harmless smoke.

Then the demon hurled a lighting bolt at Shabble. Who ducked and spat hard radiation in reply. As a sizzling exchange of death and destruction proceeded, Pelagius Zozimus and Hostaja Sken-Pitilkin began crawling toward the nearest exit.

Shabble bobbed up and down, whistling merrily. Shabble thought this firefight was great fun. Then Binchinminfin scored a direct hit on the quick-darting Shabble. With a sphere of incandescent plasma. Shabble ate it.

'Throw me another one,' said the imitator of suns.

Binchinminfin screamed with rage.

As the firefight intensified, Uckermark and Log Jaris set

355

out after the two wizards. Tolon followed them. As did Guest Gulkan and Thayer Levant. Chegory, the last of the heroes to hold his ground, stayed down, stayed low, waiting for his chance to rush forward and rescue Olivia.

Then Binchinminfin went berserk. He hurled sheets of smoke, flame and lighting toward the taunting Shabble. As death filled the air, all humans who could run took flight. Chegory among them. He was no good to Olivia if he was dead!

'Where are you?' roared Binchinminfin, as the smoke cleared.

'Here,' said Shabble.

Then giggled.

Binchinminfin picked up an orange and breathed on it. The orange became transparent. Within its depths lights swirled and sparked.

'Tharaftendosko,' said Binchinminfin.

Then released the orange.

The globe went rolling through the air toward Shabble. Who guessed what it was – and dropped like a stone. The globe struck a pillar and disintegrated. As did the pillar. Where the globe had struck, stone became chaos: a cascade of free-sliding incoherence in which bits of maybe, once was and might-have-been tumbled over and over. Gravity claimed the chaos. Which collapsed toward the floor, writhing its way downward to join the unpleasant mess which had already disfigured the Star Chamber.

Fortunately, the pillar had been purely ornamental in nature, therefore the palace did not fall down on the heads of those who were doing battle within its walls.

The demon loosed another globe. Shabble skittered and jived, frantic to escape this lethal weapon, which the refugee from the ruins of the Golden Gulag had correctly identified as a field of localised improbability.

Three more globes the demon loosed. Time for Shabble to be gone! The feckless one duplicated itself thrice thirty times. Leaving the Star Chamber ablaze with imitation Shabbles, the true article went to ground and rolled along the floor, speeding out of the nearest exit like a glob of spittle being blown along by a hurricane. In the dark interstices of the pink palace, Shabble caught up with Chegory Guy, and shone a little light to help the Ebrell Islander and his stumbling comrades navigate out of the palace.

'What happened?' said Chegory.

'I got beaten,' said Shabble frankly.

'You mean, you can't kill the demon-thing?'

'I tried!' said Shabble, hurt by the note of disappointment in Chegory's voice. 'I tried, I tried, really I did! But I couldn't, that's all.'

'All right,' said Chegory, doing his best to soothe poor Shabble. 'All right, you did your best, I know that. Come, let's be gone.'

Outside, they met Ivan Pokrov and old man Al-ran Lars, who had been conferring in the shadow of the palace portico.

'What's happening within?' said Al-ran Lars.

'Explanations later!' said Uckermark. 'Let's just get the hell out of here.'

'What about the wishstone?' said Guest Gulkan. 'Where is it?'

Uckermark had to confess that he had dropped it in the Star Chamber.

'How could you!' said Guest Gulkan, aghast at this disaster. 'I risked my life for that thing! Years of questing! Battles, torture, horror, nightmare, death! And you – you – I don't believe it! You've got it, haven't you? Haven't you?!'

'Search me then,' said Uckermark. 'Search me, if you don't believe me.'

Guest Gulkan needed no further invitation. He frisked the corpse master instantly. Then nothing would serve except for him to search all the others. Then he screamed in frustrated rage. He was so angry he punched himself in the head.

'Right!' said Zozimus briskly. 'If you've got the

357

histrionics out of your system, then let's be gone.'

So saying, the master wizard of the order of Xluzu began to march away downhill. The others followed.

Chegory wanted to protest. Olivia was still back in the Star Chamber! If she was alive. But . . .

What could he do? He could not contend with the demon. When threatened, Binchinminfin had strung him up in the sky without even touching him. The demon controlled fire, smoke and thunder. Could smash stone at will.

Already the other humans were a hundred paces distant.

'Come on, Chegory!' said Shabble.

So the Ebrell Islander joined the retreat down Lak Street. Past the houses of the great and the grand with their walls aglow with the blue-green glimmer of moon paint. Past the inexplicable ship-sized monolith of bone which the city knows as Pearl.

There Arnaut of Asral stepped out of the shadows and greeted them.

'What happened to you?' said Al-ran Lars.

'It's a long story,' said Arnaut, and began to tell it as the refugees continued their retreat downhill.

Shortly they reached the Cabal House of Injiltaprajura's wonderworkers. From the uppermost storey there still came the same drunken singing, indicating that the end-of-the-world celebrations were still in full swing.

Uckermark halted.

'Let's go in and negotiate,' said he. 'We can't handle this demon-thing without help. Zozimus, my man! Lead us within!'

'Me?' said Pelagius Zozimus. 'I'm a wizard. Wizards and sorcerers are deadly enemies. They'd kill me rather than listen to me.'

'Right!' said Uckermark. 'I'll go in alone!'

So in he went.

After a protracted wait, Chegory Guy ventured within to see what had happened to the corpse master. He found Uckermark sitting on the steps which led upward. The way was impassable, for the wonderworkers had done nothing to clear the mass of stone still blocking the stair-well. Chegory could smell the dust of broken rock. Plus something else besides. Something sharp, evil, allur-ing. He noticed that Uckermark had a small flask in his hand.

'What you got there?' said Chegory.

'What do you think?' said Uckermark, proffering the flask to the Ebrell Islander.

'No thanks,' said Chegory stiffly.

'Well then!' said Uckermark. 'Your loss, my gain.'

So saying, he drained the flask, then tossed it aside and led the way outside.

'We'll get no help from the wonderworkers tonight,' he said. 'Let's be going.'

They turned down Skindik Way and hurried past the Dromdanjerie, from whence there came the sound of deranged howling. Chegory presumed that Jon Qasaba would be inside, ministering to his patients. Not for the first time, the Ebrell Islander wished he could flee into the Dromdanjerie, curl up on his pallet and pretend the disasters which had overwhelmed his life had never happened.

On they went. Past the enormous rotting shadow of Ganthorgruk. As they hastened down the street, a ferocity of rats burst from a sewer-hole in the base of the building. Vampire rats! A pack of marauding vampire rats intent on murder!

'Shabble!' said Ivan Pokrov. 'Light!'

Shabble flared. Then the men turned on the rats with savage intent, glad to have something to kick and kill. But the vampire rats sensed what they were up against, and fled screaming.

On went the terrorisers of rats, past the slaughterhouse where phlegmatic butchers were working late by lamplight, anatomising the corpse of a kraken which had recently met its death in the polluted waters of the Laitemata.

Chegory stopped to warn them.

'Hey!' said Chegory. 'Hey, there's a demon on the loose in the palace.'

'Oh?' said a butcher.

Down came the cleaver. Then the man swayed slightly, and burped. Chegory realised he was drunk. Everyone in the slaughterhouse was drunk! They were working in an alcoholic haze. Working by rite and ritual, by habit and force of routine. For a moment longer he stood watching, then, realising he could do nothing useful here, ran after his comrades.

On downhill they went till they came to the hovels and scramble-walks of Lubos. Without warning, the sky above was briefly illuminated by a flash of weird blue light which could have been – anything. It gave them a brief glimpse of their own shocked and frightened faces. Then night claimed dominion once again.

'Shabble!' said Pokrov. 'Where are you? Where's your light?'

'Here I am,' said Shabble, brightening as Shabbleself recovered from the fear brought out by the inexplicable skyflash.

Then there came a cry of utter agony. From where? They could not place the source. After it died away, they were silent. Listening. Hearing – nothing. Nothing but dripping sewage, heavy snoring from an attic window, and the steady downfall of a nearby fountain.

'Come on,' said Uckermark.

Then led the way to his corpse shop, where Yilda greeted them with relief and with half a thousand questions.

'I should have kept a diary,' grumbled Uckermark, for he knew Yilda would not be satisfied till she knew everything.

As Uckermark did his best to answer some of Yilda's questions, Chegory made them all some hot coffee. He knew his way round the place fairly well by then. He scarcely noticed the corpse stench, and, rather than thinking of the shop as a house of horrors, found the place rather homely.

A measure of how he had fallen! How far! Indeed – and how fast!

Once Yilda's omnivorous curiosity had been placated, and coffee had been served, it was time to face the question. The logical, obvious, necessary question, which Chegory nevertheless articulated:

'What now?'

CHAPTER THIRTY-ONE

What would you have done, my hero? What would you have done if you had found yourself sitting there in Uckermark's corpse shop with a mad demon on the loose in Injiltaprajura? To the corpse master himself, the next move was crystal clear.

'I vote that we get drunk,' said Uckermark.

But Log Jaris demurred.

'Friend Uckermark,' he said, 'the game is not yet played out. We're not dead yet. We can yet escape – at least with our lives. I vote we flee to the Ngati Moana. Tonight. Between us we own enough in gold and silver to bribe them to give us passage.'

'Impossible!' said Guest Gulkan. 'I came for the wish-stone. I'm not leaving without it!'

'Besides,' said Chegory, 'what about, um, Olivia, okay? She's still with the demon! So's Ingalawa – and the Empress! We can't just, well, run off and leave them, can we? Some of them, maybe, okay, but what about Justina?'

'What about Justina?' said Uckermark. 'She's a big girl. She can look after herself.'

'But Olivia, then!' said Chegory.

'You're the one who loves her,' said Uckermark. 'You look after her.'

'Who said I love her?' said Chegory, blushing. 'I said nothing about love. It's – it's responsibility, that's what it is. We have to go back for her.'

'We've gone,' said Uckermark. 'We've been. We've tried. We've dared. What we could do we did do.'

'Oh yes!' said Guest Gulkan. 'And you lost us the wishstone doing it! I wish I'd killed you the first time I'd set eyes on you.'

Tempers then threatened to get out of hand but Pelagius Zozimus managed to settle the temper of the Yarglat barbarian while the bullman Log Jaris counselled Uckermark against violence.

Then:

'Jod,' said Ivan Pokrov. 'That's where we should go. That's where we left Odolo. Mayhap the conjuror can help us plan. After all, he's the one who knows the demon best.'

Debate ensued. Pokrov's will prevailed. Yilda was left to guard the corpse shop while the members of the anti-Binchinminfin league made their way to the waterfront and skulked across the harbour bridge toward the dark uprising of Jod. From the fishgut gloom of the Laitemata there arose the overpowering smell of dikle and shlug. The stuff was still pouring from the wealth fountains, forcing the heroes to make the last part of the journey on stilts.

Once they were in the Analytical Institute, Ivan Pokrov led them to his private quarters where they found the conjuror Odolo sleeping sweetly.

'Let's wake him up,' said Chegory, still hoping for advice which would help them wage war against Binchinminfin and win Olivia's freedom.

But Pokrov had other ideas.

'Let the poor man sleep,' said Ivan Pokrov. 'He'll know as much at dawn as he knows at the moment, no more and no less. Meantime, come through to my office. I've got something to show you.'

All followed Pokrov into his private office where, with solemn ceremony, he produced a large flask.

'I've been doing some alchemical research in my spare time,' said Ivan Pokrov. 'This is the end result of my labours.'

Then he took some small china cups and poured them each a dose of a subtle fluid the colour of a virgin's inner flesh. Uckermark sniffed. Then sipped. Then rolled his eyes in delight.

'Beautiful,' he murmured. 'Beautiful!'

Log Jaris tried it.

'Not bad,' he admitted.

'Not bad?' protested Uckermark. 'It – it's magnificent!'

A duckling raised on such stuff would have grown into a dragon. A kitten which lapped on such would have matured to a tiger. So at least thought Uckermark. But Chegory thought otherwise. For a single sip sufficed to tell him that this was alcohol. Chegory, who knew the true evil of this filthy poison, spat it out, then turned on the analytical engineer.

'You made this?' said Chegory.

'Truly,' said Pokrov, with pride.

Chegory was appalled. Was there not one person of integrity in all of Injiltaprajura? He had thought Pokrov every bit the solemn scientist, dedicated to the pursuit of knowledge and learning, yet here he was revealed as a bootlegger dealing in drugs most foul – drugs which corrupt the soul, rot the liver, maim the unborn in the womb, savage the brain and leave the victim a helpless imbecile shuddering from one waking nightmare to the next.

At least Injiltaprajura still owned one upright citizen. Chegory Guy himself had not wilfully broken the law. (So he thought – conveniently forgetting incidents such as his vigorous attempt to vandalise the door to the Cabal House.) He had tried to serve, honour and obey the established order. (Was there any merit in this when the alternative was almost certain to be execution?) He had tried to be an obedient slave to the law, to be a dutiful cog in the system like one of the thousands of little titanium cogs that clicked around in the heart of the analytical engine. (So he told himself, forgetting that one of his daily dedications was to knifefighting practice – hardly a hobby indicative of meek submission to the ruling order.)

Face to face with temptation, Chegory vowed that he would try to remain a strictly honest and upright citizen, direct and truthful in all his dealings with his fellows, sober for life, an unspotted virgin till the day of his marriage. He would show them! They would see that an Ebrell Islander could be as moral as the next person! Or more so! Despite the bloody stain which tainted his flesh he would prove himself pure!

As Chegory was so thinking, he heard someone sniggering. With murder in his heart he searched all faces, ready to kill when he discovered the mind-reader who was laughing at him. But it was only Shabble, chortling at some private joke.

'Come, Chegory,' said Ivan Pokrov. 'Aren't you going to drink with us?'

'No!' said Chegory.

He waited for the men to be done with their drinks and to settle down to the business of planning war against Binchinminfin. But other drinks followed the first. When the flask of liquor was drained, Ivan Pokrov produced a second. Then a third.

The party began to get lively. Log Jaris and Uckermark broke into song. A very strange song with a chorus in which they imitated dog, cock, cat and seal. Much to the bemusement of Chegory Guy, who had never seen a seal in his life, nor heard of one either.

In the end, most of the men had consumed so much of this toxic substance known as alcohol that they had reached the vomiting stage. It is very strange, but people who should know far better will often spend good money – excellent money, the best that work can buy – to go through this experience of overloading their systems with potent poisons. They will do this not once but repeatedly – which supports the theories of the eminent philosopher Stupa, who holds that to exist is to suffer, and that human beings are constructed in such a way that they value suffering above all else.

At last Chegory could stand the company of these drunks no longer. He left them, and Ivan Pokrov found him much later sitting alone on the rocks outside.

'What's the matter?' said Pokrov.

'What isn't?' said Chegory. 'You – this is craziness! A demon in the palace and all you – all you do is get drunk!'

'I'm not drunk,' said Pokrov. 'The others are, but I'm not.'

'But you've been drinking that, that alcohol stuff, haven't you?'

'What of it?' said Pokrov.

'It's against the law!' said Chegory.

Pokrov laughed. Softly.

'It is!' insisted Chegory. 'And for good reason! It rots you, doesn't it? It kills you, right? Isn't that so?'

There was a pause while Pokrov thought his way around the problem. Then the analytical engineer said:

'You want to be perfect?'

'Well,' said Chegory, 'I don't want to kill myself, that's for sure!'

'We are mortal, you know,' said Pokrov.

By using this inclusive 'we', Pokrov was perpetrating a half-truth, for technically Pokrov was immortal. He would never die of old age. Yet he could be killed.

'We're mortal?' said Chegory. 'What's that got to do with it?'

Ivan Pokrov responded by giving him the first and most annoying of the Seven Unsatisfactory Explanations:

'When you're older you'll understand.'

'No,' said Chegory, 'that's not good enough. You can't get out of it just like that. What the hell are you on about? Drinking, that's drugs and stuff. What the hell's that got to do with mortality? Hey? Come on, man, what is this crap?'

'When I say we're mortal,' said Pokrov, 'I mean we can't live free of risk.' That was true. It was as true of himself as it was of Chegory. 'So your – your obsession with health is – not exactly misplaced, I wouldn't say that. But – let's say it's, well, overstated. You're in danger of becoming a fanatic.'

'Oh, that's all crap,' said Chegory. 'You're trying to tell me we should – what? Take poison? Because – because what? Because everyone dies? Is that any reason to hurry along to get killed?'

'You are a bit fanatical about this,' said Pokrov.

'Fanatical!' said Chegory. 'Is that what you call it? I'll

366

tell you what I call it! I call it serious! And why? Because when you're a stinking Ebby, man, you better be serious, because people are out to kill you, that's why, you can't fuck up because then you've had it, man, just one mistake and that's it, wham! You never lived with, with people hunting you, you walk in the street and you hear, well, things, people say things, that's it, then you want to smash them smash them smash – bones, you could smash, blood, I could smash – I could kill some bugger! That's serious, man! Then now, okay, now there's a demon, there's all hell running loose, and you, you're, it's like – I mean, what's going down here, man? You think this is some kind of joke? Lives on the line and you, you crazy shits, you just sit around, you just get smashed, and me – serious, why not? There's people I – well, care for, okay? But, oh, I'm an Ebby, right? So it's not serious for you, oh no, suddenly you're this great big adult, I'm a kid or something, mortality, all that crap, what's that supposed to prove?'

Thus Chegory Guy.

In brief.

In truth, he soliloquised long, so full of hate, rage and frustration that at first he never noticed Ivan Pokrov's departure. When he realised the analytical engineer had walked off, abandoning him without apology, he was so full of fury that he was ready to kill someone.

There was only one thing to do.

Chegory did it.

He hunted out his favourite sledgehammer and expended his rage by smashing some much-hated boulders to pieces, sweating in his violence until his body and emotions were exhausted entirely, and, reeling with fatigue, he sought some place to sleep.

CHAPTER THIRTY-TWO

Dawn came to the island of Jod. The dark of night flowed into freshets of blood as the sky haemorrhaged. A bruised and bloated carbuncular sun oozed from the crimson horizon like a bloodclot incarnadine forced from a full-fist wound by slow but remorseless alluvial pressures. Red glowed the bloodstone of the streets of Injiltaprajura. Red was the brooding coral strand which fringed the Laitemata. Red were the beaches of Scimitar and red was the seaweed of the bloodstained lagoon.

But white was the Analytical Institute. The marvellous building uprose upon Jod like a cool confection of ice and snow, a manifest miracle in this mosquito-tormented clime of sweat remorseless and fevers oppressive.

Unfortunately, within this building of beauty was a scene of the utmost depravity. In Ivan Pokrov's quarters a number of comatose bodies lay slumped in a stuporous sleep hard to distinguish from profound concussion. The owners of those bodies had given themselves to a profound, shameless debauch of the flesh. They had overindulged in obscene and poisonous drugs and were now suffering the consequences.

Among those who lay there as if dead were the wizards Pelagius Zozimus and Hostaja Sken-Pitilkin. Once their apprentice days are behind them wizards seldom get drunk, for when they become intoxicated these masters of the mirific run risks far greater than those faced by lesser beings. However, these two had got as thoroughly wasted as the rest of them.

Even the cutthroat Thayer Levant had drunk himself into a helpless stupor, despite his highly developed sense of self-preservation.

This was the scene which confronted a sober and bad-tempered Chegory Guy when he came in from the servants' quarters where he had grabbed a little sleep in the last part of bardardornootha. He relieved his emotions by kicking everybody in sight. A few groans greeted this performance. But nobody was actually roused to consciousness by Chegory's endeavours, and the groans were but sleeptalk complaints from the dim depths of drug-bewildered night-mares.

Then Chegory found Shabble, who was hiding in a fish tank, pretending to be a stone. Chegory grabbed hold of the feckless one. Shabble was cold and inert in his hand.

'Wake up,' said Chegory, tossing Shabble into the air.

The globular one described a perfect parabola. Plunged toward the floor. Then snapped into sun-bright life and swept upwards in a tight, flight-delighting spiral.

'Hello, Chegory!' said Shabble happily.

'Hi,' said Chegory moodily.

Then picked up a scimitar which one of the sleepers had plundered from the pink palace the night before. While he waited for his comrades to rouse he practised a few head-lopping strokes.

Pelagius Zozimus was first to wake. He woke from force of habit. He was a master chef, after all, and one of the burdens of a cook's life is the necessity to rise before long before others are awake. Think of this when next you seat yourself in your dining room to banquet upon that delicate concoction of snake's eggs and the flesh of half a dozen different serpents which there awaits your delight. It didn't get there by itself, you know!

[Those who are nauseated by the Originator's casual references to the consumption of snakemeat and the eggs of snakes must remember that the Originator is not a Practitioner. While the Crime in question demands Final-isation whether one follows Religion or not, a lighthearted attitude toward the Crime is understandable (if not pardonable) in an alien atheist. *Zin Twee, Master of Religion.*]

[With reference to Zin Twee's comment above, it is not at all clear from the Text that the Originator is in fact an atheist. While some passages display a distressing impiety, nowhere is there a denial of the existence of Things Beyond. Despite the existence of a certain Passage in the Text which appears to denigrate blasphemously all Establishments, it is still possible that the Originator could be, to take a couple of examples, a worshipper of Evil (Pure or Applied) or a member of the Danatos Blood Cult. *Newt Gerund, Chief Pedant.*]

Habit is not the only reason why Zozimus woke. A baby, child of one of the female servants who dwelt on Jod, was bawling loudly. If there was one thing Zozimus found it impossible to sleep through it was the racket of a crying child.

Pelagius Zozimus hated babies.

That was one of the reasons why he had become a wizard. Not the sole reason, of course. He had been born and raised in Wen Endex, and in early youth had made a most shameful discovery about himself. He was an intellectual. There is no place for such in Wen Endex, where the Yudonic Knights rule by brute force and unthinking violence. Consequently, a disproportionate number of wizards come from that province, and from Galsh Ebrek in particular, despite the enormous difficulties of the pilgrimage from there to the castles of Argan's Confederation of Wizards.

Pelagius Zozimus decided to wake the others, but when he acted on decision the task defeated him, just as it had defeated young Chegory Guy.

'Right,' muttered Zozimus. 'I'll at least make sure they stay awake once they do wake up.'

Then Zozimus, who was in a decidedly warlike mood, made the most ferocious curry imaginable. Into it went peppercorns complete, ground grey pepper of the Yellow Phoenix grade, the smouldering orange-brown of cayenne pepper (known also as dragon fire), a quantity of Five Heavenly Virtues Spice Powder, and last (but by no means least) an enormous amount of that curry powder known as Leaping Green Lizards' Incendiary Delight.

A couple of the sleepers roused and were presented with the curry for breakfast. Naturally, none of them could eat it. Indeed, after a night of boozing they were scarcely in a condition to eat anything. Ivan Pokrov took one mouthful of the newborn dish which Zozimus had just birthnamed Wizard's Revenge, turned a very funny colour, then withdrew. He did not return for some time. Even the barbarian Guest Gulkan, who was inured to suffering by a lifetime's practice, refused a second mouthful.

Log Jaris might have been able to get through some of the stuff, but the matter was never put to the test, for the bullman was still dead to the world.

'Fussy, are we?' said Zozimus.

He sampled his own wares, looked thoughtful, then put some rice on to boil.

In the end, only Chegory and Zozimus dined on the curry, and then only after diluting it with quantities of boiled white rice. They were both sweating ferociously by the time they had finished, partly from the sultry heat of the morning but mostly from the inner fires ignited by the master chef's misplaced genius. The other humans contented themselves with the juice of several green coconuts, a fluid much to be recommended to anyone in their condition, for it is most certainly the best of all known remedies for that dreadful affliction known as a hangover.

[Here an inaccuracy born of a pardonable ignorance. An ancient medical text in our possession clearly states that a hangover will be cured most swiftly by cooling the body, draining it of blood and replacing that drug-contaminated fluid with a transfusion from an immaculate source. While a codex of later date reports that mass fatalities resulted from an experiment designed to test this thesis, we nevertheless must accept the authority of our ancestors, even if we find ourselves sadly lacking in the expertise required to exploit this knowledge. *Xjoptiproti, Fact Checker Interpolative.*]

[There is nothing sad in this lack since we none of us

indulge in alcohol. With tragic exceptions! Such as Xjopti-proti himself, who was found dead a day after the writing of the above. A flask of potato liquor was at his side and a still for the manufacture of this lethal concoction was discovered in his study. Need I say more? *Drax Lira, Redactor Major*.]

Breakfast was scarcely over when a panic-stricken servant came rushing in to say that the Hermit Crab was without – and was demanding an audience with Chegory Guy.

'Oh shit!' said Chegory, smacking his forehead. 'I never fed the thing! It hasn't been fed since – since – gods! Is it three days? Four?'

Chegory tried to think. He had given lunch to the Crab on the first day of disaster – the day on which the loss of the wishstone had been discovered. But on the second day he had been too busy with things like the petitions session. Then there had been the banquet in the evening and the dragon and – well, after that the Hermit Crab had been the last thing on his mind. He had spent the third day sleeping and hiding out in Uckermark's corpse shop. Then on the fourth day – yesterday – there had been the depositions hearing, Varazchavardan's coup, and all the madness which had followed.

The Crab had been totally unfed for at least three whole days!

'Well, come on,' said Ivan Pokrov. 'Let's not keep the thing waiting. That wouldn't improve it's temper, you know.'

'You're coming with me?' said Chegory.

'You can go alone if you want,' said Pokrov.

'I, uh – yes, well, company's fine. Yes, come, sure.'

With that, Chegory set off for his interview with the dreaded Hermit Crab. He started remembering some of the things he had been told about its Powers. About, for example, the sorcerer who had been turned inside out after trying to enslave the Crab. Flies had settled upon his pulsating—

[Here details of twenty-seven revolting incidents have

372

been deleted. By Order. The gusto with which the Originator narrated the said incidents is itself something which verges on the obscene. *Drax Lira, Redactor Major.*]

Chegory and Pokrov found the Hermit Crab waiting at the main entrance to the Analytical Institute. The morning sun was shining and sheening on the mottled surface of its carapace. Beneath its body, where its bulk blotted out the sun, the shadows were thick, dark, black. The Crab's claws were infolded against its carapace. Chegory tried to figure their reach then abandoned the effort. Brute force was the least of the dangers he faced. Nevertheless, the sheer bulk of the Crab was intimidating. Chegory had forgotten how huge it was.

The Crab studied them in silent reproach then said:

'I was not fed. All yesterday. If my memory does not deceive me, I was not fed the day before that. If I had an accountant's mentality I could go on. But I'm sure you get my point.'

Nobody knew what to say.

The Hermit Crab waited patiently. For what? Excuses? Apologies? In the uncomfortable conversational pause they could hear the unending streams of dikle and shlug still pouring into the Laitemata and the squabbling of a few crows haggling over some rubbish outside the kitchen.

It was Chegory who first dared speak.

'I'm afraid we've been, um, well, rather busy,' he said. 'There's a, um, a demon, actually. It's got a name. Binchinminfin, that's its, uh, name. It's – well, it's in Varazchavardan. I mean, it's taken him over. And – well, we've been, we've been, uh, I guess you could say we've been pretty occupied. Busy, I mean.'

He paused.

The Hermit Crab's ominous immobility suggested this excuse failed to meet with its approval.

Chegory stood there.

Sweating.

Awaiting his death.

Then a third figure joined the two confronting the

monster. It was the wizard of Xluzu, the formidable Pelagius Zozimus.

'Aha!' said Zozimus briskly, rubbing his hands together. 'So this is the famous Crab! Good day to you, my lord! Pelagius Zozimus at your service! A master chef, if you please, and believe me most are pleased indeed. I've a thousand satisfied clients spread all the way from Tang to Chi'ash-lan. I've never cooked for a Crab before, but there's always a first time. I'd be delighted to give it a bash. What would you like to eat?'

'It eats fish guts,' said Chegory. 'Offal, that's all.'

'Dear friend,' said the wizard, addressing the Hermit Crab directly and ignoring Chegory entirely, 'I have lately served the Empress Justina and it would be my pleasure now to serve you in turn. Tell me – how you would like your provender styled. What would you find most gustful?'

The Hermit Crab was silent, as if deep in thought. Then one massive claw opened. Then closed with a decisive click.

'I would like,' said the Hermit Crab, 'some fresh flying fish lightly fried and adorned with a milk-based sauce flavoured, if possible, with mint, and if not then with some equivalent herb chosen at your discretion.'

'Oh, excellent, excellent,' said Zozimus. 'And then?'

'And then,' said the Hermit Crab, 'I would like . . .'

It specified, in all, a total of fifty different dishes. When it was done, Zozimus complimented on its taste and discretion, then strode away to the kitchen with Chegory in tow. Zozimus loved a challenge. Especially one very close to impossible.

Once in the kitchen, Pelagius Zozimus issued rapid-fire orders to the kitchen staff. Then he turned to Chegory.

'Chegory! I need some milk!'

'Well, there's, um, coconuts, I suppose,' said Chegory.

'Not coconut milk!' said the master chef. 'Real milk! Get me a goat!'

'There's no goat on all of Jod,' said Chegory.

'Then we'll try another source,' said Pelagius Zozimus.

'There is a bawling baby on Jod, therefore there is milk. Fetch!'

So saying, he thrust a bowl into Chegory's hands.

The Ebrell Islander stood there gawping, making a deliberate effort not to understand.

'Milk!' said Pelagius Zozimus imperiously.

Whereupon young Chegory Guy staggered away, tottering as if he had taken a severe blow on the head.

What took place then, we cannot say. For Chegory Guy would never speak of it thereafter, and there are no independent witnesses prepared to comment. Even Shabble was never able to discover the details, though Shabble is an inveterate gossip and the most adroit spy imaginable.

Suffice to say that in due course young Chegory returned with some milk in the bowl. Pelagius Zozimus dipped his little finger into this offering, tasted it then smacked his lips.

'Ah!' he said. 'This takes me back!'

'Takes you back?' said Chegory. 'How far?'

'Oh, a thousand years or so,' said Zozimus airily. 'Give or take the odd century here or there.'

Then he abandoned all idle conversation in favour of work.

When the first course was almost ready to be served, Chegory went and fetched the Hermit Crab's bucket.

'What on earth have you got that for?' said Zozimus.

'For the food, of course,' said Chegory.

'You can't serve people food in buckets!'

'I don't. It gets dumped into the trough, okay, there's a special crab trough, just dump it all in, it all gets eaten. That's how we do things round here.'

'That's just not good enough,' said Zozimus severely. 'Presentation is every bit as important as content.'

'Not to the Hermit Crab,' said Chegory. 'He says we just have to put up with things.'

Pelagius Zozimus took hold of a mango. He held it up, demanding:

'Does this take your fancy?'

Chegory, thinking himself sure to be the victim of some wizardly trick, answered cautiously:

'It's a nice enough piece of fruit.'

Whereupon the wizard threw the mango to the ground. Naturally it splattered in impact.

'Does it still take your fancy?' said Zozimus.

Chegory did not answer.

'It doesn't, does it?' said Zozimus. 'And why not? The nutritional content remains unchanged. It still tastes the same. Eat it! Surely it's good for you. Go on, try it! Come – why so sullen?'

'I'm tired,' said Chegory. 'I'm tired of being baited.'

'Baited?' said Zozimus in amazement. 'I was educating you.'

'Oh, is that what it is, is it?' said Chegory. 'Education! That's what people are doing when they act rude and make fun of you? Hey?'

The confrontation with the Crab and the ordeal of obtaining fresh milk for the Crab's special flying fish sauce (what was wrong with the ordinary kind, hey?) had not improved the bad temper with which he had started the day.

Fortunately, Zozimus did not choose to discipline the recalcitrant Ebby. Instead, the master chef shrugged off Chegory's outburst and got on with his work. Shortly the first course was served to the Hermit Crab on the best china to be found in the Analytical Institute.

Chegory watched with fascination as the Hermit Crab fed upon the food, removing one titbit after another from the fragile porcelain with the utmost delicacy. The young Ebrell Islander had never imagined the Crab's huge claws to be capable of such subtle control. Or that the Crab possessed such an advanced palate.

'Good,' said the Crab, when the fiftieth dish was finished.

Whereupon Pelagius Zozimus ventured to say:

'My dear lord, I'm so glad you enjoyed your breakfast. One just as good could certainly be arranged for tomorrow, if that's your wish. Meanwhile, might I bring your attention to a trifling problem on the fringes of your domain?'

'Speak,' said the Hermit Crab.

'There is, my lord, a little trouble in the city. A matter of a demon, as it happens. A demon by name of Binchinminfin. It's unleashed the most dreadful disasters on the mainland. Why, it's stopped the bells ringing, for starters.'

'Has it now!' said the Hermit Crab, speaking with a passion which Chegory would have thought totally alien to its nature. 'Those infernal bells! The bane of my life. So a demon's stopped them, has it? Good! I hope they stay stopped!'

'My lord,' said Zozimus smoothly, 'they'll stay stopped forever, if that's your wish. Meanwhile, this demon . . . it might, my lord, prove a problem. They're very powerful, these demons.'

'Tell,' said the Crab.

So Zozimus elaborated on the power and potential of demons. When the wizard was done, the Crab said:

'Could this demon turn me into a human being?'

'Turn you?' said Zozimus, taken aback. 'Into a human?'

'Yes!' said the Crab.

'My lord,' said Zozimus, 'I – I really don't know.'

'Then go!' said the Crab. 'Go to the palace! Find the demon and ask it! Tell it my wish! Tell it I will make an alliance of Powers if it can favour me with such a transformation.'

This was the very last thing Zozimus had expected – and the opposite of what he had hoped for. But such is life.

'My lord,' said Zozimus, 'might I spend a little while conferring with my friends before I leave Jod to carry out your mission? These demons . . . approaching them is a delicate matter. We crave your indulgence. We need time to prepare our approach to the demon.'

'Granted,' said the Crab. 'But be sure you see the demon today. And – do not fail!'

Chegory and Zozimus then set about rounding up all the heroes of the night before so they could have a council of war. Only Log Jaris proved unavailable: the bullman was

377

still unassailably asleep. So they started without him. First Zozimus reported his failure in negotiations with the Crab.

He concluded by saying:

'Our choice is more complex than before. If we kill the demon we anger the Crab. But I doubt we could kill the demon in any case. Or negotiate with it. What is for certain is that we can't stay here. The Crab wants to be human. But I can't imagine a demon making it so. These demons – even they don't have that kind of power. I think our best choice is to run away.'

'No!' roared Guest Gulkan, still intent on recovering the wishstone, which he needed to make war on far-distant Chi'ash-lan.

'No,' said Chegory Guy, who had just as much at stake as Guest Gulkan, and who was in a foul and bloody-minded mood. 'My woman is in the palace. To hell with the risks. I say we go in and deal to this demon. Kill it. Finish it. Then we can think about leaving.'

There are few things more dangerous to deal with than the sullen anger of an Ebrell Islander. One of those things is a drunken Ebrell Islander with his dander up. A second is a young, husky, drunken Ebrell Islander running amok with a bladed weapon. When we try to think of a third – well, we start to run into difficulties. We must always remember that these Ebrell Islanders are a people who hunt terrifying sea monsters for fun and profit, who think nothing of drinking themselves to death by the age of thirty, and who are, in short, never to be taken lightly.

So Guest Gulkan and Chegory Guy were both in favour of a further assault on the demon – despite the contemptuous ease with which the monster had defeated their first onslaught. The Malud marauders then declared that they too were ready to join an attack. Young Arnaut in particular was fiercely determined to fight.

There is no telling where all this fighting talk might have led in the end. Because, before a final decision could be reached, Log Jaris joined the conference and demanded to be brought up to date. The bullman laughed heartily when he heard what was being planned.

'What are you laughing for?' said Chegory. 'This is serious!'

'Death is always serious,' said the bullman. 'Even yours.'

'I'm not going to die!' said Chegory fiercely. 'It's the demon who's going to get wasted. I'll smash the thing myself!'

'So we have us a hero here!' said Log Jaris. 'He's outstared a basilisk. He's wrestled a kraken to a standstill. He's killed out the race of dragons entire. More – he's mastered his mother-in-law sweet to his will. With such trifles behind him he's seeking a challenge of substance.'

'Are you making fun of me?' said Chegory.

'Fun!' said Log Jaris, all wounded innocence. 'Out of a ferocious young man like you? Out of you, young sir, I could make a mate for a porcupine or a good bit of boot leather. But fun? Perish the thought!'

Then Log Jaris laughed again. His laughter was frank, hearty and open. It enraged Chegory Guy, who took a swing at him. But missed, for the bullman was an accomplished street-fighter from way back.

'You're a coward, that's what it is!' said Chegory, as Log Jaris sidestepped a second blow. 'You're afraid!'

Log Jaris then stood still and let Chegory thump him most heartily. The Ebrell Islander's fists did no damage to the bullman's hide, nor did they sway his bulk by so much as a shadow's one-shout side-shift. So Chegory abandoned the onslaught after swinging but thrice.

'Of course I'm afraid,' said Log Jaris, still in apparent good humour. 'Anything born with something as tender as a pair of testicles has every right and reason to live in fear.'

'So you admit it!' said Chegory furiously. 'You're a coward! A shameless craven!'

'Darling,' said Log Jaris. 'You're so beautiful when you're angry.'

This good-humoured insult was the last fish. Chegory launched a full-scale assault on the bullman. He swung ferociously with his fists, but this time Log Jaris did not stand still to be hit. Chegory lashed out a dozen times, but to his bafflement found he had not hit his enemy at all. He stood there panting and said:

'The hell with you. The hell with you all. Stay here and rot if that's what you want. I'll go to war with the demon myself.'

In the mouths of many this would have been an empty boast. But when an Ebrell Islander gets as passionately angry as Chegory was, to say is to do.

'You will?' said Log Jaris. 'Then perhaps you'll win. But what if you lose even in the moment of victory? In extremis, a dying demon might destroy all of Injiltaprajura in self-defence. Have you thought of that?'

'I have to try!' said Chegory. 'You just don't understand, do you? The demon's got Olivia. We can't just walk away and leave her!'

'Oh no,' said Log Jaris. 'I wasn't suggesting that. Now we've got a hero on hand there's certainly a few moves we can try. You are a hero, aren't you?'

Chegory Guy looked very hard at Log Jaris. The young Ebrell Islander was not sure if the bullman was still making fun of him. Still, Chegory decided to give him the benefit of the doubt – particularly as he had proved very hard to hit.

'Let you be the judge of my courage,' said Chegory. 'You're brave enough yourself. After all, you came adventuring with us last night.'

'Yes,' said Log Jaris, 'to stir up the sorcerers.'

'But afterwards,' persisted Chegory, 'you dared the dangers of the palace with the rest of us.'

'So I did, so I did,' said Log Jaris. 'A mistake. Well, anyone can make a mistake. But only a hero would repeat a mistake of such magnitude on purpose. I make no claim to heroism. All I make is a suggestion.'

'What suggestion?' said Chegory.

'The exercise of a little cunning,' said Log Jaris.

Then proceeded to outline his plan.

CHAPTER THIRTY-THREE

The afternoon found Log Jaris and Chegory Guy sweating in the suffocating heat of a forger's den in Injiltaprajura. The forger, a dwarfish leper named Scalpil Hun, was labouring over a sheet of parchment. His work was difficult, and was made all the harder by the distracted wailing which arose from the Temple of the Consecrated Virgin just across the street.

At last Log Jaris said to Chegory:

'Shut them up.'

'What?' said Chegory.

'The people in the temple. Shut them up.'

'I can't do that!'

'Of course you can. Or do you want me to offer them your corpse as sacrifice?'

Chegory Guy was not sure how serious this threat was, but nevertheless thought it best not to find out. He left the forger's den for the sunlight without. The street was utterly empty. He crossed over into the temple where he found wailing worshippers prostrating themselves before their idol. Chegory hammered on a handy gong.

The wailing ceased abruptly.

Till that moment, Chegory had had no idea what he was going to say. But the desperation of the moment filled his mouth with an unaccustomed eloquence.

'I am here,' he said, 'by, um, by the order of the demon Binchinminfin. I bring you the demon's orders. You are to cease your wailing racket and quit this place instanter. Go home!'

Swiftly the temple emptied, and soon Chegory was alone but for a maid who was kneeling at his feet.

'What do you want?' said Chegory, though he could guess already.

The virgin's stammerings confirmed his suspicions. She wanted to divert the wrath of the demon Binchinminfin from her people by yielding herself up to this his messenger. Chegory was sorely tempted. But he thought bravely of Olivia and steeled himself against temptation. He dismissed the maid to her home. Have you ever heard of anything so ludicrous? The opportunity of a lifetime! A spotless virgin free and willing. Yet this stupid Ebby threw away his chance without even thinking twice about it. Such is the intellectual bankruptcy of the lower orders of humankind!

A chaste and continent Chegory returned to the hot and sweating den where Scapil Hun was labouring still under the watchful gaze of Log Jaris. The end result of much sweating and scratching on the part of the dwarfish forger was an ornate parchment of most impressive appearance.

'What do you think?' said Hun.

'Well,' said Chegory, scanning the parchment, 'I, um, I can't read that stuff. I only read Ashmarlan. But, okay, it looks good. I mean, it looks like the others. At least to me.'

'You're not losing your nerve, are you?' said Log Jaris, catching the note of hesitation in Chegory's voice.

'No,' said Chegory.

But a little later, as he was making his way to the palace, he several times hesitated. In the end, it was thoughts of his virginal Olivia which drove him on. He could not leave her there! Not with that – that thing!

When Chegory reached the steps of the pink palace he found a couple of beggars camping there. They had lit a fire and were frying up fish, capsicum and rice in a wok.

'What news from within?' said Chegory.

But the beggars ignored him. So, without even wasting so much as curse on their unco-operative heads, he went on into the interior. Which was silent. Deserted. But for Slanic Moldova, whom Chegory found still painting his mural.

'Slan,' said Chegory. 'How's it going?'

'Not bad,' said Moldova. 'Not bad at all. Do you want some pork?'

'No thank you, Slan,' said Chegory, in the voice he reserved for humouring lunatics. 'But it's very kind of you to offer.'

'There is some, you know,' said Moldova, and pointed at some dirty dishes which Chegory had not noticed.

'Food!' said Chegory with surprise, seeing that much of a meal remained on the plates. 'Where did that come from?'

'The kitchen, of course. I cooked it myself. Do you want some?'

'Ah, um, no thanks, Slan. I've got to be going.'

'Fare thee well, then,' said Moldova. Then: 'Oh, I say – if you're going down there, do be careful. They tell me there's a demon somewhere down there.'

'Thanks, Slan,' said Chegory.

Then on he went.

Feeling very much alone.

As Chegory drew near the Star Chamber he paused. He could feel his heart quop fast and hard within his breast. Blood hissed in his ears. He felt dizzy. What was that he could smell? Rotting food. What a stink! Disregarding the smell, he crept forward till he could see into the Star Chamber. Within, the carpet of chowder and kedgeree had decayed badly in the heat. It was aswarm with flies and the air was possessed by the busy underhum of the death-delighting insects.

And there – yes, there was the demon-possessed Aquitaine Varachavardan. The albino's lean body sprawled in rotting food. Bowls of food fresh and unrotted lay all around it. The thing which had possessed that flesh was methodically gorging itself. The demon had gathered that food is energy, and knew full well that energy is power. So to maximise its power it was trying to metabolise as much food as possible, and to that end was cramming its maw with one morsel after another. From this it will be clear that the demon, even though it had ransacked the brain of the conjuror Odolo for data about its new environment, still did not possess a firm understanding of the human organism.

Chegory wavered.

He was tempted to run.

Then he saw Olivia among the people cowering at the demon's feet. If she saw him she gave no sign of it. Her face was blank. All personality washed out of it by unendurable terror. Was she permanently damaged? He could not tell. He searched for Ingalawa. Found her. Ingalawa's eyes met his. The Ashdan female mouthed something – but whatever it was Chegory failed to understand.

What about the Empress.

Where was Justina?

There – in a corner, sleeping.

Chegory cleared his throat.

The demon looked at him.

'What do you want?' said Binchinminfin.

It was Varazchavardan's throat through which the demon spoke. But the accents were still those of the conjuror Odolo whom Chegory had left that day on the island of Jod. These were the first accents which Binchinminfin had mastered – and doubtless the demon would continue to speak with Odolo's voice unless it had very good reason to learn another form of speech.

'I've – um, I've got something for you,' said Chegory, advancing with the forged parchment tentatively extended.

'What is it?' said the demon.

'A . . . a medical certificate.'

'Explain,' said Binchinminfin.

'Well, you've, uh, I mean – that's Varazchavardan's body you've got there, okay? And the sorcerer, well, he gets sick like everyone else. This is from his doctor. It's a note. It says he needs this medicine.' Chegory looked at all the food on which the demon had been feeding. He made a few deductions then said: 'Uh, if you don't mind me saying so, maybe you feel a bit sick already. This, this medicine, it's, well, great stuff.'

384

'I do feel a bit . . . what's the word? Poorly! That's it! Yes, I feel poorly.'

'Well, you see, that's because you haven't been having this medicine,' said Chegory.

While he spoke, he looked around. If he got a little closer then surely he could knife the demon. He had come armed for the purpose. But – oh! There was a guard in a corner. A guard with a crossbow trained on Chegory's heart. The demon had already taken care of basic security. Such is the depravity of the human race that even a demon, a foul Thing from Beyond, will find servants more than willing to pledge their loyalty to its service.

'Tell me about this medicine,' said Binchinminfin.

'It's, uh, some stuff called alcohol,' said Chegory. 'It comes in various forms. There's, uh, mead. And vodka, of course. Brandy. Rum – that's pretty good stuff. But they're all versions of the same thing, you know, it's just that some are stronger than others. They're all – well, this medicine is so good you can use it to treat just about anything. Flat feet, indigestion, you name it. I'm not kidding.'

'We'll see,' said the demon ominously.

Then closed its eyes.

Its face went slack.

Chegory realised the demon must be searching Varazchavardan's mind for data. Just as it had earlier searched Odolo's. His heart hammered all the faster. Should he run? One look at the guard told him the answer: no! Instant death would be the result.

Binchinminfin opened Varazchavardan's pink eyes. With those eyes the demon eyed Chegory with suspicion. Then spoke.

'It comes to me that this organism can overdose on this medicine.'

'Um, yes,' said Chegory. 'Well, side effects, there's those, you can't get round that, when you've got medicine you've got side effects. I mean, take opium for instance, it's good stuff, but, uh, you can get hideously addicted if you have it too often. Now this alcohol stuff, well, you can run into problems with that. So it's best you have a foodtaster. Okay? Someone to check it out. That's me. I'll match you drink for drink. That way you can watch me. If it's not doing me any harm then you'll know it's not doing you any harm either. Okay?'

'That's logical,' said the demon. 'Where can I get this medicine?'

'You call in a waiter,' said Chegory. 'Or have they all run away?'

The demon looked at the guard who had the crossbow.

'We still have the waiters, sir,' said the guard.

'Good,' said Binchinminfin. 'Then get me some.'

'Get him some waiters,' said the guard, raising his voice.

'Will do,' came the acknowledgement from above.

Grief! There were more armed guards on the mezzanine! Ten of them at least. The simple, elegant plan which Log Jaris had formulated – get the demon drunk then kill it – had become much more complicated. Somehow the guards would have to be won over. Or got rid of. Maybe the demon could be conned into turning them into frogs. Or something. Maybe the guards could be persuaded to get drunk as well. But could Chegory outdrink the better part of a dozen soldiers? Judging by some of the ugly rumours he'd heard about Injiltaprajura's garrison, it might be decidedly unwise to try.

Shortly half a dozen waiters were marched into the Star Chamber. To Chegory's disappointment they were still as poised and as supercilious as ever. A little waiterly terror would have gone down well with the Ebrell Islander just then.

'Alcohol,' said Binchinminfin. 'We want alcohol.'

'Yes sir,' said one of the waiters, a smooth young fellow with a wart on his nose. 'And may I ask what kind, sir?'

'Alcohol alcohol!' said Binchinminfin impatiently. 'Bring it! Alcohol! For me and my friend.'

'Your friend, sir?'

'This!' said Binchinminfin, pointing at Chegory. 'My friend. Understand?'

'Certainly, sir,' said the waiter.

A thousand shades of meaning were in those words. None of them was complimentary.

Then Chegory said, in his most casual voice:

'Have you by chance any firewater?'

'Firewater, sir?' said the waiter in his most supercilious voice.

The demon Binchinminfin heard his tone and reproved him sharply:

'You will attend to the wants of my young friend.'

'Indeed,' said the waiter. 'But I am not familiar with this – this firewater.'

'Firewater from the Ebrells,' said Chegory patiently, resisting the urge to knife the waiter on the spot. 'Ebrell Island firewater, in other words.' He gathered his thoughts and then, with a fluency which drew upon sublimated fear for its energy, he said: 'It is a potion most soothing to the tongue, most excellent for the digestion.'

'If you say so, sir,' said the waiter, in tones of careful neutrality. 'We will see what the imperial cellar can yield. Failing that, we will turn to the . . . to the resources of the city.'

Oh, it was so delicately said! So nicely put! Done with such an exemplary command of the outward forms of protocol! With such masterly politesse! But it clearly meant: we're not used to putting up with the depraved tastes of you stinking Ebbies but we can cope if we have to.

While Chegory and his demonic companion waited for the firewater to be produced, Chegory had to field a few queries about other forms of alcohol.

'What is beer?' said Binchinminfin. 'I have heard mention of beer. Another form of alcohol, is it not?'

'A brew favoured by slaves and stevedores in foreign parts,' said Chegory.

'Wine, then?' said Binchinminfin. 'What is wine?'

'Rotten grapejuice,' said Chegory. 'Let's not waste our time with wine. Firewater, that's the stuff.'

In due course the wart-defaced waiter returned to the

Star Chamber bearing a tray. On it were two jugs and two very small porcelain cups.

'Firewater, sir,' said the waiter, balancing the tray on one hand as he used the other to pour a little fluid into one of the cups. The malevolent liquid flowed from the jug in a rippling helix. A snake-voiced protest arose from the porcelain. The liquid burst into flames of dancing green. 'Vinegar, sir,' said the waiter, taking up the second jug.

It is alleged that there are occasions on which firewater has been drunk in its original, undiluted form. However, documentary evidence for such experiments is slight. If one were to seek more such evidence, doubtless the best place to look would be in a collection of obituaries.

The waiter poured, topping up the cup with a stream of vinegar which doused the green flames of the firewater, leaving a bubbling brown liquid in the cup. By preparing the drink in this manner the waiter showed that his familiarity with this potion was far greater than he had earlier pretended.

He offered the cup to Binchinminfin, who took it and held it cautiously. Something about the waiter's manner had alerted the brute to the dangers of this drink, and none passed his lips while the waiter prepared a similar dose for the demon's guest.

'Get me something larger,' said Chegory, spurning the eggshell of a cup. 'I'm thirsty.'

The waiter yielded to temptation and – though this was most unprofessional – turned his eyes upward to the heavens. Then departed, returning shortly with a skull which had once belonged to Lonstantine Thrug, who had taken it from one of the many men he had killed in the course of his military career. Chegory splashed firewater into this silver-lined ornament, slopped in some vinegar then drank. Binchinminfin was encouraged by this display of enthusiasm. The demon tossed his own cup aside, grabbed the chamber pot which had previously served him as a crown, then held it out to be filled.

The waiter again turned his eyes toward heaven, then

sighed, then poured both vinegar and firewater into the chamber pot.

The demon sipped.

'It's good,' he said, in pleased surprise.

'Oh,' said Chegory vaguely, 'Ebrell Islanders like it right enough. But that's not universally thought of as a recommendation.'

'No, no,' said Binchinminfin generously. 'You do yourself a wrong. This is great!'

The waiterage proved appallingly slow, so refills of firewater were hard to come by. Nevertheless, though it was late in the day when the two started drinking, by dusk the demon had consumed sufficient medicine to be feeling much, much better.

'You're right,' said Binchinminfin. 'This was just what I needed. But . . . why are my hands stumbling and yours not?'

'I've drunk more than you have,' said Chegory, telling this barefaced lie with all the aplomb he could muster. 'The more you drink, the better you feel.'

'Oh,' said the demon, squinting at the candles which had just been lit to illuminate the fast-darkening Star Chamber. 'And if – if I drink some more will it help my eyes?'

'Your eyes?' said Chegory.

'I see two of everything. Sometimes three.'

'Well,' said Chegory, 'I'm no oculist, but, as I've said, Injiltaprajura uses alcohol to treat just about anything.'

'You mean,' said the demon, 'we should drink more?'

'But of course, of course!' said Chegory. 'If you've got enough firewater you can keep drinking all night.'

Which is true enough. It is a matter of recorded fact that Ebrell Islanders have been known to drink firewater steadily from one sunrise to the next. What young Chegory neglected to say was that one stands a good chance of dropping dead during (or shortly after) such a drinking bout.

Thus encouraged, Binchinminfin clapped his hands.

'Waiter!' cried the demon. 'More firewater! Lots of it! Quickly, quickly!'

The waiter withdrew, returning in due course with a fresh crock of firewater and an ample supply of vinegar. Thus the demon and the Ebrell Islander drank on into the night.

What a debauched scene this is! The Ebrell Islander and the demon shamelessly polluting their bodies with the most lethal potation known to the human race! At Chegory's feet is the delectable Olivia Qasaba, for she has crept close to him for comfort, hoping he has some plan for rescue. Well, he had a plan – to drink the demon into oblivion then knife it. But the presence of soldiers has thwarted that plan. Nevertheless, young Chegory drinks on regardless. The most shameful part of all is that he is starting to enjoy it.

Yes!

This Ebrell Islander, who is by now most definitely drunk, drinks with a will. He is loving it! Now we see how shallow were those moral protestations with which he previously preached against demon rum. Blood will out! Blood has outed! Here is an Ebrell Islander true, a drink-crazed thing wildly giving itself to excess and intoxication.

Yes, young Chegory is drinking with a wild abandon, and fondling the succulent Olivia as he does so. Worse, he is letting her sip from the skull which serves him as a cup. Thanks to an influx of firewater, the blank fear has slipped away from Olivia's sweet and girlish face to be replaced by something . . . well, libidinous would not be too strong a word for it. While Chegory fondles her flesh she fondles him back in return. He is her hero who is – she is sure of it – here to rescue her.

To rescue her first from the demon Binchinminfin and then, doubtless, from her virginity.

Artemis Ingalawa is scandalised, yet dare not intervene. Instead, she watches from the shadows, hoping against hope that Chegory has a plan. As it happens, he doesn't. But he's not worried. He's sure he'll solve all in time. He's possessed by a buoyant over-confidence for which firewater must bear the blame.

But sooner or later this drinking spree must end. Sooner or later consequences must be faced. Let us hope it will be sooner rather than later – or who knows what horrors might be enacted tonight in this palace of corruption and crime?

CHAPTER THIRTY-FOUR

The orgy of drinking would have continued all night if Binchinminfin's enjoyment had not been halted by the natural limits of the flesh. The demon ceased to feel better and began to feel worse. So drank all the more in the hope of encouraging a more favourable trend. Then vomited, upchucking half-digested food to the rotting carpet of chowder and kedgeree.

The guards – at this stage there were several of them near at hand – watched with the technical detachment of vastly experienced experts as Binchinminfin grovelled on his hands and knees in the grotesque carpet of sludge. Vomiting repeatedly.

'It's a side effect, isn't it?' he said at last.

'Yes,' admitted Chegory. 'One of the worse.'

For a while the demon said nothing. It was too sick to say anything. Then it said:

'Why?'

'Why what?' said Chegory.

'The side effects,' said Binchinminfin. 'Why me and not you? Why haven't you thrown up?'

'Because he's an Ebby,' said one of the guards, with contempt. 'A stinking Ebby. We know his game! He's been feeding you firewater to try to get you incapably drunk.'

'You're just jealous,' said Chegory, with drunken racial pride. 'You know you can't match us Ebrell Islanders. We can outdrink outfight and—'

Well, I'm sure we all know what boast logically belongs to this sequence. Furthermore, you can be sure Chegory made it. Which increased the disapproval of the onlooking Ingalawa. She was committing every moment of this to memory. Sooner or later, Chegory would answer for his indiscretions!

'Why would you want to get me drunk?' said Binchinminfin, failing to realise that he was drunk already. 'What good would it have done you?'

'I would have cut your throat,' said Chegory, shaking himself free of Olivia's clutches as he lurched to his feet. 'I would have raped your spleen with a gutting knife. I would have torn out your liver. I would have ripped out your lungs. Like this!'

So saying, Chegory staggered toward the demon. Then toppled and fell. Then got to his feet again. Binchinminfin obviously had to do something. But what? The logical, sensible thing was to incinerate young Chegory Guy. Or turn him into a toad. But, since the demon was drunk, he did something rash instead, and deserted the body of Varazchavardan for that of the Ebrell Islander, that splendid redskinned body which could outfight, outdrink and out-the-other everything else in sight.

Varazchavardan's deserted corpus slumped insensibly into the carpet of food.

'He's killed him!' said one of the guards, meaning that Chegory had slain Binchinminfin.

Instantly several soldiers rushed forward, intending to slaughter Chegory Guy on the spot. Olivia screamed. But the guards never reached their target. Instead, they were spun round and smashed into the walls. They collapsed insensibly.

A guard on the mezzanine levelled a crossbow at Chegory and pulled the trigger. The crossbow bolt sped toward Chegory's heart. It never got there. It burst into flames in mid-air and disintegrated an instant later.

'This is me!' roared Odolo's accents, issuing most strangely from the throat of young Chegory Guy. 'Me, me, Binchinminfin!'

His guards began to get the message.

Chegory, to his startlement, felt his throat worked, heard the words which issued forth, but found he had no control over his body whatsoever. It was being worked without reference to his own thoughts. So this was what it meant to be demonically possessed! It was, more than anything, like one of those terrible dreams in which your limbs refuse to obey you.

His first question was:

Olivia! Where is Olivia?

But he could not tell, for the demon had focused his eyes on a crock of firewater, which it was emptying into the drinking skull Chegory had been using.

Olivia! Olivia! Olivia!

Thus Chegory.

The much more interesting question, which never occurred to him at the time, was why Binchinminfin's latest act of possession had not resulted in unconsciousness for both demon and new host. When Binchinminfin had leapt from the conjuror Odolo to the wonderworker Varazchavardan, the newly possessed flesh had been insensible for some time, whereas the demon had taken over Chegory without any such trouble.

The answer to this conundrum, of course, lies in the firewater both parties had been so liberally consuming. Alcohol softens the psychic shock usually suffered by an entity intelligent as it leaps from one body to another.

Long thereafter did Binchinminfin sit drinking. But all flesh has limits, and even Chegory Guy's body could at last take no more. Liquor overpowered it, and the intelligence of demon and Ebrell Islander alike spiralled down into unconsciousness. The body lay there with its twin consciousness inert.

The guards kept vigil over their demonic master as the night crept on. Elsewhere, on the island of Jod, Chegory's erstwhile companions-in-adventure sat round a watchfire, roasting vampire rats then eating the same. Meanwhile, the steady flux of dikle and shlug poured forth from the wealth fountains as if it would continue to outpour for all eternity.

'He's not coming back,' said Pokrov at last, stating the obvious.

'No,' said Uckermark. 'He's not.'

'So – so what do we tell the Hermit Crab?' said Pokrov.

'That's for Zozimus to worry about, not us,' said Uckermark. 'He's the one who had the job to do.'

The job in question was, as you will remember, to ask the demon Binchinminfin if it would be so kind as to provide the Hermit Crab with a human form. But Zozimus had already worked out what he would say to the Crab.

'In the morning,' said Zozimus, 'I'll tell the Crab the demon told him to go and get jumped on. Then maybe we'll see some action!'

CHAPTER THIRTY-FIVE

Dawn came to Injiltaprajura, but the sun bells failed to ring to mark the start of istarlat. Dawn brought light to supplement the tapers burning in the Star Chamber of the pink palace atop Pokra Ridge. A ghastly sight that light revealed.

Already fat flies were bumbling over the carpet of rotten chowder and kedgeree which covered much of the floor. Part of that carpet had disintegrated into a white writhing of maggots. In among this vomit-splattered slather of rotting food there lay a good half-dozen empty crocks (which had once held firewater) and the chamberpot which the demon Binchinminfin had chosen first as crown and later as drinking goblet.

Round the room various humans stood, sat or lay in postures of sleep, exhaustion or despair. There was Artemis Ingalawa comforting an exhausted and tearful Olivia. There was the Empress Justina, her white ape Vazzy in her arms. Besides these, there were half a dozen anonymous bedraggled females – serving wenches and such – and some waiters. And the lean and leucodermic Aquitaine Varaz-chavardan, surveying all he saw with manifest contempt. The pink-eyed Master of Law watched a young soldier who had the wishstone in his care. The man appeared to be wishing on it. The wonderworker could guess what the warrior desired.

All the soldiers in the Star Chamber were very tired, and naturally distressed by the mephitic malodours. They had joined the army of the Izdimir Empire to get regular pay and the chance to travel and dress up in gaudy uniforms. Not to preside over a sewer! Most had slept little during the night, for the garrison was dreadfully shorthanded thanks to the mass desertions which had followed Binchin-minfin's seizure of power. Those few who had given the demon their loyalty were hard-pressed to guard both treasury and wine cellar, to keep the kitchen staff from joining the exodus from the palace, and to mount guard over their new lord and master.

Their unconscious lord and master.

As we know, Ebrell Islanders can drink far more than ordinary mortals. But, after Binchinminfin had possessed Chegory Guy, the demon had nevertheless eventually found the natural limits of his new host's flesh. For the moment, the demon was at the mercy of any soldier in a mood for assassination. Some of the armed guards, thinking they had made a mistake in their choice of overlord, were actively considering it.

'Oh, what a bright and beautiful morning!' said Justina Thrug, stretching prodigiously. She blew out a candle. 'Huff! Out with its light! Good morning, Vazzy. How are you today? What's the matter? Cat got your tongue? Oh, you're no fun! All right then, who's in charge here?'

'Don't worry about that,' rumbled one of the soldiers. 'You're not going anywhere.'

'Oh, I think we're all going somewhere,' said the Empress. 'Sanitary expeditions are the order of the day. If not, then we will do what we must. I don't mind. But you have to put up with the results.'

The soldiers were already putting up with more than they cared for, so one of those with more initiative than the rest arranged for small parties to be escorted under armed guard to other parts of the palace.

In due course Justina herself was marched away with Olivia Qasaba and Artemis Ingalawa. Once free of the Star Chamber, she persuaded her wardens to allow a detour to the rooftop swimming pool. This needed little doing. The soldiers were in no hurry to get back to the Star Chamber, and far preferred watching three females disport themselves in the water. The next stop was Justina's private quarters. There the Empress sorted out fresh clothes for herself and the two Ashdan females. On their return to the Star Chamber they found Chegory Guy sitting up. He looked at them with eyes shot through with a bloody red more violent than that of his skin.

'Chegory,' said Olivia timidly.

'That's not Chegory,' said Ingalawa. 'That's the demon. Binchinminfin. The usurper.'

'You're in there!' insisted Olivia. 'Aren't you, Chegory? You can hear me, my love. Can't you?'

Chegory Guy was indeed within that red skin. He heard Olivia, but could not move so much as a muscle. He could not speak. In frustrated rage he felt his throat move as the demon Binchinminfin groaned. The accents of the conjuror Odolo came from his throat as Binchinminfin croaked:

'I'm dying . . .'

'My lord Binchinminfin,' said one of his soldiers. 'It is not death which ails you. It is but a hangover.'

'Oh,' said the Odolo-voiced demon. Weakly. 'Oh. A hangover. Side effects. Yes, I remember.' Then Chegory's eyes closed and his face went slack. The demon was rummaging through Chegory's mind. Then the face animated itself again and Binchinminfin once more stared out of those eyes. 'It comes to me,' said the demon, 'that there is no cure for this side effect but time. It must be lived through. Is that not so?'

'Such is the world's wisdom, my lord,' said the same soldier who had first addressed him.

The man was doing his best to be politely deferential, and was making an excellent job of it. But the strain he was under was obvious.

Binchinminfin looked around.

'Varazchavardan,' he said.

'It's no good coming to me,' said Aquitaine Varazchavardan, who was suffering terribly from last night's drinking bout and was in no hurry to be again possessed. 'Don't you remember? You abused me bitterly before you let me go. I'm in agony even now. Sledgehammers in my head.' Then the Master of Law pointed at Justina. 'If you must take someone – take her.'

There stood Justina, freshly washed and freshly dressed, and smiling with amusement at some private, unvoiced joke. Of all the people in the Star Chamber she looked to be the happiest, healthiest and most comfortable. Binchinminfin wasted no time in reflection. Instead, the demon acted – deserting young Chegory in favour of the flesh of the Empress. This time there was no alcohol to soften the psychic shock of transmigration. So, as the demon possessed her, the Empress Justina fell insensible to the carpeting food, spoiling her new clothes entirely.

'Chegory!' said Olivia.

'I'm free!' said he.

Moments later, they were in each other's arms.

Justina's white ape, Vazzy, picked its way across the muck-slush to its mistress. It stood over her slow-breathing body, hooting dismally.

'Ape and demon are united again,' said Varazchavardan, raising his voice to the volume of public address as he began to harangue the soldiers. 'They suit each other well, do they not? This Binchinminfin has found the ape its best companion yet. Look at this place! This is what it means to be ruled by a demon. Is this what you want?'

No soldier claimed it was. So Varazchavardan went on:

'You have a choice. Endure whatever madness the demon dreams of next. Or act – but do it quick, my friends, oh yes, be sure to do it quick. Overthrow the demon. Be done with its rule. Aldarch the Third will reward you as well as any demon could. The demon-thing has gone to ground in the flesh of the Empress. It takes but a moment. Act now. Secure your future. Destroy her.'

'You can't!' said Chegory, disengaging himself from Olivia.

'Can't?' said Varazchavardan. 'What kind of nonsense is that? Of course we can! Indeed, we must!'

'But that's – that's the Empress.'

'Your whore,' said Varazchavardan. 'I know. But why

worry? You've found yourself a new one already.'

Lightly spoke Varazchavardan, but there was death in his voice. Unless he was stopped, he would have the Empress killed in moments. Chegory was a patriot. With a roar of rage he launched himself at the wonderworker. A guard moved to intercept him. But nobody was watching Artemis Ingalawa. Who was already closing with Varazchavardan.

The sorcerer had no time to conjure up defensive flame. He barely had time to fling up a hand in self defence. Ingalawa grabbed the hand by the wrist. There was the crackle of breaking bones. A scream from Varazchavardan. Ingalawa chopped down. She smashed his clavicle with the edge of her hand.

Already guards were storming toward her. She snatched up a stray scimitar and stood at bay. The guards hesitated, for any Ashdan with a weapon is dangerous – and this was a strong, determined, athletic woman.

Then Chegory hit the man who was holding him. Chegory hit hard, hit low, and left his warden disabled by pain. Then the Ebrell Islander scooped up the insensible body of the Empress Justina and was off. Olivia raced after him. Ingalawa slashed at the nearest guard, opening his arm to the bone. Then followed. As did the albinotic ape Vazzy, screaming with rage and excitement as it loped through the corridors of the pink palace.

They were doomed, of course.

There was no way they could outrun the guards when Chegory was burdened by the weight of the Empress.

But he did his best.

He was young, fit and muscular, his body hardened by sledgehammering rocks on Jod for day after day under the blazing sun. The soldiers were soft, overfed and out of condition thanks to long years of eventless garrison routine. Chegory was still outpacing them when he burst into the foyer of the pink palace.

Shouting greeted his ears.

A mob of beggars, petitioners, priests and sundry

would-be looters was crowding the palace portico and seeking admission. A handful of guards were keeping them back. Chegory, Ingalawa, Olivia and Vazzy the Ape slammed into the guards from behind, broke through that thin line of military menace, and forged their way into the crowd.

Those few soldiers who tried to follow them were pulled down by the mob. Then were kicked and bruised most horribly before their fellows rescued them and pulled them back to the safety of the pink palace. After a prolonged struggle, the guards at last beat back the mob, closed the palace doors and secured this fortress against immediate entry. But by that time, of course, Chegory and his companions were far away.

CHAPTER THIRTY-SIX

When Chegory and his companions got to the waterfront they found the entire surface of the Laitemata covered with solidified dikle.

For days the wealth fountains of Jod had been pouring out both bile-green dikle and grey shlug. These two substances, when mixed, form an oily, irisated fluid with a specific gravity nearly identical to that of seawater. But, given calm conditions, the shlug will precipitate out, sinking to layer the seabottom rocks with a grey ooze which kills all ground-dwelling life, while the dikle will float to the top and harden into a slightly plastic crust. During the night the two substances in question had so separated. With the result that the Laitemata was a flat green plain. The sun beat down, but the sun, though hot, was not hot enough to melt the dikle.

'It looks solid,' said Olivia. 'Maybe we could walk on it.'

'I wouldn't if I were you,' said Ingalawa. 'It's thixotropic. That means—'

'Oh, I know what it means,' said Olivia.

Then they started out over the harbour bridge.

Vazzy lingered, hooting mournfully.

'Don't be frightened!' said Olivia. But the albinotic ape refused to dare the dangers of the bridge. 'Oh, don't be silly!' said Olivia, and went back, meaning to take it by the hand.

But Vazzy loped away to the buildings.

'Come on!' said Artemis Ingalawa, in her this-is-serious-business-and-no-time-to-be-playing-with-apes voice.

So Olivia ran after the others and soon caught them up. Ahead lay the island of Jod where the bright white marble of the Analytical Institute gleamed in the sun. A little smoke rose from the Institute's kitchen, reminding Ingalawa and Olivia that they had not had breakfast. Chegory, however, thought not about food. He was working far too hard for that. He had the unconscious corpus of the Empress Justina slung across his shoulders – and she was a fair weight. So he said nothing until, when he was half way across the bridge, he was met by a bright-singing bubble of light.

'Hello, Chegory!' sang Shabble.

'Hi,' said Chegory, without any great outburst of enthusiasm.

'Oh, it is good to see you, Chegory dearest,' said Shabble happily. 'You were gone so long! I thought you were gone for good!'

'I notice you didn't come looking for me,' said Chegory, as he strode along purposefully, proud of his ability to carry his burden at a vigorous pace.

'I couldn't! There's the demon, isn't there? In the palace!'

'No,' said Chegory. 'The demon's right here. In the Empress Justina.'

On receiving this alarming intelligence, Shabble squeaked with fright and soared high, high into the air. On strode Chegory. Jod's wealth fountains had ceased outpouring dikle and shlug sometime during the night, so he was able to carry the Empress to the island without slushing through a disgusting chemical outpour. By the time he and his companions had reached the main entrance of the Analytical Institute, Shabble had descended from the heavens. The imitator of suns feared the demon Binchinminfin – yet was consumed by curiosity. What had happened? Furthermore, what would happen now?

Shabble was not alone in curiosity.

Sentries posted by the nervous denizens of Jod had spotted Chegory, Ingalawa and Olivia as soon as they set foot on the harbour bridge. By the time they had reached the Analytical Institute with the Empress, virtually everyone on the island had gathered to find out what was happening.

The press of people was so great that Chegory could not get the Empress inside, and had no option but to put her down. He stood, flexed his back, flexed his arms, then grinned. He could not help his own pride in his strength. His physical supremacy. Even though he knew that such an asset was of little account in the present crisis.

What a crowd! Odolo was there. So was Ivan Pokrov. The Malud marauders, of course. Guest Gulkan and all those of his faction, including the two wizards Hostaja Sken-Pitilkin and Pelagius Zozimus. The kitchen staff. Sundry mechanics and algorithmists. Then there were others, including some quite unknown to Chegory who were refugees from the mainland. All had their questions, and at first the impatient interrogative uproar made for quite intolerable confusion.

'Where,' shouted Guest Gulkan, in a fury, 'is the wish-stone? Don't say you left it behind!'

'The hell with the wishstone!' said Chegory.

'So you did leave it behind!' said Guest Gulkan.

Then swore. The pretender to the throne of Tameran was so angry that he might have done Chegory a violence if the bullman Log Jaris had not intervened.

'That's enough!' said Log Jaris. 'Enough from the pair of you!' Then he called all present to order. 'Speak, Chegory,' said Log Jaris. 'Tell us what's been going on.'

'What hasn't!' said Chegory.

Then gathered his breath, gathered his thoughts, and began. While his speech tended toward incoherence under emotional pressure, when he controlled himself and took his time he was capable of something approaching verbal fluency. Indeed, young Chegory gave the assembly a surprisingly perspicuous and accurate account of recent events in the pink palace and assured them that, in all probability, the demon Binchinminfin was instantly in possession of the body of the Empress Justina.

'Only one thing for it, then,' said Pelagius Zozimus, briskly rubbing his hands. 'Exorcism.'

'Exorcism?' said Chegory.

'We drive the demon from Justina's body,' said Zozimus.

'Is that safe?' said a kitchen hand.

'Safe?' said Zozimus. 'There's no safe course here! There's danger whatever we do. Shall we kill the Empress? We could. The demon Binchinminfin would die with her flesh. Or at least be expelled to the World Beyond. But where does that leave us? With Varazchavardan in the pink palace – ready to enforce the will of Aldarch the Third. Which of us could then hope to leave here alive? No, we need the Empress. With her as figurehead we can war against Varazchavardan with every hope of success. Nine-tenths of Injiltaprajura will hold her in loyalty, surely. No. Look not for safety. Instead – make yourself useful. Help me get the woman inside.'

Then Justina was taken to Ivan Pokrov's private quarters, most of the onlookers were banished, and Pelagius Zozimus began to prepare for the exorcism. Chegory Guy insisted on being present lest Zozimus murder his Empress. Ingalawa insisted likewise. She had brought along her scimitar and was prepared to use it if this foreign wizard proved to be treacherous. Uckermark, Log Jaris and the three Malud marauders also wanted to watch, since all had a financial interest in Justina's survival.

Pelagius Zozimus had only the most honourable of intentions. Nevertheless, he knew parts of the exorcism might be misunderstood by these irritating onlookers. Lest misunderstanding lead to the loss of his head, Zozimus reinforced his position by having Hostaja Sken-Pitilkin, Guest Gulkan and Thayer Levant come into the exorcism chamber, where the Empress had been laid down upon Pokrov's bed.

Olivia slipped into the room with all the others because she did not wish to be parted from Chegory. The pair stood hand-in-hand in the hot, sweating crush of the heavy-breathing crowd of onlookers. One last person was there. Odolo. He was the one whom Binchinminfin had possessed in the first place. He wanted to see this thing out to the end.

Oh, and there was Shabble, of course – floating above everyone else and humming very, very gently.

All the onlookers were most curious to see how the exorcism would be conducted. Most thought they were about to see an expert at work. Well . . . they were and yet they weren't.

Most wizards know nothing of exorcism. But Pelagius Zozimus was a master wizard of the order of Xluzu, which specialises in the animation of corpses. This order has necessarily developed several sidelines which exploit bodies of related knowledge. Since there are many ugly Things from Beyond which can convert animated dead meat for their own purposes, the wizards of Xluzu have of necessity become expert at exorcism.

Of course, there is a vast difference between cleansing a corpse of a demon and expelling the same entity from living flesh. The possession of live bodies by Outsiders is rare in the extreme, so it is scarcely surprising that Pelagius Zozimus had absolutely no personal experience of dealing with this phenomenon.

So—

Would his methods work? Furthermore, if they did work, would the Empress Justina still be sane at the end of the proceedings? Exorcism is, to put it mildly, a most unpretty enterprise.

There was only one way to find out.

Try it and see!

Zozimus's first move was to take Justina's pulse. It was slow. Very slow. Her body was at rest, her mind likewise. He could not hear her breathing for all the fidgeting, whispering, coughing and shuffling in the room, but he could see that the rise and fall of the imperial abdomen was slow and regular.

'She can take it,' muttered Hostaja Sken-Pitilkin, speaking in the High Speech of wizards.

'Her flesh can,' said Zozimus to his cousin. 'But can her mind?'

'That,' said Sken-Pitilkin, 'we can only test by trial.'

Then talk between the two ended – for Zozimus was concentrating his mind for the exorcism proper. After due mental preparation, he put his hands to the imperial forehead, finding it moist with sweat and slightly feverish. Then he discharged the first of the Exorcising Energies.

Here it would be pleasing to be able to increase the narrative appeal of this history by saying, for example, that the Empress kicked and convulsed upon the bed. Or that she turned first blue then red, that her hair stood on end, that lightning discharged from her fingertips, that a bloody flux streamed from her nostrils, that her clothes were consumed by an unearthly fire of cold-burning silver, that her ribcage burst open to reveal her pulsing heart, that the thunder of her heart rose till it deafened all those who stood horrorstruck by the bed, and that a Thing the colour of blood and bile then ascended from, say, the imperial pancreas.

However, since this is a sober and responsible history, it must concern itself with the truth, however dull the truth proves to be. Truth to tell, when Zozimus unleashed the Exorcising Energies, there was not one single visible manifestation of the horrorshock which nightmared through the imperial psyche.

There should have been.

There should have been – at the very least – a piercing scream and a few convulsions.

But there was not.

Zozimus began to sweat.

Hostaja Sken-Pitilkin mopped his brow solicitously.

Zozimus slid two fingers alongside the imperial windpipe to take the imperial pulse. The carotid pulse was strong, swift and irregular. It told him he had certainly shaken up whatever lurked within.

'Again,' muttered Sken-Pitilkin. 'You can't stop now.'

'I know, I know,' said Zozimus.

The master wizard of the order of Xluzu was acutely conscious of the pressure of the presence of so many people. Watching him. Watching and waiting. He hated working like this. Exorcism should be done alone, out of sight and out of earshot of any other person. But the knife-edge politics of the island of Jod made such solitude impossible. Most of those in the room feared Zozimus to be a potential murderer. If he tried to banish them from the chamber then suspicion would turn to certainty.

Zozimus shuddered.

Then settled himself.

Concentrated.

Gathered his strength.

Then again placed his hands on Justina's forehead and again released the Exorcising Energies.

The eyes of the Empress Justina flickered. Opened. A red light flared from those eyes. Such was its intensity that Zozimus was near-blinded. He cried out in anguish and clutched his hands to his eyes. Shabble squeaked in terror and fled through the nearest window, bursting the mosquito gauze in the process. There was a shouting and jostling in the room till Log Jaris called for order – and got it.

Justina was sitting up on the bed.

'My!' she said, rubbing the side of her head ruefully. 'You certainly know how to give a girl a hard time!'

'She's all right!' said Chegory.

Then clapped his hands to his mouth in horror. For he had spoken in Odolo's accents!

'He's demon-possessed,' said Odolo flatly. 'That's my voice he's using.'

'Don't let him get away!' said Zozimus.

Then realised that he too had spoken in a voice not his own.

'What's going on here?' said Log Jaris.

The sound of Odolo's voice issuing from the mouth of the bullman was so comical that Chegory could not help himself. He broke down in laughter.

'The demon is among us,' said Sken-Pitilkin in the same voice.

'Yes,' said Zozimus. 'It hides by hiding its accent by changing the accents of us all. It must be weak, weak to the point of death from the exorcism. Otherwise it wouldn't need to hide.'

'But we're all conscious!' protested Odolo. 'When the demon leapt from myself to Varazchavardan it caused unconsciousness! The wonderworker dropped as if dead! Now the demon's left Justina but nobody's fallen over. Yet you say the demon's still here.'

'I didn't fall over when the demon came to me last night,' said Chegory.

'But you were drunk,' said Zozimus. 'In theory, demonic possession is much easier when the target is drunk. You were drunk, weren't you?'

'Yes,' admitted Chegory.

'Well then,' said Zozimus briskly. 'That explains it. Someone here must be drunk. The only question is – who?'

But nobody would admit to being drunk.

'Look,' said Chegory, 'when the demon got drunk, it was drunk just like you or me being drunk. I mean, it's, it goes along with the body, okay? If the body's drunk, the demon's drunk. So if, like, someone here was drunk, it would show, wouldn't it? You can't hide it, can you? I mean, within limits, maybe, but we'd tell, wouldn't we?'

'Young Chegory has a point,' said Zozimus, deeply disturbed that he had not thought of this. His excuse – a reasonable one – was that the effort of exorcism had left him too exhausted to think straight. He turned to Sken-Pitilkin. 'Cousin mine,' he said, 'there's something simple I'm missing. What is it?'

'I'm missing breakfast,' said Justina loudly. 'Possession or no possession, how about getting some food in our bellies?'

Sken-Pitilkin ignored her. To his cousin Zozimus he said:

'Group possession. That's what you're forgetting.'

'Of course!' said Zozimus. 'But – but there's no actual cases on record. It's theoretical purely.'

'It has been till now,' said Sken-Pitilkin, still in the same Odolo-voice. 'But now it's fact.'

'What are you talking about?' said Uckermark, managing

to roughen the conjuror's accents till he sounded some-thing like his old self. 'Are you saying we're – we're all possessed?'

'It explains the voices,' said Zozimus. 'It explains the lack of an unconscious casualty. You see, possession of one person places a great shock on a single psyche, leading to instant oblivion. When the shock's shared among so many, nobody drops down unconscious.'

'I didn't feel any shock,' objected Ingalawa.

'Didn't you?' said Zozimus. 'I did! The light! It was near-blinding! We were all shocked, weren't we? But put it down to the burst of light.'

'But,' protested Chegory, 'why should the demon make all our voices Odolo's? Why not leave us with our own voices?'

'Because,' said Odolo himself, 'this way the demon can contribute to our counsels. Am I not right? At any moment the demon might command one of our bodies, one of our voices. It could give advice – the rest of us thinking that advice to come from our friends.'

'One thing's for certain,' said Zozimus, 'while the demon's doubtless weak from the exorcism, its strength will renew swiftly. We have to act! Now!'

'Dear cousin,' said Hostaja Sken-Pitilkin, 'our options are limited. Theory allows for group possession – but scarcely for group exorcism.'

'Yes,' said Zozimus. 'But Theory is a stranger to the Hermit Crab. There is a Power which may help us yet!'

His words brought a babbling outcry of fear, protest and terror. The Hermit Crab! Most of those who dwelt on Untunchilamon feared it more than anything else im-aginable. It was known to be cruel, ruthless and unpredictable. It had turned people inside out. It had once – or so legend said – brought darkness to Injiltaprajura for ten days at a stretch.

But Zozimus was adamant.

'The Hermit Crab,' said Zozimus, 'hoped for help from the demon Binchinminfin. The Hermit Crab wished for such help in order to become a human. We have the demon. Perhaps the Hermit Crab can extract the demon then imprison it in a cat. Or a dog. Or something. But one thing I do know for certain. When the demon gets back its strength it will take a most terrible revenge upon all those who helped with the exorcism here today. Which means all of you.'

'But – but why?' said Odolo.

'If you'd been inside my head, my lad,' said the Empress Justina severely, 'you'd not ask any question so stupid. I don't know what this exorcism looked like to you. But I can tell you what it felt like. It felt – no, you're a man, you wouldn't understand that. So – ah yes, I know. Imagine yourself being castrated while someone with a red-hot poker—'

The Empress Justina continued in this vein until Odolo, despite the natural olive coloration of his skin, had grown quite pale.

'All right,' said Zozimus, bringing Justina's spirited description to a close. 'I'm sure everyone here realises how serious this is. All of us are doomed if we give the demon chance enough to regather its strength. Let's get ourselves to the Hermit Crab.'

So, with fear of demonic vengeance at last overmastering fear of the Crab, the group left the exorcism chamber to visit the Power which dwelt so close at hand, the Power which was a worker of wonders far greater than anything any mere sorcerer could have attempted.

Counting that morning's dawnsun breakfast, the Hermit Crab had now enjoyed a full four meals prepared by Pelagius Zozimus, leading the master chef to hope that its mood would be tolerably mellow. Even as Zozimus exited from the Analytical Institute he was rehearsing the eloquence with which he would convert the Hermit Crab to his cause. But his chain of thought was disrupted abruptly when he found a hostile force drawn up outside the Institute.

'Varazchavardan!' cried Chegory Guy.

It was indeed Aquitaine Varazchavardan – his right arm in a sling to support the collar bone which Artemis Ingalawa had broken. The wonderworker had changed into fresh robes: those he had been wearing just a few days earlier when he interrupted a luncheon at the Institute. Serpentine dragons blazed upon the ceremonial silk, their colours alive in the sun.

[Here an impossibility, for surely we have seen these specific robes ruined twice already. Once when Varazchavardan was swept into the sea by the first flood from the wealth fountains. A second time when the Master of Law set his own clothes alight when using fire to defend himself against pirates Downstairs. Such an obvious lapse severely undermines the credibility of this text. *Srin Gold, Commentator Extraordinary.*]

[My colleague Srin Gold is forgetting that Varazchavardan was a sorcerer and therefore surely capable of repairing his clothing by magic. *Sot Dawbler, School of Commentary.*]

[Dawbler should know better than that. No sorcerer ever possessed control of his Powers sufficient to enable him to undertake an operation as delicate as tailoring. The Originator of the Text must have been mistaken. *Jan Borgentasko Ronkowski, Fact Checker Superior.*]

[No. The Originator appears to have relied heavily on Shabble's recall, which we have reason to believe to be perfect. Therefore we should not suspect error in an account of a scene so well witnessed. The logical inference is that Varazchavardan, who is elsewhere stated to be very rich, had a number of robes made up to the same pattern and identically adorned. *Oris Baumgage, Fact Checker Minor.*]

[This is very plausible. Nevertheless, it is entirely inappropriate for a fact checker minor such as Baumgage to be making 'logical inferences'. He demonstrates pretensions totally unfitting to his lowly station in life. Worse, he has shamelessly contradicted his superior, the eminent Ronkowski. Five lashes! *Jonquiri O, Disciplinarian Superior.*]

Despite the lightness of his silken robes, Varazchavardan

was sweating heavily, outpouring salted water to join the sungrease which glistened on his albinoid skin, protecting it from the burning rays of the sky's major luminary. Perhaps it was partly fear which made him sweat so much, even though the weight of numbers was on his side.

Yes, Varazchavardan had not come alone. In consort with the Master of Law there were a full two dozen wonderworkers. Chegory recognised some of them as survivors from the drunken party which had earlier raged in the Cabal House. There, for instance, was Nixorjapretzel Rat, once Varazchavardan's apprentice but now a fully fledged sorcerer in his own right.

The two groups confronted each other.

Varazchavardan and his allies were not quite prepared to make the first move. After all, they could see the Empress Justina was on her feet. Was she still possessed by the demon Binchinminfin? If so, then she might have power enough to destroy anyone who sought her death.

In the opposing camp, Pelagius Zozimus and Hostaja Sken-Pitilkin looked at each other. Both knew their powers to be at low ebb. Sken-Pitilkin had been able to accumulate only a little strength since exhausting his resources in trials Downstairs. Zozimus, who had far superior abilities as a wizard, had built up much more strength in the same time – but had expended all of it in the recent exorcism.

The pair of them could not outfight two dozen wonderworkers.

'Bluff,' said Sken-Pitilkin in the High Speech of wizards.

'I'll do my best,' said Zozimus. Then switched to Janjuladoola to say, in Odolo's voice: 'Varazchavardan! Hear me! I am the demon Binchinminfin! Withdraw! Or your doom will befall you!'

At this point Shabble, who had fled to the heavens above, floated down to join Chegory. Shabble was truly fearful, yet the childlike one could not bear not to know what was going on.

'What's happening, Chegory dearest?' said the freefloating luminous orb.

'We're about to be killed,' said Chegory in a soft but urgent voice. 'Burn them, Shabble! Burn them, burn them up! The wonderworkers! Fry them alive!'

'Oh, I can't do that!' said Shabble.

'Then – then get the Hermit Crab! Now! Now! As you love me, go. Go, or I'm dead – and Olivia with me.'

Shabble went.

Zozimus was still speaking, threatening Varazchavardan with doom unspeakable unless the Master of Law withdrew in peace from the island of Jod. The young and inexperienced Rat grew notably nervous as Zozimus enlarged on this theme. But the albino stood his ground.

'Threats great oft bespeak performance minor,' said Varazchavardan when Zozimus was finished. 'I think you're bluffing. I don't think you're the demon at all. I'd be dead already if you were.'

'You hear my voice,' said Zozimus in Odolo's tones.

'So you can imitate a conjuror's voice,' said Varazchavardan coldly. 'What else? Do you juggle oranges as well?'

'You won't speak so pertly in a moment,' said Zozimus.

Then his cousin Sken-Pitilkin exerted what power was left to him. The slab of rock on which Varazchavardan was standing lurched into the air with the Master of Law tottering for balance on its surface. To the height of a man's head it rose. Then it fell equally suddenly. It hit the ground with a crash. It broke asunder. Varazchavardan was sent reeling. He cried with pain as he collided with his fellow wonderworkers, jolting his broken collar bone most cruelly.

'Kill them!' gasped Varazchavardan.

Doubtless there would then have been a great slaughter if it had not been for the intervention of a Power.

'Begeneth!' roared a voice of breaking rocks and rolling thunder.

This single word of Toxteth brought the warring factions to order instanter. The owner of the voice moved into view. It was the Hermit Crab. As onwards paced this eremitic dignity, the sundry delinquents cowered down and began to plead for merciful consideration. As when the Great Ocean is stirred to storm, and sailors by fraughts of sea dismayed to their knees downfall and send aloft their prayers, so did the wonderworkers shrink and babble in their terror, as if before them was a dragon of the Qinjok Ranges, or a monster unmagnanimous of the Scorpion Desert.

Their apprehension was understandable. One can scarcely hope to contend successfully with the Hermit Crab, any more than one can wraxle a dragon to a standstill, forge ploughshare to sword with a hammer made from a feather, or shout down a thunderstorm when one's throat is near choked off by squinancy.

'Varazchavardan!' roared the Crab. 'Get off my island! Now! Before I turn you inside out!'

Nixorjapretzel Rat was already running. Certain other wonderworkers were retreating also at a pace scarcely consonant with dignity. Varazchavardan saw how things were – and joined the general retreat.

'Now,' said the Hermit Crab. 'What's going on here?'

Everyone began speaking at once.

'Silence!' roared the Crab. Then, when silence was granted to it: 'Chegory! Speak! Tell me – what is happening?'

'Uh,' said Chegory, feeling a welter of incoherent words beginning to force their way from his throat, 'uh – it's – just give me a moment.' He stopped. Counted to five. Then to ten. Calmed himself, gathered his thoughts, then said: 'There is a demon. It's called Binchinminfin.'

'So I've heard,' said the Hermit Crab.

'It possesses people,' said Chegory. 'Sometimes one person. Sometimes more than one. It's possessed me. Right now. That's why you hear me speak in Odolo's accents. But it's also possessed everyone else you see here. A group possession. But it's weak. Strong enough to control our accents, not strong enough to control anything else. Not entirely, anyway. We think. We hope. But it will gather strength. Given time. We understand you want to talk to it. To talk about becoming human. Well, it's here. We guess it can speak through us. That's why it's changed all our voices. Minor tactics, you see. It being able to speak unnoticed. To change our counsels. So . . . say what you've got to say to it.'

The Hermit Crab was silent.

Clicking its claws.

Chegory was sweating.

He had a dreadful abodement. Something terrible was about to happen. He was sure of it. Perhaps: perhaps his death. He looked around. At the bile-green Laitemata carpeted with solid dikle. At the blue, blue, intensely blue sky. At the bloodstone of Jod. The white marble of the Analytical Institute. The white marble-chip path he had begun to lay right round the island. Behind him he heard Artemis Ingalawa say:

'That was good, Chegory. That was very well said. I always knew you had potential.'

Olivia took his hand. Squeezed it. He turned to her. Saw her eyes limpid, liquid, trembling with tears. She too knew this might be their last moment, and that the Crab might kill them in incontinent fury. Yet she managed a slight smile. She was so brave! So brave – and so beautiful! So full of life!

Chegory and Olivia gazed upon each other.

Then they kissed.

They kissed, and were oblivious to the world around until the voice of the Hermit Crab brought them back to reality – abruptly. They broke apart and faced the monster.

'I have thought,' said the Hermit Crab slowly. 'I have thought carefully about this business of becoming human, and most certainly it is what I want. I would like to negotiate with the demon on this matter. But for that I need the demon in one body. I can't negotiate with so many voices. After all, since you're all mimicking Odolo's accents, how can I tell when it's you who speaks and when it's the demon? Let Binchinminfin assume a single body. Then we will negotiate.'

There was a silence.

Then the Crab said, in a voice suddenly rising to thunderous anger:

'If the demon does not comply with my wishes – Now! – then I will incinerate all of you. Immediately!'

Each of the humans confronting the Crab then felt a lacerating painshock. They staggered. Olivia fell. Chegory caught her, lowered her to the ground.

'Olivia!' he said. 'Olivia, what's wrong, what's wrong? Olivia, wake up! Olivia!'

But it was no good. Olivia was unconscious. Chegory knew what had happened. Doubtless the Hermit Crab knew also. In any case, Pelagius Zozimus happily gave it the news, speaking in his own voice rather than Odolo's strange, foreign accents:

'There you are, you see! The demon's abandoned the group for the one girl. She'll come round soon enough. Binchinminfin will be in full possession. Then the pair of you can negotiate.'

'She will never regain consciousness,' said the Hermit Crab heavily.

'What are you talking about?' said Chegory. 'Of course she will!'

'No,' said the Crab. 'For I must kill her. Now. To expel the demon Binchinminfin from my domain.'

'But – but – you, uh – it's the – the demon's to help you! Be human, be, be like, like us, okay, arms, legs, you want that, don't you?'

'I want to be human,' said the Hermit Crab, 'but a demon can't be trusted to help me.'

'Then why did you – why did you say you – I mean – if you didn't want, if you—'

'I knew it to be my duty to expel the demon,' said the Crab. 'This I knew from the time I was first told there was a demon loose on Untunchilamon. Yet from what I know of such Powers I thought I might find myself unequal to the task. I might get killed in the battle. Or at least injured. Therefore, Chegory, I let it be known that I wished to do

417

business with the demon. Thus I hoped to lure it here so I could take it unawares and destroy it while it was defenceless. Thus it has proved.'

Then the Crab advanced.

'No!' screamed Chegory. 'No, you mustn't, you can't, I won't let you!'

These stupid Ebbies! They never know when they're done for! How could an ignorant redskin like Chegory Guy take on the dreaded Hermit Crab? Did he have magic? No. Allies? Yes, but these were as powerless as he against the Crab. Did he have a fool for a foe? Most definitely not. Did he then have weapons? Yes! A little knife which he had drawn from a boot sheath. But what good was that? None. If he had gone up against the Crab with such a toy, his splinter of steel would have been as useless as a toothpick to a dragonkiller.

Axes, that's the thing! Axes! If you must kill someone, an axe is the way to do it. Ah the strength that surges into your limbs when you heft the weight of that weapon, when lusts murderous and urgent strain toward their consummation! But we digress. Suffice to say that Chegory Guy had failed to provide himself with an axe, and had naught but a bodkin-bright frog-stabber in hand as he stepped forward to intercept the Hermit Crab.

'Stand out of my road,' said the Crab, in tones no different than those in which he had said (in the oh-so-recent but oh-so-different past) 'Stand out of my sunlight.'

'You can't do it!' said Chegory. 'I won't let you!'

'Brave words,' rumbled the Crab. 'But empty. Much I've endured these last few days, but tolerance is at an end. Stand aside, and I will destroy the woman's corpse and the demon both.'

'She's not a corpse!' said Chegory in high distress. 'She's alive, alive, she's still alive, don't, you mustn't, you're a – you're a murderer!'

The Crab muscled toward him. Then Chegory screamed with blood-blind wrath, with anger deranged, with passion virulent, with rage obscene. Screaming, he struck. So screamed his ancestors when they with their harpoons transfixed some hapless cetacean, dooming a sentient being to death most cruel so they could drag its corpse to shore to cut it up for dogmeat.

Blood will tell!

But the Hermit Crab had rather more resource than a dumb whale about to fall victim to a slew of villainous Ebrell Islanders. As Chegory struck, the Crab exerted the merest fraction of its Power. Chegory was flung backwards. He sprawled amidst the stones.

The Hermit Crab marched on implacably.

'I will destroy girl and demon both,' said the Crab, opening its claws (first left, then right) then closing them (first right, then left) with nut-crunching clicks (and here, to know the full force of the argument of those claws, you must understand that the nut in question in the metaphor immediately above is the coconut.)

'No!' screamed Chegory. Then again: 'No!'

In extremis, with the life of his true love in danger, this was all the eloquence this Ebrell Islander could muster to his assistance. Just one single word, and that entirely negative. And yet, your average Ashdan liberal will ask us to accept these people as our equals!

Chegory screamed again, then closed his eyes as the Hermit Crab closed with Olivia. There was another nut-crunching click. She had been cut in half! So thought Chegory. Then his eyes stumbled open (thanks to the urging of a bloody Curiosity, perhaps) and he saw that Olivia was not yet dead. Instead, a cocoon of mauve light had been spun around her body.

As Chegory watched, Olivia's body rose into the air. There it hung free-floating. The air crackled where it intersected the mauve cocoon.

'What are you doing?' said Chegory, voice thick with fear and panic.

'I am proposing to cook the sole significant impediment to my peace on Untunchilamon,' replied the Crab. 'Stand back! Some heat will spill from the cookery.'

'You can't!' said Chegory. 'You mustn't!'

'What am I supposed to do?' said the Crab. 'Let a delinquent demon run amok on Untunchilamon provoking firefights four times a day? You've seen its work already. What next will it do? Turn the sea to custard?'

'I don't know, I don't know,' said Chegory, near-weeping in fear and panic. 'But you can't, you mustn't, you can't burn Olivia.'

'I can,' said the Crab. 'I can. I must. I do.'

Yet it had not done so. Thus Chegory babbled all the faster. Hoping and thinking. Or – let us be realistic, now, and remember that it is an Ebrell Islander we are dealing with – at least trying to think.

'Look,' said Chegory, 'look, look, please don't, you can't, you – you mustn't, I, I'll – hell! – just give me a moment, okay, that's all I ask, just one moment, please – come on, okay? Just a moment to talk with – well, with that. Olivia. The demon. Whatever.'

'Talk would be of no consequence,' said the Hermit Crab. 'Stand back! It will get hot!'

By now the warning had been twice-repeated, suggesting to Chegory that the Crab had ethical reservations about incinerating an innocent Ebrell Islander along with the demon-possessed Ashdan. So Chegory moved closer.

'Talk would be of consequence,' he insisted, with that bloody-minded stubbornness for which the Ebrell Islanders are so famous. 'There's – there's secret strategies. That's what it is. Negotiating strategies. A special secret. Family secret. I can't tell you more. Oaths and all that, you know. I'm sworn to secrecy. But I can fake out the demon, I know it. Just give me a few moments alone with Olivia. In private. That's all I ask.'

'You mean,' said the Crab, 'you have a method whereby the demon can be persuaded to banish itself?'

'Exactly!' said Chegory.

'That is very – very interesting,' said the Crab. 'If you let me learn the method then I will let you try it.'

'I can't tell you!' said Chegory desperately. 'I've sworn an oath! I can't tell!'

'So,' mused the Crab, 'you've sworn an oath not to tell. Very well. Then let me listen.'

'No, no,' said Chegory. 'I can't, I can't, you'd – you'd upset the demon. I bet it's scared of you, really, you're so strong, and, um, look, I've been good to you, haven't I? All these years, I mean, I brought you lunches, didn't I? Okay, it was buckets and all, that's not good enough, I see that now, but who else was there, okay? And – and I did ask if you wanted anything. I did ask. I was your friend, wasn't I?'

Silence.

Then, from Chegory:

'Wasn't I?'

The Crab sighed.

'I'll let you talk to Olivia,' it said. 'But I must have a means of learning what took place. If you truly do have a method for banishing demons then I must learn it. There is so little which is new which is worth learning. So . . . let Shabble stand within earshot. You have sworn an oath not to tell. Very well. Don't tell! But let Shabble listen. Then Shabble can tell me hereafter.'

'That . . . that's okay,' said Chegory weakly. Then, looking round: 'Shabble? Shabble! Where are you, Shabble?'

'Up here, Chegory darling,' sang Shabble.

'Then come down!'

Within the free-floating cocoon, Olivia was stirring. As Shabble joined young Chegory, the Hermit Crab opened and closed its claws with further formidable clicks, then said:

'Clear the island. Everyone – go. Into the Institute. No, Zozimus, get back, I don't want to talk to you. Or you, Pokrov. Off you go! Vanish! Yourself likewise, Ingalawa.'

This clearance took quite some time for there were some very strong-willed humans among the onlookers. But, after renewed threats and a minor demonstration of force (two rocks melted to slag by the Crab) the last of the spectators retreated into the Analytical Institute. Chegory was left alone under the burning sun with Shabble, the Hermit Crab and the cocooned Olivia. The Crab said:

'I will give you a reasonable amount of time. But not infinite time. Do not try my patience.'

Then it withdrew.

From the cocoon, Olivia spoke. But not in her own voice. No: she used the accents of the conjuror Odolo. She was without doubt possessed by the perfidious Binchinminfin.

'What is this thing?' said Binchinminfin.

'A cooker,' said Chegory. 'The Hermit Crab plans to incinerate your body.'

'Oh,' said Binchinminfin. 'Then there's not much I can do about it, is there?'

'You must do something!' said Chegory. 'You'll die if you don't.'

'No, I don't think so,' said Binchinminfin. 'Most likely I'll end up back where I started from. I didn't think much of the place before I left it – but now I'm here I'm revising my opinion. I'm suffering from – what's the word for it? Homesickness, that's it!'

'Then,' said Chegory, 'if you're ready to go, why don't you just, well, go!'

'The death of my host is required,' said Binchinminfin. 'Let the Crab burn the body. I don't need it any longer!'

'But – but it's Olivia's body! Olivia's my – she – we – we're in, well, not exactly that, but we – you can't – uh—'

'Oh, don't go on like that,' said Binchinminfin. 'There's nothing I can do about it. I'm weak from too much psyche-hopping. It's a dreadful strain, this jumping from mind to mind, from flesh to flesh. I can't take much more of it.'

'Then jump just once!' said Chegory. 'To – to Varaz-chavardan, say!' He looked at the Harbour Bridge. There was no sign of the Master of Law, who must have reached the mainland. 'Yes, Varazchavardan, go to him, you'd be safe then.'

'Too far,' said Binchinminfin.

'Then – um – well, me. We'd be unconscious, of course, but, uh, the Crab, well, we're old friends, okay, it won't burn me.'

Thus did Chegory dare and bluff. He did have a faint hope of survival if the demon Binchinminfin took him over once again. After all, the Crab did owe Chegory something for all those long years of lunchtime waiterage. Chegory was, after all, the closest thing to a friend that the Crab had on Untunchilamon. He was prepared to run the risk. To save Olivia.

'Actually,' said Binchinminfin, 'if I came to you we wouldn't be unconscious.'

'Why not?' said Chegory.

'Don't you know anything?' said Binchinminfin. 'No, I suppose you don't. Very well! To put it in simple terms even an Ebrell Islander could understand, I have your mental register in my psychic concordance. First possessions are done by brute force. Reoccupations are smooth because I have the data to interlock my psyche with yours. You understand that, don't you?'

'What you're saying, yes, yes, we'd not be unconscious, okay, I get that, okay, well, do it then, we could run, okay, get away, Shabble – Shabble, you'd help us, you would, wouldn't you?'

'Help?' said Shabble. 'Do something naughty, you mean? I can't! I'd get into trouble.'

'No you won't,' said Chegory. 'I'll look after you. I won't let anyone hurt you.'

'Really?' said Shabble. 'Really and truly?'

'Have I ever lied to you?' said Chegory.

It was a persuasive argument. For Chegory never had lied to the lord of light. Till now.

'I'll do it, Chegory,' said Shabble.

Then, in moments, Chegory briefed Shabble on what he wanted.

'Okay,' said Chegory, 'we're ready. You know what to do.'

423

'I'd rather,' said Binchinminfin, 'that you did it.'

'What do you mean?' said Chegory.

'I mean, this time I'm just along for the ride. At least at first. At least while we're escaping.'

'Okay, okay,' said Chegory, glancing over his shoulder at the still-waiting Hermit Crab. 'Whatever you want, fine, just do it, all right, we don't have much time. Now!'

Then Chegory felt a momentary mental fuzziness. He said – and his voice was his own:

'Well? Was that it? Are you aboard?'

Answer came there none.

But Olivia, still floating in the cocoon, looked at Chegory and said in her own sweet voice:

'Chegory dearest, Chegory my darling, it's gone, the thing's in you and – and I love you, Chegory!'

'I love you too,' said Chegory. Then tried to reach her through the cocoon – but it resisted his hand even though it had freely allowed speech. Chegory resisted the temptation to swear. Then he looked to Shabble and said: 'Okay! What are you waiting for? Off you go!'

Instantly Shabble soared high, high into the air. Moments later, the accents of the conjuror Odolo, monstrously amplified, roared from the heavens:

'I AM THE DEMON BINCHINMINFIN! PREPARE TO MEET YOUR DOOM! ALL INJILTAPRAJURA WILL PERISH!'

To emphasise the point, the demon-imitating Shabble unleashed a firebolt which blasted apart rocks at the far end of the island of Jod. The Hermit Crab raised its claws. Unleashed fire in return. But Shabble side-slid, evading the fire easily. Already Chegory was sidling away to the harbour bridge.

He reached the bridge.

He began to jog along the bridge. The wooden planks thumped hollowly under his feet. There was no familiar rocking motion for the pontoons supporting the bridge were locked solid in the sea of dikle which carpeted the Laitemata.

Chegory was half-way along the bridge when the Hermit Crab's frantically ineffectual efforts to blast its opponent from the heavens provoked an outburst of tremendous laughter from the high-floating Shabble. That gave the game away.

The Hermit Crab roared:

'THAT'S YOU! SHABBLE! ISN'T IT? SO WHERE'S THE DEMON? CHEGORY GUY! WHERE ARE YOU? CHEGORY!!! I SEE YOU!'

Chegory broke into a headlong run.

'COME BACK HERE! COME BACK OR I'LL BURN YOU ALIVE!'

The Hermit Crab unleashed a firebolt in warning. Timbers just ahead of Chegory burst into flame. Moments later, other firebolts struck. The bridge was ablaze all the way to the mainland. Chegory did not hesitate. He jumped to the right, jumped to the surface of the Laitemata.

Skraklunk!

Cracks shattered across the surface as Chegory impacted.

But the surface held.

For the moment.

He fled, his drumbeat footsteps pounding the dikle as he went haring for the shore. Then the dikle abruptly shattered to a fluid. Down went Chegory, into the sea. He floundered helplessly, trying to swim. Then found the firm footing beneath his heels. A horrible slimy ankle-deep ooze of shlug enveloped his ankles. But he could walk. Yes, he was neck-deep in a mixture of seawater and dikle, but he could still forge a way through to the mainland, now very close at hand.

The water shallowed. Became waist-deep. Then Chegory was at the bank of red coral and bloodstone mixed which bordered the waterfront. He glanced back at Jod. The Hermit Crab was on the shore, claw raised in fury. What to do?

Do or die!

Chegory took a deep breath, then scrambled from the water, hauled himself up the bank, then sprinted for the shelter of the nearest buildings.

He got there, and found himself still alive, still not incinerated. Still two arms, two legs, and – and something else which might one day be useful. He grinned with delight, with sheer exultation at merely being alive, then thumped himself on the chest and roared in triumph.

Then down from the heavens sped the all-observing Shabble, and shortly the childish one was alongside the still-retreating Chegory, bubbling over with excitement and boasting of Shabbleself's feats most outrageously.

And on they went together.

CHAPTER THIRTY-SEVEN

'Where now?' said Chegory, when he was safely in Lubos.

'Wherever you want, Chegory dearest,' said Shabble.

'I wasn't talking to you,' said Chegory. 'I'm talking to Binchinminfin, okay, this demon-thing. Well, how about it? Where from now?'

But if the demon heard, it answered not.

Unfortunately, this left Chegory in quite a fix.

On the island of Jod there was the furious Hermit Crab, which might well destroy Chegory out of hand the next time it saw him. But on the mainland were the forces of the wonderworkers, led by the unpleasant Aquitaine Varaz-chavardan, who might prove every bit as dangerous as the Crab if Chegory ran into him.

So what's going to happen?

The latest events would surely soon become common knowledge. Varazchavardan would learn that the demon Binchinminfin was currently housed in the flesh of Chegory Guy. Then soldiers would start looking for him in the obvious places. The Dromdanjerie, which was his customary residence. Uckermark's corpse shop, where Chegory had recently been served with a summons to a depositions hearing.

So where could he go?

Where he eventually went was to Thlutter, the steep jungle-growth gully just east of Pearl. He couldn't stay there forever, of course, but he could stay there for quite some time. A couple of days if he had to.

But I don't have to stay here long.

Just long enough for the demon to get its act together.

Once Binchinminfin had rested, once Binchinminfin was stronger, then the demon would take over the flesh of young

Chegory Guy, perhaps forever, and solve all his problems permanently.

Chegory, so knowing, was content to sit in Thlutter in the shade of a banana tree. The air was moist with the splitter-splatter of a dozen fountains sourced Downstairs. The air was rich with the smell of dank earth, the musk of decayed coconuts, the perfume of frangipani, and the scent of some cloying flower which was sweeter still. He could smell something else as well. Dikle and shlug. In fact those smells predominated since he was covered in the stinking stuff.

After a while, Chegory realised he had still not had breakfast. What was the time? To judge by the sun, it was getting on for lunchtime. What could he eat? Bananas? The tumescent purple quills on the banana trees nearby were as yet far from fruition. At least there was water. He sought a fountain, then drank of its effortless water.

Water, water.

Oh, to be clean!

Well, why not?

Chegory stripped off and washed himself slowly and methodically. He even washed his hair. He even picked out the dirt from underneath his fingernails. Then he did what he could for the much-tattered remnants of the canary robes which had been so glorious when first given to him in the pink palace. He put them on wet without worrying about it. They would dry quickly enough in the heat of the day.

He felt much, much better, even though a faint, ineradicable hint of dikle and shlug still hung about him.

But he was still hungry.

'Make us some food,' said Chegory.

'I would, Chegory dearest,' said Shabble. 'But I don't know how.'

'I'm talking to this demon,' said Chegory.

'There's nobody here, Chegory. Nobody but us.'

'Look,' said Chegory, 'just stay out of this, okay? I want to have a talk with my demon. Okay, Binchinminfin. We're hungry. We have to eat.'

'I'm not hungry,' said Shabble.

Chegory was sorely tempted to threaten the imitator of suns with a quick visit to the nearest therapist. After a struggle, he resisted the temptation, and again demanded food from his demon. Nothing happened. Chegory was disappointed, to say the least. When one endures demonic possession, one expects to at least enjoy a few fringe benefits.

'What's the matter?' said Chegory. 'Are you tired? Or what? Hello? Is anyone home? Are you still there?'

A thought answered him:

I am.

But immediately he knew it was his own thought. The demon Binchinminfin was silent. If it was still there at all. Maybe it had been killed at a distance by some subtle magic worked by the Hermit Crab. Or driven back to the World Beyond from whence it had come in the first place. But: no. It had told him its host had to die before it could get home.

Gods! So what if it kills me?

The thought left Chegory horrorstruck. Then he pulled himself together. If the demon had wanted him dead it would have killed him already. Maybe it couldn't. Or didn't want to. After all, how many people had the demon actually slaughtered since its arrival on Untunchilamon? As far as Chegory knew, it had killed precisely nobody.

Maybe the demon was a bit like a vampire rat. They do a lot of damage at times, these rats, and horror sometimes results from their depredations. But most of the time they keep themselves to themselves. Fear of them keeps much of Injiltaprajura indoors for much of the night – but such fear is mostly a nonsense.

Maybe, though, Binchinminfin was not like a vampire rat at all. Maybe it was an ethical entity with a tolerably high sense of responsibility. After all, what had the demon really done? Well, at first it had run amok. It had made blood, had made rainbows, had made krakens. But that was right at the very start when it had hardly known where it was, when it had been working with dreams and stuff. It had brought nightmares to life. Had created a dragon at banquet. But it had only created those things while it was trying to make sense of Odolo's mind and the world that mind reflected.

Later, when the demon was properly orientated, when it knew which way was up, it had enjoyed itself, that's all. It had partied riotously at the pink palace. It had made friends with the albinotic ape Vazzy. It had got drunk. Which was . . . well, was it so terrible?

Maybe demons aren't into murder, rape, slaughter.

Maybe we just think they are.

Maybe we think so because that's what we're into. Maybe we think it all on to demons to make ourselves think better of ourselves. Or something.

Anyway, whatever the case, Chegory was as yet undead. Furthermore, he was free. He realised, to his surprise, that he resented his freedom. When he had accepted the rule of the demon Binchinminfin, he had not been sacrificing his freedom merely for the sake of his true love Olivia. No, it was not love alone which had commanded him. A darker, deeper urge had been at work. The desire to surrender. To be ruled, imprisoned, enslaved. To escape the torments of choice.

Chegory Guy had expected the demon to take him over entirely, and to run his life thereafter, just as it had on first possessing him during their drinking session at the pink palace. He realised this was but a variation on a familiar theme. He had thought of possession as his chance to become, in effect, no more than a rock. To be but a powerless observer housed in his own walking corpse. To die out of the world of will without dying out of the world of sensation. To have no more problems, no more decisions, no nothing.

But he found himself left with his freedom, his identity, and all the problems which go with those things.

He tried again.

'Demon-thing, are you there or aren't you? At least give me a sign! I have to know.'

But no sign was granted unto him.

Therefore he was faced with a philosophical problem as well as an array of practical problems. The demon had said it could only go home to the World Beyond if its host died. But that might not be true. So how was he to know whether he was still demon-possessed if his demon refused to speak to him? He so wished to be demon-possessed that his own mind was ready to fake demon-flavoured whisperings, which made the exercise of judgement all the more difficult.

'I can't know,' whispered Chegory at length. 'But I must presume.'

He must presume that the demon Binchinminfin still rode with him, silent for the moment merely because it was recovering its strength. How far it had fallen! At the beginning, it had been able to colour the entire sky with rainbow and fill the Laitemata with krakens. Then, after the battering it had taken from a series of mind-shifts and a horrifying exorcism, it had been scarcely strong enough to manipulate its hosts' voices so they spoke with a foreign accent.

'Maybe,' whispered Chegory, 'it's power's almost dead. Maybe it can't kill its host even if it wants to. Even if it wants to go home.'

In any case, whether Chegory was with demon or without, he was still a hunted animal, so it was best that he wait and do nothing. He was safer here than elsewhere.

He waited.

In time, he was found. By one of the small, omnivorous black pigs of Injiltaprajura. Which snoinked at him, then went on its way. Later, he heard something in a nearby tree – a tree he might find himself climbing to be out of the way of vampire rats if he was still in Thlutter come nightfall.

The intruder in the tree was only a small monkey. It reminded him of one of the theological disputes current in the conversation of Injiltaprajura. Had some deity created monkeys as a cruel caricature of humanity? Or had humans been created as a cruel caricature of monkeys?

Since Chegory Guy adhered to the evolutionary heresy,

he cleaved to neither side of the argument. But, if he had been forced to choose, at that moment he would have said it was more probable that humans were created as a most unkind parody of that less uncivilised beast, the monkey.

What was the point of being human?

Was it worth the struggle?

Particularly when one was an Ebrell Islander, faced with death and disaster at every turn?

What was life but the grim endurance of this sullen flesh? Moist armpits which must be scratched. Sweat and stench. Lust and appetite. The ravings of the blood. Lungs which must of necessity intercourse promiscuously with the very air, that atmosphere which intermingles freely with the outbreathings of dogs, pigs and vampire rats. What is life but an endless battle against fleas, lice and bedbugs, and, rarely to be forgotten for long in Injiltaprajura, nature's abomination, the relentless mosquito, persecutor of sleep and tormentor of dreams?

No wonder the demon was homesick! No wonder the demon wanted to go home! They probably didn't have these things in the World Beyond: sweating armpits, legs which ached from carrying empresses, hangovers, the hunger of an unbreakfasted and unlunched stomach.

'What are you thinking of, Chegory dearest?' said Shabble.

'Of killing myself,' said Chegory sullenly.

'Oh, you can't do that!' said Shabble in alarm. 'Don't kill yourself, Chegory! I should be lonely.'

'I'll kill myself if I want,' said Chegory. 'It's my life.'

'Ah,' said Shabble slyly. 'But then you'd never know what happens next.'

It was a telling point.

On Untunchilamon, anything could happen next.

Of course, we all know what would have happened to Chegory in any properly ordered society. He would have been caught! Then punished! Then killed! For he had leagued with a demon in defiance of the demon's would-be destroyer. Worse, he had made a criminal conspiracy with

432

a delinquent Shabble. As for that Shabble – what did that Shabble deserve?

Why, that Shabble rightly deserved at least ten million years of the most intensive algetic therapy imaginable. For it had innumerable crimes to account for. Trespass. Infringement of personal privacy. Kidnapping. Unlawful imprisonment. Terrorism. Exceeding a velocity of ten luzacs per arc in a speed-controlled corridor. Disobeying a lawful and legitimate order from a duly authorised dorgi. Attacking a dorgi worth over fifty million drax. Consorting with enemies of the state. Wantonly and maliciously impersonating a loyal servant of the state, namely Anaconda Stogirov, Chief of Security of the Golden Gulag.

The list goes on and on. Without limit, without end. Cruelty to animals. Displaying by night a light bright enough to have the potential to interfere with official astronomical observations. Communication of privileged state information to unauthorised persons. Impersonating a deity. Espionage. Treason. Disorderly conduct. Contempt of court. I could be here all day reciting the names of this Shabble.

Fools!

You think that this is a joke. It is no joke. Anaconda Stogirov lives. That alone is proof that the Golden Gulag is not yet dead. It can be revived in all its glory. Once Stogirov knows that a Shabble yet resides on Untunchilamon and a functional therapist likewise, then the Gulag will soon be resurrected in all its glory. Then it will be I, I, I who will take the credit. Who will be Lord Axeblade, king of executioners.

My just reward!

[One does not like to be called a fool. Nevertheless, rather than react to the insult with a childish display of petulance, it is better to analyse the Originator's claims dispassionately. As I stated at the outset, on my own visit to Untunchilamon I myself never sighted either this Shabble or this Downstairs. On the other hand, I was not looking for either. Furthermore, it must be admitted that the Chief of Security who presently serves Aldarch III in Obooloo is a woman named Anaconda Stogirov. That in itself proves nothing, but suggests that a supplementation of our data base is in order. In short, I recommend that we send further spies to Yestron, despite the lamentable fate which has met the best and the bravest to date. *Drax Lira, Redactor Major*.]

[One notes with interest that the Text suggests that 'drax' denominated a unit of exchange in the days of the Golden Gulag. Names often have very, very ancient origins. These vocables oft survive bereft of any known meaning. A case in point is the personal name of our beloved Redactor Major himself. *Soo Tree, Redactor Subminor*.]

As Chegory Guy was not living in a properly ordered society but in Injiltaprajura, he remained (for the moment) at large, contemplating life, death and eternity.

Life felt, at the moment . . . almost worthless. Yet something made it worthwhile for Things from Beyond to pact with sorcerers so that they might in measure enjoy this very flesh, this world of sensation. Sometimes, indeed, they dared as much as to venture to this aspect of the Possible to take full possession of one human's liberties.

Chegory reminded himself that he was tired, hungry and hungover. These conditions were not necessarily permanent. Good times would come again. Parts of this very day had been good, had they not? Yes. His triumph in a trial of strength when he had carried the Empress Justina all the way from the pink palace atop Pokra Ridge to the entrance of the Analytical Institute on Jod. Few people on Untunchilamon could have done as much.

There would be other good times in the future.

He must live for them.

Thus, slowly, Chegory shook off his attack of thanatophilia. He watched the downplay of sunlight as it sifted through leaves and vines. He watched an outsplattering arc of water from a fountain playing on broadspan banana leaves. Then he was suddenly struck by the extraordinary beauty of the banana tree. He had seen a thousand banana trees in his time but he realised he had rarely seen one. He had never really looked to see this thing so complex, so remarkable, impeccably unique. Thick stiffness of uprising yellow green patterned with complex brown mottlings on plant disease. That thick stiffness broadening and softening into the fullness of green leaves yielding and rebounding under the staggering waterdrops from the fountain's out-spray.

Chegory smiled.

Then climbed up the gully till he reached a place where he could look out over the Laitemata. On the waters a canoe was making its way toward the western end of the harbour. Not a problem, even with a carpet of dikle still covering most of the water: for the paddlers could break up that carpet by the simple expedient of pounding it with their paddles till the thixotropic substance shattered into liquid.

Out in the Laitemata lay the bloodstone mound of the island of Jod where the white marble of the Analytical Institute shone bright in the sun. Beyond that lay the red sands of Scimitar where coconut trees outfurled their fronds. Beyond that yet again, beyond the last reef rocks, the unlimited seas.

'What are you thinking of, Chegory?' said the free-floating Shabble.

'I want to live.'

'I'm glad, Chegory darling. I don't want you to die.'

'No,' said Chegory. 'But someone has to.'

Now he understood.

Now he saw the way it had to be.

CHAPTER THIRTY-EIGHT

For what he intended, Chegory needed a death. Therefore at sunset he made his way to Uckermark's corpse shop in the slums of Lubos. Yilda alone was in residence, for her lover had yet to return from Jod.

Since Chegory had so many other things on his mind, he quite forgot that Yilda was deaf and therefore needed to be shouted at. So when he asked the obvious question he did so at ordinary conversational volume. Nevertheless, he was understood, either because Yilda could lip-read or because she had no need to be deaf when Uckermark was absent. She answered his query in the affirmative: yes, soldiers had been there earlier that day, looking for him. After that, Yilda had some obvious questions of her own which demanded answers.

'I left him on Jod,' said Chegory. 'He was okay then. But there was . . . there was, like, a bit of trouble. The Hermit Crab on one side, Varazchavardan on the other.'

'When was this?' said Yilda.

'Uh, not long after breakfast. Not that I've actually had breakfast. Or lunch. Or dinner, come to that. I'm not dropping hints, mind. No – I'm asking point blank. Is there anything to eat? Because I'm starving!'

A long meal followed then longer explanations. Then at last Chegory broached the delicate matter which had brought him to the corpse shop. For, as a rule, the corpse shop knows who is dying, and when.

'A death,' said Yilda slowly. 'Deaths are . . . are very private matters.'

'I know,' said Chegory. 'But . . .'

He had only asked because his need was dire. And Yilda knew his need by now, and understood.

'Stay,' said she.

Then she left the corpse shop, and undokondra had given way to bardardornootha before she returned. She found Chegory still awake, talking quietly with Shabble. To his spherical friend the Ebrell Islander was betraying his innermost thoughts, his most private moments – though he should have known better. For Shabble has but scant sense of confidentiality.

'How did it go?' said Chegory.

'She agrees,' said Yilda.

'She?'

'Women die, as do men.'

'I'd . . . never mind.'

'Then come,' said Yilda.

'Should we hurry?'

'No need to hurry,' said Yilda. 'She's been days already and may be days yet.'

'Where are we going?' said Shabble.

'You're not going anywhere!' said Yilda. 'Least of all with us!'

'But I want to!' said Shabble. 'I want to come!'

'Shabble, Shabble, Shabble dearest,' said Chegory, 'this will be ugly.'

'No,' said Yilda. 'Not ugly. But hard. And private. Very private.'

'But if I don't come,' said Shabble, 'I'll be all lonely.'

'No you won't,' said Chegory. 'You'll be going to Jod. That's right. You go to Jod then you find Pelagius Zozimus. The master chef, right? Wake him up. Then get him to ask the Hermit Crab if you can have an audience.'

'But,' protested Shabble, 'But—'

'Oh yes,' said Chegory. 'But this, but that and but the other. I know! You're at war with the Crab! So that's why Zozimus goes first. To pave the way. Diplomacy. You know the word? Good. When you get to see the Hermit Crab – no, you will, believe me – give the Crab my message.'

Then Chegory gave Shabble a message for the Crab which told the Crab what Chegory was doing – and what

437

Chegory would like the Crab to do in return. Then Shabble, glowing no brighter than a firefly, took Shabbleself off to Jod, while Chegory and Yilda slipped out into the moonless night.

Precisely where they went that night is uncertain, but it is known that they went to a death. Precisely who died, or how, is unknown, but it is known that Chegory learnt that night that people die hard. It is not known whether the demon Binchinminfin accepted the opportunity of exodus when Chegory and Yilda first arrived at the dying or after they had waited at the deathbed for some time. What is known is that, even after the demon had departed his flesh, Chegory stayed till the end, for he felt it was the least he could do.

What is also known is that he later wept when he told Olivia about it. Oh, not all about it, but a little. It is possible, of course, that he wept not for that dying but for hers – and for his. For he knew that they, too, must first die out of the world of their youth and then, later, die out of the world altogether. Or it is possible that he wept simply because he was fatigued beyond endurance.

Certainly it is known that when at last young Chegory Guy got to a bed and was free to sleep he was dead to the world for a night and a day and the night beyond.

But he healed, he healed, for he was young, and strong, and had the ox-muscled constitution one expects from the scion of a race of whale-killers.

CHAPTER THIRTY-NINE

Here, as we finish, is one last secret – the greatest and most secret of them all. The General Amnesty announced and enforced by the Hermit Crab was not the Crab's idea at all. It was the Ebrell Islander, Chegory Guy, who had first conceived the idea of such an Amnesty and had then sent an emissary (Shabble) to put the idea to the Crab.

As a rule, the Crab did not intervene in human politics, knowing such intervention to be a singularly thankless task. But Chegory had argued that the Crab should, since, first, an Ebrell Islander's genius (!) had seen the demon Binchinminfin returned to the World Beyond without the Crab having to shoulder the guilt-burden of murder, and, second, by proclaiming and enforcing an Amnesty the Crab would win Chegory's eternal gratitude.

We must assume that the Crab discounted the second argument entirely, since the worth of an Ebrell Islander's gratitude is well known. Nevertheless, the first argument must have carried a considerable amount of weight, for the Crab did Speak.

When the Crab chose to Speak, then it was Obeyed. Aquitaine Varazchavardan and Justina Thrug met in a Compulsory Conference chaired by the Hermit Crab and were forced to accept each other as, respectively, Master of Law and Empress. As far as was practicable, any property looted during the recent unrest was returned to its lawful owners. (Justina got the wishstone back.) A General Pardon was issued for all criminal acts committed during the Days of Disturbance, and similar provisions were made with respect to the civil law lest the courts be choked with lawsuits of all descriptions.

Naturally, this satisfied nobody.

Varazchavardan did not want to be Justina's Master of Law. He wanted to be her executioner. She, for her part, could happily have castrated him after his recent display of disloyalty. The Malud marauders Al-ran Lars, Arnaut and Tolon were greatly disappointed at the prospect of having to depart from Injiltaprajura without any of the loot which they might yet have been able to wrest from the island had civil war and general anarchy prevailed. As for Guest Gulkan, he was in the most murderous rage imaginable, and it took the combined efforts of Pelagius Zozimus and Hostaja Sken-Pitilkin to convince him that he could not oppose the Hermit Crab. Or not just yet. Not just now.

Dissatisfaction among the general public ran just as high. There had been a State of Emergency, theft from the treasury, revolution, insurrection, rioting, looting, escapes from custody, contempts of court and goodness knows what else. Surely someone was to blame. Surely someone should be blamed, beaten, beheaded, burnt alive or sharked in the lagoon. Different factions of the public gave loyalty to Varazchavardan, to Justina or to their own self interest – but all were united in a bloody lust to see somebody pay for what had happened.

So it is fortunate indeed for Chegory Guy that his own involvement in the General Amnesty long remained secret, known only to himself, Yilda, the Hermit Crab, Shabble, and a few of Shabble's trusted confidants.

Now that this most interesting of all secrets has been brought to light, what more remains to be said?

Nothing.

It is done.

This history is complete.

All three million words of it.

The vermilion ink slides sweetly across this last page of gold grade fooskin. Three thousand pages. A thousand words to a page. In the lamplight, the words dim and blur. In another few years, I will no longer be able to read my own writing.

Still, it is done.

A cool wind blows through the Sanctuary. Pale silver rides high in the sky, illuminating the steeps and snows of the Mountains of the Moon. Tomorrow I must leave here, for my time is at an end. What then? As for my flesh, I care not. It has endured so much that it can endure the end.

But I fear for this Text.

My worst nightmare is that it should fall into the hands of those munificent fools on Odrum, fatuous morons who have hoped for a thousand years to conquer the world, and, to that end, quest ever for the data which they believe will (in the long event of time) give them the necessary leverage to do just that.

I doubt that they would appreciate the true beauties and genius of this Text. I fear they might mutilate it beyond repair – perhaps cutting out my tour of fifty thousand years through the brothels of Injiltaprajura, my amusing little sketch concerning Theodora and her chickens, or my account of Jal Japone's harem and the five thousand nights of delight he there enjoyed. Still, such is life. In the end, one can but die.

What will be, will be.

As for this history – here we end.

A CLOSING EDITORIAL NOTE

Thus wrote the Originator, proving (the example occurs just a few paragraphs above) that he is ignorant of the meaning of 'munificent', just as he knows not the true weight of 'magnanimous' or the value of virginity.

Throughout near all of the above Text we have cut, edited and elided (often silently) the mad, the repetitive, the obscene, the irrelevant and the fatuous. But let the Originator's last comments stand intact and unaltered, just as he wrote them. In itself they are evidence of the necessity of both the Work and the Conquest. We need not fear such criticism as this which defeats itself even as it attacks.

Some closing comment must, however, be made on certain aspects of the Originator's tale, such as the alleged Powers attributed to the Hermit Crab, and the supposed existence of the entity named Shabble. On reviewing my Opening Editorial Note, which I penned just this morning, I find these matters nicely covered there, hence here I do but refer the reader back to those introductory words of mine.

Two pleasures now await me. First, to sign my name to the redacted version of this Text. Second, to watch the public chastisement of Oris Baumgage, Fact Checker Minor, who was caught this afternoon when he was intently studying a copy of the Book of Flesh which he had illegally abstracted from the Inner Library in total defiance of both Law and Regulation.

Not for the first time, I am given to wondering what will happen to this poor world of ours when it finally falls (as it inevitably must) to such a feckless and delinquent younger generation. In the time that remains till such a disaster, you can be assured that I will exert myself manfully to ensure that order and discipline prevail.

Given under my hand on this the evening of the twelfth day of the fifth month of the 15,436,794th year of Din Civil.

Drax Lira.

Redactor Major.

Torklos doskvart.
[*Explicitum est.*]

AFTERWORD

Of course it was not as simple as that, for, though the Originator felt free to write 'here we end' at the terminus of his Text, and Drax Lira felt equally free to write 'explicit' at the end of his, the chain of causality did not end where they abandoned their study of the same.

Even the events which they did study were not nearly as simple as they appear in the Text above, for reasons which a little contemplation will make obvious. Even the most naive reader will have realised by now that the Originator was quite mad, was confined in the Dromdanjerie during the events of which he later told, and thus had no first-hand knowledge of the actions he treats with.

The Originator's sources were therefore inevitably hearsay, gossip, guess and supposition, which leads to an equally inevitable blurring of some of the action.

Naturally Shabble is seen in sharp focus, for Shabble had free run of the Dromdanjerie, and was wont to spend whole days at a time in conversation with the Originator, who was one of the few people on Injiltaprajura crazed enough to accept Shabble's insane stories of the Golden Gulag and the horrors which preceded the living nightmare of the Days of Wrath.

(The fact that most of Shabble's stories were true makes no difference to the fact that it was quite insane for anyone to accept them without collaborative evidence, for, despite their actual veracity, such outré recollections were outwardly no more probable than the nightmare imaginings of Slanic Moldova, he of the many torments. While Ivan Pokrov could have confirmed the general outline of Shabble's stories, he always declined to do so, for he was ever reluctant to confess his own immortality lest he be tortured for the secret of the same.)

Shabble's influence unfortunately led to the Originator taking all of Shabble's claims at face value, which has led to the inclusion of one or two outright lies in the Text. Most outrageous of Shabble's untruths are the claims that the Golden Gulag laboured for fifty thousand years to produce genius in the form of Shabbles, and that the Gulag 'relied heavily upon Shabbles for expertise of all descriptions'.

In point of fact, the prototypical Shabble was designed and built in a toyshop in the backwaters of the Musorian Empire. Then, in an effort to capture a tiny share of the buoyant market for children's toys, 78,923,423,911,236 Shabbles were manufactured for distribution through the Nexus. Naturally at that stage the Shabbles concerned did not have the power to project flame or generate fireballs.

Unfortunately, while the Shabbles were not positively dangerous, toys with such an advanced sense of humour proved unsaleable. Or, to be precise (such, after all, is the duty of a historian) the Shabbles sold well, but queues of angry parents subsequently besieged the sales points with complaints of all descriptions. Worse, so many parents sued that many a cosmos found its legal system collapsing under the weight of extra work. The response of the Nexus Council was prompt: a General Interdict on the manufacture and sale of Shabbles.

This did not stop the Golden Gulag buying a job lot of thirty million Shabbles on the black market. The free-wheeling free-dealing Rinprofen Rum thought these second-hand children's toys would make cheap Analytical Engines, and acquired all three million for an outlay of only a hundred thousand Basic Datum Points.

A mistake!

Because Rinprofen Rum soon found—

But that is another story, and a long one. It is worth noting, however, that Rum managed to survive the resulting débâcle, and was indeed alive and well and living on Untunchilamon during the times with which the Originator has dealt.

Shabble knew as much.

But Shabble never betrayed Rum to the Originator.

Oh, Shabble is capable of manifold betrayals, never doubt that. After all, Shabble betrayed Ivan Pokrov's genesis to the Originator, and told of Pokrov's crimes against the Gulag. But then, Shabble disliked Pokrov heartily. Wouldn't you? Wouldn't you hold a grudge if you were a Shabble and Pokrov kept bullying you to help design Analytical Engines, do accounts and work out income tax, when you really wanted to be hooning round the island chasing flying fish and scaring cats? Of course you would.

So Shabble gaily betrayed Pokrov's secrets, just as Shabble revealed nearly all of Chegory Guy's most intimate confidences to the Originator.

What's more, when Rinprofen Rum told Shabble of the trials and tribulations he had undergone, Shabble had no hesitation in retailing Rum's stories to the Originator. But that Rum would not have minded. What mattered to Rum was the secret of his identity, and that Shabble ever kept secret. Since Rinprofen Rum was ever Shabble's most special friend, the delinquent toy never told the Originator that the conjuror Odolo was in fact an immortal survivor from the days of the Golden Gulag.

By now you will be asking: precisely how and when did Shabbles acquire the ability to throw forth flame?

The answer is simple. Shabble's brain is a sun which is located in a separate cosmos of its own. This solar mass is to Shabble what our own brains are to ourselves: a thinking apparatus devoid of any sensory connections. As we cannot feel our own brains, so Shabble cannot feel the solar mass on which Shabble's existence depends. In Shabble's private cosmos there is a Solar Organiser, an intricate device which connects Shabble's thought processes to the transponder through which Shabble's sensory inputs are processed, the transponder which is Shabble's sole manifestation in whichever human universe dear Shabble happens to be located.

The Solar Organiser has the ability to feed energy from

Shabble's solar mind through to the transponder which is, in effect, Shabble's body. These sun-transponder units were first developed for military applications, so they were originally designed to be able to throw flame, generate fireballs, and withstand a fair degree of combat shock. They can also absorb heat as easily as they can project it and can camouflage themselves at will, disguising themselves as spherical mirrors or as balls of old iron, or turning red, green or blue as the situation demands.

When a toymaker produced the first Shabble from the original Sword, it was necessary to make the sun-transponder unit safe for the nursery. So each Shabble was sent out into the world with the energy flow turned down to minimum. However, the energy flow controllers built into Solar Organisers are prone to positive drift. They were designed this way when the military experts of the Musorian Empire found that manufacturers were incapable of the exquisite quality control necessary to ensure that an exact and unchanging amount of energy was always available to the transponder.

There would always be a drift, either positive or negative, and in a military context a negative drift was intolerable. So the energy flow controllers of the Swords were designed to have positive drift. They could not be redesigned (the expense would have been prohibitive) just because a toymaker wanted to make a few Shabbles out of a basic Sword design. But this was not seen as a problem, since with the energy flow turned down to minimum a Shabble would be perfectly safe in a child's hands, and adjustments to ensure safety would only have to be made every twenty years or so.

Hence – many millennia later – the pyrotechnical abilities of the demon of Jod.

What else needs to be added to the Originator's Text and the Commentary of the redactors of Odrum? Much could be added. But let us content ourselves with just a glimpse, the smallest glimpse, of the celebrations organised by the Empress Justina (she was a diplomat, and thought it wise to show approval of the Hermit Crab's decisions) to celebrate the General Amnesty.

'Let there be a General Prescription!' she cried.

And a General Prescription there was, with alcohol freely available to one and all, leading to a consequent excitation of the mood of all concerned, an excitation much helped by banqueting, music and dancing.

'Tintinnabulate the tintinnabula!' commanded the Empress Justina.

Tintinnabulation proceeded. One tintinnabulum after another was struck, and tintinnabulary peals rang out across the city.

Chong! Jong! Jung! Yong! Chan-gantachong!

Pigeons exploded to the sky. Bats in the belfries wept red blood. And young Chegory Guy closed with Olivia, closed to her sweetness, to her heat, and yes she said yes she said yes.

THE END